KT-143-712

PRAISE FOR BESTSELLING AUTHOR STEPHEN LEATHER

'A writer at the top of his game . . . The sheer impetus
of his story-telling is damned hard to resist'
Sunday Express

'An aggressively topical novel but a genuinely thrilling
one, too'
Daily Telegraph

'Explores complex contemporary issues while keeping
the action fast and bloody'
Economist

'As tough as British thrillers get . . . gripping'
Irish Independent

'A master of the thriller genre'
Irish Times

'Masterful plotting . . . rapid-fire prose'
Sunday Express

'Action and scalpel-sharp suspense'
Daily Telegraph

'Fast-moving, lots of atmosphere'
Mail on Sunday

'Leather is an intelligent thriller writer'
Daily Mail

If you'd like to find out more about these
and future titles, visit www.stephenleather.com.

STEPHEN LEATHER

Last Man Standing

HODDER

First published in Great Britain in 2019 by Hodder & Stoughton
An Hachette UK company

This paperback edition published in 2019

1

A CIP catalogue record for this title is available from the British Library

A format ISBN 978 1 473 67189 8
B format ISBN 978 1 473 67188 1
eBook ISBN 978 1 473 67187 4

Typeset in Plantin Light by
Palimpsest Book Production Ltd, Falkirk, Stirlingshire

Printed and bound in Great Britain by Clays Ltd, Elcograf S.p.A.

Hodder & Stoughton policy is to use papers that are natural, renewable
and recyclable products and made from wood grown in sustainable forests.
The logging and manufacturing processes are expected to conform
to the environmental regulations of the country of origin.

Hodder & Stoughton Ltd
Carmelite House
50 Victoria Embankment
London EC4Y 0DZ

www.hodder.co.uk

Last Man Standing

I

Matt Standing was lying on his bunk listening to an Arabic language lesson through earphones when a Navy SEAL pulled back the flap of his tent and called his name. Standing sat up and switched off his iPod. The SEAL was Rick Lopez, a keen-as-mustard Hispanic demolitions expert and a member of the team Standing had been embedded with for the past four months. 'We've got a live one,' said Lopez. 'We're moving out in three minutes.' Lopez hurried away without waiting for a response.

Standing put on his flak jacket and reached for his weapon, a Heckler & Koch 417 assault rifle. He ducked out of the tent and jogged over to where his platoon was assembling, close to the three four-door Toyota Tacoma pick-up trucks that the SEALS used as their preferred transport. They called them NTVs – Nonstandard Tactical Vehicles – and modifications included belt-fed machine-gun mounts, grenade launchers, roll bars, infrared headlights, satellite communications, and tracker units. The NTV was a monster and as it resembled a Syrian rebel truck, it could often pass through high-risk areas when a military vehicle would have been fired on.

Two more SEALs hurried over. There were sixteen men in the platoon and Standing made seventeen. He had been embedded with the SEALs for more than three months as part of a special forces exchange programme. His place in the SAS had been taken by a SEAL who was presently on operations in Afghanistan.

The lieutenant in charge was a year or so older than Standing, brown-haired with hazel eyes, and taller than the average SEAL with bulging forearms, and a six-pack that he liked to show off by going bare-chested in the camp as often as possible. Now he was in full combat gear including a Kevlar vest and helmet. His name was Skip Dunnett and while he usually appeared relaxed and laid back, his easy-going nature belied a tough profes-sionalism and a fierce loyalty to his men. 'This is a chance to get one of yours, Matt,' said Dunnett. 'A guy from London who's been in our Top Ten for the past three months.' He showed Standing a printout of a bearded twenty-something Asian holding an RPG as he posed in front of an ISIS flag. 'They call him the Axeman because—'

'I've seen the videos,' said Standing. 'Where is he?'

'We've had intel that he's meeting with an ISIS commander in a village some fifty clicks south of Manbij. So, two birds with one stone. There's a drone in the air but it's for observation, the top brass want them taken alive for questioning.' He put the printout into a pocket on his protective vest. 'We'll drive to within a mile of the target and proceed on foot. Normally we'd wait until dark but we don't know if the bad guys plan to overnight there, so we're going to strike while the iron's hot.'

'How good is the intel?' asked Standing.

'It's come through the MID and they've requested that we take action rather than the Syrian Army,' said the Lieutenant. The Military Intelligence Directorate was the country's military intelligence service, which reported directly to the president.

'Because they know the locals will only fuck it up,' snarled Warrant Officer Andy Wirral. 'All they know is how to gas civilians and bomb hospitals.'

'There isn't a Syrian unit available,' said the Lieutenant. 'They're asking that we hand any ISIS combatants over to them, but my orders are that we take any prisoners straight to our airbase in Kharab A'sheq. Should take us just over an hour if we're lucky. The CIA will give them a grilling there before deciding whether or not we hand them over to the Syrians.'

Lieutenant Dunnett climbed into the lead vehicle, followed by four of the SEALs.

Standing was in the middle vehicle. Wirral was already in the front passenger seat as Standing climbed into the back. The driver was the oldest member of the team, Leeman Jones, who had just celebrated his thirtieth birthday. Jones was a New Yorker, broad-shouldered and square-jawed, his eyes hidden behind impenetrable wrap-around Oakley shades. Jones gunned the engine and black smoke belched from the exhaust.

Lopez climbed in after Standing. They were joined by Bobby-Ray Barnes. Standing had trained with Bobby-Ray during a one-month stint at the unit's base in California prior to being sent out to Syria and the two men had become firm friends. He was close to Standing's age but a couple of inches taller and ten kilos heavier. He was from Los Angeles and had the look of a surfer, blond-haired and blue-eyed with gleaming white teeth. 'So they've found the Axeman,' Bobby-Ray said as he dropped down next to Standing. He patted him on the leg, close to the Glock 19 in its nylon holster. 'What the fuck is it with your Asians? Why are they so keen to leave the UK and fight in this shithole?'

'They're not my Asians, Bobby-Ray.'

'You know what I mean, dude. We don't see American Asians over here. They know that the US of A is the best fucking country in the world and they're lucky to live there. But your Asians, they must fucking hate the UK, right?'

'Again, they're not my Asians. No one understands these guys. And they're a very small minority at best.'

The jihadist known as the Axeman was a British-born Asian, Abdul Khan, the only son of a Leicester doctor who, up until the age of seventeen, had seemed to be destined to follow his father into the medical profession. Khan had been radicalised at his local mosque and a few days after his eighteenth birthday had flown to Syria to fight for ISIS. He had appeared in several ISIS propaganda videos, bearded and waving an AK-47, but in recent months had taken to executing prisoners using a large axe. Bobby-Ray was right: Khan was a wild animal that needed to be put down, the sooner the better.

The final space in the back of the truck was taken by Ryan French, his skin tanned brown from tours in Syria, Iraq and Afghanistan and the proud owner of a bushy beard that reached halfway down his chest. He was a skilled sniper and cradled a Knight's Armament Mark 2

Sniper Weapon System that he was capable of using at well above its usual one thousand-yard range. 'Off to work we go,' he said, grinning.

Lopez stood up and grabbed the machine gun. He pushed his sunglasses up his nose and loosened the red and white checked scarf around his head. 'Rock and roll!' he shouted.

The gates opened and the three vehicles drove out of the camp. The operational command centre had been set up on the outskirts of the town of Ayn Dadad in 2016, not long after the area was seized by the Kurdish militia. It had initially been used to monitor the movements of opposition groups affiliated with the Free Syrian Army but was now used as a springboard for US special forces to mount search and destroy missions in the north of the country.

All the houses within a quarter of a mile of the base had been demolished and the rubble removed. The land was used by local farmers to graze their goats and for local kids to play football. A dozen or so young men were kicking a ball around but they stopped to watch the convoy drive by. One of the men pulled a mobile phone from his pocket and began talking into it. Standing turned to stare at the man. A call from his girlfriend or tipping off ISIS that the Americans were heading out? There was no way of knowing, but Standing feared the worst.

'Phone a friend, do you think?' asked Bobby-Ray as if reading his mind.

'Happens everywhere,' said Standing. 'Afghanistan, Iraq, anywhere there are troops there's always a hostile with a phone ready to call in troop movements.'

The man put the phone away but continued to stare at the convoy. French casually sighted his rifle on the man. 'Bang, bang,' he said.

The convoy kept at a steady thirty miles an hour. The traffic was light and the vehicles behind the convoy held back, intimidated by the fire power. The drivers coming from the opposite direction stared openly at the Americans, some with undisguised hostility but most were simply curious.

Once they were a few miles from the town the traffic thinned out to just the occasional pick-up truck or agricultural vehicle. The fields either side of the road were mostly bare of crops. Food production had dropped by half since the civil war had erupted in 2011. The conflict disrupted the State system that subsidised farming and provided seeds to farmers, and the country had moved from being an exporter of grain to an importer. The majority of the millions of refugees who had poured out of Syria were former farmers and their families who were no longer able to make a living from their land, and many of the buildings either side of the road had been abandoned.

Standing's earpiece crackled. 'Heads up, guys, there's something in the road ahead.'

Standing peered over the top of the cab. The wreckage of what had once been a people carrier was lying across the road, riddled with bullet holes. It was on its side and a child was hanging from the window. At first Standing thought the child was dead but an arm twitched. It was a boy, and his white robe was spotted with blood. Just behind the people carrier was an old pick-up truck, its doors open and steam feathering from the engine.

The three US vehicles slowed to a halt. Lopez kept his machine gun moving as he scanned the surrounding area.

'Stay frosty, guys,' said the Lieutenant.

Standing looked around. The nearest high ground was several miles away but there were several dozen buildings within sniper range. Most had flat roofs and open windows. Bobby-Ray was following his example and scanning their surroundings. Jones was tapping his gloved hands on the steering wheel. 'What are we waiting for, that kid needs help,' he muttered.

'We're on a mission,' said Wirral. 'This is a distraction.'

Jones turned to look at the warrant officer. 'That kid's dying,' he said.

'The LT's doing the right thing,' said Wirral. 'This could be an ambush. Don't get too close in case we have to move quickly.' He twisted around in his seat. 'Stay alert, guys!' he shouted.

The child stopped moving. Blood dripped down from his arm to the road.

'Everyone stay put,' said the Lieutenant in Standing's ear. 'I'm sending a medic over. Keep your engines running and your eyes open.'

One of the SEALs in the lead vehicle dropped onto the road and jogged over to the people carrier. He was carrying a first-aid kit in his left hand, his carbine in his right.

Standing continued to scan the surrounding area, his trigger finger in position. Lopez had the machine gun aimed in the general direction of the two damaged vehicles. Standing knew that every second that passed meant a sniper attack was less likely – any sniper in the vicinity would have started firing as soon as the convoy had come to a halt.

The other two machine guns were moving left and right, covering the sides of the roads.

'We've got company,' said Jones, checking his wing mirror.

Standing twisted around. Two saloon cars were heading towards them.

'LT, we've got two vehicles fast approaching at the rear,' said Wirral over the radio.

'Make sure they're not hostiles and keep them back,' said the Lieutenant.

'Roger that,' said Wirral. He climbed out of the cab and walked around to the rear of the truck. 'Matt, Bobby-Ray, with me,' he said. 'Ricky, keep the gun on them but hold your fire until I say otherwise.'

Lopez turned the gun to aim down the road as Standing and Bobby-Ray jumped down and walked to stand either side of Wirral.

As they walked to the last truck, three more SEALs piled out and joined them, fanning out to block the road. The warrant officer held up his left hand to stop the cars while Bobby-Ray and Standing raised their weapons.

Standing felt reasonably relaxed. Both cars looked well cared for and their windows were up. The front car had a man driving and a female passenger, her head covered with a hijab. There were two men in the second car, both elderly. The cars braked smoothly a hundred feet or so from the final truck in the convoy. The second car was directly behind the first, which was another good sign.

'Stay back!' Standing shouted in Arabic. 'Stay where you are!'

'The kid is still alive,' said the medic through Standing's earpiece.

'That's not our problem,' muttered Wirral.

'We can't just leave the kid to die,' said Bobby-Ray.

'Kids are dying all over this godforsaken country,' said the warrant officer. 'The best way to stop that happening is to take out as many of these ISIS scumbags as we can.'

'Well, it's the LT's call,' said Bobby-Ray.

The lead car edged forward and Standing raised his hand again. 'Stay where you are!' he shouted in Arabic. The SEALs had their weapons pointed at the cars. 'It's okay guys, they're just nervous,' he said.

'We should tell them to turn around,' said one.

'They're cool,' said Standing. He smiled and waved. The passenger in the front vehicle waved back.

'Everything under control at the rear?' asked the Lieutenant.

'All good,' said Standing.

'We've got three vehicles heading this way from the north,' said the Lieutenant. 'Matt, you and Bobby-Ray move to the front. Gator and T-J, go with them.'

'Roger that,' said Standing. He and Bobby-Ray ran along the road towards the front of the convoy. Lopez had turned the machine gun around and was covering the two cars. Wirral raised his hand to tell the two cars to stay where they were.

Ed 'Gator' Hebert, a native of Louisiana, jumped down from the lead truck, followed by T-J Hamelin, a Texan who favoured a black cowboy hat when he wasn't on duty.

As Standing reached the lead truck, he saw the medic

pulling the child out of the people carrier and lowering him gently on to the ground. The boy was covered in blood but his chest was moving. The medic knelt down and opened his first-aid kit.

The SEAL manning the machine gun on the lead truck was pointing the barrel down the road. Beyond the two damaged vehicles blocking their way were three trucks, each leaving plumes of dust behind them. Standing had a bad feeling the moment he saw them. They were powerful pick-ups, not too dissimilar from the ones that the SEALs were using. Unlike the NTVs, the approaching trucks didn't have machine guns mounted on them, but there were men sitting in the back. They could have been workers heading to or from work, but if that had been the case Standing would have expected the vehicles to have slowed.

'I don't like this, LT,' said Standing, shouldering his weapon.

'Hold your fire, Matt,' said Lieutenant Dunnett.

Standing looked across at Bobby-Ray. Bobby-Ray flashed him a worried smile. He was clearly as apprehensive as Standing.

Standing bent down to talk to the Lieutenant through the open window. He looked up at Standing. 'They might just be in a hurry,' said the officer before Standing could say anything.

Standing shook his head. 'They're hostiles, LT. I'd bet the farm on it.'

'Have you got a farm?'

'It's an expression.'

The Lieutenant pointed down the road. 'Make it clear they're to stop,' he said. 'If necessary fire a warning shot.'

Standing nodded and jogged towards the damaged vehicles. The medic had ripped the shirt off the little boy and was applying a dressing. The boy's chest didn't look as if it was moving any more.

The trucks were about a quarter of a mile away and showing no signs of slowing despite the fact they must have seen the damaged vehicles blocking the road.

'What do you think, Matt?' asked Bobby-Ray, slipping his finger over the trigger of his weapon.

'I think a warning shot's not going to do a blind thing,' said Standing.

T-J and Gator stood to their left and shouldered their weapons. Standing and Bobby-Ray moved apart. Bobby-Ray raised his hand. The trucks were too far away to hear him, so he didn't shout anything.

The trucks continued to speed towards them, then suddenly the rear trucks moved, one left and one right, so that all three were abreast as they sped down the road.

'LT, this isn't good!' shouted Standing.

'Fire a warning shot,' said the officer.

Bobby-Ray fired a quick burst in the air above the middle of the three trucks. As Standing turned to look at Bobby-Ray, he saw movement on the second floor of one of the buildings behind him. There was someone in one of the windows. There was a glint of sunlight, from a sniper's scope or binoculars maybe, and there was definitely a figure standing there. Bobby-Ray lowered his weapon, then turned to see what Standing was looking at.

The house was about three hundred yards from the road, an easy enough shot for a half-decent sniper. But if it was a sniper he could have taken a shot at any time,

Standing knew. So maybe it wasn't a sniper? What then? An observer? Someone who had called in the trucks? The options raced through Standing's mind in less than a second.

He turned back to look at the three trucks, now just a hundred yards away. The men in the back of the vehicles stood up, brandishing AK-47s.

'Hostiles!' shouted Standing. He dropped to one knee and brought his weapon to bear on the middle truck. He fired a quick burst at the driver's side of the windscreen. The glass exploded and he fired a second burst. The truck continued to race towards him, so he lowered his aim and fired another burst at the offside front tyre. Almost immediately the offside of the truck dipped and it crashed into the vehicle next to it in a shower of sparks. Standing slapped in a fresh magazine and fired again, this time at the truck to the left, the first burst at the windscreen followed by a second at the tyres. The truck spun off the road, spilling out the men in the back. It bucked along the rough ground and came to a halt. The men in the back were shaken but not injured and they jumped out. There were five of them, their faces covered with scarves and sunglasses. T-J and Gator fired and cut the men down with a series of short, controlled bursts.

The middle truck was now careering along the road, swerving crazily, then it crashed onto its side, spilling out the men in the back.

There was only one truck still heading their way. Bobby-Ray and Standing fired together. The windscreen exploded and the offside tyre burst; the bonnet flicked up and steam poured skywards. The truck ran off the road. T-J and Gator had finished picking off their targets and turned their attention to the final truck, spraying it with bullets. In a matter of seconds all the armed men in the back were dead.

Standing lowered his weapon. The Lieutenant climbed out of his vehicle and walked over. 'Shit,' he said.

'What do you think, LT? Was this whole thing a set-up?'

'It's starting to look that way,' said the officer. 'Fuck. So there is no ISIS officer and no Axeman.'

'It could be a coincidence,' said Standing.

'Yeah? Or it could be that they ambushed the cars and placed the kid in the window knowing that we'd stop.'

Bobby-Ray was looking over at the house again. 'There's somebody in there,' he said.

The Lieutenant went over to join him. He shaded his eyes with his hand. 'I can't see anyone.'

'There was a flash. Off glass.'

Standing stared at the house. He nodded when he saw movement in one of the top-floor windows. 'There's definitely someone in there,' he said.

He dropped his gaze to the lower floor. The building was featureless concrete with white paint peeling off the shutters and doors. A stray dog cocked its leg against the side of the building.

'LT, can I use your binoculars?' asked Bobby-Ray.

The officer handed them over. He put them to his eyes and focussed on the front door. 'There's a wire running out of the front door,' he said. He lowered the binoculars.

A figure appeared at the window. A man, his head swathed in a black and white headscarf. 'Sniper!' shouted the Lieutenant, but Standing could see that the man wasn't holding a rifle. There was something in his hand, though, and Standing realised what it was. A trigger.

'IED!' he shouted at the top of his voice.

He turned to look at the two damaged vehicles. The medic was still attending to the boy. To the left, dirt had been spread across the road. Standing knew with a terrible certainty that the dirt was to cover the wire that ran from the house, across the field and into the car. He reached over to grab the Lieutenant and pull him away. Bobby-Ray was moving, too, stretching out his arms and putting himself between them and the car.

'IED!' Standing screamed again.

The medic looked over but made no attempt to leave the boy. Standing looked over at the lead truck in the convoy. The driver gunned the engine but there was no way he would be able to reverse the vehicle with the second truck blocking its way. 'Get out!' he yelled.

The SEAL operating the machine gun turned and threw himself off the back of the truck. The SEALs with him followed suit.

Bobby-Ray was pushing the Lieutenant, his shoulders hunched against the explosion he knew was to come.

Standing looked over at the medic. He had scooped up the boy and was turning to carry him away from the people carrier. His eyes locked with Standing's and there was the briefest of smiles before the car exploded in a mass of fire and flames. Metal and glass ripped through the air and the medic was thrown to the side. The blast hit Standing a fraction of a second later and he fell backwards, his shoulders hitting the road first. Bobby-Ray crashed onto him and the impact forced the air from his lungs. His right hand managed to keep hold of his weapon and he used his left to roll Bobby-Ray off him. He staggered to his feet, ears ringing. The Lieutenant was lying on his back, blinking in shock, but he didn't appear to be too hurt. Bobby-Ray was on his side. His flak jacket had protected his chest and vital organs but his legs had been hurt by the shrapnel. His eyes were closed but he was breathing, albeit noisily. 'Medic!' Standing shouted. He stood up and looked over at the people carrier. It had been shifted by the explosion and had shielded the SEAL medic from some of the blast but not enough to save his life. The explosion had torn through one leg and he lay on his side, blood still pooling from his left thigh. The small boy lay next to him like a discarded doll. 'Medic!' Standing screamed again.

A SEAL emerged from behind the lead pick-up truck and ran over. 'Take care of Bobby-Ray,' said Standing.

The Lieutenant was coughing. 'What the fuck happened?' he gasped as he got to his feet. His cheek had been ripped open and blood trickled down his neck.

'IED in the car,' said Standing. He took a trauma pack from his belt, ripped it open and slapped it against the Lieutenant's cheek. The Lieutenant used his hand to keep the dressing pressed against the wound. 'You'll be okay,' said Standing.

The medic cut away what was left of the material around Bobby-Ray's injured legs. Standing looked over at the house where he had seen the trigger-man. He started to run. As his feet pounded on the road he heard the Lieutenant shout something but Standing didn't catch it. He hit the side of the road and his boots slapped against bare earth. The man had gone from the window but Standing hadn't seen him emerge from the building, which either meant there was a back way out or that he was still inside.

His chest was burning from the exertion but he quickened his pace. Something thwacked against the ground to his left and he looked over at a three-storey building. There was a man on the roof with a rifle. Another round hit the ground a few inches from Standing's foot, kicking up dirt.

Standing planted his right foot hard and twisted to the left, then immediately went down on one knee and fired a quick burst at the sniper. The rounds went low and smacked into the wall just below the roof. Standing adjusted his aim and the next burst blew the sniper away in a red mist. The sniper was still falling backwards when Standing was on his feet and running full pelt towards the house.

He caught movement in his peripheral vision to the right and he swung his weapon in that direction, his finger already tightening on the trigger. He relaxed immediately when he spotted the two boys, one of them holding a football, staring at him open-mouthed.

He heard a brief rattle of gunfire behind him, a single shot from a Kalashnikov followed by rapid fire from HKs.

He was less than a hundred feet from the house now. There was no movement at the upper windows and the front door remained firmly shut. The shutters on the ground-floor windows were closed. As he ran he heard an engine burst into life. He slowed and the engine roared. A second later a white SUV sped from behind the house, its wheels spewing up dirt. He dropped onto one knee again, took aim and shot at the heavily tinted windscreen.

It imploded and he caught a glimpse of a dark-skinned man wearing sunglasses behind the steering wheel. Standing fired a single shot and the man's face transformed into a pulpy mess. The SUV continued to accelerate, so Standing assumed the man's foot was jammed on the accelerator. He let loose a quick burst at the nearside wheels, ripping the tyres to shreds. The rear window of the SUV slid down and the barrel of an AK-47 emerged, but Standing was already taking aim and he fired a burst into the rear of the vehicle before the Kalashnikov discharged.

The car bucked over the rough ground then spun to the left, towards Standing. He leapt to the side, rolled on the ground and came up firing, two long bursts that shattered the remaining windows. The vehicle slammed into a tree and the bonnet sprang open. There were three men in the SUV, two behind the driver, and all three were dead.

Standing slapped in a fresh magazine and ran towards the house, his weapon at the ready. He was breathing heavily but far from tired. As always when he was in combat, everything seemed to have slowed to a crawl. All his senses were in overdrive. He heard shouts from the road and the crackle of burning vehicles, and he could smell the cordite in the air. He glanced to his right as he ran. The two boys were still watching him with wide eyes, too shocked to move. His eyes flicked back to the upper windows of the house. Still no one there. Most likely all the occupants had been in the SUV, but he needed to make sure.

More shouts from behind him. His name being called. He took aim at the front door and fired a burst that splintered the lock. The door sagged on its hinges. As he ran towards it he looked over to his left at the house where the sniper had been. There was another man on the roof now, this one wearing a black headscarf and sighting down an RPG-7. Standing stopped and turned, raising his Heckler to his shoulder.

The RPG-7 was an anti-tank rocket-propelled grenade launcher, capable of hitting a target a thousand metres away but not particularly accurate beyond two hundred metres, which is about how far away he was from it. Time stopped as Standing took everything in. It hadn't been fired yet because there was no puff of blue-grey smoke. When the trigger was pulled a gunpowder booster charge would send the grenade hurtling through the air towards its target at just over a hundred metres a second. There was no guidance system, so once it was launched, that was that. After ten metres the rocket motor would ignite and the grenade would speed up to close to three hundred metres a second. Which meant that it would take almost two seconds for the grenade to reach its target. It wasn't a long time, but it was enough.

Standing raised his weapon. If he was lucky he would get a shot off before the man fired. He wasn't. He saw the puff of smoke. The trigger had been pulled.

A fraction of a second after he saw the smoke he heard the 'whoof' of the charge. He took three quick steps to the right and threw himself onto the ground. As he hit the soil the grenade slammed into the front door of the house and carried on inside before exploding. The thick walls of the house absorbed most of the explosion, though shards of wood flew out and thudded around Standing.

The air was thick with choking dust as he stood up. He swung up his carbine and sent a quick burst towards the roof. The man was still there, staring down to survey his handiwork. The man ducked as Standing's bullets whined overhead but he made the mistake of straightening up. Standing put a bullet in his chest.

He heard the sound of a second engine starting up and he sprinted around to the rear of the building. Three men, their heads wrapped in scarves and holding Kalashnikovs, were climbing into the rear of a rusty red truck. The driver's jaw dropped when he saw Standing come around the corner. He stamped on the accelerator and the truck leapt forward, spilling the passengers out of the back. The driver was cursing as he aimed the truck at Standing, but Standing just stared impassively as he fired three single shots. The first shattered the windscreen, the second and third hit the driver in the face. Standing stepped to the side and flattened himself against the wall of the house as the truck sped by, then stepped back and swung up his Heckler. The men who had fallen out of the back of the truck were scrambling to their feet but they were too slow and Standing took them out with three quick double-taps to the chest. He watched as they slumped to the ground, then turned and hurried back to the front of the house. The red pick-up truck slammed into one of the neighbouring houses. An old man in a thawb robe hurried out shouting and waving his fist, but he took one look at Standing and rushed back inside his house and shut the door behind him. Standing looked around for any other potential threats, but other than a few curious onlookers there was no one in the vicinity who looked like they wanted to cause him harm.

He looked over at the three men he'd shot behind the house. Two were definitely dead and the third wouldn't last much longer. Standing went over to the injured man and kicked his AK-47 out of reach. The man stared up at him with unseeing eyes. Blood was pouring from a fist-sized wound in his side and soaking into the soil. Death was only seconds away.

Standing turned and walked back to the road. It had been less than a minute since he had left the convoy but in that time he had killed a sniper, the RPG fighter, three men in the SUV plus the driver and three gunmen in the pick-up truck. At no point had he been scared or even worried. He never was, in combat. Whenever bullets started flying, his instincts took over. It was as if his conscious mind took a back seat and allowed his subconscious to function without inhibitions. He didn't fully understand the process but it had never failed him.

He began to jog, his Heckler in his right hand. Two of the SEALs were carrying Bobby-Ray to the lead vehicle as the medic fussed over him. Two more SEALs were carrying their dead comrade over to the vehicle Standing had been in. The Lieutenant turned to look at Standing as he reached the convoy. 'What the fuck, Matt? Didn't you hear me calling you?'

Standing shrugged. 'I guess I got caught up in the moment.'

'You could have gotten yourself killed.'

'Could've. Should've. Would've.'

'I'm serious, Matt. That's not how we do things in the SEALs. We're a team.'

'They were getting away, LT. I had to move quickly.'

'Was that an RPG they fired?'

Standing nodded and Lieutenant Dunnett shook his head in astonishment. 'And you just jumped out of the way?'

'It's not the first time I've avoided an RPG,' said Standing. 'The trick is to let them target you, then move as soon as you see the smoke. It doesn't work if you're in a vehicle, obviously, and you need to be at least a couple of hundred yards away.'

The officer shook his head in amazement. 'You are one mad son of a bitch.'

'I knew what I was doing, LT. Trust me, I was never in any danger.'

'And the sniper? That was just dumb luck.'

'He wasn't a sniper. Not really. Just a bad guy with a rifle going for a long shot. Look, LT, all's well that ends well, let's leave it at that.' He nodded towards the SEALs who were gently easing Bobby-Ray into the back of the truck. 'How is he?'

'His legs are all cut up and he's having trouble breathing but he's going to be okay. The medic says he might have a collapsed lung but they can fix that back at the base.'

'He put himself between us and the bomb.'

The officer nodded. 'I know that.'

'Hell of a thing to do.' Standing sighed. 'What about the mission?'

The Lieutenant grimaced. 'We were set up,' he said. 'No question. There is no mission.'

'That's what I thought. Whoever gave you the intel, they need looking at.'

'That will happen, don't worry.' He gestured at the

vehicles. 'Okay, mount up, we'll head back to base. And Matt, next time I give you an order, I'd be obliged if you'd follow it.'

Standing grinned and flashed him a salute. 'Aye, aye, sir,' he said, before he jogged over to his vehicle.

2

SIX MONTHS LATER

Standing's boots pounded on the grass. There were two men ahead of him, blocking his way. They were in their late forties and their hair was starting to go grey, but they were fit and there was no fear in their eyes. He looked left and right, then waited until the last possible moment before planting his left foot hard and pushing right. The manoeuvre took them by surprise and he sprinted by them. The man closest to him cursed and stuck out his foot but Standing was too quick for him.

He looked over to his left. Ginge Maclean was about fifty feet away and looking around, assessing the situation.

'Ginge!' shouted Standing.

Ginge looked over, grinned, and kicked the ball, sending it spinning through the air towards him. He caught it on his chest, let it drop to his feet and turned to face the goal. The keeper had played for Liverpool during the late Eighties and was already moving towards Standing, his arms out to the sides. Standing pushed the ball forward with his left foot and then hit it hard with his right. The ball went straight into the arms of the keeper, who took two quick steps and threw it hard and fast to one of his own defenders.

Ginge let loose a barrage of abuse about Standing's parentage but Standing waved it away. 'To my feet next time, you wanker!' he shouted.

Ginge laughed and went haring after the defender. Standing stood with his hands on his hips. He'd never been good at football, rugby was his game of choice, but the Regiment was short-handed and he'd been called in to make up the numbers on the Pilgrims team. The opposition was a team of the great and good of British football, though few of the names were familiar to Standing. Most of the players were in their sixties but they were still better at the game than any of the SAS men, as shown by the current score of 4-1 with just ten minutes to go. The SAS team were fitter and stronger and even after eighty minutes of running they were still relatively fresh, but the former professionals had the edge when it came to skill and strategy. The SAS spent most of their time running, the ex-professional footballers were more about passing and shooting.

As Standing watched, the defender sent the ball to the feet of a former Manchester City player who was now a pundit on Sky TV. The pundit wrong-footed a sergeant who had just returned from Afghanistan, sporting sunburnt skin and a shaggy beard, and sent the ball over to the far side of the pitch where a former Chelsea striker had all the time in the world to take the ball down the sideline before crossing it over to the goalmouth, where the pundit made a quick dash and knocked it home with a perfect header.

The small crowd of spectators burst into applause and the pundit did a mock bow to them. The annual football match was one of the few occasions when civilians were allowed onto the SAS base at Credenhill. It was a fund-raiser, with proceeds going to the SAS's Clocktower Fund, which helped support former members of the Regiment who had fallen on hard times. A couple of hundred specially vetted visitors were allowed into Stirling Lines to see SAS demonstrations, watch the match, and have a black-tie dinner in the Sergeants' Mess. During the dinner there was an auction of SAS memorabilia including wines and spirits with the SAS insignia, and afterwards the visitors were taken to the clock tower for a group photograph, one of the few times that picture-taking was allowed on the base.

For a group of VIPs – including the dozen or so former players – the day had started much earlier and they were allowed to live-fire weapons on the outdoor range, take part in exercises in the Killing House and get behind the wheel of some of the Regiment's specialist vehicles. Standing had been assigned to the Killing House in the morning, following the VIPs through carefully rehearsed scenarios as they fired at terrorist targets, basically making sure that no one got hurt. Lunch had been bacon sand-wiches washed down with coffee, after which they had changed for the game.

The event was always popular and the SAS men enjoyed the chance to show off their skills to outsiders. Their soldier skills anyway – there wasn't much to be proud of when it came to football.

The game ended with the visitors 7-1 ahead, and Standing was pretty sure they could have made double figures if they had wanted to. The players shook hands, acknowledged the applause from the spectators, then ran over to the changing rooms. There were still a few hours to go before dinner, so Standing pulled on his camouflage fatigues. Like the rest of the SAS men, he had a holstered Glock on his hip.

He was just finishing buttoning his shirt when his mobile buzzed to let him know that he had received a text message. It was from an American number. 'IS THIS MATT STANDING?'

Standing frowned. His phone didn't recognise the number and neither did he. 'WHO WANTS TO KNOW?' he typed.

A few seconds later, he received a reply. 'MY NAME IS KAITLYN. I AM BOBBY-RAY'S SISTER.'

Standing's frown deepened. Bobby-Ray Barnes hadn't mentioned he had a sister, but then they had shared very little personal information during their time together, something Standing welcomed as he was never happy discussing his family, or lack of it. The hairs on the back of his neck stood up as he realised that there was only one reason that Bobby-Ray's sister was contacting him – she had bad news for him. He walked outside and hit the button to call her number, and she answered on the third ring. 'Kaitlyn, hi this is Matt Standing—' he began, but she started speaking over him.

'I can not hear you,' she said. Her voice was stilted, as if she was having trouble forming her words.

'It's Matt Standing,' he said again. 'Is there—'

'I can't hear you,' she said, interrupting him again. He stopped talking as she continued. 'I am deaf, so I can not talk on the phone. But you can text or we can FaceTime.'

The line went dead and Standing frowned at his phone. If she was deaf, how would FaceTime help? He shrugged and placed a FaceTime call. It was answered almost immediately by a blonde girl with freckles across her nose and cheeks. She grinned showing perfect white teeth. 'Kaitlyn?' he said.

She nodded. 'Can you hold the phone a bit closer to your face,' she said, in her stilted voice. 'I have to be able to read your lips.'

Standing did so. 'How's that?' he asked.

'Better,' she said.

'Has something happened to Bobby-Ray?'

She nodded, 'Yes. He's in trouble and needs your help.'

'What happened?' asked Standing.

'Can you come to LA?'

Standing wondered if she had missed what he'd said, so he repeated himself. 'What happened?'

'Bobby-Ray says I can't say over the phone. He will meet you in LA.'

'Is he hurt?'

'I can't tell you. He says it's dangerous to say anything over the phone. But he needs your help, Matt. He says you are the only one he can trust.'

Standing didn't hesitate. Bobby-Ray had damn near saved his life in Syria and the injuries he'd received, while not life-threatening, had ended the man's military career. 'I'll be there,' he said. 'I'll text you my flight number.'

'When can you get here?' she asked.

Standing looked at the Rolex Submariner on his wrist. If he left for London as soon as the group picture was taken, he'd be able to catch a morning flight to Los Angeles. 'Tomorrow,' he said.

'Thank you,' she said. 'Thank you so much. I'll pick you up at the airport.'

He ended the call, then jogged over to the administration office. Debbie Gilmore, the wife of one of the Regiment's sergeant majors, looked up from her computer.

'Debbie, can I see Colonel Davies? It's important.'

She looked at him over the top of her glasses. 'How important?'

'It's not life and death, but it's close.' She waved him to a seat but he just smiled. He wanted to stand. 'I'll tell him you're here.' She picked up her phone, spoke to the Colonel, then nodded at the closed door. 'You're to go straight in,' she said.

'You're an angel, Debbie.'

'And don't you forget it.'

Standing knocked on the door and let himself in. The Colonel was sitting at his desk, the sleeves of his fatigues rolled up above his elbows. He was in his early fifties but without an ounce of fat on him, whippet-thin with steel-grey hair cut close to the scalp and his nose and cheeks flecked with broken blood vessels.

Soldiers didn't salute officers in the SAS but Standing stood with his back ramrod straight and his hands behind his back as a sign of respect.

'What's up, Matt?' asked the Colonel, sitting back in his chair.

'I know this is short notice, boss, but I need some time off. I've plenty of days due.'

'You've got a problem?'

'A friend in need, boss.'

'Regiment?'

'No, boss. But he's a good friend.'

'How long do you need?'

'A week, maybe longer.'

'How are you fixed, task-wise?'

'I'm clear this week. Next week I'm down for the training with the Met's CTSFOs and hopefully I'll be back by then but really I wouldn't be missed.' The Metropolitan Police's Counter Terrorist Specialist Firearms Officers were the elite members of the capital's armed police and they did much of their training with the SAS.

The Colonel tapped on his computer keyboard and looked at his screen. 'You haven't taken any leave in the past twelve months,' he said.

'I've been busy,' said Standing. 'We all have.'

'I hear that,' said the Colonel. 'Okay, I'll do the paperwork. When do you want to go?'

'As soon as I've finished tonight,' said Standing.

'How's it going out there?'

'Really well.'

'The Pilgrims lost seven-one?' said the Colonel.

'Our best players are all overseas at the moment,' said Standing. 'It shows you how desperate they are when they have to put me on the team.'

The Colonel looked at the chunky TAG Heuer on his wrist. 'I'll be at the dinner,' he said.

'It'll be a good night,' said Standing. 'That Liverpool comedian is always good for a laugh. Thanks, boss.'

'Just make sure you don't get yourself into any trouble, Matt.'

Standing smiled. 'I'll do my best, boss,' he said, though he didn't feel as confident as he sounded.

3

The LAX immigration queue was longer than any Standing had ever seen and it took him the best part of an hour to reach the front of the line, where a pretty Hispanic girl with bright red lipstick asked him what the purpose of his visit was. Standing shrugged. 'Holiday. Vacation, I guess you'd say.'

'On your own?'

Standing shrugged again. 'I prefer my own company.'

For the first time she smiled. 'Good looking guy like you, I'm sure you'll find company if you want it.'

Standing wondered if she was hitting on him, but even if she was it wouldn't matter because he was in the US for only one reason, and that reason didn't involve any sort of romantic attachment. She gave him back his passport and her face was impassive again. 'Enjoy your vacation,' she said, and waved over at the next passenger. She wasn't hitting on him, Standing decided, and actually felt a twinge of disappointment as he walked away.

He'd flown into LA on a Virgin Atlantic plane. He'd managed to get a seat in Premium Economy, which gave him a little extra legroom, but the three beers he'd downed in the departure lounge meant he had slept most of the way. He had brought with him a backpack containing just the essentials – a change of clothes and a washbag.

He walked through sliding doors into the arrivals area and spotted Kaitlyn Barnes immediately. She was wearing a denim jacket over a white halter top and faded blue jeans. She was small; even in her high heels she barely reached his shoulder. He guessed that she was in her very early twenties. She beamed at him as he walked up to her. 'Matt?' she said and he nodded. 'Thank you so much for coming,' she said, and she reached for him and hugged him, burying her cheek in his chest. He wasn't sure how to react and ended up just patting her on the back.

'Do you have a car or do I need to hire one?' he asked. It was only when she didn't react that he remembered that she had to read his lips. He waited for her to break away, made eye contact again and repeated the question.

She nodded. 'Yes,' she said. 'My car's outside.'

'And what about Bobby-Ray?' he asked. 'Can I talk to him?'

She nodded again. 'I'll take you to him,' she said.

'Kaitlyn, what's happened? Why all the cloak and dagger?'

She looked around, then back at him. 'There are too many people here,' she said. 'Let's grab a coffee.'

She took him to a café in the arrivals area. Standing bought her a latte and himself an Americano and a sandwich. They sat down and Standing bit into his sandwich as she began to talk, keeping her face close to his and her voice low. 'Bobby-Ray was working as a bodyguard, what they call close protection. The client was killed three days ago. They say that Bobby-Ray killed him.'

Standing stopped chewing. 'What?'

'It was Bobby-Ray's gun. The client was killed and so were three of the bodyguards.'

Standing frowned. 'I didn't see anything on the Internet.'

'The cops haven't released his name or description. But they're looking for him. And so are the Russians.'

'Russians? What Russians?'

'The client was a rich Russian. An oligarch. Rich as God. Friend of Putin, they say.'

'Okay, so why was Bobby-Ray on his personal protection team? Those guys usually have their own people.'

'They did,' said Kaitlyn. 'But the client had just flown in from the UK and they wanted some locals on the team.'

'How did they find Bobby-Ray?'

'One of his buddies, a former SEAL. Kurt Konieczny. Kurt worked for a company called Redrock and he brought Bobby-Ray on board.'

'And where's Kurt now?'

'Kurt was killed. They're saying that Bobby-Ray killed him, but that's just not possible, Matt. They were joined at the hip.'

Standing put down his sandwich. 'So this Kurt hired Bobby-Ray to be part of a close-protection team, and now they're saying that Bobby-Ray shot the client and killed Kurt?'

Kaitlyn nodded.

'So why doesn't Bobby-Ray just go to the cops? If he didn't do it, he must know who did, right?'

'He says one of the other bodyguards did it and was trying to frame him. Like I said, it was his gun that was used to kill the client. His prints are all over it. And the bodyguard told the police that it was Bobby-Ray. So it's Bobby-Ray's word against his.'

'Still, the cops will have to listen to him. He's a war hero.'

Kaitlyn shook her head fiercely. 'Bobby-Ray says they won't believe him. And he doesn't trust them. He thinks they're in on it.'

'The LA police department? That sounds a bit unlikely, Kaitlyn. Look, call your brother and let me talk to him. His best bet is to talk to the police as soon as possible.'

'I can't call him. He was adamant about that. He says they're tracking his phone.'

'So how do you contact him?'

'I don't. He FaceTimed me once, but as soon as he'd finished he destroyed the SIM card. That number doesn't work any more and he wouldn't give me a new number. But he told me the motel where he was staying.'

'You know the room number?'

She nodded. 'Yes.'

'So call the motel's landline and they'll put you through to his room.'

She shook her head again. 'I can't use landlines,' she said. 'But anyway, he said no phone calls. No contact.'

Standing held up his hands in surrender. 'Okay. So take me to him. But it sounds to me like all he has to do is tell his side of the story.' He drained his coffee. 'Let's go.'

She took him to the short-term car park. She was driving a black VW Polo. It was stiflingly hot and she put the aircon on full as soon as she had started the engine. There was a SatNav on the dashboard and she pressed it and scrolled through to their destination. The Sunset Motel. 'If he's serious about staying off the grid, you really shouldn't be putting Bobby-Ray's location in the

GPS,' he said. She didn't react and he realised she wasn't looking at him. He reached out and gently touched her shoulder. She turned to look at him and he repeated what he'd said.

'Why?' she said.

'Because if he's really worried about people knowing where he is, the SatNav is an easy way to find him. The sort of people who can monitor phone calls wouldn't have any problems tapping into a GPS.'

She bit down on her lower lip and nodded, then deleted the address from the SatNav. She drove out of the airport and onto a freeway. There was a truck in front of them that was moving at exactly the speed limit and traffic was passing them on both sides. It was impossible to talk to her while she was driving, so he settled back in his seat. There was a row of white wind turbines in the far distance, turning slowly.

They were heading north on the 405, passing Santa Monica on their left, when he first realised they were being tailed.

Kaitlyn had finally overtaken the truck and a black SUV with tinted windows had matched their manoeuvre, causing a car behind them to sound its horn. Standing had seen the SUV in the wing mirror. Having overtaken the truck, the SUV slowed and allowed another car to overtake it, then another.

Kaitlyn had changed lanes again a few minutes later, and this time Standing was watching. The SUV followed suit. The vehicles between them meant he couldn't read the licence plate and the tinting was heavy enough that he could only make out the vague shapes of the driver and front-seat passenger.

Tailing a car was nowhere near as easy as they make it look in the movies, Standing knew. To do a professional job you needed at least two vehicles, ideally more. The black SUV was a bad choice, the best cars to use were nondescript saloons, the type of cars that you saw but didn't remember.

Standing spotted the second tail about ten minutes after the first, helped by the fact that it, too, was a black SUV. It was ahead of them and to the right. Like the one behind, it maintained a pretty much constant distance from them.

He tapped Kaitlyn on the knee. When she looked at him he asked her how much longer they would be on the freeway.

'Another twenty miles,' she said. 'What's wrong?'

He smiled. 'Nothing'.

She went back to looking at the road. Standing spent the next five miles checking for another tail but it seemed as if there were just the two SUVs. That suggested it wasn't a surveillance operation because nobody used black SUVs to tail a target, not long-term anyway. It could always be his imagination, of course. There was only one way to know for sure.

He tapped Kaitlyn on the knee again. Conversation was always going to be difficult when she was driving because the only way she could see what he was saying was to take her eyes off the road.

'I need you to take the next turn-off,' he said.

'What?' She looked back at the road and then at his lips again.

'I think we're being followed. Two black SUVs, one four cars ahead, the other three cars behind.'

She looked back at the road. 'Okay,' she said. The next turn off was three miles ahead.

He tapped her on the knee and waited for her to look at him. 'But leave the turn to the last moment and don't indicate.'

She frowned, then looked back at the road. 'But we're in the wrong lane.'

She looked back at him. 'I know,' he said. 'But I want to see what they do. It'll let us know for sure that we are being followed.'

A car was trying to push in front of them, so he pointed forward. She looked ahead and braked to allow the car in. 'Okay,' she said. 'I understand.'

The turn-off was two miles away. She kept glancing in her rear-view mirror. One mile. When they were within sight of the turn-off, she eased off on the speed. He tapped her knee and she looked at him. 'Keep your speed the same,' he said. 'Don't slow down.'

'I get it,' she said, and pressed her foot down on the accelerator.

The exit was fast approaching. He checked the wing mirror. There was a car just behind them, fifteen feet at most. The driver was a woman and she was alone in the car but talking animatedly, probably using her phone hands-free.

He tapped Kaitlyn's knee again to get her attention. 'Right at the last second, use your turn indicator,' he said. 'Make it look as if you changed your mind. Okay?'

She nodded. 'Okay.' She looked back at the road and her knuckles whitened on the steering wheel. He wanted to tell her to relax but didn't want to distract her. He checked the wing mirror again. The woman was driving with one hand on the wheel and waving the other, clearly totally involved in her conversation.

The SUV was still four cars behind.

The exit was a hundred yards away. Cars ahead of them were indicating that they were leaving the freeway. If the occupants of the SUV ahead of them were a tail they would be checking their mirrors looking for any signs that they were going to exit.

Fifty yards.

Kaitlyn flicked the turn indicator on and yanked the wheel to the right. Several horns immediately sounded and the woman on the phone slammed on her brakes. Kaitlyn had to brake to avoid hitting a pick-up truck ahead of her and there were more angry horns blaring behind her.

The SUV ahead of them had missed the turn and continued north but the one to the rear followed them. The driver didn't have time to indicate as the SUV cut across the north-bound traffic and several drivers vented their anger on their horns.

The SUV followed them off the freeway but slowed to put distance between them. Standing reached over to the SatNav and used it to search for the nearest gas station. He pressed the button for the route. It was just two miles away.

Kaitlyn turned to look at him, frowning. 'We don't need gas.'

'If they think we turned off for gas they might not realise we've made them,' he said. 'So drive as if you're trying to save fuel.'

'Clever,' she said.

Standing laughed. 'If I was clever I'd have spotted them

at the airport,' he said, but she had already turned her attention back to the road.

Standing reached over to the SatNav again and zoomed out the display. The next turn-off on the freeway was eight miles away, so it would take the other tail at least fifteen minutes to get back.

He checked the wing mirror. The black SUV was hanging back, matching their speed at a steady forty miles an hour. He was sure they would be on the phone to the other car and trying to work out whether or not they'd seen them.

Standing had a whole load of questions for Kaitlyn but they'd have to wait until she'd stopped driving. He saw the gas station ahead of them. Shell. There was a KFC outlet next to it.

Kaitlyn drove to the pumps and parked. Standing got out of the car, unscrewed the filler cap and shoved in the nozzle. He pulled the handle but nothing happened. Kaitlyn wound down the window. 'You've got to put your credit card in,' she said. 'Or go inside and pay first.'

Standing took out his credit card, inserted it into the slot and tapped in his PIN number. The pump started to vibrate. He tried again and this time fuel poured into the tank. He looked around casually. The SUV was parked outside the KFC outlet. He saw movement in the back. So at least three of them. Possibly four. He looked at his watch. The others were at least ten minutes away.

It only took four gallons and the tank was full. He put the handle back on the pump and got back into the car.

'They're waiting to see what we do,' he said to her. 'Seems to me that they've bought the premise that we turned off to look for fuel. If we go back to the freeway that'll confirm it for them. But we can't go and see Bobby-Ray, not while they're tailing us.'

'So what do we do?'

That was a very good question. Three against one was never good odds, four against one would be worse, and this was America where guns were a right guaranteed under the Constitution. Having said that, Standing was well trained and combat ready and if he caught them unawares he had a good chance of disabling them without them doing too much damage. But Kaitlyn was with him and he was never a fan of innocent bystanders getting caught up in violence. They could lead them on a wild-goose chase, and at some point they would probably be able to lose them, but then they wouldn't know who their followers were or why they were being followed. 'Are you hungry?' he asked.

'Not really,' she said.

'I think we should pay Colonel Sanders a visit,' Standing said.

She frowned. 'But they're watching us.'

'Exactly,' said Standing. 'They're following us, which means they're not going to hurt us. I'm guessing it's Bobby-Ray they're after. If we head on over and park near them then go and eat, it'll convince them that we don't know they're following us.'

'You're the expert,' she said.

He grinned. 'Hopefully.'

She started the engine and then drove slowly over to the KFC. She reversed into a parking space four slots away from the SUV. He patted her on the knee. 'When we get inside, you get the food, I'll get us a table so we can watch them.'

She smiled. 'You want fries with that?'

He laughed. 'I'll have the works,' he said. 'I'm a big fan of KFC. Get me the beans and coleslaw, as well, please.'

They got out of the car and went inside. There were half a dozen tables occupied but there were two free by the window and Standing took one. He could see two shapes in the back of the SUV. So four against one. He wondered what they would do next because four men sitting in a parked vehicle looked a little off. He took another look at his watch. The other SUV would be here in a few minutes. If they were smart, though, they would keep well away: two black SUVs might not stick out on a busy freeway, but two parked together in a car park would definitely be a red flag.

As he watched, the rear doors opened and two men got out. Former military, he was sure, just from the way they carried themselves, though the close-cropped hair and impenetrable sunglasses were another clue. Both men were in their late twenties, wearing bomber jackets and cargo pants. The jackets were short, so if they were carrying guns they'd be in underarm holsters.

The front passenger door opened and a third man climbed out. A decade older and twenty pounds heavier, his hair greying and wearing glasses to correct his vision rather than to hide his eyes. The two others turned and waited for him to join them – proof if proof were needed that he was running the show. He was wearing a dark jacket and an open-necked checked shirt and had a chunky watch on his left wrist.

The driver stayed in the car as the three men made their way inside the restaurant.

They went over to the counter together and lined up behind Kaitlyn, who was waiting for her order.

A young girl opened up a cash register and asked the three newcomers what they wanted. Kaitlyn noticed them for the first time but seemed unfazed. She looked back at the middle-aged man who was putting two large paper cups of Pepsi on her tray. She thanked him and carried it over to Standing's table.

'Is that them?' she said quietly as she sat down opposite him.

'Three of them,' said Standing, barely speaking because she was reading his lips. 'There's one more in the car.'

'Are we in trouble?'

'I don't think so,' he said. 'There are too many people here for them to start something, plus there's CCTV. And if they planned to do us harm, they could have done that on the road on the way here.' He reached for one of the boxes of chicken and took out a drumstick. He took a bite and then ripped the lid off a tub of coleslaw.

'You really are a fan of Colonel Sanders,' she said.

'He's the only officer I've any respect for,' said Standing. He put a forkful of coleslaw into his mouth and slotted in a few potato wedges.

Kaitlyn had ordered popcorn nuggets for herself and she nibbled on them. The three men carried their trays over to the far side of the restaurant. Standing had his back to them, which is probably why they'd chosen that table.

'What are we going to do, Matt?' Kaitlyn asked.

'I'm giving it some thought,' he said. 'One thing's for sure, we can't go anywhere near Bobby-Ray while they're tailing us. I'm pretty sure they think we don't know they're following us. We're just stopping for fuel and food. So we could just drive back to the freeway after this and go somewhere else. Maybe check into a motel of our own and see what happens.'

'Can't we lose them?'

'Probably. But as soon as they see anything that looks like counter-surveillance they'll know we're onto them.'

'So?'

'So they might decide to up the ante.' Standing shrugged. 'I'm guessing they don't know you're deaf, by the way.'

'Why do you say that?'

'They obviously thought they were being clever sitting behind me, but that means you can see them. Can you read their lips from there?'

'Pretty much,' she said. 'The further away, the less accurate I am. But I can see their lips.'

'Keep an eye on them, without making it obvious,' said Standing.

She sipped her Pepsi. Standing looked over at the SUV. The engine was still running but that was probably just to keep the aircon cold. There was still no sign of the second vehicle.

'They're wondering who you are,' said Kaitlyn. 'The older one says he's sure you're special forces.'

'Good guess,' said Standing.

'He says they need to get a photograph of you.'

Standing nodded. So they didn't know who he was. Or why he was there. He was still an unknown quantity as far as they were concerned and hopefully he would stay that way.

'The other guy I can see says you might be a body-guard. Hired muscle. But the older one says no. If I were going to have a bodyguard it'd be someone local. Or one of Bobby-Ray's Navy SEAL buddies.' She smiled. 'The younger one has just suggested that you might be my boyfriend.' She took another sip of her Pepsi and grinned at Standing, then her eyes flicked back to their table. 'The older one just said maybe.' She looked at Standing and tilted her head on one side. 'Little do they know you're not my type,' she teased.

'Really?'

'Too clean cut,' she said. 'And I do like tattoos.'

'So a kiss would be out of the question?' he said.

She laughed, but he reached over and held her hand. 'I'm serious,' he said. 'If they really are confused about our relationship, maybe now's the time to add to their confusion.'

She met his gaze for a couple of seconds, then leaned over and began kissing him. Her hand slipped behind his neck and she pressed her lips against his, though she kept her mouth firmly closed. She watched him with amused eyes as she broke away. Standing chuckled and popped another couple of wedges into his mouth. 'I see what you did there,' he said.

She sipped her drink. She seemed to be looking at him but he knew her gaze was over his shoulder at the table behind him. 'The younger one is saying he was right.'

'And the older one?'

'He's nodding, but I'm not sure if he's convinced. Maybe we should try it again.'

Standing laughed and held up a potato wedge. 'I think once is enough.'

Her eyes narrowed playfully. 'Was there something wrong with my technique?'

'I just don't want to overplay our hand,' he said. 'They might start wondering why we're getting so affectionate over fried chicken but not at the airport.'

'I hugged you,' she said.

'Yes. You did. It would be nice if they bought the boyfriend-girlfriend scenario, but that won't stop them tailing us.'

He tucked into his baked beans while she continued to nibble on her popcorn.

'So what do you do for a living?' he asked.

'My main job is teaching sign language,' she said. 'But I also help the local police with lip-reading. They call me in to look over CCTV and surveillance footage where there's no sound.'

'You're clearly very good at it,' said Standing.

'Because I wasn't born deaf,' she said. 'So I can remember what words sound like, which is a big help. People who are born deaf have no sense of what sound is. I was six years old when I lost my hearing, so I was lucky in that sense.'

'What happened?' asked Standing, picking up another chicken drumstick.

'Meningitis,' she said. 'I went swimming in a creek with Bobby-Ray. I got sick and he didn't. I was in hospital for more than a week and it was touch and go for a while. I recovered but ever since I've been as deaf as the prover-bial post.'

'I'm sorry,' said Standing.

'There's nothing to be sorry about,' she said. 'I could have died. Every day since then has been a bonus.' She sipped her Pepsi again. 'Bobby-Ray always blamed himself. He taught himself sign language to talk to me, even though I was good at reading lips from the start.' She looked over at the table behind him. 'The older one's on his cellphone. It's covering his mouth so I can't get a read on him.'

'Probably talking to the occupants of the other car,' said Standing. 'Okay, so where were we heading before we turned off the freeway?'

'Van Nuys,' she said. 'Bobby-Ray's in the Sunset Motel there.'

'We can't go there while we're being tailed, obviously,' said Standing. 'I don't suppose you live out this way?'

She shook her head. 'Venice Beach.'

'So what reason could we have for heading this way?'

'Sightseeing with my boyfriend? It would just about make sense that we were taking the 405 to 101 and then heading west to Santa Barbara.'

'Sounds like a plan,' said Standing.

4

S tanding used Kaitlyn's smartphone to check out the Santa Barbara area on Google Maps, then found a bed and breakfast with a view of the ocean, the sort of place a couple might choose for a romantic getaway. He booked a double room online as Kaitlyn turned off the 405 and onto the 101, the Ventura Freeway.

The two SUVs were back in play. The one containing the guys from the KFC outlet was now a quarter of a mile behind them. The second vehicle had been waiting for them at the approach to the freeway and was now half a dozen cars ahead. The longer the surveillance went on, the more convinced Standing became that they meant them no harm, at least until they had located Bobby-Ray.

It took almost ninety minutes to reach Santa Barbara and the SatNav took them straight to the bed and breakfast, a pretty wooden-sided detached house halfway up a hill overlooking the ocean. There was a paved area with parking for a dozen cars and Kaitlyn brought the Polo to a halt next to a white Mercedes. One of the black SUVs had been a hundred or so yards behind them and it drove on by.

They were checked in by a middle-aged man with slicked-back hair who introduced himself as Milton.

Kaitlyn used her credit card to pay for one night. Milton offered to carry Standing's bag but Standing said he was okay.

'Do you have any other bags?' asked Milton.

'In the car, we'll get them later,' lied Standing.

Milton took them upstairs and showed them to their room. There was a king-size four-poster with Egyptian cotton bedding, a modern low sofa and a large antique wardrobe. By the window was a Victorian dressing table with an ornate mirror. 'You'll love this,' said Milton, picking up a remote control. He pressed it and a television slid out of a cabinet at the foot of the bed. Another press on the remote and it slowly slid back into the cabinet. Milton handed it to Standing. 'Not that our guests come for the TV,' he said with a sly wink. 'Breakfast is between seven thirty and nine downstairs. Enjoy your stay.'

He left and closed the door behind him. Standing put his bag on a small table by the wardrobe. 'You can have the bed, I'll have the sofa,' he said.

'I'm smaller than you,' said Kaitlyn. 'You should have the bed.'

'I probably won't be sleeping much anyway,' said Standing. He went over to the window and looked out over the Pacific Ocean. There were a group of islands to the west.

'That's Santa Cruz Island,' said Kaitlyn, pointing to the largest of the group. 'They've reintroduced bald eagles there.'

'I'd suggest we go over and do some sightseeing,' said Standing. 'But we've got more pressing matters to deal with. Do you think Bobby-Ray will call you again?' He sat down on the bed.

'I don't think so,' she said. 'He was quite definite that the phone was too dangerous.'

'But your cellphone is the only way of getting in touch?'

She nodded. 'I don't have a landline.' She smiled. 'Obviously. I can only use texts or FaceTime.'

'But the way things stand, he's expecting you and me at the Sunset Motel?'

She nodded. 'He said he'd wait there. He said he wouldn't call us and I wasn't to call him.'

Standing rubbed his chin. Bobby-Ray's suspicion of phone communication was well founded, but intercepting calls was usually done by law enforcement and Standing was fairly sure the men in the black SUVs weren't police or FBI.

'The guys in the restaurant were speaking English, right?'

Kaitlyn frowned. 'Of course.'

'I don't suppose you could tell if they had an accent?'

She laughed. 'I'm good, Matt. But I'm not that good. To be honest, a lot of lip-reading is guesswork. Only about a third of the sound comes from the lips, so a lot of the time it's a matter of knowing the context. But accents, no. Why?'

'I was wondering if the guys following us are Russian, that's all.'

'Working for the client that died?'

'It would make sense. If it were the cops, they'd be more likely to pick us up and question us. This cloak and dagger wouldn't make much sense. Did the cops come and talk to you, after the shooting?'

'Just once. The day it happened. They wanted to know when I'd seen him last. He phoned me a few hours after they'd left.'

'Has there been much on TV or in the papers?'

'On the day of the shooting it was everywhere, but Bobby-Ray's name wasn't mentioned. Then it went quiet.'

'Can I use your phone again?' He held out his hand. Kaitlyn tapped in her password and gave it to him. He searched for Bobby-Ray's name but nothing came up. 'The Russian, what was his name?' asked Standing.

'I don't know. I mean, I read it but I can't remember.'

'Can you Google it?' He passed her the cellphone.

'Sure.' She busied herself for a moment and then handed it back to him. It was an article in the *LA Times*. 'RUSSIAN BUSINESSMAN AND THREE BODY-GUARDS SHOT DEAD IN HOME INVASION' read the headline. The story was on the front page but contained very little in the way of information. The businessman was named as Mikhail Koshkin but other than that there was hardly any detail, not even his age. There was even less detail about the bodyguards – they weren't even named. According to the newspaper article, the police had responded to a call that shots had been fired at a mansion in Bel Air and when they had arrived, four bodies had been discovered. The killers were believed to have fled the area in a car but there was no description of the killers or the vehicle. There was a photograph of the mansion with emergency vehicles parked outside, and a single picture of the deceased, a head-and-shoulders shot of a stern-faced man with a wide chin and jug-like ears, which looked as if it had been used in company publications.

Standing tapped the Russian's name into Google and the search engine came up with more than a dozen relevant hits. The *LA Times* and the *Los Angeles Daily News* both ran stories with more information on Koshkin – he was a former associate of the Russian president, who had lived in London for more than a decade. He had recently moved to Los Angeles and rented the mansion in Bel Air where he and his three bodyguards had died. Police suspected robbery was the motive and that a large amount of cash and jewellery had been taken.

There were more detailed stories in the British Press, including articles in *The Times*, the *Daily Mail* and the *Daily Telegraph*. But most of the information was about the man's companies rather than the man himself. Koshkin had run several oil and pharmaceutical companies in Russia before he had moved to the United Kingdom. He had been granted British citizenship and two of his children were at Oxford University. There was no mention of the fact that he had left the UK. In fact, there was very little in the way of hard information, and the only photograph of him was the same one that had been used in the *LA Times*. Standing handed her back the phone. 'Mikhail Koshkin,' he said. 'Bobby-Ray isn't mentioned in any of the stories about the killing.'

'He said they didn't want any publicity, so they hadn't released his name or photograph.'

'Bobby-Ray said that?'

She nodded.

'Who did he mean by "they"? Did he say?'

She shrugged. 'The cops, I guess.'

'Seems a strange way of going about an investigation, especially when you're hunting for a suspect.'

She slipped her phone into her pocket. 'We didn't talk for long,' she said.

'The papers don't say that the cops are looking for

him. They make it seem like it was a home invasion and robbery. And that more than one person was involved.' He shrugged. 'It's weird, the whole thing.' He looked at his watch. 'I could do with a shower,' he said. 'After that, we should go out and eat.'

'Is that a good idea?' she said.

'It's what a couple would do,' he said. 'I saw an Italian place down the road. We can walk.'

Standing showered and shaved and put on fresh clothes, then they went downstairs and out onto the road. Standing looked left and right but there was no sign of the SUVs, though he was sure they would be close by. They headed down to the main road and along to the restaurant, a single-storey building with a pitched roof and a terrace overlooking the ocean and the islands beyond. 'Let's sit outside,' said Standing. It was a warm evening and the terrace also gave them a good view of the road. There was still no sign of the black SUVs.

A young woman in a red dress took them out onto the terrace and gave them menus. The sun was starting to go down but there was an hour or so of light left. Standing ordered a bottle of Frascati. 'Are you okay to drink?' he asked Kaitlyn.

'I'm twenty-two,' she said.

'I mean do you drink?' said Standing. 'A lot of Californians are teetotal, right? And vegetarian.'

She laughed. 'I'm a steak and wine girl,' she said.

'Shall I cancel the Frascati and order red?'

'Frascati's fine,' she said. She looked over at the islands, then back to him. 'This is lovely.'

'It is. Yes.'

'But we're not on vacation, are we?'

He nodded. She was right. The setting was idyllic but the circumstances were anything but relaxing.

'So Bobby-Ray says you were like a British Navy SEAL?'

Standing nodded. 'SAS,' he said.

'What does that stand for?'

'Special Air Service.'

'So you're like a pilot?'

He smiled and shook his head. 'No. Though I've jumped out of a fair few planes. I don't know why it's called that. There's an SBS, too. Special Boat Service. They're mostly sailors and do a lot of their work at sea. I guess the SBS would be more like the Navy SEALs than the SAS.'

'He said you were with him in Syria.'

Standing nodded. 'He didn't tell you what happened?'

A waitress came over. Standing ordered the sea bass and true to her word, Kaitlyn ordered a Steak Pizzaiola. He waited until the waitress had walked away before continuing. 'He saved my life, pretty much,' said Standing. 'Got between me and the IED that injured him. Saved me and the officer who was with us.'

'He never said.'

'He isn't one for telling war stories,' said Standing. 'I didn't think his injuries were that bad and I was surprised to hear that he'd left the SEALs.'

'The explosion collapsed one of his lungs. A pneumothorax they call it. They fixed it and he was out of hospital in a week, but it meant that he could never dive again.' She sighed. 'I never understood why he was out there in Syria. It's not America's fight. It's not England's fight. And both sides seem as bad as each other.'

'It's messy,' agreed Standing.

'Which side were you guys on?'

Standing laughed. It was a good question. 'We were fighting ISIS,' he said.

'The Muslims?'

'The bad Muslims, you might say. The ones that throw gays off roofs and set fire to prisoners. But ISIS were fighting the Syrian government and you couldn't really call them the good guys because the president was killing a lot of his own people while we were there. Gassing civilians, bombing hospitals, messy doesn't come close to describing it.'

'And what were you doing out there?'

'What did Bobby-Ray tell you?'

'Not much. He said it was classified.'

'That's probably true,' said Standing. 'Basically, we were hunting down bad guys. And there were a lot of them.' He sipped his wine as he checked out the road. Still no sign of their tails.

He continued to look over at the road as they ate their meal. Plenty of cars drove by but there were no black SUVs with tinted windows. The sky darkened and waitresses placed lit candles on the tables.

Standing and Kaitlyn finished their meals and the wine and drank coffee as the sun dipped below the horizon. Standing paid the bill and they walked back to the bed and breakfast. Their followers had to be around somewhere, unless they had simply abandoned the surveillance, but that made no sense.

It was as they were walking up the stairs to their room that he realised what had probably happened. They had put some sort of tracking device on Kaitlyn's car, which meant they could follow the vehicle without staying close. He waited until they were in the room before telling Kaitlyn of his suspicions. 'They could have done it while we were at the restaurant,' he said.

'Could you find it?' she asked.

'Probably, but I've got a better idea,' he said.

5

Standing dozed on the sofa while Kaitlyn slept on the bed. He had jammed a chair under the door knob but he didn't expect anyone to break in. It was clear that the men in the SUVs were more interested in tracking down Bobby-Ray than they were in doing him harm. At least in the short term.

He'd set his phone alarm to wake him at seven. He shaved and showered and went down to the restaurant for a cup of coffee while Kaitlyn continued to sleep. Avis in Santa Barbara opened at eight o'clock sharp and at one minute past the hour Standing was on the phone ordering a rental car to be delivered to the bed and breakfast as soon as possible. The super efficient woman on the end of the line assured him the car would be with him before nine, and she was as good as her word. A young Hispanic man with a nametag that said his name was Jesus drove up in a white Ford Escape at precisely eight thirty. Standing had been waiting for him in the car park. Another Avis employee was with Jesus, driving a Ford Fiesta. The car park wasn't overlooked and Standing took Jesus in through the back entrance and along to the reception area where they did the paperwork and Standing showed him his driving licence and credit card.

After Jesus had left in the Ford Fiesta, Standing went back to the room, where Kaitlyn was showering. He waited until she had finished and dressed, before explaining what he planned to do, then they went downstairs and had breakfast. 'You're sure about this?' she asked as she spread jam on a slice of toast.

'I don't see we've any choice,' said Standing. 'I'll lead them on a wild-goose chase and you can go and talk to Bobby-Ray. I can arrange to meet you later.'

'But it's you Bobby-Ray wants to talk to.'

'Sure, but I'm not happy about the guys in the SUVs following you. This will give you a clear run, hopefully.'

Kaitlyn didn't look convinced but Standing was sure that he was right. She reached into her pocket and took out a set of door keys and took one off the ring. 'You should keep this, in case we get separated,' she said. 'It's the key to my condo.'

'What about you?' he asked.

'It's a spare. You'll need to get someone to let you into the building but anyone will do that.'

She held out her hand. 'Give me your phone.' He did as she said, and she tapped in her address and gave it back to him.

'We won't get separated,' he said.

'Just in case,' she said.

They finished their breakfast, then Standing went upstairs to get his bag. Milton was at reception and he shook them both by the hand and said that he hoped they'd visit again soon.

'I'm sure we will,' lied Standing. 'You have a lovely place.' That much was certainly true. Under other circumstances Standing was sure he would have enjoyed himself.

Standing put the bag on the back seat of the Polo and gave the keys to the Escape to Kaitlyn. 'Wait until I text you,' he said.

She threw him a mock salute. 'Aye, aye, sir.'

'I'm serious,' he said. 'We need to be sure that both vehicles are after me before you head out. And keep your eyes open. If at any point you even get the feeling you are being followed, text me and head back home.' She was clearly worried, so he patted her on the shoulder. 'It'll be okay,' he said. He climbed into the Polo, started the engine and drove out of the car park. He headed down the hill and turned onto the 101, driving east to Ventura. He spotted the first black SUV a mile outside Santa Barbara. It kept its distance, confirming his suspicion that they had placed a tracking device on the car. The second SUV was waiting outside Ventura and it drove ahead of him on the way to Camarillo. He picked up his mobile and sent Kaitlyn a text message. 'GOOD TO GO.'

A few seconds later he got a thumbs-up and a smiley face.

Kaitlyn would also be driving along the 101 but she would be several miles behind. They had agreed that once she got to Ventura she would head north-east on the 126 to Santa Clarita and then drive down to Van Nuys.

Standing's eyes kept flicking to his rear-view mirror. The SUV behind was hanging well back, which suited him. The windows of the Polo had a slight tint but even so, if the followers got close they would see that he was alone in the car. The front SUV was almost half a mile ahead, there was no way they would be able to see that the passenger seat was empty. Standing smiled to himself. So far so good.

The freeway passed by Ventura and he began to relax. Kaitlyn wouldn't be following him beyond Ventura, she would be out of harm's way.

The traffic wasn't heavy and there wasn't much lane switching going on. The SUV behind kept its distance, but the one ahead had slowed and Standing was gaining on it. He eased off on the accelerator. He wondered if the narrowing of the gap was calculated or just random. Five minutes later both vehicles were even closer and he decided it was deliberate.

Standing considered his options. If they kept getting closer, at some point they would realise he was alone in the car and that they had been duped. It would be too late for them to go back and look for Kaitlyn, which meant they would have to stick with him. But their mission was to find Bobby-Ray and they wouldn't know whether or not Standing knew where the former SEAL was hiding, which meant there was a good chance they would move from surveillance to a more pro-active response.

The forward SUV was now a dozen cars ahead of him. There was just one man in the back seat and he could make out another passenger in the front. So three. And probably four in the SUV behind him. Seven in all. The best way of improving those odds was to lose one of the SUVs.

He looked over at the SatNav. Ahead was Thousand Oaks, and to the south were several nature reserves. The nearest freeway exit was Newbury Park, just two miles away. Standing was in the middle lane. The SUV ahead of him was in the left-hand lane, the one to his rear was on the right. If he did another rapid exit they'd know that something was wrong, but they'd know that anyway once they saw that Kaitlyn wasn't in the car.

His eyes flicked to the rear-view mirror. His pursuers were about a hundred yards behind him. There was no way he would be losing them.

The Newbury Park exit was just a mile away. He accelerated and moved over to the left lane to give the impression that he was going to continue on the freeway. The tail behind stayed where it was but the SUV ahead of him also accelerated. They were now all doing just over sixty miles an hour.

Time seemed to slow. He continued checking both wing mirrors and the rear-view mirror, watching his tails but also keeping himself aware of what other traffic there was. He wouldn't be indicating this time, he would just cut across the lanes at the last possible second. There were no police vehicles in the area and unlike British highways there weren't any CCTV cameras. His only real concern was hitting another car.

The exit was only a couple of hundred yards away. He resisted the urge to brake as any change in speed would alert his followers. He checked his mirrors. Two cars in the right-hand lane indicated that they were leaving the freeway. The SUV ahead of him went by the exit and immediately he wrenched the wheel to the right and stamped down hard on the accelerator. There was plenty of space in the middle of the highway but there was a large truck barrelling down the inside lane. Its horn blared as Standing cut across the freeway, the rear of the Polo missing the truck by inches.

The two cars that had turned off the freeway ahead of him were travelling at about half his speed and he shot past them on the inside of the ramp. Both drivers pounded on their horns and the truck continued to sound its disapproval as it powered down the freeway towards Thousand Oaks.

Standing eased down on the brake to get his speed back to sixty. His eyes flicked to the rear-view mirror. The black SUV behind him had made the turn but was now trapped behind the two saloons.

The ramp curved to the right but he kept his speed up. In a perfect world he'd lose his tail and meet up with Kaitlyn in Van Nuys, but Standing had dealt with enough cock-ups in his life to know that the world was far from perfect. The ramp joined a road and he accelerated. The SUV cut around the two saloons and also accelerated. It looked as if they had given up any pretence and were openly in pursuit now. He figured they had gotten close enough to him on the ramp to see that he was alone in the car. He smiled to himself. They were probably as mad as hell right now.

He was heading south on South Moorpark Road, towards what his SatNav identified as Los Robles Open Space, which appeared to be some sort of wilderness area. There wasn't much traffic around and the SUV came up behind the Polo, close enough so that he could see the grey-haired guy in the front passenger seat. He, like the driver, was wearing glasses.

They drove through an estate of detached houses, each on a pristine lot, then the houses were gone and there were rocky hills either side of the road. Standing's eyes flicked between the rear-view mirror and the wing mirrors. The SUV was getting closer by the minute and that meant they were planning something. Standing was breathing slowly and evenly and his hands were relaxed on the steering wheel. They were alone on the road now and the SUV pulled out and accelerated.

Standing tensed, knowing what was going to come next. Their plan was to run him off the road, which wouldn't be too difficult as the SUV was a much heavier and more powerful vehicle than the Volkswagen. There was a clump of bushes ahead to his right – if he were in the SUV that's where he'd make his move. He accelerated and the SUV matched his speed. He had both feet at the pedals now, the right foot on the accelerator while the left hovered over the brake. He waited until the bushes were just fifty feet away before easing his foot off the accelerator and simultaneously stamping down on the brake. The Polo slowed and the SUV went ahead. As the rear of the SUV passed the Polo's bumper he flicked the wheel to the left, and hit the accelerator at the same time as he took his foot off the brake.

The Polo hit the nearside wheel arch and Standing pressed the accelerator to the floor. The Polo was much lighter than the SUV but the surge in power pushed the rear of the SUV to the right. If the driver had been paying attention he'd have turned his steering wheel to the right to keep his vehicle straight but Standing had carried out his manoeuvre so quickly that, before the driver could react, the rear of the SUV had shifted to the right and the vehicle flipped onto its side in a shower of sparks.

Standing immediately took his foot off the accelerator and pressed down on the brake pedal. As the Polo slowed, the SUV continued its roll, crashing along the tarmac in a screeching of tortured metal.

Broken glass splintered across the road and the sides

of the SUV buckled under the stress, and all the time the engine roared like an animal in pain. The roll took the SUV off the road and onto the grassy verge, where it made one more complete revolution and finally came to a halt, upside down. Standing pulled up behind it and climbed out of the Polo.

The SUV's airbags had inflated and the wheels were still turning. The rear offside door opened and Standing hurried over. The man in the back had his seat belt still fastened and was hanging from it. He had a semi-automatic in his hand. A Glock 19. The man was shaken from the tumble and he was blinking as he raised the gun and aimed it at Standing. Standing kicked the door and it slammed against the man's arm. The impact made the man's finger tighten against the trigger and a shot rang out, the round burying itself in the grass. Standing kicked the door again and this time the gun fell from the man's nerveless fingers. Standing bent down and picked up the Glock. He pulled the door open and hit the man with the butt of the weapon, smashing it against his temple. The man went limp. The passenger next to him was stunned, hanging upside down with all his weight on his seat belt.

Standing reached inside the jacket of the man he'd hit and patted him down. The pockets were empty. He felt for the man's trouser pockets and in the right-hand one he found a wallet. He pulled it out and shoved it inside his own jacket, then straightened up. The road was still clear of traffic.

The SUV's engine coughed and spluttered and died, and the wheels slowly stopped spinning. Standing pulled open the front passenger door. The airbag was keeping the grey-haired man pressed against his seat and he seemed to be unconscious. But as Standing patted his jacket looking for a wallet, the man's eyes opened. He snarled at Standing, pushed his hand away and reached inside his jacket. Before the man could grab the gun from his underarm holster, Standing punched him, twice and hard. The man's eyes rolled back in their sockets. Standing grabbed the man's gun from its holster. Another Glock. He shoved it into the waistband of his jeans and then patted down the man's trousers. He found a wallet, put it in the pocket with the first one and slammed the door shut.

He hurried back to the Polo, climbed in and drove off, pulling a U-turn and heading back to the freeway. The road was still deserted and it was a full two minutes before he saw another vehicle, a UPS van driving in the opposite direction. The UPS driver would report the damaged vehicle but it would take the emergency services at least half an hour to get to the scene. He smiled to himself as he wondered what the occupants of the SUV would say by way of explanation.

He reached the freeway and headed east. He wanted to contact Kaitlyn but it was more important to put plenty of distance between himself and the SUV, so he stayed in the middle lane at just above the speed limit and drove to Thousand Oaks before pulling off the freeway and sending her a text message saying that he wanted to talk to her.

He took out the two wallets he'd taken and went through the contents as he waited for her to FaceTime him. The guy in the front passenger seat was John Keenan. Just about to turn sixty and living in Pasadena, according to his driving licence. The guy in the back was half Keenan's age. His name was Marcus Reams and he lived in Anaheim. So both were local. Neither man had a business card or anything in the way of personal mementos, just driving licences, credit cards and cash. Both men did have blue key cards with the same logo on them, a rocky peak in a circle. Standing put the wallets in the glove compartment, along with the guns he'd taken.

His phone rang. It was Kaitlyn, and he held the phone up so that she could see his lips clearly before telling her that the two SUVs had been following him but that he was now in the clear. 'Where are you now?' he asked.

'Just outside Van Nuys,' she said.

'Wait where you are and I'll come to you,' he said. 'Best we go see Bobby-Ray together.'

She had parked outside a diner and she gave him the name and address. He tapped it into the SatNav. It told him that she was twenty-four miles away and that it would take precisely twenty-seven minutes to reach her. It turned out the estimate was optimistic as he hit traffic on the Ventura Freeway and slowed to a crawl. The SatNav constantly updated his time of arrival and when he finally pulled up next to the rental car, more than an hour had passed.

They went inside for coffee. After the waitress had filled their mugs, Standing explained what had happened. He realised again the advantage of her deafness as he was able to lower his voice to the slightest of whispers and she was still able to follow what he said. 'So who are they?' she asked.

'They both had security key cards with a logo on,' he said. 'A rock thing in a circle. I haven't checked but I'm thinking Redrock, the company that employed Bobby-Ray.' He took out his phone and used Google to search for Redrock and then checked for images. He found the logo and clicked on the page it was from. Redrock Solutions, a security company headquartered in Washington DC. He showed her the screen. 'That's it,' he said, but she was looking at the phone and didn't hear him. He waited until she looked back at him. 'That's the logo,' he said.

He scrolled through the website. Redrock Solutions had government security contracts in Iraq and Afghanistan, and provided advice to governments around the world, predominantly regarding airports and ports. They also had a personal protection division and an alarm and CCTV company. According to the website they had more than two thousand employees around the world.

'Why would the company that hired Bobby-Ray be following me?' asked Kaitlyn.

'I assume because they think he'll contact you,' he said. 'Did they ever reach out to you?'

Kaitlyn shook her head. 'No.'

'That's what I don't understand,' said Standing. 'I would have expected them to get in touch officially rather than following you around. You'd expect them to be on Bobby-Ray's side.'

'Unless they think he killed the client.'

Standing shrugged. 'Even so . . .' He sipped his coffee. 'Hopefully Bobby-Ray will know what's going on. How far is the motel?'

'About half an hour,' said Kaitlyn.

'I think we should leave your car here,' said Standing. 'We can use my rental.' Standing paid for the coffees and they went out to the car park. He opened the front passenger door of the Polo and took the two guns and wallets out of the glove compartment, hiding them inside his jacket as he walked over to the rental. He got into the driver's seat and she climbed in next to him. 'They had guns?' she said when he leaned over and put the Glocks in the glove compartment.

'Yeah,' said Standing.

'That's not good.'

'I thought all Americans had guns.'

'California has some of the most restrictive gun laws in the country,' said Kaitlyn. 'And it's not easy to get a licence to carry a concealed gun.'

'Those guys were pros,' said Standing. 'Probably former cops or ex-military.' He fastened his seatbelt and started the engine.

'But you beat them?'

'Yeah.'

6

They arrived at the Sunset Motel in the early after-noon. It was a two-storey flat-roofed building with rooms either side of a central reception area. A large sign in the middle of the roof had the name of the motel under a cartoon of a setting sun. Underneath it was a sign that read VACANCY.

There was a car park behind the motel with half a dozen vehicles lined up. Standing drove in and parked. 'Is one of those Bobby-Ray's?' he asked.

Kaitlyn shook her head. 'He has a Ford F-Series.'

'What's that?'

'A pick-up truck. A red one. I don't see it.'

Standing rubbed his chin as he considered his options. If Bobby-Ray was in hiding, he'd almost certainly have checked in under another name. If they both went in and started asking for a guest based on just a description it would look suspicious. 'Maybe you should go talk to the desk,' he said. 'I don't suppose Bobby-Ray told you what name he's used to check in?'

She shook her head.

'Maybe tell them some story about him owing money and you're there to help him. Have you got any pictures on your phone?'

'Sure,' she said. She took out her cellphone and showed him a picture of her on the beach with Bobby-Ray, him in baggy shorts with pineapples on them and her in a white bikini.

'Nice,' he said. 'I'll wait here, you go and get the room number.'

She forced a smile and nodded.

'It'll be okay,' he said. 'Don't worry.'

She nodded again and got out of the car. He watched her walk around the side of the building. He practised square breathing for a couple of minutes, a relaxation technique that he used whenever he felt himself tensing up. He inhaled slowly for four seconds, held the breath for four seconds, exhaled for four seconds, then held his breath for four seconds before repeating the process. He felt himself relax as he concentrated on counting off the seconds.

Kaitlyn returned after five minutes. 'He's not answering his phone, the clerk thinks he's out.'

'Does he remember seeing Bobby-Ray's truck?'

She shook her head. 'No, he has one of the rooms at the back. Number twelve.' They drove around to the rear of the motel. Each room had its number burnt into a wooden block at the side of its door. Number 12 was to their left on the ground floor. 'That one,' she said, pointing at it. The curtains were drawn and there was a DO NOT DISTURB sign hanging from the handle.

'What did you tell the clerk?'

'Just like you said. I showed him the picture on my phone and said he was my brother. The clerk said he'd checked in as Billy Jones and had paid in cash. He checked in three days ago and the clerk hasn't seen him since. He called the room for me but there was no answer.'

'He didn't seem suspicious?'

'He didn't seem to care. What are we going to do, Matt?'

It was a question that Standing was struggling with. If Bobby-Ray had gone out, their only option was to wait for him to return. But they had no way of knowing how long that would be, and somebody would notice them eventually. But it didn't make sense for Bobby-Ray to be driving around if the cops were after him. The sensible thing to do would be to lie low. 'Why don't you knock on the door? He might just not be answering the phone.'

Kaitlyn got out of the car and walked over to the door. She knocked, and knocked again. She peered in through the window, then knocked on the door again. She put her face close to the door for several seconds and Standing figured she was calling out to him. One more knock and then she walked back to the car. He could see from the look on her face that something was wrong.

'What?' he said as she got back into the car. She wasn't looking at his face, so she didn't see his lips move. She pulled the door shut. He put his hands on her shoulders and turned her so that she was facing him. 'What's wrong?' he said.

Tears were welling up in her eyes. 'He's lying on the floor. I think he's dead, Matt.'

She began to sob and Standing held her. Her body shook and he patted her on the back. 'It's definitely him?' he asked.

She didn't answer. He stopped hugging her and pushed her back so that she could read his lips.

'Are you sure it's him?' he said. 'You saw his face?'

'I just saw his legs,' she said, blinking away tears.

'It might not be him, Kaitlyn,' said Standing.

'It's his room. Who else could it be?'

'One step at a time,' he said. 'Let's see for ourselves.' He leaned past her and opened the glove compartment. He took out one of the Glocks.

'I want one,' said Kaitlyn.

'You don't need a gun.'

'If you do, I do.'

'Kaitlyn, no offence but in the wrong hands a gun is more dangerous to the shooter than the person they're shooting.'

'I could shoot before I could walk, pretty much,' she said.

'I'm sure that's an exaggeration.'

'Bobby-Ray taught me when I was nine.'

'So you were a late walker?'

She laughed despite the tears. 'Okay, I exaggerated. But trust me, I can shoot.' She held out her hand and he gave her the second Glock. She ejected the clip, checked that the barrel was clear, then quickly and efficiently broke the gun down into its major components, placing them on her lap. Then she just as quickly reassembled the weapon, slotted the magazine back in and pulled back the slider to insert a cartridge.

Standing nodded, impressed. 'Okay,' he said. 'You can have that one.'

They got out of the car. Standing tucked his gun in the waistband of his jeans. The Glock's trigger safety mechanism meant that the weapon was almost impossible to fire accidentally. Kaitlyn shoved her gun down the back of her jeans. Her denim jacket was just long enough to conceal it.

They walked over to Bobby-Ray's room. Standing looked around but couldn't see any CCTV cameras. He went to the window and peered through a narrow gap in the curtains. Kaitlyn was right. There was someone on the floor. He stepped back and looked left and right to make sure there was no one around, then he kicked the door hard, just below the handle. There was a splintering sound but the door didn't move. He kicked again, and again. On the third kick the door flew open and slammed against the wall. Standing stepped inside with Kaitlyn close behind. The body was on the floor, face down. Kaitlyn hurried over to it as Standing closed the door.

She knelt down and rolled the body over. 'It's not him,' she sighed. 'Thank God!'

The dead man was in his forties with receding hair, wearing a grey suit and a shirt that was matted with blood. When Kaitlyn rolled the man over she revealed a Smith & Wesson semi-automatic with a bulbous silencer attached.

'Let me have a look,' said Standing. Kaitlyn stood up and Standing took her place. There was a towel on the bed and Standing used it to pick up the gun. He sniffed the silencer and the gun. It had been fired. He ejected the magazine and did a quick count. By the look of it four shots had been fired. He put the gun back on the floor. He could see three brass cartridge cases immediately and then saw a fourth under the bed.

He patted the man down. There was a holster on the man's hip. In his pocket were two wallets, one containing money and credit cards, the other an FBI badge.

'He's a Fed!' Kaitlyn gasped.

Standing nodded. He pulled out the man's driving

licence. Roy Johnson. He was local to Van Nuys. He put the card back in the wallet and slid the wallets back into the dead man's pockets.

'Matt,' said Kaitlyn, her voice shaking.

He looked around. Kaitlyn was staring wide-eyed at the bathroom. He stood up and walked over to the bathroom door. It was ajar and through the gap he saw a man slumped on the toilet. At first glance he thought it was Bobby-Ray – the man was about his friend's height and build – but as he pushed the door open he realised he was older and darker skinned.

The man had been shot in the chest, twice, and his shirt was red with dried blood. There was another gun on the tiled floor. A Beretta. He went over to the man and patted him down. He was also carrying an FBI badge and was wearing a shoulder holster. His driving licence said he was Michael Kelly and that he lived in Santa Clarita, to the north of Van Nuys. Blood had pooled around the base of the toilet and Standing was careful not to touch it as he put the badge and wallet back.

'Do you think Bobby-Ray did this?' asked Kaitlyn.

'I can't believe he'd shoot FBI agents,' said Standing. He used the towel to wipe the bathroom door handle. 'But that's what it looks like. Come on, we need to get the hell out of here.'

He wiped the front-door handle and kept the towel on it as he pulled it open. A bald man in shirtsleeves and brown trousers was standing there, holding a pump-action shotgun. He had a name badge clipped to his shirt pocket. ERIC. He gestured with the barrel. 'Hands up, mister,' he said.

'We didn't do this,' said Standing quietly.

Eric smiled without warmth. 'Looks to me like you kicked in the door,' he said. 'Now where's the woman? The one saying she was Mr Jones's sister.'

'She's inside,' said Standing. 'Look, sir, we haven't done anything wrong.'

'You broke into a guest's room,' said Eric. 'That there is wrong for a start. What were you planning to do? Steal from the guy? How low can you get?'

Standing took a step towards Eric but stopped short when he aimed the barrel at Standing's chest and tightened his finger on the trigger. 'Put your hands in the air or I swear to God I'll blow your head off!' he shouted.

Standing did as he was told. 'Where is the woman?' asked Eric.

'She's deaf,' said Standing. 'Let me talk to her.'

'I know she's deaf. Now you stay where the hell you are.'

Kaitlyn came up behind Standing and flinched when she saw the shotgun. Standing twisted his head so that she could see his face. 'It's okay,' he said slowly. 'Just put your hands in the air, don't be scared.'

She nodded nervously and raised her hands. Standing turned to look at Eric. A car drove around from the road but Standing kept his eyes on the shotgun. 'Listen to me, Eric. When you see what's inside that room you're going to get a shock, but you need to know that we didn't do it.'

The man's eyes narrowed. 'You been smashing the place up, is that it?'

'No, Eric. It's worse than that. But we had nothing to do with it.'

Standing stepped to the side and Eric moved to get a better look inside the room.

The car stopped. Standing heard the engine of a second car.

Kaitlyn was blocking Eric's view of the room. He waved the shotgun at her. 'You get out here, missy,' he said. 'And keep your pretty little hands in the air where I can see them. You didn't think I bought your story about being his sister, did you?'

Kaitlyn stepped outside. Standing looked over at the cars. They were SUVs. One was white. The other was black. Both had tinted windows. The white one had stopped at the side of the motel, the black one was driving slowly parallel to the building. Standing's eyes narrowed. They clearly weren't police or FBI. Were they more Redrock vehicles?

Eric moved to his left and craned his neck. He could see into the room now but Standing knew that he wouldn't be able to see the body on the floor.

'Sir, can we step inside for a moment?' asked Standing.

'You stay where you are!' said Eric. He moved further to the left.

The windows of the black SUV slid down.

Standing turned to look at Kaitlyn. 'When I say now, get down on the ground,' he mouthed silently. She frowned. 'Understand?' he mouthed. She nodded.

Eric took another step and his jaw dropped when he saw the body. 'Who's that?' he said. 'Is that Mr Jones?' He looked back at Standing. 'You killed him? Is that what's going on here? You broke in and killed him?'

A gun appeared in the front window of the SUV.

Standing turned to look at Kaitlyn. 'Now!' he shouted.

She immediately dived to the side and hit the floor. Standing turned back to look at the SUV. A second gun had appeared in the rear window. An Uzi or a Ruger MP9. Both were capable of spraying a lot of bullets in a short space of time. The gun at the front was a Glock. Less of a threat but still fatal.

Eric aimed his shotgun at Kaitlyn, his mouth open wide in confusion, and Standing lashed out with his foot, kicking Eric's ankle and knocking him off balance.

He heard the rat-tat-tat of automatic fire and the motel window shattered, followed almost immediately by two rounds thwacking into Eric's back. Standing was already moving, diving to throw himself next to Kaitlyn so that he could shield her from the bullets.

The shotgun fell to the ground. The rounds had gone through Eric's back and exited, blowing bloody holes in his chest. His mouth worked soundlessly and for a second he looked uncomprehendingly into Standing's eyes.

The SUV was still moving and now both guns were firing. The machine pistol was still aiming high and a second window exploded but the Glock was being fired low with rounds ricocheting off the tarmac around him. Standing pulled out his gun and held it with both hands as he brought it to bear on the vehicle.

The machine pistol was doing the most damage but the man firing it was aiming high and would soon have an empty clip. The guy in the front seat was a better shot and so was the more immediate threat. Standing sighted on the front window and fired twice. Almost immediately the Glock was pulled back inside the vehicle. Standing switched his attention to the rear window. He fired twice. The machine pistol continued to fire and then stopped. Standing jumped to his feet and ran towards the SUV. He fired two more shots through the back window and this time was rewarded with a scream of pain.

The white SUV was moving now, and Standing dropped into a crouch to make himself a smaller target as he swung the Glock around. He aimed at the passenger side of the windscreen and fired once. The glass shattered and he saw a man with a crew cut and dark glasses holding a machine pistol. Standing fired twice and the man's head exploded.

The white SUV picked up speed. Standing could easily have shot the driver but he wanted them to leave because if they stayed he would be outgunned. He fired twice more into the vehicle but kept his shots to the left. The SUV pulled a U-turn and headed back around the motel to the road, its tyres screeching.

Standing looked back at the black SUV. Another gun appeared at the window, a semi-automatic, presumably in the hands of the other backseat passenger. Standing moved to the side to make himself a harder target and fired twice. The SUV stopped. Three shots rang out and rounds whizzed by him and thudded into the wall of the motel. He fired two more shots. He had been counting instinctively. He had fired fifteen times. The Glock's magazine held seventeen rounds which meant he only had two shots left.

The gun disappeared and the SUV went into reverse. It headed back the way it had come and then pulled a tight one-eighty handbrake turn before accelerating away. Standing kept his gun trained on the vehicle until it had disappeared around the side of the motel, only then did he hurry over to Kaitlyn. 'Are you okay?' he asked.

She nodded at him shakily. 'I'm okay.'

He helped her to her feet and then went over to the motel employee, who was lying on his back, his hands clutched to his chest. The rounds had penetrated his lungs, deflating them so that he couldn't breathe. Bloody froth was trickling from between his lips. His eyes had gone blank and Standing could see that he was only seconds away from bleeding out. He held his hand. 'It's okay, Eric, just relax,' he said softly. He wasn't sure if Eric could hear him but he continued to speak. 'Think of the people you love,' he said. 'Think of them, think of them around you.' Eric squeezed his hand once and then went still. His mouth fell open and his eyes stared sightlessly up at the sky. 'Sorry, mate,' said Standing.

He stood up and put his arm around Kaitlyn, who was staring down at the corpse in horror. He tilted her head so that she could see his lips. 'We've got to go,' he said. She nodded and allowed him to lead her to the car. He eased her into the front passenger seat and then climbed in next to her. He glanced at the motel windows as he started the engine. There didn't appear to be anyone watching. Maybe he'd been lucky. He just hoped that if anyone had seen the shoot-out they wouldn't have the presence of mind to note down his registration number.

He drove around the side of the motel and slowed as he reached the road. He looked left and right to make sure there was no sign of the SUVs, then headed for the 405 South back to Los Angeles.

7

S tanding drove south. He really wanted to talk to Kaitlyn but the fact that he was driving made it impossible. He reached Venice Boulevard, where he had the choice of heading east to Los Angeles or west to Santa Monica. Kaitlyn was clearly upset; she sat with her head down and her arms folded, biting her lower lip. He decided to take her to the beach. He drove to the ocean and found a parking space close to the pier. 'We need to eat,' he said.

She shook her head. 'I can't face food.'

'You're in shock,' he said. 'You need to get your blood sugar up.'

She seemed a little unsteady on her feet, so he held out his arm and she linked hers through his as they walked along Ocean Avenue. He found a quiet seafood restaurant, and a pretty Asian girl showed them to a table with a view of the ocean and gave them menus.

'I'm really not hungry, Matt,' she said. 'My stomach's churning.'

'It's stress,' said Standing.

'Damn right it's stress,' she said. Her voice was loud, so he motioned with his hand for her to keep it down. 'Sorry,' she said.

Standing reached over and held her hands. He could feel her trembling. 'What you're feeling is totally natural,' he said.

'How can you be so calm?'

'I've been well trained.'

'They were shooting at us. I couldn't move. I only got down because you told me what to do. I would have been frozen to the spot, like the motel guy.' Her eyes filled with tears. 'I can't believe they killed him.'

'They didn't mean to,' said Standing. 'It was us they wanted.'

'Weren't you scared?' she said. 'When they were shooting at you?'

Standing shrugged. 'Not really. I was reacting instinctively, I didn't really have time to be scared.'

'How did you know what to do?'

Standing grinned. 'Kaitlyn, I've been well trained. So has Bobby-Ray. We train and we train hard so when stuff like that happens the training kicks in and you just do what you have to do.'

'You could have been killed.'

'You don't think about that. But to be honest, firing a gun from a moving vehicle is not an easy thing to do. One of the guns was a machine pistol and they're not accurate above a couple of dozen feet, and the others were pistols and again they're not very accurate.'

'They killed the motel guy.'

'They sprayed bullets everywhere and he was just unlucky. They call it spray and pray. You spray bullets and pray that some hit their target. I'm a bit more . . . methodical.'

'Is that what you call it?'

A waiter appeared and they both smiled up at him, though Kaitlyn's eyes were still wet with tears. Standing let go of her hands as the waiter rattled off the specials. Kaitlyn clearly wasn't interested in food, so Standing ordered the swordfish special for them both, and Coke to drink, figuring the soft drink would be the quickest way of raising her blood sugar, while he could do with the caffeine.

'Is that what it's like when you're in combat?' asked Kaitlyn after the waiter had left.

'It's not usually as close as that,' said Standing. 'Generally, you know where the enemy is and you go after them. They only attack you if something has gone badly wrong on the intel side. And when they attack you in places like Syria or Afghanistan they usually do it with AK-47s and RPGs. More bang for the buck.'

'And how do you feel, when you're being attacked?'

Standing shrugged. 'I don't really feel anything,' he said. 'You just try to work out what your options are and which of those options has the best possible outcome. You assess the threat and then decide how best to react. There's no time to have any feelings about what's happening. That's for afterwards, when the shooting's over.'

She held out her hands. They were still shaking. 'Look at me,' she said. 'I'm a mess, but you were like ice then and you're still . . .' She shrugged, struggling to find the right words. 'It's as if it doesn't mean anything to you.'

'I wouldn't say that,' he said. 'But as I keep telling you, I've been trained by the best. Your brother's the same. When the shit hits the fan you just do what you have to do. You might talk about it over a beer afterwards, but you don't let it worry you. That'd be the quickest way to a nervous breakdown.'

'You didn't even seem affected when the motel guy died.'

'There was nothing I could do,' he said.

'You held his hand.'

'Sure. Maybe it made it a bit easier for him.'

She looked at him earnestly. 'Have you seen a lot of people die?'

'Some,' he said. 'But usually the enemy, so there wasn't much hand-holding going on.'

The waiter returned with their Cokes. Kaitlyn sipped hers. 'So is there a girlfriend back in the UK getting worried about what you're up to?' she asked.

'The work I do, it's hard to keep a relationship going.'

'So have you got a girl in every port?'

Standing laughed. 'The sort of places we tend to be sent, the women are covered from head to foot and they are stoned if they so much as look at an infidel.'

'But what about at home?'

'Our base is at Hereford, near Wales, but these days we're not there much and when we are there we're training and don't really get out of camp.' He sipped his drink and grimaced. It was way too sweet, but that was what Kaitlyn needed just now. 'What about Bobby-Ray? Does he have a girlfriend here? Someone he might go to?'

'There was one girl he was seeing. Lucky.'

'Lucky?'

'Her name's Lucy but she misspelled it in a text to him once, so he called her Lucky ever since. She's a paralegal. I think he met her in a bar.'

'You've met her?'

'A couple of times.'

'Do you think he might be with her now he's left the motel?'

She shrugged. 'It's possible. Maybe.'

'Do you have her number?'

'No, but I know where she lives. We picked her up at her home a few weeks ago and went to the beach. Here actually. Santa Monica.' She leaned forward. 'Matt, what do you think happened at the motel? Those men were FBI agents. Do you think Bobby-Ray killed them?'

Standing grimaced. That was exactly what he thought. Which put Bobby-Ray in a whole world of trouble. 'I guess so,' he said. 'But he might have had just cause.'

She frowned, not understanding.

'The guy on the floor, his gun had a silencer,' said Standing. 'FBI agents and cops don't use silencers. So you have to wonder what that guy was doing with a silencer on his gun.'

'They were definitely Feds?'

Standing nodded. 'The shields seemed real enough. The question is, were they there officially or not? I think not.'

'I don't understand.'

'I'm guessing they identified themselves as FBI. Bobby-Ray lets them in. But that right there doesn't feel right because if the FBI knew he was at the motel they should have gone in with a SWAT team. They'd assume that Bobby-Ray was armed and dangerous and he's a former SEAL. I can't see they'd go in alone. Not unless they had some other agenda.'

'They were there to kill him, is that what you mean?'

'Why else would they have a silencer? It looked to me

as if the guy on the floor was killed with his own gun. There was bruising on his right hand as if the gun had been twisted around. I think Bobby-Ray realised what they intended to do, grabbed the gun in the man's hand and shot the agent by the bathroom. That agent staggers back and sits down on the toilet, bleeding out. The gun goes off again and the other agent dies. There were four shell casings on the floor and they look like they were from the cop's Smith & Wesson. And that would explain why nobody heard any shots. So the good news is it wasn't Bobby-Ray's gun. And with the motel guy dead, hopefully there's no one who can identify Bobby-Ray. But it's messy, all right. Very messy.'

The waiter returned with their food. They thanked him, and Standing waited until he'd left before continuing.

'There are a lot of unanswered questions,' he said. 'How did they know where he was? Why did they try to kill him? Who were the guys in the SUVs? And how did they know about the motel?'

'Do you think they were working together? The SUV guys and the Feds?'

'If they were, they'd have gone in together. The SUVs turned up later, so I think they were following us.'

'But how? They couldn't have known about the rental car.'

'I don't know. They were following the Polo this morning and they left you alone. They were definitely only tailing me. So something must have happened for them to have known we were at the motel.' He shrugged. 'I just don't know.'

'So what do we do now?'

Standing toyed with his fish. Kaitlyn had the knack of

asking the questions that were upmost in his mind. Unfortunately he didn't have much in the way of answers. 'There were no clothes or a bag or anything in the hotel room, so Bobby-Ray must have taken everything with him,' he said. 'That's a good sign. Is there any other way that Bobby-Ray might try to get in touch?'

'Email maybe.'

'Can you check?'

'Sure.' She put down her knife and fork and tapped away on her iPhone. Eventually she shook her head. 'Nothing. Why hasn't he been in touch?'

'I'm guessing he thinks they're tracking all communications,' said Standing. 'And the fact that the FBI turned up at his motel has probably made him even more careful.'

'Is that how they found him, you think? By tracking his phone?'

'I guess it depends on whether he was using his own vehicle or not. But if he'd ditched his truck and was using a car that couldn't be linked to him, then there aren't that many options.'

'So we just have to wait for him to contact us?'

'We can go and talk to Lucky, see if he's been in touch with her,' said Standing. 'Unless you can think of somewhere else he might be holed up.'

She shook her head. 'I just hope that wherever he is, he's okay.'

Standing wanted to say something, anything, that would put her mind at ease, but Bobby-Ray was most definitely not okay.

8

They walked back to the car in silence. Standing got behind the wheel and tapped it as he considered his options. If the men in the SUVs had been following Kaitlyn, there was a good chance that they were also watching Bobby-Ray's girlfriend.

'What's wrong, Matt?' asked Kaitlyn.

He turned to look at her. 'I'm wondering what's the best way to approach Lucky.'

'You think they'll be watching her?'

'That's exactly what I was thinking,' he said. 'Maybe phoning her is the way to go. Do you know where she works?'

Kaitlyn shook her head. 'No.' She shrugged apologetically. 'Sorry.'

'What about her family name?'

She shrugged again. 'All I know is Lucky. And Lucy.'

'But you can find her place?'

Kaitlyn nodded. 'She's three roads up from the beach.'

Standing looked at his watch. It was just before three, so it would probably be a couple of hours at least until Lucky got back from work. 'We could do with a change of car, and a change of clothes,' he said. 'The car rental company has an office here, let's get that sorted first.'

He drove the car to the rental company and told an earnest young man with thick-lensed glasses that the vehicle he had kept making a grinding noise at high speeds. There was a scrape on the front bumper from where he'd pushed the SUV off the road but the man didn't mention it. Standing opted for a different model and colour, choosing a grey Chevrolet Cruze. The man amended the paperwork and five minutes later he and Kaitlyn were back on the road. 'Do you have charity shops in LA?' he asked Kaitlyn but realised she couldn't see his lips. He made sure the road ahead was clear, turned to look at her, and slowly repeated the question. 'The American Cancer Society has a store on Wilshire Boulevard,' she said.

She gave him directions and he followed, constantly checking for tails. He was reasonably sure they weren't being followed, so he drove to the charity store and parked close by.

'I've got money,' she said as they walked to the store. 'We can buy new, you know.'

'It's not about money, it's about not looking as if we're walking around in brand new clothes,' he said.

They went inside. Standing headed straight for the men's clothing section and chose a pair of faded blue jeans, a couple of dark work shirts and a brown wool jacket. He also grabbed a couple of baseball caps, one advertising Coors Beer, the other the LA Lakers.

'You need something, too,' he said. 'Different style and colours to what you're wearing now.'

'Second-hand clothes?' she said. 'Seriously?'

'They'll help you blend in,' he said. 'They've already seen us, so we need to look as different as possible. If it helps, think of it as vintage rather than second-hand.'

She wrinkled her nose and went over to a rack of shirts. She selected a couple, then chose a pair of jeans and a leather jacket with a pink fringe across the back. He shook his head at the jacket. 'Nothing distinctive,' he said. 'You don't want anything memorable.'

'Like an LA Lakers cap?' she said.

He held it up. 'First of all, you see LA Lakers stuff all over town,' he said. 'But second of all, if I ditch the LA Lakers cap and change it to the Coors cap, that alone will fool a lot of tails. Most of the time a follower will pick on one thing and stick with that. Alter that one thing and it's as if you've disappeared. So grab a few hats yourself.' There were a dozen or so wigs hanging on the wall and he gestured at them. 'They might come in handy, too.'

Kaitlyn took a long black wig and a shorter, curly, brown one. She also took a faded denim jacket, a short denim skirt and a pair of white shorts.

Standing found a scuffed Samsonite backpack and added it to his purchases. They carried everything over to the counter where a middle-aged black woman wearing bifocals scanned everything and put them in two large carrier bags.

'Can we use your changing rooms?' asked Standing.

'Sure,' said the assistant, who was already serving another customer.

There was only one changing room, so they took it in turns. Kaitlyn went in first and changed into her denims, then Standing put on his jeans, one of the work shirts and the jacket. They put the rest of their clothes in the backpack and went out to the car.

'We need to check out where Lucky lives,' he said as he got behind the wheel. 'If she is under surveillance it's going to make reaching out to her that much more difficult.'

Kaitlyn gave him directions to Lucky's apartment. He drove past slowly but didn't see anyone waiting in a vehicle outside. She lived in a four-storey block with a metal shutter gate leading to an underground parking garage.

Standing took a series of right turns and drove by the block a second time. It still looked clear, so he found a parking space and pulled up at the side of the road.

'Is it okay?' asked Kaitlyn, twisting around in her seat and looking out of the rear window.

'Maybe,' said Standing. 'The street seems clear but they could be watching from a building.' He realised that she hadn't been looking at him, so he tapped her on the shoulder and once she was looking at his lips he repeated what he'd said. She nodded. 'How about this?' said Standing. 'You go and get her, then bring her out and walk her to the pier. I'll follow and check if she's being followed.'

'Why don't we just talk to her inside?'

'Because if she is being watched and the watchers are good, they'll have bugged her apartment. And tell her to leave her phone in her apartment.'

Kaitlyn nodded. 'Okay,' she said.

'You're sure? You're okay with this?'

She nodded, more confidently this time. She climbed out of the car and walked to the apartment block. She pressed a button on the console at the side of the door, and a few seconds later pushed the door open and went inside.

Standing continued to scan the pavement as he waited.

No one else went into the building or came out. After five minutes Kaitlyn reappeared with an Asian girl with waist-length black hair wearing a University Of Southern California sweatshirt and cut-off jeans. They left the building and headed towards the ocean. Standing climbed out, locked the car and went after them, pulling on his LA Lakers cap.

He kept on the opposite side of the road, checking all pedestrians and vehicles as the two girls walked down to the beach, then turned left and went to the pier. Standing was certain that no one was following them. As they walked onto the pier and headed towards the amusement section at the far end, Standing hurried after them. He caught up with them and Kaitlyn introduced him to Lucky. They shook hands. She was a pretty girl with high cheekbones and olive skin and a pair of sunglasses pushed high up on the top of her head. Her hand felt tiny in his but she had a strong grip. 'I don't understand what's happening,' she said. 'Is Bobby-Ray in trouble?'

'What did he tell you?' asked Standing.

'Just that he had a problem, that I wasn't supposed to believe anything I read in the papers or saw on television, and that he would be back in touch with me when it's safe.'

'He didn't explain what had happened?'

Lucky shook her head. 'No.'

Standing looked at Kaitlyn, wondering how much they should tell her. 'He had a problem at work,' said Kaitlyn. 'One of his clients was killed and the police think he did it.'

Lucky put her hands up to cover her mouth, her eyes wide. 'No way.'

'It's all a mistake,' said Kaitlyn, reaching out to touch

her on the shoulder. 'Bobby-Ray's innocent, but he has to stay hidden until it's resolved.'

'How does hiding from the police resolve anything?' said Lucky, taking her hands away from her face. 'He needs a lawyer and he needs to tell the police everything.'

'It's complicated,' said Standing. Two men walked by wearing baseball jackets. One of them had a white earpiece. It was probably a Bluetooth unit but it didn't match with the man's casual attire and gleaming white Nikes. Standing turned to watch them walk by as he continued to talk to Lucky. 'There's some confusion about what actually happened.'

'He can tell the police what happened, and if he didn't do it then he'll be okay.'

'It's not as simple as that,' said Standing. The two men walked towards the big wheel. One of them reached out and held the other's hand. If they were on surveillance and it was a cover move, it was a clever one. 'He thinks the best thing is for him to stay hidden for a while.'

'Why hasn't there been anything on the TV or in the papers?' asked Lucky.

It was a good question, Standing knew. And one that he didn't have an answer to. 'We don't know,' said Standing.

'If they were looking for him, surely they would release his picture?'

'Lucky, you're right. But this isn't a normal case. There is something very strange going on here, which is why Bobby-Ray is lying low. Do you have any idea where he might be?'

She shook her head. 'He said I shouldn't call him or look for him, and that he would call me when it was over.'

Kaitlyn nodded. 'That's what he said to me.'

'What about the police, did they talk to you?'

Lucky shook her head. 'No.'

'What about the FBI?'

Lucky frowned. 'The FBI?'

'Did anyone from the FBI talk to you?'

'No. Nobody.' She folded her arms. 'I don't understand any of this,' she said. She looked at Standing. 'Kaitlyn said you're a friend of Bobby-Ray's.'

'I was with him in Syria.'

Her eyes narrowed. 'Are you the guy who was with him when he got hurt?'

Standing nodded. 'There was an IED. A booby trap.'

'He hated having to leave the SEALs but they said he couldn't dive again. They wouldn't even let him stay on as an instructor.' She sighed. 'None of this would have happened if he hadn't left the SEALs.'

'Was he happy in his new job?' asked Standing.

'Not really,' said Lucky. 'But he didn't have many options.'

'How long had he been working for Redrock?'

She frowned. 'What's Redrock?'

'That's the company he was working for?' said Standing.

'He didn't tell me the name, he just said he was going to be working with Kurt, bodyguarding some rich Russian guy.' Her eyes narrowed. 'Was that the client who died? The rich Russian?'

Standing nodded. 'Did Bobby-Ray tell you anything about the job?'

'Just that the guy they were bodyguarding was an asshole. He treated everybody like shit.' She smiled nervously. 'He did actually say once that he could understand why someone would want to kill him, but he was only joking.'

'What about the guys he was working with?' asked Standing. 'How did he get on with them?'

'Kurt got him the job. Kurt Konieczny. They were in the SEALs together. Have you spoken to Kurt?'

'Kurt's dead,' said Kaitlyn.

'What? How? No.'

Kaitlyn nodded. 'He was killed when the client was killed.'

'What about the other bodyguards, the Russians?' asked Standing. 'Did he tell you anything about them?'

Lucky was still shocked at learning of the death of Kurt Konieczny, so Standing had to repeat the question. 'He said they were a surly bunch,' she said. 'He thought that the Russians resented the Americans. But Bobby-Ray said they needed people with local knowledge. They had two American drivers. One was called Paul, I think. He and Kurt didn't socialise with the Russians but they had a few arguments as to who should do what. Bobby-Ray said they liked to throw their weight about and sometimes that caused problems in LA.' She frowned. 'You think he fell out with them and had some sort of fight?'

Standing shook his head. 'Bobby-Ray wasn't the sort to lose his temper like that,' he said. 'And he's certainly not the type to shoot an unarmed man, no matter what the provocation.'

'So what's going on?' asked Lucky.

'I wish I knew,' said Standing. 'Look, if he does contact you, let us know straight away. And if the police contact you, tell us.'

'I will,' she promised.

They walked her back to her apartment block and waited on the pavement until she was safely inside.

'What are we going to do, Matt?' asked Kaitlyn.

'I need to talk to Bobby-Ray's pals, see if they've any idea what he was up to. I know a few people at their base in Coronado. I'll drive down.'

'I'll come with you,' she said.

'I think it's best I go alone,' he said. 'I'm fairly sure I can get on the base, but you're a civilian.'

'I can't go back to my apartment, not after what's happened.' She bit down on her lower lip and he could see she was scared.

He realised she was right. 'How about this? We drive down to the base and we check you into a motel? Depending on what happens, we can stay there tonight. I figure a room close to a Navy SEAL base is as safe as it gets.'

Kaitlyn forced a smile. 'That works.'

9

It was a two-hour drive south from Los Angeles to the Naval Amphibious Base at Coronado. It was just across the bay from San Diego, reached by driving across a massive steel girder bridge. Standing had spent a month at the base before flying to Syria with the SEALs. The base was one of eight separate military facilities, covering more than 230 square kilometres stretching from San Clemente Island, seventy miles west of San Diego, across to the Mountain Warfare Training Camp, sixty miles to the east. Through an architectural oversight in the late Sixties, six of the buildings on the base had been erected in a swastika-shape when seen from the air. The design quirk was only spotted when Google Earth became widely available and despite some modifications and landscaping, the base still sported one of the largest swastikas on earth. There were more than twelve thousand military personnel and reservists at the base and it dwarfed the SAS's camp in Hereford.

As soon as they had driven over the bridge, they stopped off at the El Rancho Motel and Standing used his credit card to book a room for Kaitlyn before he drove on to the base. He was stopped by a uniformed guard, who scrutinised his UK military identification and listened to his request, then pointed him in the direction of a car park outside the base. When he returned to the guard post on foot, the same guard made an internal call and spoke to the administration office for SEAL Team Six. After a few minutes he waved Standing over and handed him the receiver.

'Matt Standing? Seriously? Is that you? This is Skip Dunnett. What the hell are you doing here? Haven't heard from you in months.'

'Sorry to drop by without an appointment, LT,' said Standing. 'Is there any way you could spare me a few minutes? It's important.'

'Sounds mysterious,' said the Lieutenant. 'Let me talk to the guard there.'

Standing gave the receiver back to the guard, and a few minutes later he was walking through the base with a visitor ID clipped to his jacket pocket.

Lieutenant Dunnett was based in an administration office a short walk from the guardhouse. He had to wait in an outer office for a few minutes, then the Lieutenant threw open his office door and came out. He was wearing desert fatigues and had a Glock in a holster on his hip. Standing saluted and Dunnett laughed and returned the salute, then hugged him and clapped him on the back. 'How the hell are you?' asked the officer. He had a small scar on his cheek from where he'd been hit by shrapnel from the IED in Syria.

'Keeping busy,' said Standing. 'You?'

'They've got me training at the moment, but word is I could be back in Syria in a month or two.'

'I'm sorry about the surprise visit, LT.'

'I'm just glad you didn't come in through the window after throwing in a couple of flashbangs,' said Dunnett. 'I'm just on my way to the firing range. Walk with me.'

The two men walked out of the administration office and across a grassy area. 'I'm here because of what happened to Bobby-Ray,' said Standing.

'So it's not a social visit?' He clapped Standing on the back. 'Sounds like Bobby-Ray's got himself in a right mess.'

'Did the cops talk to you?'

The Lieutenant scowled. 'Yeah, we had a couple of LAPD detectives here asking questions. They seemed sure that Bobby-Ray had killed his client and the other bodyguards in his team. I tried to point out that they'd be better waiting to hear Bobby-Ray's side but they looked at me like I'd farted.'

'It was Bobby-Ray's gun, right?'

'That's what they said. But that means nothing. Anyone could have grabbed his weapon. And one of the body-guards he was supposed to have killed was a friend of his. Former SEAL, Kurt Konieczny. I didn't buy it for one minute.'

'Yeah, me neither.'

'So do you know where he is?' asked the Lieutenant.

Standing shook his head. 'I haven't spoken to him.'

'So no offence, why are you here?'

'His sister called me. She doesn't know what to do.'

'Has she spoken to Bobby-Ray?'

Standing's mind raced. He didn't want to lie to the Lieutenant, but admitting that Bobby-Ray had been in contact with his sister might well get her into trouble. And the attack on the way from the airport suggested that they would be better off staying below the radar. 'She's got no way of contacting him, and hasn't seen him since three days before the Russian was killed.' That much was true, so he figured he hadn't actually lied to the officer.

'So where do you think he is?' asked the Lieutenant. They reached a large metal-sided building with a sign above the door that said LIVE FIRING RANGE and a smaller sign that said HEARING PROTECTION MANDATORY.

'I don't know him well enough to hazard a guess even,' said Standing. 'He's obviously lying low. My thought was that if I could at least prove he wasn't responsible for killing the Russian, he could turn himself in.'

'If he isn't the killer, he should do that anyway,' said Dunnett.

'That's what I said to Kaitlyn. But she thinks the cops have Bobby-Ray in their sights and won't consider any alternatives.'

'Yeah, that's the impression I got. They didn't seem interested in looking for anyone else.'

'And they know he's a former SEAL. Which means if they do catch him, it'll likely be a hard arrest and they'll go in with guns blazing.'

The Lieutenant nodded. 'I hear you.' He rubbed the back of his neck. 'How about I talk to the guys here that he was close to and get them to talk to you. They might have some thoughts about where he'd hole up.'

'Sounds like a plan.'

'There's an Irish pub on Orange Avenue. McP's. Owned by a former SEAL, Greg McPartlin. Swing by there this evening and I'll send the guys to talk to you.'

'Thanks, Lieutenant.' Standing saluted and Dunnett returned the salute, but then shook hands with him before turning and entering the firing range. Standing headed back to the guardhouse. He handed in his badge, collected his car and drove off the base and to the El Rancho Motel.

Kaitlyn was watching through the window and opened the door the moment he'd parked the car. 'How did it go?' she asked as soon as he reached the door.

'He's going to put me in touch with some of Bobby-Ray's friends here,' said Standing as he slipped inside the room. 'The cops have been to the base but didn't learn anything. The LT I spoke to doesn't know where Bobby-Ray is but his mates might.' He lay down on one of the two beds in the room. The television was on but the sound was muted.

'When can we see them?'

'Tonight. The LT'll send them to a place called McP's.'

She grinned. 'I know McP's. I've been there with Bobby-Ray.'

'Where is it?'

'About a mile away. Can I come?'

'I don't see why not.' He looked at his watch. It was five o'clock. 'The LT said this evening but didn't say when exactly. Why don't we head there now and we can grab something to eat?'

She grinned. 'You eat a lot, you know that?'

'It's an army habit,' said Standing. 'You grab food when you can. You never know when you might not be so lucky.'

'Sure, when you're in Syria or Afghanistan, but this is

the US of A and there's plenty of food here, twenty-four seven.'

'Okay, if you're not hungry, we can get a coffee.'

Her grin widened. 'No, I can eat,' she said.

10

McP's was a single-storey white building with a green turret at the entrance, from which hung a stars and stripes. Across the road from the pub was the Coronado Museum of History and Art. They left the Chevrolet in the car park and walked inside. The décor was that of a typical Irish pub – or at least what Americans thought an Irish pub looked like – with a smattering of Navy SEAL memorabilia, including flags, patches, shields and framed photographs of news reports of major SEAL operations. A U2 song was playing in the background. Like most soldiers, Standing wasn't a fan of the Irish group.

They went to the bar and picked up a menu. Standing grinned at the Ol' Dubliner burger – a half-pound burger, corned beef, Swiss cheese, grilled onions, Thousand Island dressing and sauerkraut. He'd visited Dublin several times on undercover operations and had never been offered a burger like that. Kaitlyn ordered a grilled chicken Caesar salad and a Coke and Standing asked for a beer and a shepherd's pie. The barman gave them their drinks and they headed outside to the patio, where there were circular tables and chairs shielded by large green umbrellas. They sat down at a table overlooking the car park. A group of dog owners were sitting at a table with their pets at their feet. Two German Shepherds, a Rottweiler and a yappy Jack Russell.

Standing was halfway through his beer when a waitress brought out their food, and he was halfway through his shepherd's pie when Kaitlyn looked over at the entrance to the patio and smiled. 'I know one of those guys,' she said, pointing with her knife at three men who had just walked out of the pub holding bottles of beer.

Standing turned to look. They were definitely special forces with super-fit physiques and tans that suggested they weren't long back from somewhere hot and sunny, and with beards that meant they were probably heading back that way sooner rather than later. They were all wearing cargo pants and tight-fitting polo shirts that showed off their muscles. One of the men spotted Kaitlyn and waved and all three headed over to their table. Kaitlyn got to her feet and rushed to the guy who had waved. He laughed and picked her up and twirled her around.

The tallest of the three walked over to Standing's table. 'You Matt?' he asked. He had a square jaw with a cleft in it and the close-cropped hair that most SEALs favoured. He had a pair of Oakley sunglasses hanging from the neck of his shirt.

Standing nodded and got to his feet. 'Matt Standing,' he said, offering his hand.

The man shook, squeezing hard. 'I'm Fenn,' he said. 'Stephen Fenn.'

The SEAL who had grabbed Kaitlyn let her go and he nodded at Standing. 'This is John McNally,' said Fenn. He gestured at the third man, who was standing watching them with his hands on his hips. 'And this is Simon

Farrant.' Farrant's beard was straggly and unkempt and he had a thick rope-like scar on his right arm. He had a chunky steel TAG Heuer watch on his wrist.

Standing shook hands with McNally and Farrant.

'They call me Camels,' said McNally. 'Because of the cigarettes I smoke, nothing to do with the animal.' His beard was neatly trimmed and he had a tattoo of a frog's skeleton on his left arm, a shout-out to the days when the SEALs were known as frogmen. He grinned at Farrant. 'You never met Bobby-Ray's sister?'

Farrant shook his head and offered his hand to Kaitlyn. 'Pleasure,' he said.

Kaitlyn shook hands with Farrant, and with Fenn. Fenn and McNally pulled over chairs and they all sat down at the table.

'You guys want to eat?' asked Standing.

'We already ordered,' said Fenn. He waved at their plates. 'You should eat, our food'll be a while. So, the LT says you're a friend of Bobby-Ray's?'

'I was embedded with his group in Syria,' said Standing. He picked up his fork and began to attack his shepherd's pie again.

'You're the Brit he saved, right?' asked McNally.

Standing nodded. 'Got between me and an IED.'

'That's why he was injured?' said McNally. He was holding a set of ranger beads, small black beads on a length of paracord, separated into one group of nine and one group of four. The beads were a special forces technique of counting distances, developed long before GPS came along. A soldier worked out how many paces made up a hundred metres. Then he would count off one bead for each hundred metres. When he got to one kilometre he would count off one of the small group. So the beads on the paracord would allow him to accurately count off five kilometres. McNally seemed to be using his like prayer beads, letting them slip through his fingers one by one.

'Yeah. Took the blast himself,' said Standing.

'They're talking about giving him a medal,' said Fenn, stretching out his legs.

'He deserves it,' said Standing. 'My Regiment is putting him up for a medal, too, but the powers that be are saying no because he's a Yank. Bastards.'

'Bobby-Ray wouldn't give a damn about a medal,' said Fenn. 'Medals mean nothing, we all know that. Just a way of prettying up an officer's uniform.'

'When was the last time you saw him?' asked Standing.

'Me? Two months ago. It was here. I came in and he was sitting at the bar. He was with Kurt Konieczny.'

'Arsehole,' grunted McNally.

'You didn't like Konieczny?' asked Standing.

'I think Bobby-Ray was the only one who did,' said McNally.

'What was the problem?' asked Standing.

'He was a nasty piece of work,' said Fenn. 'Wasn't always that way, to be fair. Three years ago I was with him in Afghanistan and he was as good as gold. But a year or so later he was in a team that was pinned down by an ISIS hit squad in the middle of nowhere. Two of Konieczny's team were killed, and not in a good way.'

'How so?'

'There were two snipers and not a lot of cover. One of his team was out in the open and they kept shooting him in the arms and legs. There was nothing they could do to help him. Took over two hours for him to die. They called in air support and the ISIS unit was killed, but Konieczny was never the same after that.'

'I guess you can understand why,' said Standing.

'Shit happens,' said Fenn. 'You deal with it. But he dealt with it by treating every Haji as if they were Johnny Jihad. He'd be on patrol and he'd just take pot shots at the locals. Took every opportunity to get physical. Okay, we know that there's no way we're going to be winning hearts and minds out there, but he was intent on causing as much pain as he could. He was spoken to a few times but if anything he got worse, and eventually he was let go.'

'He was kicked out?'

'The record shows that he resigned, but yeah, he was given his marching orders.'

'And he went private?'

Fenn nodded. 'Joined some Blackwater-type operation, but even they had to keep him out of the Sandpit.'

He looked over at McNally. 'What was that company called? Redrum?'

'Redrock,' said McNally.

Farrant nodded. 'Yeah, Redrock Solutions or something.'

'They moved him to personal protection and he said he was doing really well,' continued Fenn. 'He used to drop around to McP's and hand out his business card to the guys, telling them to give him a call.'

'Arsehole,' said McNally again.

'But Bobby-Ray was friends with him?'

McNally nodded. 'They went through training together. Bobby-Ray always said that if Konieczny hadn't been there he'd never have made the cut. I thought that was BS but what can you do?'

'You know the cops are saying that Bobby-Ray shot Kurt?'

'Can't see that being right,' said McNally. 'I mean, the guy's an arsehole but he was still a SEAL and once a SEAL always a SEAL. SEALs don't go around shooting each other.'

The other two men nodded in agreement.

Kaitlyn had been eating her salad in silence, watching their lips carefully so that she could follow their conversation. 'Do you have any idea where he might have gone?' she asked. 'Anyone you can think of who might be hiding him?'

'Haven't heard any chatter,' said Fenn. 'And I'm pretty sure the cops will have been checking all the obvious places. He hasn't reached out to you?'

'Once, just after it happened,' she said. 'But he's off the grid now. He told me he thought the cops were monitoring his phone, so he dumped it.'

'But at some point he'll get back in touch?' said Fenn.

'I hope so,' said Kaitlyn.

Fenn took a long drink of beer. 'This is such a clusterfuck.'

'Tell me about it,' said Standing.

'Anything we can do, just ask,' said Fenn. McNally and Farrant nodded earnestly.

'Thanks, guys,' said Standing. 'I appreciate that.' He sipped his beer. 'So the last time you saw Bobby-Ray, he was okay? He didn't seem worried about anything?'

'Seemed happy enough,' said Fenn. 'Good salary, health benefits, they were talking about sending him to Iraq.'

'Iraq?'

'The company they were working for made its money from government contracts out in Iraq and Afghanistan. A couple of former Blackwater managers left in 2007 when they got caught up in the shitstorm in Baghdad, remember? Fourteen civilians were killed?' Standing nodded. He remembered the incident. Two years later Blackwater was renamed as Xe Services and two years after that it was acquired by a group of private investors and renamed Academi, still providing services to the US Federal Government and the CIA. 'The managers were involved on the periphery, they weren't charged but Blackwater let them go. They got a big payoff and they used the money to set up Redrock. They've got two thousand or so employees and about fifty are ex-SEALs or former Delta.'

'And most of Bobby-Ray's work was close protection?'

Fenn nodded. 'That's what he said. But they were talking about him heading up their Iraq bodyguarding division.' He tilted his head on one side. 'You know, thinking about it, that did seem to put Kurt's back up.'

McNally nodded. 'Yeah, I picked up on that,' he said. 'Like he was jealous.'

'The Iraq job was a promotion?' asked Standing.

'That's how I read it,' said Fenn.

Standing sipped his drink. 'It doesn't make any sense, does it? They worked together, they were friends, and yet the cops are sure that Bobby-Ray killed him.' He shrugged. 'So if it wasn't Bobby-Ray, who could have done it?'

'The cops told you what went down, right?'

'I haven't spoken to them,' said Standing.

'The way we understand it, they were at the Russian's house getting ready to stand down for the night and

Bobby-Ray went in and started shooting. Shot the client, shot Kurt, and shot two of the Russian bodyguards.' Fenn scowled. 'If the mission was to kill the client, it was one hell of a messy way of doing it,' he said. 'He could have just waited until he was alone with the client and popped him. Or done it in the car. If Bobby-Ray was following protocol he would have been in the front passenger seat. He could have just turned around in his seat and shot the guy in the heart. Bang bang, dead as a doornail. Instead he goes all gunfight at the O.K. Corral, almost as if it was a spur of the moment thing.'

'Is that possible?' asked Standing. 'He just went crazy?'

Fenn laughed harshly. 'Come on, man. You know Bobby-Ray. He's a rock solid operator. Cool as a cucumber no matter what you throw at him. He wasn't happy at having to leave the SEALs but he was doing okay and earning good money. No way would he lose it in the way they're saying he did.' He frowned at Standing. 'Are you thinking he did it?'

Standing shook his head. 'I don't know what to think,' he said. 'But he told Kaitlyn he didn't, and so far as I know he's still in LA. If he had done it he'd have had his exit strategy in place and be well away by now. But if it wasn't Bobby-Ray, then who? And why is everyone so keen to blame him for the shootings?'

The three SEALs shrugged but no one had an answer. 'Who was Kurt's boss at Redrock?' asked Standing.

'A guy called John Keenan,' said Fenn. 'Another former SEAL but he's been out fifteen years or more. He was with Blackwater in Iraq back in the early days when it was the Wild West and security guards were picking up a thousand dollars a day.'

Standing nodded slowly but his mind was racing. John Keenan was the grey-haired man sitting in the front of the SUV that he had pushed off the road. So the men tailing him had definitely been from Redrock. But why were they trying to kill him and Kaitlyn?

'I never met Keenan, before my time, but he was very highly regarded,' said Fenn. 'He was in Bosnia in 1999 helping to track down war criminals, then he was in Afghanistan during Operation Enduring Freedom as part of Task Force Sword. You ever hear of that?'

Standing shook his head.

'It was a US special forces initiative, basically a black ops unit working directly to Joint Special Operations Command. They were tasked with hunting and killing senior leaders of al-Qaeda and the Taliban. Word is that Keenan had half a dozen confirmed kills on that operation.'

'Why did he leave the SEALs?' asked Standing.

'He was wounded in 2002,' said Fenn. 'He was part of a SEAL team protecting President Karzai and he took a bullet during an assassination attempt. Left not long after but he was snapped up by Blackwater. You're thinking about maybe talking to him?'

'I doubt that Bobby-Ray has been checking in with his employer, not with the cops after him for killing a client. He's more likely to reach out to his family or friends.'

'He hasn't spoken to any of us,' said Fenn. He looked at his colleagues and they both nodded in agreement.

They seemed to be telling the truth, and that worried Standing because if Bobby-Ray was in trouble, the obvious people to ask for help were his former SEAL colleagues. Once a SEAL always a SEAL was a mantra he'd heard time and time again when he was embedded with them. But Bobby-Ray hadn't reached out to them, he'd gone to Standing, more than five thousand miles away. There had to be a reason for that.

'He had a girlfriend, right?' said Fenn, looking at Kaitlyn. Kaitlyn nodded. 'Lucky. We've spoken to her. She doesn't know where he is.'

A waitress carried over three burgers for the SEALs. She clearly knew them all and said their names as she placed their food in front of them.

'So what's your plan, Matt?' asked Fenn as he picked up his burger with both hands. McNally was already chewing on his.

Standing shrugged. 'I'm not sure. Bobby-Ray asked me for my help, but now he's gone to ground and seems to be avoiding me.'

'I don't understand that,' said Fenn. 'You come all the way here to help, why doesn't he get in touch?'

Standing didn't want to tell the SEALs about the two dead FBI agents, so he just shrugged again. 'Good question,' he said. He nodded at Kaitlyn. 'We should get back to LA,' he said.

They stood up and all three SEALs shook Standing's hand. 'I meant what I said, you need anything, just ask,' said Fenn. 'Give me your phone.' Standing handed over his mobile and Fenn tapped in his number. 'You need us, we're there for you,' he said, and gave the phone back to Standing.

Standing went to the bar and paid his bill, and also paid for the food and drinks of the three SEALs. 'We need to go to Pasadena,' he said as they walked back to the Chevrolet.

'Pasadena? Why?'

'That's where John Keenan lives. The guy that was following your Polo. I took his driving licence. I need to talk to him.'

'Now?'

'I figure if we drop by in the middle of the night we're more likely to catch him at home,' said Standing.

John Keenan lived in a small Spanish-style single-storey house in a quiet street on the outskirts of Pasadena. Standing parked some distance away and looked at his watch. He had left it until just before three o'clock in the morning before driving to the house, figuring it was the best time to make an unannounced home visit. Kaitlyn was sitting in the front passenger seat, wearing the long black wig that they had bought in the charity shop in Santa Monica. She looked totally different. Standing had one of the Glocks in his lap. He couldn't see any security cameras around the house but there was a burglar alarm box and as Keenan was in the security business, Standing was fairly sure the house wouldn't be easy to break into.

'I should take my gun,' said Kaitlyn.

'Best you don't,' said Standing. 'Leave it in the car. Just ring the bell.' He shoved a roll of duct tape in his jacket pocket. 'Once he comes to the door, you get back in the car and wait for me.'

'What are you going to do to him?'

'Ask him a few questions, that's all.'

'Are you going to hurt him?'

'I'm not planning to.' He grinned. 'Not much, anyway. Kaitlyn, this guy is trying to kill your brother. If I have to slap him around a bit to find out what's going on, then so be it.'

She nodded solemnly. 'Okay.'

They got out of the car. The street was deserted and well lit. They walked across the road and up the driveway to the front door. There was a small porch and Standing stood to the side and pressed his back against the wall. He nodded at Kaitlyn. She stepped forward, pressed the doorbell, and stepped back. They waited for thirty seconds and when nothing happened he motioned for her to ring again. This time they heard footsteps and the door opened a few inches. It was on a security chain. 'Who is it?' growled a man.

'I'm so sorry to bother you, but my dog has got into your back garden. Can I get her, please?'

'What?'

'My dog. Sasha. She's pregnant and she's got a bladder problem, so I have to take her out all the time and she ran off. She went into your garden.'

The man unlatched the chain and opened the door wide. 'Do you have any idea what time it is?' It was Keenan. Standing moved quickly and jammed the barrel of his Glock under Keenan's chin. He pushed him into the hallway and kicked the door shut behind him.

'Is there anyone else in the house?' Standing hissed. 'Tell me, because if there is and they burst in on me, I'll have no choice other than to shoot them.'

'There's no one here,' said Keenan. 'Just me.' He was naked underneath a blue towelling bathrobe.

Standing kept the gun jammed into the man's neck as he marched him through to the sitting room. He made him sit down on a wooden chair with arms, and gave him the roll of duct tape. 'Tie your ankles to the chair,' he said, gesturing with his gun.

'You're the Brit,' snarled Keenan. His face was bruised and one of his eyes was puffy from where Standing had hit him after his car had crashed off the road.

'Just keep your mouth shut and do as I say,' said Standing. 'Tie your ankles to the chair.'

Keenan glared at Standing, and then did as he was told. He used the duct tape to bind his left ankle to the chair, then did the same to his right. Standing gestured with his gun.

'Now tape your left arm to the arm of the chair.'

'It'd be easier if you did it,' said Keenan.

'Yeah? And it'll be a lot more painful if I put a bullet in your arm. Just do as you're told.'

Keenan opened his mouth to say something but then had a change of heart and followed Standing's instructions. Once the left arm was secured, Standing stepped forward, placed the gun on the table and quickly bound Keenan's right arm to the chair.

'What the fuck is this about?' asked Keenan. He didn't seem the least bit frightened and he stared unflinchingly at Standing.

'Why are you trying to kill Bobby-Ray?' asked Standing.

Keenan's forehead creased into a frown. 'Say what?'

'You heard me. You were following us from the airport.'

'That's right. We had the sister under surveillance.'

'Because you want to find Bobby-Ray.'

'Damn right. He killed a client. And one of my men.'

'So you want revenge, is that it?'

Keenan's frown deepened. 'What the fuck is your

problem?' he hissed. 'You ran me off the road, remember? You tipped over our car and damn near killed us.'

'You were trying to get me off the road.'

'To talk to you. We'd realised that the sister wasn't with you and that you were on to us.'

'So you decided to kill me.'

'You've got this the wrong way around. You tried to kill us. Any one of us could have easily died in that crash.'

'And what about the drive-by shooting at the motel?'

'What motel?' Keenan seemed genuinely confused by the question.

'The Sunset Motel in Van Nuys,' said Standing. 'Where Bobby-Ray was holed up. Two SUVs armed to the teeth killed a motel employee and nearly took out me and Kaitlyn.'

'That wasn't our people,' said Keenan.

'So you say. But then you would say that, wouldn't you? Seeing as how you're tied to that chair and I'm holding a gun.'

'Why would Redrock want to hurt you or Bobby-Ray's sister? It's Bobby-Ray we want. And when I say "want" I mean to talk to, not to hurt. We just want to know what happened.'

Standing stared at Keenan in silence. The man appeared to be telling the truth, and it had never made any sense that Bobby-Ray's employers would try to kill them.

'What happened at this motel?' asked Keenan.

'Bobby-Ray had told Kaitlyn he'd wait for her there. We looked through the window and saw a body on the floor. We thought it was Bobby-Ray so we broke in, but instead we found two dead FBI agents. A motel employee pulled a shotgun on us and two SUVs turned up and started shooting.' He shrugged. 'Kaitlyn and I were okay, so we got out of there.'

'Two FBI agents, you say?'

'Roy Johnson and Michael Kelly. They'd both been shot.'

'By Bobby-Ray? Are you telling me that Bobby-Ray killed two FBI agents?'

'I'm not psychic, how would I know?' said Standing. 'It looked to me that whoever did it used Johnson's gun.'

'Bobby-Ray would have been more than capable of that,' said Keenan.

'But do you think he'd shoot Feds?'

'I don't know what to think any more,' said Keenan. 'We've got a dead client and three dead bodyguards and Bobby-Ray's on the run. If you'd asked me a week ago if I thought he'd go rogue I'd have laughed in your face. But now? I don't know.'

'If he had gone rogue, he wouldn't have called me for help, surely.'

'But if he's done nothing wrong, why not talk to me? Why not talk to the cops or the FBI? If he's got nothing to hide, all he's got to do is tell us his side of the story.' He nodded at his bound wrists. 'Why don't you untie me and we talk about this over a drink?'

Standing stared at the man for several seconds, and then nodded. 'Okay, but you won't be offended if I keep the gun?'

'We're on the same side,' said Keenan. 'What did you say your name was?'

'I didn't. But it's Matt.'

'Okay, Matt. There's a letter opener over there on my desk. Get this tape off me and I'll open a very good single malt.'

Standing went over to the desk and picked up a minia-
ture silver sword. He used it to cut the tape from Keenan's
ankles, and then did the wrists. He moved away, the letter
opener in one hand, the gun in the other. Keenan grinned
as he rubbed his wrists. 'You can relax, Matt.'

'I'm relaxed.'

'I'm not going to jump you.'

'You're welcome to try.'

Keenan looked him up and down. 'Former special
forces?'

Standing said nothing.

'SAS?'

'How about you open that whisky,' said Standing.

'See no evil, hear no evil, speak no evil,' said Keenan.
'I get it.' He stood up and walked over to a cabinet. As
he took out a bottle of whisky and two glasses, Standing
put the paperknife back on the desk. Keenan splashed
whisky into the glasses and then handed one to Standing.
'Here's to you, Matt,' said the American and they clinked
glasses and drank. Standing nodded his appreciation. It
was a very good whisky.

Keenan waved him over to two winged chairs close to
the window and they sat down. 'Who was the girl at the
door?' he asked, then realisation dawned. 'That was
Bobby-Ray's sister? Why don't you invite her in?'

'Let's just leave her where she is,' said Standing. He
put the gun on a side table. He watched Keenan thoughtfully as he sipped his whisky again. 'How much do you
know about what happened at the Russian's house?' asked
Standing.

'We've only got the word of the surviving Russian
bodyguard, and we haven't been allowed to talk to him.

So the intel we have is second-hand, courtesy of the LAPD. The bodyguard told them that they had arrived home in the late afternoon. They were in two vehicles. The client and five bodyguards in total.'

'Including drivers?'

Keenan shook his head. 'Plus the drivers. Bobby-Ray was in the client's vehicle, front passenger seat. Kurt Konieczny was in the front passenger seat of the lead vehicle. There were two Russian bodyguards in Kurt's car and one in the car with Bobby-Ray and the client. They drove up to the house and Bobby-Ray and Kurt went inside with the client, along with the three Russians.' He sipped his whisky. 'Once the client was safely inside, the cars drove to the garage area and parked up. The client was in for the night, so normal procedure is for the team to make sure that the house is clear, check the alarm system and then leave. One of the bodyguards went upstairs to check the bedrooms and while he was there Bobby-Ray shot Kurt and the two Russian bodyguards and then shot the client. The surviving Russian came downstairs and Bobby-Ray shot at him and ran off.'

'Ran off? Literally? He just legged it?'

'There were two security guards at the driveway entrance and they heard the shots but didn't see Bobby-Ray. He got out through the garden at the rear of the house.'

'And the bodyguard who went upstairs, did he shoot at Bobby-Ray?'

'He says so.'

'And the cops checked it out?'

'There's bullet damage that backs up his story. That's what the cops said.'

'And it was Bobby-Ray's gun that was used to kill the client and the bodyguards?'

'No question of that. The cops have the gun.'

Standing frowned. 'So Bobby-Ray left the gun behind?'

Keenan nodded. 'The magazine was empty.'

'Even so. You don't throw away a perfectly serviceable weapon. Especially if you've just used it to shoot people.'

Keenan shrugged. 'He was under pressure. And under fire.'

'Yeah, about that,' said Standing. 'Bobby-Ray shoots three trained bodyguards, one of whom is a former Navy SEAL, shoots the client, and then somehow fails to hit the bodyguard on the stairs? Does that sound likely to you?'

'Like I said, he was under pressure. The cops found Bobby-Ray's gun in the garden. His fingerprints and DNA were on it, and it was definitely the gun that killed the client and the bodyguards. And it matched rounds in the hallway where he'd shot at the bodyguard on the stairs.'

'And knowing that, he still dropped his gun?'

Keenan held up his free hand. 'I hear you,' he said.

'But do you? You seem to think that Bobby-Ray killed the client and three other men, including a friend and a former colleague.'

'That's not true. I've got an open mind. But the fact that Bobby-Ray didn't immediately come to me or the cops suggests he has something to hide.'

'Or that he doesn't trust you.'

Keenan's eyes narrowed. 'What are you getting at?'

Standing smiled coldly. 'Like you, I'm keeping an open mind. But if Bobby-Ray has done what they've said he's done then I don't see why he'd be calling me.'

'Maybe he wants you to get him out of the country.'

'Maybe,' said Standing. 'After it happened, he didn't call you? He didn't get in contact?'

Keenan shook his head. 'He ditched his company phone. Never heard from him again.' Keenan took another sip of whisky. 'We could spend all day talking about maybes and ifs,' he said. 'But until we talk to Bobby-Ray, we're just whistling in the wind.'

'We need to talk to the surviving bodyguard.'

'We tried. It's not going to happen.'

'Because?'

'Because he's left the country. He's back in London.'

Standing put down his drink. 'How the hell was that allowed?'

'He's not a suspect. He's a witness. He has no criminal record and the cops had no reason to detain him. He was fully cooperative and has promised to come back in the event of a trial.'

'That's very public-spirited of him. The cops should have at the very least told him not to leave town.'

'I don't think they had any reason to do that.'

'Because they're sure that Bobby-Ray is the killer?'

Keenan nodded but didn't say anything.

'What's the guy's name?' asked Standing.

'Nikolai. Nikolai Lipov. But if you're thinking of talking to him, forget it. We sent one of our people to talk to him in London and Lipov beat him to a pulp. These dead FBI agents you found, what did you say their names were?'

'Roy Johnson and Michael Kelly,' said Standing.

Keenan went over to his desk and immediately Standing's hand went for the gun on the side table.

Keenan froze and smiled. 'I'm getting a pen,' he said. 'It's a very nice Montblanc but it's no match for your Glock.'

Standing nodded but kept his hand close to the pistol as Keenan reached out for a black pen and a small leather-bound notebook. He wrote down the names. 'I haven't heard anything about two Feds being shot but I'll check,' he said.

'There's something you need to know about that,' said Standing. 'There was a silencer on Johnson's gun.'

Keenan frowned. 'Silencers are illegal in California,' he said.

'Legal or not, what would a Fed be doing with one?'

'They were definitely Feds?'

'They had FBI shields.'

Keenan chuckled. 'You can buy them online,' he said. He put the pen and notepad away. 'Let me check them out. So what are you planning to do?'

'I don't have many options,' said Standing. 'Like you, I want to talk to Bobby-Ray. And the way things stand, I don't see that happening.'

'He hasn't contacted his sister?'

'Just the once, after it happened. He told her to contact me and to take me to the motel. Obviously he's gone to ground again and I assume he thinks that whoever is trying to kill him is able to tap phones and monitor emails.'

'That's not as easy as it sounds.'

'It is if the government is involved,' said Standing.

'What are you thinking? FBI? CIA? NSA?'

'Who knows?' said Standing. 'It might just be someone who has access to their technology, officially or otherwise.'

Keenan frowned. 'I don't follow you.'

Standing drained his glass. 'Everyone's so busy looking for Bobby-Ray that nobody seems to be taking any interest in the victim. He's a Russian, right? A Russian who only recently moved to the States. And someone fearful enough to be hiring bodyguards. Maybe he had enemies in high places.'

'There was an attempt on his life in London,' said Keenan. 'That's why he moved to the States.'

Standing frowned. 'There was nothing in the papers about that.'

'It was hushed up,' said Keenan. 'Some sort of poison, that's what he said.'

'You met him?'

'I had a preliminary briefing with him to assess his needs. He had minimal security in London, which he realised was a mistake, obviously. We put together a security proposal and as part of that Bobby-Ray was assigned to his inner circle.'

'Who did he think wanted him dead?'

Keenan shrugged. 'He didn't say.'

'Did you ask?'

'Of course I asked, but he was vague. Said that all of the oligarchs are under threat.'

'From the Kremlin?'

'He wasn't specific and he made it clear he didn't want to go into details. He said our job was just to protect him and that it didn't matter where the threats came from.'

'Is that normal?'

'It depends,' said Keenan, pouring himself more whisky. 'We are sometimes paid to look after some pretty shady characters. It's understandable that they wouldn't want to go into the details of who they've pissed off.'

'And you think Koshkin fell into that category?'

'Difficult to say for sure. But yeah, maybe.' He sipped his whisky. 'You realise we're on the same side here, right? It's in my best interests to prove that Bobby-Ray didn't go rogue and kill our client. If I can't prove that, no one is going to trust my company ever again.'

'I hear you,' said Standing.

'Do you think he will get in touch with you? Or his sister?'

'I don't know,' said Standing. 'I think that after whatever happened in that motel with the FBI agents, he can't trust anybody.'

12

S tanding walked out of the house and climbed into the car. 'How did it go?' asked Kaitlyn.

'He wasn't trying to hurt Bobby-Ray,' said Standing. He put the duct tape and the Glock in the glove compartment. 'And he's not convinced that Bobby-Ray killed the client and the other bodyguards.'

Kaitlyn frowned in confusion. 'You said he was chasing you.'

'Yeah, well he claims that he was just following me.' He started the engine. 'We need somewhere to crash tonight,' he said.

'I don't want to go back to my apartment,' she said. 'Not after everything that's happened.'

'Sure, no problem,' said Standing. 'We'll find a motel.'

They checked into a Best Western on the outskirts of Pasadena, and the clerk who booked them in seemed surprised at Standing's request for single beds. As soon as they were in the room, Kaitlyn locked herself in the bathroom and started showering. Standing lay on one of the beds, connected his phone to the hotel's Wi-Fi and hit the Internet.

He Googled Mikhail Koshkin's name but there was nothing about him being poisoned in London. He frowned. Keenan had been definite that the Russian had been attacked before he moved to the States. He Googled 'poison attack' with 'Russian' and 'London' and got more than twenty million hits which made him smile.

He spent the next half an hour following the most popular links. The most talked-about attack was that on Alexander Litvinenko, back in 2006. Litvinenko was a former KGB agent who was employed by the Federal Security Service but left under a cloud and devoted his life to slagging off his former bosses, including Putin. He died in London after drinking a cup of tea laced with radioactive Polonium 210. Most of the stories he read said that MI5 was sure that the Russian president ordered the attack. The general view seemed to be that anything involving Polonium had to be government sanctioned. The radioactive material wasn't something you could buy over the counter.

In the same year there was a much less sophisticated killing of a Putin critic. Anna Politkovskaya wrote a book accusing Putin of turning the country into a police state. She was shot in the lift of her building in Moscow by five men. It was a professional job but the Russian cops never found out who paid for the hit. Standing visited more than a dozen sites to read about the Politkovskaya assassination. She didn't have any bodyguards but he couldn't help thinking there were similarities to what happened to Koshkin.

Standing couldn't understand why Putin would bother using contractors when he had the resources of the Federal Security Service to draw on. He denied having Politkovskaya killed, obviously, but it seemed to Standing that killing the writer in such an obvious way caused

Putin more problems than anything she had written as a journalist. A false flag operation seemed more likely. Politics was a dirty business at the best of times and there were plenty of people – and countries – who were throwing shit at Putin in the hope that at least some of it would stick.

The most recent poison attack in the UK occurred in March 2018 when former Russian military officer and double agent Sergei Skripal and his daughter Yulia were poisoned with a Novichok nerve agent in Salisbury. Novichok was developed by scientists in the Soviet Union in the nineteen seventies, the name meant 'newcomer' because it marked a breakthrough in chemical weapons and was the most powerful nerve agent in the world. Again, it seemed unlikely that the chemical could have found its way to the UK without some sort of Russian government involvement.

While the attempt to kill Skripal had been a hi-tech attack, most of the assassinations Standing read about were very basic. One of Putin's most vocal critics, Boris Nemtsov, was shot in the back four times within sight of the Kremlin in 2015. He had been deputy prime minister for a while but fell out with Putin. In 2009 a human rights lawyer called Stanislav Markelov and a Russian journalist Anastasia Baburova were shot by masked gunmen, again near the Kremlin. Two members of a neo-Nazi group were found guilty of the murders but no one really believed they did it. But a lot of commentators wondered if Putin would be stupid enough to sanction murders so close to his place of work. Standing smiled as he read that. No one had ever accused the Russian president of being stupid.

He closed the browser on his phone and stared at the ceiling. If Koshkin had been attacked in London, why was there no mention of it anywhere on the Internet? And why was it being reported that Koshkin and his bodyguards had died in a home invasion in Bel Air? If the police truly believed that Bobby-Ray was responsible, why hadn't his details been released to the media?

Kaitlyn came out of the bathroom. She was wearing a long T-shirt and had a towel wrapped around her head. She dropped down onto the other bed. 'So what do you think?' she asked.

'I think somebody is going to a lot of trouble keeping a lid on this,' said Standing. 'And those same people are the ones after Bobby-Ray.'

'So what do we do?'

Standing sighed. 'I think I'm going to have to go back to London for a few days,' he said. 'What happened in London is the key to what's happening here, I'm sure of that. Something happened to Koshkin there, which is why he came to LA.'

'And how are you going to find out what happened in London?'

Standing smiled. 'I know a man who should be able to help,' he said.

'A friend?'

'Sort of.'

13

S tanding arrived at Heathrow at just after ten o'clock in the morning, after an uncomfortable eleven-hour flight. The immigration officers on duty were a lot less attractive than the Hispanic girl who had checked his passport in the US. The men and women of the UK's Border Force were dressed in blue uniforms so dark that they were almost black, and several had tucked their trousers into their boots to give them a military look. Standing was old enough to remember when immigration officers wore suits and smiled as they checked passports – these days they looked more like Nazis and had facial expressions to match. Standing used the automatic gates, which meant he didn't have to interact with anyone – he just placed his passport on the scanner and facial recognition did the rest.

He only had his carry-on bag, so he went straight onto the Heathrow Express to Paddington Station and a Bakerloo Line train to Waterloo.

The Union Jack Club was next to the station, a private members' hotel for former and serving members of the armed forces. The hotel had more than 260 rooms and suites and was one of the cheapest places to stay in the capital. Standing used his military ID card to check in.

His room was on the fifth floor, facing the station, and as he opened the door he heard a train rattling out. Noise never bothered Standing; like most soldiers he could sleep through an earthquake if necessary. His room was one of the cheapest, which meant that he shared a bathroom, but the room was only a place to sleep and Standing wasn't looking for luxury. The £40 a night he was paying was a bargain, but more importantly all the guests were present or former military, which meant he wouldn't be bumping into outsiders. He dropped his bag on the bed and went back outside. He found a phone shop and paid cash for a cheap Samsung smartphone and a pay-as-you-go SIM, then went into a Starbucks and ordered an Americano and a cheese salad sandwich. He sat at a table by the window and set up his phone. Once it was up and running it took him less than a minute to get a phone number for MI5. The Security Service had a website and its phone number was prominently displayed, though it was quick to point out that anyone wanting to report a crime should call 999 or the anti-terrorist hotline. Standing called the number and it was answered within seconds by a woman with a strong Scottish accent. Standing gave his name and said that he was a former colleague of Daniel Shepherd and requested a call back. The woman had him spell his name and then ended the call.

Standing ate his sandwich and went to the counter to buy another. He had almost finished it when his phone rang. The caller was withholding his number but it could only be one person. 'Thanks for calling me back, Spider,' said Standing.

'What's up?' asked Shepherd.

'I need help,' said Standing.

'What sort of help?'

'Advice,' said Standing. 'And guidance.'

'Are you in London?'

'Yeah. Near Waterloo.'

'I'll see you at the Tattershall Castle at five thirty.'

'Sounds grand,' said Standing.

'It's a boat they use as a pub,' said Shepherd. 'It's on the Thames, opposite the London Eye, between Westminster and Embankment Tube stations.'

'I'll see you there,' said Standing.

He finished his second sandwich, then went back to the hotel and shaved and showered in the shared bathroom.

He arrived at the Tattershall Castle shortly before the arranged time, and Shepherd was already up on the deck. The Tattershall Castle was a huge paddle steamer built in the nineteen thirties, which had been converted into bars and function rooms. It was a good place for a meeting, Standing realised, as everyone had to enter and leave along a narrow gangplank and could clearly be seen from Shepherd's vantage point on the deck. Standing nodded at Shepherd and Shepherd raised his glass in salute.

Standing walked on board and went over to Shepherd's table. He was already getting to his feet. Average height, with brown hair that was starting to grey at the temples, he was wearing a fleece jacket over a denim jacket and black jeans. He was a good decade older than Standing, but definitely fit. The old hands at Hereford still laughed and shook their heads when they talked about Shepherd's habit of running around the Hereford base with a rucksack full of bricks wrapped in newspaper on his back.

The two men shook hands. 'How are you doing, Matt?' asked Shepherd. 'Keeping out of trouble?'

'Got back from Syria last month,' he said. 'I'm on a short break, then it's back to Hereford for training.' He nodded at the bar. 'What can I get you?'

Shepherd held up his half-empty glass. 'Jameson's, ice and soda,' he said.

Standing went inside to the bar. There were several dozen customers, a mix of office workers in suits and tourists, including four Japanese girls who were busy taking selfies. He was served quickly and was soon back on the deck. He gave Shepherd his drink and sipped his lager. 'What about you?' he asked. 'Busy?'

'Over-stretched and under-staffed, we're running around putting out fires left, right and centre,' said Shepherd. 'It's never-ending. And it's like the IRA said to Margaret Thatcher after they just missed assassinating her in Brighton back in the Eighties – they only have to be lucky once. We have to be lucky every time.'

'It's getting worse?'

Shepherd nodded. 'They go off to fight in Syria or Afghanistan or wherever, then they waltz back into the UK and start planning an atrocity here. Most of the time we know who they are and where they live but we just don't have the resources to keep tabs on them all. So far we've managed to keep on top of it, but if the public knew how close we've come to major terrorist attacks over the past year, they'd be a lot less complacent.' Shepherd shrugged. 'It's bad at the sharp end, where you are, but at least you're trained to handle it. Here we've got a nation of sitting ducks.'

'So what's the answer?'

Shepherd laughed harshly. 'There is no answer, Matt. The genie's out of the bottle and there's no putting it back. Fifty years down the line, maybe we won't have home-grown terrorists, but it's not going to change in the near future.' He sipped his drink. 'So what do you need from me?'

'I'm helping a mate who's got into a spot of bother in the States. He's a former Navy SEAL who got injured out in Syria and moved into personal security. Now he's been accused of killing his principal.'

'Ouch,' said Shepherd.

'I'm pretty sure he didn't do it, but he's in hiding and there are bad guys with guns after him.'

'You do get into scrapes, don't you?' said Shepherd.

Standing shrugged. 'It's not by choice,' he said. 'But if I don't help him I don't see that anyone else will.' He leaned closer to Shepherd. 'The principal was a Russian who used to live in London. Mikhail Koshkin. There was an attempt on his life here, I'm told.'

Shepherd's eyes narrowed. 'Who told you that?'

'The guy who helped put together his security detail in LA. It doesn't seem to have been made public.'

'It wasn't,' said Shepherd. 'It wasn't my case but I saw a few memos. There was a D-notice on it, so the details aren't widely known.'

'So what's the story?'

'Some sort of poison got into his system and he was in intensive care for two weeks. He nearly died. A journalist he was talking to also got sick.'

'There was nothing online about that,' said Standing. 'I did read about that former Russian double agent and his daughter who got poisoned not that long ago.'

Shepherd nodded. 'Sergei Skripal. It's generally assumed that the attempted hit on Skripal was ordered by the Kremlin, but these days who knows? I've also been told that Mossad were behind it in an attempt to smear the Russians.'

'How was Koshkin poisoned?'

'He was in a restaurant talking to a journalist. They reckon it was in his food. They both fell ill and were treated in a private hospital. Koshkin had some pretty good connections and it was all kept quiet. The authorities were happy enough to keep a lid on it as these poisonings often lead to panic.' Shepherd sipped his drink.

'That's why they slapped a D-notice on it?'

'I assume so. Why do you ask?'

'Because the details of what happened in LA are also being withheld. Instead they're saying it was a home invasion. That's what the media are being told. But the cops are looking for Bobby-Ray and he's the only suspect.'

'Bobby-Ray?'

'Sorry, that's his name. Bobby-Ray Barnes.'

'What reason would Bobby-Ray have for killing him?'

'None that I know. I think the assumption is that someone paid him to pull the trigger.'

'Is that possible?'

'Bobby-Ray's a straight arrow, Spider. He isn't assassin material.'

'So who do the American cops think wanted Koshkin dead? Who footed the bill?'

'They didn't say.'

Shepherd frowned. 'You'd think they'd want to know. Whoever paid for the hit is as guilty as the man who carried it out.'

'Yeah. I thought the same. I got the feeling they wanted to find Bobby-Ray first and that he'd tell them who hired him.'

Shepherd sipped his drink. 'So they're firm in their belief that he did it?'

Standing nodded. 'I'm told they're not looking for anyone else.'

Shepherd put down his glass. 'Who should they be looking for?'

'What do you mean?'

'You're convinced that Bobby-Ray didn't kill Koshkin. And I believe you. So if he didn't do it, who did?'

Standing shrugged. It wasn't a question he could answer.

'Who survived the attack in the house?' asked Shepherd.

'One of the bodyguards.'

'Russian?'

Standing nodded.

'So he must have seen what happened?'

'He says not. He was upstairs and by the time he was downstairs it was all over. He fired at Bobby-Ray and Bobby-Ray fired back. Again, I only have that second-hand.'

'So the guy's dead?'

'Very much alive.'

Shepherd frowned. 'So a former Navy SEAL shot and missed. That doesn't happen very often.'

'That's what I thought.'

'Is there any way you could talk to that guy?'

'I could try,' said Standing.

'Because if Bobby-Ray didn't do it, someone else must have. Look, are you sure that Bobby-Ray isn't dead?'

Standing sighed. 'That's a distinct possibility.'

'Let's assume the worst,' said Shepherd. 'What will you do?'

'What can I do?'

'Exactly. I'm serious, Matt. Is this a revenge thing? Is that what this is about?'

Standing pulled a face. 'If they've killed Bobby-Ray, I should just let it go?'

'That would be your call. I know you've got form when it comes to revenge, and I'm not in a position to throw the first stone. But you need to proceed with care.'

Standing smiled thinly. 'I'm not scared, Spider.'

'It's not about fear. It's about putting yourself in the firing line.'

Standing held up his hands. 'One step at a time,' he said. 'I said it was a possibility that Bobby-Ray was dead. But until I know for sure, I'm working on the premise that he's lying low. Which means my priority is to prove he didn't do it.'

'Okay, all good,' said Shepherd. 'Putting my cop hat on, I'd say your best bet is to find out who had the most to gain from Koshkin's death. That should lead you to whoever took out the contract, and that in turn should ID the killer.'

'And we're saying that it probably wasn't political?'

'If it was a Kremlin-sanctioned hit, they would probably have been cleverer about it.'

'So who then?'

Shepherd shrugged. 'I don't know. Sorry. Other than a few memos that passed over my desk, I know next to nothing about the case.'

'Can you find out?'

Shepherd grimaced. 'Not without explaining why I had an interest,' he said. He sipped his whisky. 'But I could put you in touch with one of the cops that was on the case.'

'That would be helpful,' said Standing.

'But it'll have to be on the QT.'

'No problem,' said Standing. 'My lips are sealed.'

'They better had be,' said Shepherd.

14

Standing's phone rang as he was walking out of Waterloo Station towards the Union Jack Club. The caller was withholding his number but Standing took the call. It was Shepherd again. 'I've had a word with one of the detectives who investigated the attempt on Koshkin,' said Shepherd. 'He's happy to have a chat with you.'

'You're a star,' said Standing.

'His name's Matty Stogdale. So you're both Matts. He's a DS, a detective sergeant. I'll text you his phone number. All he knows is that you need a briefing on the case. He won't ask who you are or why you're interested, and best you don't tell him. And everything he tells you is absolutely off the record.'

'Understood,' said Standing. 'Thanks, Spider. I owe you one.'

Shepherd laughed. 'You don't owe me anything, Matt,' he said. 'We never met and we never had this conversation.'

The line went dead and a few seconds later a text message arrived with the phone number. Standing called it and Stogdale answered almost immediately. Standing told the detective who he was and Stogdale arranged to meet him in a Soho pub at nine o'clock that evening.

Standing caught an Uber to Soho. It was only when he walked into the Coach & Horses that Standing realised he didn't know what DS Stogdale looked like. The pub was busy, every seat was taken and there were a dozen or so men at the bar. He looked around. There were several gay couples sitting at the tables, young men in fashionable clothes, with expensive haircuts and glowing skin, deep in conversation over glasses of wine, but there were mixed couples, too, and groups of office workers winding down after a hard day in front of their computer terminals.

There were several men drinking at the bar but only two turned to look in his direction. One was in his thirties with a receding hairline and shoulders and arms that looked as if they would have no problems bench-pressing a couple of hundred pounds. The other was taller and thinner with gold-rimmed spectacles and with a leather briefcase at his feet.

The taller man looked away but the weightlifter nodded at Standing. Standing nodded back. The man walked over, carrying a glass of something clear with a slice of lemon and ice in it.

'Matt?' said Standing.

'Back at you,' said the man. He transferred his glass to his left hand and the two men shook. 'You a smoker?' asked Stogdale. He was wearing a dark pin-striped suit and well-worn shoes with laces.

Standing shook his head. 'No.'

'Well, I am,' said the detective. 'Grab a drink and I'll see you outside.'

Standing went to the bar. It took him the best part of five minutes to order and receive a pint of lager and by the time he joined the policeman outside he was already three-quarters of the way through his cigarette. There were four other smokers in a group near the door but Stogdale had moved to the other side of the pub. Standing joined him. 'So, you're interested in what happened to Mikhail Koshkin?' said the cop.

Standing nodded.

Stogdale blew smoke at the darkening sky. 'See the Italian restaurant over there?'

Standing looked across the road at a small restaurant with tables with red and white checked tablecloths and he nodded again.

'That's where it happened,' said Stogdale. 'Koshkin was eating with a Russian journalist. The journalist got sick, too. While they were in there someone put something in their food, but the boffins still aren't sure what it was. They're saying it was some sort of organo-phosphorus compound but they're having trouble nailing it down. The one thing they know for sure is that it didn't get into his system accidentally. Somebody was trying to kill him.'

'If it was an assassination attempt, how come Koshkin didn't die?'

'That's a bloody good question,' said the detective, flicking ash into the gutter. 'It could be that they got the dose wrong, could have been because he went straight to hospital.' He shrugged. 'Could have just been lucky.' He nodded over at the restaurant. 'It was Friday evening so the restaurant was full, and the streets were busy. There's no CCTV in the restaurant itself and people were coming and going all the time Koshkin was in there. We checked all the staff and they seemed clean.'

'Checked for the poison, you mean?'

The detective shook his head. 'Background checks. PNC checks. Police National Computer. By the time we knew he'd been poisoned the staff had all gone home and the place had been cleaned.'

'In the past these sorts of attacks have been linked to the Russian government, right?'

'Sure. But those attacks involved nerve agents like Novichok or radioactive poisons like polonium. Stuff like that can only come from a government lab. The poison used on Koshkin could probably be knocked up in your average kitchen. That's why they've had problems nailing it down, it was pretty impure.'

'But do you think Koshkin was targeted by the Kremlin?'

'It's possible,' said the detective. He threw away what was left of his cigarette. 'But when the Russians want someone dead they tend to send a message. They use stuff like Novichok so the world knows who was behind it. Fuck with us and we'll fuck with you. Not exactly a confession, but the method tells everyone what they need to know.' He shrugged. 'The fact that they used poison might indicate that it was some sort of false flag operation. Someone wants to make the Russians look bad. I tell you, it makes my head hurt. It's so much easier when a husband snaps and strangles his wife or she sticks a knife in him. You know where you are with a domestic.'

'Did you look at Koshkin's wife?'

'Of course,' said Stogdale. He put his glass on the windowsill and lit another cigarette. He blew smoke then picked up his glass again. 'They were getting divorced.

He'd been fooling around and she'd signed up with a big City legal firm.'

'So there's a motive.'

Stogdale shrugged. 'Not really. Lawyers were involved but he's seriously rich and could afford any settlement. Most of his money is offshore – the Cayman Islands, Panama, Bermuda, Monaco – so if anything, his death would make it harder to get at the cash. They lived in a big house in Notting Hill and he'd already agreed to let her have it, plus their homes in Marbella and Paris.'

'Kids?'

'Grown up, so they weren't an issue. I spoke with Mrs Koshkin and while she was hardly the grieving widow I didn't have her down as a woman who had hired an assassin.'

'But it's possible that she could have paid for him to be killed?'

'It's possible, sure. Anything's possible. But she's pretty low down our list of suspects.'

'So who'd be at the top of that list?'

Stogdale flicked ash onto the pavement. 'I always thought his business partner was the most likely candidate. Guy by the name of Erik Markov. I say business partners, they fell out a year or so back and there was no love lost between them. They both invested in a riverside property development in Battersea. So far as we can tell, Koshkin fucked Markov over on the deal and ended up owning the whole shebang.'

'How much was the deal worth?'

'Millions. Worth killing for, that's for sure. But again, suspecting and proving are two different things and Markov has an army of lawyers. We managed to get an interview with him but his lawyers did all the talking and it was no comment right down the line. Whoever tried to kill Koshkin was a pro, and I doubt the killer would have ever gone near whoever hired him. If it was Markov who paid for the hit, there'd be no paper trail to follow. He'd have used a middleman, probably wouldn't even know who was doing the job for him.'

'But if it was about revenge, why go to the trouble of using a poison? Why not just shoot him in the back of his head or put a bomb in his car?'

'To muddy the waters,' said the detective. 'The more it looked like a government hit, the less we'd be looking for other motives. But that's also hypothetical. There's no evidence, circumstantial or otherwise.'

'What about the journalist? The one who was also poisoned.'

'He made a full recovery, too,' said Stogdale. 'The doctors reckoned he was exposed to less of the toxin.'

'Wrong place, wrong time?'

'Seems that way,' said Stogdale.

'What's his name?'

'Anton Vasilyev. He works for a Russian website. He was interviewing Koshkin for a feature about Russians living in London.' He sighed. 'Anyway, water under the bridge and all that. Now that Koshkin is dead, our case is closed.'

'The Americans haven't spoken to you?'

Stogdale shook his head. 'We made contact and offered our assistance but they said they had a suspect and hoped to have him in custody sooner rather than later.'

'So they weren't linking the London attack with what happened in LA?'

'They didn't seem interested. Anyway, their murder trumps our attempted murder so, like I said, case closed. Anything else you need?'

Standing flashed him a tight smile. 'Thanks, I'm good. I appreciate your time.'

'Not a problem,' said the detective. 'Any friend of Spider's . . .'

The two men shook hands and Standing walked away as the detective went back into the pub.

15

Mrs Anna Koshkin lived in an imposing stucco-fronted house in Notting Hill. It was on three floors with a large garden surrounded by a high wall. The gate was twelve feet tall and solid metal painted black so that only the upper floors were visible from the road. Standing figured that she wouldn't speak to him if he rang the intercom at the gate, so he ordered an Uber cab to meet him in the street a short distance away. He was wearing a dark suit, white shirt and red tie that he'd bought in an Oxfam shop. In the city, a suit was just as much camouflage as desert-pattern fatigues were in the Middle East. The driver who turned up was called Mohammed and was driving a white Toyota Prius. He had a white woven skullcap and a long beard that was flecked with crumbs from his last meal. Standing offered him a fifty-pound note plus whatever the Uber App priced the journey at and said that he wanted to wait for the owner of the house to leave. Standing told the driver that he was a journalist working on an article, and Mohammed was happy enough with the arrangement. 'The customer is always right,' he said as he slipped the fifty-pound note into his pocket. 'Especially a customer with money.'

An hour passed and the gates remained closed. Standing gave Mohammed another fifty-pound note, which the driver accepted with a grin. They listened to Smooth Radio and Mohammed busied himself on his smartphone.

Fifteen minutes after Standing had handed over the second banknote, the gate rattled open to reveal a BMW 5 Series. The driver was wearing dark glasses, as was the heavily built man in the front passenger seat.

As the car pulled out and turned into the road, Standing caught sight of the woman in the back. She was in her forties, with high cheekbones and blonde hair. There was another heavy sitting next to her, shaven-headed and wearing the ubiquitous dark glasses.

'That's them, Mohammed,' said Standing. 'Don't lose them but don't get too close.'

'I'm on it, sir,' said Mohammed.

The white Toyota Prius was one of the most common cars on the streets of London, the make that was favoured by the bulk of Uber drivers, so Standing doubted that he'd be spotted as they followed the BMW east. After driving for a little under twenty minutes, they reached their destination – Selfridges. The BMW pulled up at the rear of the department store. The heavy in the front passenger seat got out first. He walked quickly to the rear and opened the door for Mrs Koshkin. The other heavy was just as quick on his feet and both men walked her to the entrance as the BMW moved away.

Standing thanked Mohammed and got out of the Prius. He hurried over to the department store and rushed inside, just in time to see Mrs Koshkin and her two minders heading for the Chanel store. He slowed and headed after them.

Mrs Koshkin was wearing a long fur coat. He had no idea what animals had died to provide her with the garment but he figured there had been a lot of them. The soles of her shoes were a bright red, which he knew was the signature of some famous designer whose name he couldn't remember, and the bag hanging off her right shoulder looked expensive. There was a confident swing to her hips as she walked, and she held her head high. She was tall, and in her heels was an inch or so taller than her bodyguards.

She walked into the Chanel store and was immediately attended to by a young black man in a black suit. He began showing her a selection of bags while her two protectors stood guard outside, hands clasped over their groins, eyes watchful behind the dark lenses.

Standing sauntered by, his hands in his pockets, running through what he was going to say to her. He'd only get the one chance, but approaching her in public gave him a greater chance of success, as the bodyguards would be limited in their actions.

He wandered over to the Prada store and watched Mrs Koshkin in the reflection of the main window. She chose a bag, paid for it with a credit card, and waited as the assistant wrapped it and put it in a Chanel carrier bag.

As she left the store flanked by her two heavies, Standing walked towards her, taking his hands from his pockets and opening them so that the heavies could see he wasn't carrying a weapon.

He smiled, and as their eyes met she also began to

smile, perhaps thinking that she knew him from some-where. 'Mrs Koshkin, I'm sorry to bother you but I really need to talk to you about your husband,' he said.

'Who are you?' she asked, taking a step back, her hand moving up to her throat as if she feared he was going to grab the diamond necklace there.

A hand seized Standing's left arm. 'You need to walk away, now,' growled the taller of her two bodyguards.

The man gave Standing a cold stare that would prob-ably have scared most people but it just made him smile. 'Let go of my arm,' said Standing.

The grip tightened and the man's fingers dug into his arm. Standing was still smiling when he stamped down on the man's instep. The bodyguard yelped and Standing pulled his hand free, grabbed the man's wrist and twisted it up behind his back. He smiled at Mrs Koshkin. 'Just a quick chat,' he said. He pushed the man towards the second bodyguard and for a second they were in a lover's embrace, their faces almost touching.

Mrs Koshkin actually laughed, then hurriedly covered her mouth with her hand.

The two bodyguards untangled themselves and turned to face Standing, their hands clenching.

Standing turned to look at Mrs Koshkin, raising his hands to show that he wasn't a threat. 'I just need a few minutes of your time,' he said, keeping his voice soft and low as if he was soothing a spooked horse. 'I only want to talk to you.'

'About what?'

'Your husband's death,' he said. 'And my condolences, for your loss.'

The two bodyguards moved towards Standing but Mrs

Koshkin stopped them with a wave of her hand. She spoke to them in Russian. It wasn't a language Standing spoke anywhere near fluently, but he got the gist – she was furious at them. She turned to look at him and smiled coldly. 'Who are you?' she said.

'My name is Matt Standing. I'm a friend of the man who is being accused of killing your husband. There's something you need to know about what happened in LA. I'm sure you only know what you've been told, and I have every reason to believe that you haven't been told the truth.'

She stared at him for several seconds, then she nodded. 'I need a drink,' she said.

Standing grinned. 'You and me both.'

She said something to her bodyguards, then turned and walked off. Standing followed her. The bodyguards trailed behind them. She took the escalator up to the first floor and walked to the Champagne Bar, where she was clearly a regular because she was greeted warmly and shown to a table, even though there were several people waiting. She took off her coat, draped it over the back of her chair and sat down. 'Do you drink champagne, Mr Standing?' she asked.

'I'm a beer man, but I can drink bubbly,' said Standing, sitting down next to her.

Mrs Koshkin ordered two glasses of champagne and fifty grams of Beluga caviar. 'So you know the man who killed my husband?' she said as the waitress walked away.

'He's alleged to have killed him, but I don't think he did.'

'And what possible reason would you have for wanting to talk to me?'

'Because I think something stinks about the whole business, and I figure you would want to know the truth about what happened.'

'Will the truth bring Mikhail back? I don't think so.' Her two bodyguards were standing at the entrance to the bar. The one Standing had hit was glaring in their direction. 'How did you do that?' she asked. 'They are professionals.'

'So am I.'

'They are bigger than you and probably stronger. But the way you handled them . . . you are a bodyguard, too?'

'I have done protection work before, but I'm not a bodyguard.'

'I would hire you, Mr Standing. Based on what I've seen, you'd do a better job than the men I have.'

A waitress returned with a bottle of champagne and two glasses. They waited as she opened the bottle and poured.

As the waitress walked away, Standing smiled and raised his glass in salute. 'Thank you for the compliment,' he said. 'But I'm gainfully employed.'

She picked up her own glass and narrowed her eyes. 'You're a soldier,' she said. 'Special forces.'

'Why would you think that?'

'Some of our bodyguards in the past have been former special forces. Spetsnaz. They have a way of carrying themselves. A confidence.'

Standing shrugged. He knew exactly what she meant. It was partly the way special forces men carried themselves, but the eyes were also usually a clue. The two men currently responsible for protecting Mrs Koshkin were tough, there was no question of that, but Standing was sure they had never served in special forces.

She looked around the bar as she sipped her champagne. 'How did you know I'd be here?' she asked.

'I followed you from your house,' he said.

She sighed in annoyance. 'And they didn't spot you? What use are they?'

'They're not to blame, Mrs Koshkin. I was in an Uber cab and I was the only passenger. There's no way I would have appeared to be a threat.'

'You could have had a gun.'

'Are you expecting an attempt on your life?'

She laughed. 'Of course not.'

'Because if you are, then you'd need more than a two-man detail. You'd need at least four, plus drivers and at least one more vehicle. Plus, you wouldn't take the direct route to your destination.' He shrugged. 'Your security operates just fine for what you want.'

'They didn't stop you getting close to me.'

He smiled. 'They tried. But I was never a threat to you. If they had seen me looking as if I was about to harm you, they would have reacted differently, I'm sure.'

She put down her champagne flute. 'You think I wanted Mikhail dead, don't you? That's why you wanted to talk to me.'

'I don't know what to think. But what happened, someone must have paid for it.'

'And you think I did?'

Standing shrugged. 'You're in the middle of a divorce, aren't you?'

'And you think I'd have Mikhail killed? For what?'

'For money? Or maybe you were arguing over the children?'

'Our son is twenty-one, our daughter is nineteen. They are both studying at Oxford. And as far as money goes, my husband has left more than enough money to keep me and the children in the style to which we are accustomed.'

'So you weren't fighting? The divorce was amicable?'

She laughed and there was a harshness to the sound. 'Far from it. I'm as angry as hell at the way he refused to keep his dick in his pants during the last ten years of our marriage. But men are men, right? I was his second wife. I was his PA for five years and for three of those he was sleeping with me behind his wife's back, so I always knew what I was getting into. But I never stopped loving him.'

The waitress returned with the caviar. Mrs Koshkin waved at the dish. 'Please, help yourself.'

Standing was even less of a fan of caviar than he was of champagne, but he used a small spoon to heap some of it onto a cracker and popped it into his mouth. It tasted of salt and fish and wasn't in the least bit pleasant, but he forced a smile and nodded his approval. The waitress refilled their glasses and moved away. Standing washed away the taste of caviar with his champagne. 'So who do you think killed your husband?' he asked.

'According to the Los Angeles police, it was a rogue bodyguard. Your friend, apparently.'

'As I said, I'm sure it wasn't him.'

'Was he also a member of special forces?'

Standing nodded. 'He used to be a Navy SEAL.'

'So he would have had the necessary skills to kill Mikhail.'

'No question,' said Standing. 'But he wasn't a killer.'

'I thought that was the whole point of being in special forces.'

He looked at her, trying to work out if she was joking or not, but she stared back at him impassively, waiting for him to answer. 'He wouldn't kill for money?' she asked eventually.

'He would kill for his country, that's what soldiers do. But he wasn't the type to be a hitman. Trust me, Mrs Koshkin.'

'Mr Standing, if I didn't trust you, I wouldn't be sitting here talking to you.'

Standing nodded. 'Suppose the killer was a paid hitman,' he said. 'Who do you think would pay to have Mikhail killed?'

Mrs Koshkin looked around as if she was worried about being overheard, then leaned towards him and lowered her voice. 'You need to be very careful when you ask questions like that,' she said.

'You think the Russian government wanted him dead?'

She frowned. 'There you go again, putting words in my mouth. Why would you think the Russian government would want my husband dead?'

'I heard that someone tried to kill him in London and it's common knowledge that many enemies of the Russian State have ended up dead in the UK.'

'My husband was not an enemy of the Russian State, as you put it. And he has always been a good personal friend of the Russian president.'

'So who tried to kill him here in London?'

'Mr Standing, unlike you I'm not in the business of throwing around unsubstantiated allegations.'

'I understand that. And I'm sorry if I spoke out of turn. But I truly believe that my friend has either been set up or framed and to stand any chance of clearing his name, I need to find out who wanted your husband dead. What did the police say?'

She shrugged. 'Nothing. To be honest, I think they were relieved that Mikhail died in America because it meant they no longer had to investigate the attack on his life here.'

'They said that?'

'Not in so many words. But after his death, I never heard from the investigating detectives again.'

'What happened here in London?'

'You don't know?'

'He was poisoned, that much I know.'

She nodded. 'He very nearly died. He was in hospital for two weeks.'

'The Russian government often uses poison to take out its opponents.'

'So you say. But I've already told you that my husband was not an opponent of the Russian government. Quite the opposite, in fact.'

'And when he recovered he left the country. Why?'

'He didn't think he would be safe here.'

'But he had bodyguards already?'

'Oh yes. We've always had security. In Russia and here, and when we travel.'

'So he was scared of being attacked?'

She shook her head fiercely. 'Mikhail was scared of nothing,' she said. 'But he was prudent. He knew that our family was at risk of kidnapping, especially the children.'

'The bodyguards who went with him to Los Angeles, they had been with him for a long time?'

She nodded. 'He hired Max and Boris when we moved to London. Nikolai joined us a few years after that. So Max and Boris for eight years, Nikolai for two. Eighteen months, maybe.'

'And why did he hire bodyguards when you moved here?'

'Oh, Mikhail has always had bodyguards. We had a big team in Russia but he wasn't able to bring them all to England. There were problems with their visas.' Standing nodded. Mrs Koshkin leaned towards him. 'Do you think the bodyguards had something to do with my husband's death?'

'No,' said Standing. 'At least not Max and Boris because they died with Mikhail. But Nikolai was upstairs when it happened. And he's the only witness.'

'So you think Nikolai was somehow involved?'

Standing shrugged. 'I am sure that my friend didn't kill your husband. So if Nikolai says that he did, then Nikolai must be lying.'

'That's all you have?'

'I'm afraid so. Mrs Koshkin, I'm told that Nikolai is now back in London. Has he been in touch?'

She shook her head. 'No.'

'I'd have thought he might want to talk to you about what happened. Express his condolences.'

'We were never friends, Mr Standing. He was an employee.'

'But he was there when your husband was killed. I just thought . . .'

She shook her head again, more emphatically this time.

Then she sipped her champagne and studied him over the top of her glass. 'You realise that it doesn't matter, Mr Standing. Not in the grand scheme of things. Someone wanted my husband dead. It doesn't matter who that someone was, not to me. All that matters is that he's dead. And nothing will change that.'

'There's justice.'

She smiled sadly. 'Justice is very over-rated, in my opinion. My husband was no saint, I've always known that. When the Soviet Union fell apart, he was a factory worker. A worker, with zero prospects. But the collapse of the Soviet Union provided opportunities for men with the willingness to do what had to be done, and Mikhail was one of those men. He took over the factory and became its boss. And how do you think he did that? By smiling and asking nicely?' She shook her head. 'Mikhail took what he wanted and woe betide anyone who got in his way. He took over the factory and then took over three more. By then he had people working for him who would do what needed to be done, but it was still Mikhail who gave the orders. He always said that you were either a sheep or a wolf, there was nothing in between.'

'He made enemies?'

She smiled coldly. 'If anyone chose to become Mikhail's enemy, he dealt with them, Mr Standing. And he wasn't alone in that. But you talk about justice. There are those who might say that what happened to my husband was justice. It all depends on your viewpoint, I suppose.' She smiled when she saw the look of confusion on Standing's face. 'You expected a grieving widow?'

'You seem very . . . relaxed,' he said.

'Mikhail was Mikhail,' she said. 'I took him from his wife, another woman was taking him from me. During our marriage he was never faithful.' She paused. 'But I can't say I didn't know what I was getting into. His company was one of the biggest in Russia and he was on good terms with the president. But we were always aware that at any point it could all be taken away from him.'

'How so?'

She chuckled. 'I'm sure you know,' she said.

'This is a whole new world to me,' said Standing.

'Running a business in Russia is not the same as in the UK, or the US,' she said. 'Mikhail was close to the president. He had been for years. But the president is known to be fickle. Hundreds of oligarchs are in prison. Mikhail was always careful to stay on the president's right side, but it was a dangerous game.'

'Is it possible that the president had turned against him?'

She shrugged. 'Anything is possible. The last time we spoke was two months ago, before he was poisoned. And that was on the phone. I haven't been in the same room as him since Christmas.'

'You had Christmas together?'

'We had a Christmas lunch, with the children. So if he was having problems, he'd be unlikely to say anything to me.'

Her mobile rang and she took it out of her bag and apologised before taking the call. She spoke in Russian and several times covered her mouth with her free hand as she giggled. Standing had the impression that she was talking to a man and that he was flirting with her.

He took another sip of champagne, wishing it was a lager. Eventually she finished her call and put her phone away. 'I have a friend on her way to see me, Mr Standing,' she said. 'It might be best if you're not here when she arrives.' She flashed him a cold smile. 'No offence.'

'None taken,' he said. He stood up. 'Thank you for your time. And I'm sorry about your loss.'

'Thank you for your sympathy,' she said. 'I had lost Mikhail long before he was killed. But his children lost a father they loved, and that is something I can not forgive.' She motioned for him to come closer and he bent down and leaned across the table towards her. 'Mr Standing, if in the course of your investigation you find out who had my husband killed, I will pay you a hundred thousand pounds if that person meets a similar end.'

Standing frowned. 'You want to pay me to kill the man who had your husband killed?'

She smiled sweetly. 'Why, Mr Standing, that's not what I said. That would obviously be totally illegal. I was simply telling you that if the man who had my husband killed meets a similar fate, you will benefit to the tune of a hundred thousand pounds.' She raised her champagne glass. 'Good hunting,' she said.

Standing straightened up. She met his stare and continued to smile. He nodded and walked away.

The two bodyguards glared at him as he walked out of the bar. Standing grinned. 'She's all yours, lads,' he said. 'You have a nice day.'

Standing waited until he was outside the store before calling John Keenan in Los Angeles. The call went straight through to voicemail and Standing realised it was probably the early hours in LA. He left a short message asking for Lipov's address in London.

16

Anton Vasilyev was easy to track down and when Standing told him that he had information about the murder of Mikhail Koshkin in Los Angeles, the Russian journalist readily agreed to a meeting in a coffee shop around the corner from his office.

Standing watched from across the road as Vasilyev arrived at the coffee shop, recognising the man from a by-line photograph on the website. He was a small man, barely five and a half feet tall, with a neatly trimmed beard and bright-blue framed spectacles. He was wearing a dark-green corduroy jacket and brown trousers and Timberland boots, with a black North Face backpack slung over one shoulder. Standing watched the journalist enter the coffee shop and waited a couple of minutes until he was sure that the man wasn't being followed, before crossing the road and pushing open the door.

Vasilyev had bought himself a cappuccino and was sitting at a table in the far corner. He looked up as Standing walked over. 'Mr Vasilyev? I'm Colin Peckham.' Standing had decided against using his real name in case the journalist wrote an article mentioning him. On the phone he'd said that he was a private detective working on the Koshkin case and he intended to stick to that cover story.

Vasilyev shook Standing's hand. His grip was weak, the flesh of his fingers soft and white. 'Let me get myself a coffee and I'll join you,' said Standing. He went over to the counter and ordered an Americano, taking a quick look through the window to assure himself that no one was loitering outside. A young woman with dyed blonde hair and a badge that said her name was Lena gave him his coffee and took his money and he went back to sit at Vasilyev's table. Standing sat with his back to the wall, side on to the door. The man at the table next to them was peering at a copy of the *Evening Standard* through thick-lensed glasses. He had a walking-stick leaning against his chair and he was picking at a chocolate muffin as he read his paper.

'So you're a private detective?' said the Russian. He had an accent but it wasn't heavy, which suggested he'd been in the UK for several years.

Standing nodded. 'I'm looking into the attack on Mikhail Koshkin.' He smiled. 'And on yourself, of course.'

'And who would your client be?'

'Our company has been approached by another firm of investigators in Los Angeles, where Mr Koshkin met his untimely end.'

The Russian frowned. 'Why?'

'Why?' repeated Standing, not understanding the question.

'Why are private investigators investigating a murder? Isn't that what the police are for?'

'The authorities in Los Angeles suspect that the man who killed Mr Koshkin was a hired assassin but don't seem to be in any hurry to find out who might have paid for the killing.'

Vasilyev nodded thoughtfully. 'But who is the client? Who is so interested in finding out who wanted Koshkin killed?'

'Aren't you curious?' asked Standing. 'They almost caused your death, too.'

'Of course I'm curious,' said Vasilyev. 'But I'm not paying a firm of private investigators to look into the matter. Is the client a family member?'

Standing shrugged. 'I really don't know. I was just asked to talk to you and to make contact with the authorities here. I wasn't told who the original client is. But I'm not making much headway on that front. The police here seem as disinterested as their American counterparts when it comes to finding out who wanted Mr Koshkin dead.'

'Even less so, after he was killed in LA,' said Vasilyev.

'There was almost nothing about the attack here in the papers,' said Standing.

'The government wanted it kept quiet,' said Vasilyev.

'But there was nothing on your website, either.'

'As I said, the government wanted it kept quiet. I was told in no uncertain terms that if I did publicise what happened, my journalist's visa would be revoked.'

'Told by whom?'

'By a man in a grey suit who knew everything about me and my family.'

'Your family?'

'My sister married a Brit and is in the process of being naturalised. I was told that if I didn't do as I was told, she would not be allowed to live in the UK either.'

'So you kept quiet?'

'I had no choice. You're British, right?'

Standing nodded. 'Of course.'

'You Brits always assume that your own government is so much more respectable than the Russians or the Chinese or the despots in the Middle East. The trust you have in those who govern you is laughable. If I had disobeyed my instructions, I would have been on the next plane out of the UK. And considering the nature of my recent reporting, I doubt I would survive for long in Russia.' He shrugged and sipped his coffee. 'But I did as I was told, and here I am. And in four years' time my sister will be a British citizen.'

'Why were you interviewing Mr Koshkin?' asked Standing, not wanting to be drawn into a discussion about the pros and cons of the British government.

The journalist shrugged again. 'Nothing much. I was writing an article about oligarchs in London. I spoke to several rich Russians.'

'Did you ever write the article?'

'It's a work in progress,' said Vasilyev.

Standing stared at the man for several seconds. 'I don't believe you,' he said eventually.

The Russian froze. 'Excuse me?'

'I believe in calling a spade a spade,' said Standing. He leaned towards the journalist, his eyes hard. 'I've looked at your website. You don't write soft features about Russian businessmen. You're an investigative reporter. You dig for dirt. So what dirt did you have on Koshkin?' The journalist stared at Standing for several seconds, then got to his feet. Standing's hand lashed out and his fingers fastened around Vasilyev's wrist. 'Sit down,' he said.

Vasilyev tried to pull his hand away but Standing was too strong for him. Standing's fingernails bit into the man's flesh and he winced. 'Who are you?' said Vasilyev.

'I'm the man who's going to break your wrist if you don't sit down and talk to me.'

The Russian sat down. Standing let go of his wrist and Vasilyev massaged it as he stared fearfully across the table. 'I could call the police,' said the journalist, but there was no conviction in his voice.

Standing smiled. 'Look, Anton, I'm not the enemy here. I'm not the one who poisoned you. I just need some information from you and then I'll leave and you'll never see me again.'

Vasilyev looked to be close to tears. 'You can't talk to me like this,' he said. 'There are laws in this country.'

'I'm sorry,' said Standing. 'But I can't let you leave, not without telling me what happened. There's too much at stake.'

'Why does it matter? Koshkin is dead.'

'I want the man responsible for Koshkin's death to be brought to justice and punished,' said Standing, and that much was true, though he was more concerned about getting the dogs off Bobby-Ray.

'All I know is what I read. There was a home invasion and he was shot, along with three of his bodyguards.'

'That's what the cops are saying, but I'm not sure that's true.'

The Russian frowned. 'What do you mean?'

'I mean that the cops might not be telling the truth. I think that Koshkin's death is connected to what happened here in London.'

'Somebody wanted him dead, that's for sure.'

'Who?' asked Standing.

The Russian shrugged. 'If I knew, I'd have told the police.'

Standing sat back in his seat. 'Maybe you would have, maybe you wouldn't,' he said.

The Russian frowned. 'What do you mean?'

'Maybe you decided that you'd be better off not telling the police anything,' he said. 'You were lucky last time, you might not be so lucky if they tried again.'

'It wasn't me they were trying to kill,' said the journalist.

'They didn't seem to care about collateral damage, though,' said Standing. He sipped his coffee. 'Of course, it could have been you who gave the poison to Koshkin.'

'I was poisoned, too,' said the Russian indignantly.

'You might have taken some yourself, to make it look as if you were also a victim.'

'I WAS a victim!' hissed Vasilyev. 'I could have died.'

Standing shrugged. 'Maybe.'

'There's no "maybe" about it,' said Vasilyev. 'Whoever poisoned Koshkin also poisoned me.'

'If that's true, how did they know Koshkin would be in the restaurant with you?'

The Russian's eyes narrowed. 'What are you getting at?'

'You were poisoned in a crowded restaurant. That takes planning. So how did they know you would be there?' Vasilyev didn't answer and Standing leaned towards him. 'Did you tell anyone you were meeting him?'

Vasilyev shook his head. 'No.'

'How far ahead was the meeting planned?'

'It wasn't. I rang him up and said I wanted to interview him. He suggested we have dinner.'

'The restaurant was his choice?'

The journalist nodded. 'He suggested the place and the time.'

'And the phone call was how far in advance of the meeting?'

Vasilyev shrugged. 'A couple of hours.'

'Do you think your phone is tapped?'

'I called him on my mobile.'

'Mobiles can be tapped.'

'It's possible, I suppose. But it'd be more likely that it was Koshkin's phone that was being tapped.'

'Why do you say that?' asked Standing.

The Russian shifted uncomfortably in his seat.

'The sooner you tell me, the sooner I'll be out of your hair,' said Standing.

Vasilyev nodded slowly. 'You know who he was, right? He was a nobody before the Soviet Union broke up, and he emerged as one of the richest men in Russia. You don't do that without making enemies, both in the government and elsewhere.'

'Elsewhere?'

'Jealous rivals. The Russian mafia. When you're rich, you're a target.'

'Mafia? The Russian mafia were after him?'

'He had connections with the Solntsevskaya syndicate, one of the nastiest Russian gangs. It's an open secret that they have links to the Kremlin.'

'Putin?'

'Allegedly. But these things are almost impossible to prove.'

'You say connections. What sort of connections did Koshkin have with them?'

'That's the billion ruble question. He denied it, obviously.'

'That's what you wanted to interview him about?' asked Standing.

'Partly. He had a business partner, Erik Markov. Markov was definitely in bed with the Solntsevskaya.'

'Koshkin fell out with Markov, didn't he?'

'Big time.'

'So it is possible that Markov used the Russian mafia to kill Koshkin?'

'I don't know,' said Vasilyev. 'But that wasn't why I interviewed Koshkin. I was more interested in rumours I'd heard that Markov was involved in the manipulation of the American elections.'

'What?'

'It's a long-running story, you know that? The Russians are said to have manipulated the elections in the United States, but to date there hasn't really been a smoking gun. I was working on a story that the Solntsevskaya organisation was the conduit and that Markov was using one of his companies to fund it. I was hoping that the fact that Koshkin had fallen out with Markov would mean that he might help me.' He shrugged. 'I was wrong.'

'Wrong that he was involved, or wrong that you thought he'd talk to you?'

The journalist forced a smile. 'The latter. In fact he tried to bribe me to not write the story. He was clever about it, though. Said he'd pay me to write the story exclusively for him. He'd pay for world rights.'

Standing frowned. 'Does he own a newspaper?'

'No, that was the point. He was offering to pay me so that the story wouldn't get published anywhere.'

'Which suggests that he was involved, obviously.'

'Not necessarily,' said Vasilyev. 'He denied that he had anything to do with election-rigging but said that any bad publicity for Markov would reflect badly on him. I think he was scared of Markov. After what happened, it looks like he had good reason.'

'So why are you still alive?' asked Standing.

The Russian's face creased into a frown. 'What do you mean?'

'If Koshkin was killed to keep the Russian involvement in the US elections under wraps, wouldn't they want you silenced as well? Why just kill Koshkin and leave you alive?'

Vasilyev shrugged. 'Without Koshkin, I really don't have a story. Just the same rumour and speculation that everyone else has.'

Standing sat back and stared thoughtfully at the journalist. 'So was it Markov who wanted Koshkin dead, or the mafia, or the Kremlin? Or all three?'

'You're asking a question I can't answer,' said Vasilyev.

'Someone told me that if it was the Kremlin they would have used something like a nerve agent or a radioactive substance, something that let the world know it was them.'

The journalist nodded. 'Putin does like his enemies to know that he can reach them whenever he wants to.' He reached for his cup. The door opened and two men walked in. The hairs on the back of Standing's neck stood up as he looked over at the door. Both men were wearing dark glasses and were looking in his direction. One stood by the door, his right hand up across his stomach. His dark-green bomber jacket was open. He had a black wool hat on, pulled low so that it covered most of his head.

Vasilyev saw Standing's eyes narrow and he began to turn to see what he was looking at.

The man nearest to their table already had his hand inside his jacket. He had on a baseball cap and his cheeks were pockmarked with old acne scars. He had a moustache that looked as if it had been glued on and was wearing a light-brown leather jacket and beige cargo pants. And gloves. It was a warm day and if Standing needed any proof that the men weren't there for the coffee, the gloves were all he needed.

Standing twisted to his right and grabbed the walking-stick that was leaning against the chair next to him. The owner of the stick opened his mouth to protest but Standing was already getting to his feet.

The gloved hand was emerging from the leather jacket now, gripping the butt of a semi-automatic. It was a Glock, a 36, one of the smallest and lightest guns around. It weighed just twenty-seven ounces and was just seven inches long, making it the perfect concealed weapon. Its small size meant that it held only six .45 ACP rounds. It looked like a toy in the man's hand, but Standing knew that it packed a punch that outweighed its size. It also had a silencer screwed into its barrel.

Standing raised the stick and smacked it against Baseball Cap's elbow. There was a satisfying splintering sound and the man grunted in pain.

The other man was reaching inside his bomber jacket. Vasilyev had his hands up in front of his face, an instinctive reaction that would do nothing to help him.

Standing pulled back the walking-stick and stabbed it into Baseball Cap's chest, just below the sternum. The gun fell from his hand and clattered on the floor as the man staggered back and fell against a table, spilling the coffees of two young mothers.

Customers were screaming now and several were ducking down under their tables.

Bomber Jacket had his gun out now. It was another Glock, a 22 Gen4, an inch longer, seven ounces heavier and with fifteen .40 calibre rounds in the magazine. Bomber Jacket was also wearing gloves and his finger was tightening on the trigger.

Standing threw the walking-stick and it spun through the air. Bomber Jacket moved to the side but the stick still caught him on the shoulder before it smashed against the window.

Baseball Cap regained his balance and staggered forward, bellowing with rage. He bent down, groping for his weapon with his left hand.

Standing stepped around the table. One of the baristas dropped down behind the counter, the other stood transfixed, her eyes and mouth open in horror. Most of the customers were screaming, but Standing was barely aware of the noise.

Baseball Cap had his left hand on the butt of his gun.

Standing pushed Vasilyev off his chair, getting him out of the line of fire.

Bomber Jacket was still bringing his gun to bear on Standing. Standing was definitely the target, not the journalist, but then they were professionals and would probably be reacting to the only threat.

Baseball Cap had grabbed the gun but he'd had to bend double and it was an effort for him to straighten up. Standing took two quick steps and seized the gun with both hands. He twisted the man around so that he was facing the door. Baseball Cap resisted but Standing jabbed his elbow into his throat, hard. He slipped a finger over the trigger and aimed at Bomber Jacket's chest. He fired two shots and both hit the man dead centre. The silencer dampened the sound to a dull pop. Bomber Jacket slumped to the ground.

Baseball Cap tried to head-butt Standing and caught him a glancing blow on the temple. Standing twisted the gun around, jammed the silencer under his chin and pulled the trigger. Blood and brains and bits of skull plastered across the ceiling and the man fell to the ground in an untidy heap.

Standing looked down at Vasilyev, who had scuttled to the side of the room and was sitting with his back to the wall. He was shaking and there was a blank look in his eyes. Standing knew he had only seconds to decide what to do next. If he stayed, then the police would take him in for questioning and while he was absolutely sure that everyone in the coffee shop would confirm that it was self-defence, he would still have a lot of explaining to do and the Regiment wouldn't be happy.

He nodded at the Russian, then put a finger up to his lips. The Russian nodded back. 'Not a word,' said Standing and Vasilyev nodded again. Standing tucked the gun into the back of his trousers and walked quickly to the door, keeping his head down. He stepped over the body by the window, pulled the door open and walked out into the street.

The sound of the silenced shots hadn't been heard over the noise of the traffic. It was a busy road and a major bus route and there was construction work going on in a building opposite. Standing kept his head down as he walked to the first intersection and took a right, then a left. In the distance he heard a siren, then another.

He was breathing slowly and evenly and he walked at a steady pace. His heart was beating at its normal rate and his mind was clear. He took another right and then flagged down a black cab. He had it take him to The Strand and he got out close to Charing Cross Station where he caught another cab back to his hotel.

17

S tanding sat on his bed and popped the tab on a can of lager. He kicked off his shoes and sat with his back to the headboard as he sipped his drink. The gun was on the bed next to him, not for protection but because he wasn't sure what to do with it. He used the remote to turn on the television and flicked through the channels until he got to Sky News. He wanted to phone Kaitlyn to check that she was okay and was trying to work out what time it was in Los Angeles when his phone rang. He didn't recognise the number but he took the call. It was Spider Shepherd. 'What's going on, mate?' asked Shepherd calmly.

Standing didn't bother pretending not to know what Shepherd was talking about. The man was a professional and deserved Standing's respect, plus he was an SAS living legend who wouldn't take kindly to being lied to. 'They came after me,' said Standing. 'I was having coffee with Anton Vasilyev and they burst in with guns.'

'Were they after you or Vasilyev?'

'They were going for me, but I was on my feet so I was the obvious one to hit first. There were two of them and they both had guns with silencers, so it was clearly a hit.'

'You took one of the guns?'

'It had my prints and DNA on it; I could hardly leave it behind. How much trouble am I in, Spider?'

Shepherd chuckled dryly. 'Surprisingly little, at the moment,' he said. 'There were two dozen witnesses in the coffee shop and two dozen different descriptions. They can't even agree on what jacket you were wearing and one had you down as a ginger.'

'They were in shock, and shock does things to your memory,' said Standing.

'Sure. But they're all in agreement that they came in and started waving guns and that you saved the day. There was no CCTV in the shop and the cameras in the street had nothing useful.'

'What about Vasilyev?'

'He's saying nothing. He told police you were a contact who'd called him up with a story but that you didn't identify yourself. He said he agreed to meet you in the coffee shop. He told the cops he didn't have your mobile number but you need to dump your SIM card ASAP and get rid of the phone.'

'Is it going to be on the TV or in the papers?'

'Maybe. But other than the fact that a mystery man took out two men with guns, they don't have much in the way of facts. The cops have no idea what was going on.'

'Do they realise that Vasilyev and I were the targets?'

'Not yet, but at the very least Matty Stogdale is going to figure it out. I'll call him and keep him on track, but at some point they're going to realise that it was Vasilyev they were after. It has to be, right? No one knows you're in London.'

'Who were they?' Standing asked.

'Professionals,' said Shepherd. 'They had no ID on

them, the gun you left behind was unregistered and their mobiles were throwaways with pay-as-you-go SIMs. Fingerprints have come back not known and they've sent DNA samples off but I'm going to assume they're not on file either.'

'So we don't even know if they're Russians or Americans?'

'Or homegrown hitmen,' said Shepherd. 'No, they're blank slates.'

'Did they have a car outside?'

'Neither of them had car keys on them, so the cops are assuming they had a vehicle waiting for them outside with a driver. Look, we need to meet, Matt.'

'Not a problem,' said Standing. 'Where and when?'

'Hyde Park Corner, opposite the Hard Rock Cafe,' said Shepherd. 'In two hours' time.'

'Fancy a burger, do you?'

'Just be there, Matt.'

'You wouldn't be trying to set me up, would you, Spider?'

'If I was, I'd have done that already,' said Shepherd. 'This is as much about protecting the Regiment as it is about helping you.'

'Good to know.'

'I'm serious, Matt. I'm not sure what you've got yourself involved in, but I want you out of it as quickly as possible. I'll see you in two hours. And ditch that gun. You do not want to be caught with that in your possession.'

Shepherd ended the call. Almost immediately Standing's phone buzzed to let him know that a text message had arrived. It was from John Keenan in LA. It was an address in St John's Wood.

18

S tanding got to the Hard Rock Cafe ten minutes before he was due to meet Shepherd. He'd dumped the throwaway phone in a skip after removing the SIM card, breaking it in half and flushing it down the toilet. He had broken the gun down into its component parts but had left them under the mattress in his room. He'd need to take more care of disposing of the pieces and the silencer. He spotted Shepherd on the other side of the road, clearly watching to see if Standing was being followed. Standing walked past the restaurant, then turned and doubled back. He looked over at Shepherd and Shepherd motioned for him to cross the road. Standing jogged over.

Shepherd was wearing a black raincoat over a dark-blue suit. His hands were in his coat pockets and he didn't offer to shake hands. 'So no burger then?' asked Standing.

Shepherd gestured at an open-topped tour bus. His right hand appeared from his coat pocket holding two tickets and he gave one to Standing. 'I'm not a tourist,' said Standing.

'No, but everyone else on the bus will be and they'll be listening to the commentary on earphones,' said Shepherd.

'Clever,' said Standing, following him onto the bus.

'I do my best,' said Shepherd.

They showed their tickets to the driver. Most of the sightseers had gone upstairs but Shepherd went straight to the rear of the bus and sat down. Standing sat next to him. Other than the driver, they were the only people downstairs.

The doors hissed closed and the bus pulled away from the kerb.

'Okay, so Matty Stogdale is up to speed,' said Shepherd, getting straight to the point. 'He's not happy, obviously.'

'He doesn't blame me, does he?'

'It's not about blame. It's about having an off-the-record chat with you only to have you go off and shoot two men in broad daylight.'

'In self-defence.'

'Of course it was self-defence. That's not the point. The point is that the police are trying to find out who you are, and he knows. So by not providing the investigating officers with that information he's being derelict in his duty.' Shepherd sighed. 'He's onside, there's no need to worry on that score. He's spoken to the investigating officers, who were already coming around to the idea that Vasilyev was the intended target. But Vasilyev is sticking to his story that you were just someone who had information for him and that he doesn't even have your name. Matty is going around to see him as we speak to make sure that he doesn't deviate from that line.'

'You realise they were probably after me, too?'

Shepherd grinned. 'I'm not a virgin at this,' he said. 'Of course it was you they were after. If it was Vasilyev they'd have taken him out at the same time as they killed Koshkin. They only sent in the killers when you arranged to meet Vasilyev. But there's no need for anyone else to know.'

'What's going on, Spider? Why was Koshkin killed? And why are they making such an effort to make it look as if Bobby-Ray did it?'

'Matty told you about Koshkin's business partner?'

'Erik Markov?'

Standing nodded. 'Sure. And Vasilyev seemed to think that either Markov, the Russian mafia or the Kremlin wanted Koshkin dead. Or a combination of all three.'

'I've been checking the files since we last spoke, and I agree that Markov is a likely suspect,' said Shepherd. He reached into his coat and took out a manila envelope. 'I've got some details here.'

He passed the envelope to Standing. Standing opened it. There were two photographs – one a head-and-shoulders shot and the other of a middle-aged bald man climbing out of the back of a Mercedes – and two type-written sheets.

'Markov is definitely in bed with the Solntsevskaya. There are photographs of Markov meeting with Solntsevskaya godfathers in London, Moscow and New York. They're not for public consumption, obviously. But I've seen them.'

'Is it something you'd take an interest in?'

'MI5, you mean? Markov is on our radar, obviously. But he pays taxes here and is a major donor to Labour and the Conservatives and is close friends with the usual suspects in the House of Lords.'

'But you think he had Koshkin killed?'

'Thinking and being able to prove are different things,' said Shepherd. 'And with Markov's connections, no one is going to go off half cock. There's no evidence at all linking him to the attack in the UK, and the cops in LA seem sure that your pal Bobby-Ray did the dirty deed.'

Standing's eyes flicked over the first typewritten sheet. Markov's full name in English and Russian, date of birth, passport details, a brief CV and a list of addresses.

'You'll be interested to know that two days after Koshkin left for LA, Markov flew out to New York on his private jet. He was on the ground for just six hours before flying on to LA, which is where he is now. He's taken a full floor of the Four Seasons.'

Standing looked up from the sheet. 'That can't be a coincidence, surely?'

'That he was in town when Koshkin was killed? Who knows? Coincidences happen. But coincidence or not, you're going to have to be careful.'

'I always am.'

'I'm serious,' said Shepherd. 'How much do you know about the Solntsevskaya?'

'Russian mafia.'

Shepherd nodded. 'But they're not just a gang of thugs. They're a sophisticated, well-organised, well-connected criminal organisation. They're the most powerful crime syndicate in Russia, bar none.'

'Okay . . .' said Standing. He looked at the second sheet of paper. It was a list of Russian names and addresses. He frowned, wondering what they were.

Shepherd tapped the paper. 'I thought it might be

helpful if you had those. It's the main Solntsevskaya players in the US.'

There were a dozen names on this list, mainly in New York.

'The organisation was set up in the late Eighties by a former waiter turned fraudster,' said Shepherd. 'Within ten years the gang was big enough to challenge the Chechen mafia and shortly afterwards they expanded into the east coast of America. They moved into banking and started laundering money for the oligarchs. Then they set up in Israel and now they do a lot of laundering through Israeli banks. In the last ten years they've expanded their drugs operations by linking up with the Colombians. Drugs, arms, extortion, people trafficking, there's nothing they won't do to make a profit. And there's nothing they won't do to keep their operations secret.'

'I hear you,' said Standing.

'What I'm saying is, if they did kill Koshkin and they think you might be on to them, they'll come down on you hard.'

'You think they were the ones who attacked me today?'

'It's possible. Just watch yourself, Matt. Especially when you get back to the States.'

'What are you doing to stop them?'

'Me personally?'

Standing chuckled. 'Your guys. MI5.'

'There's a section within Five devoted to the Russian mafia, and they do what they can. But the Solntsevskaya is a tight group, you almost never get an informer or a man on the inside. If they get caught they don't deal, they just serve their sentence. The only time anyone has ever turned informant, they've been dead within the year, usually tortured along with their families and friends. They're a vicious bunch.'

'And what about this Markov?' He held up the photographs. 'Are you after him?'

'Markov isn't the sort to get his hands dirty.'

'Plus he has friends in high places?'

Shepherd grimaced. 'It's the way of the world,' he said. 'We don't put people in jail without evidence and a trial. That's why so many of the oligarchs choose to live here, it's a safe place for them.'

'Even when they're gangsters. That sucks.'

'If the cops get evidence they make a case. But guys like Markov, as I said, they never get their hands dirty.'

'And anyone who grasses on them gets killed?'

Shepherd nodded. 'I'm afraid so.'

Standing held up the papers and photographs. 'Can I keep these?'

'Sure. But for your eyes only.'

Standing put the papers back into the envelope and slid the envelope into his jacket pocket.

'So what's your plan now?' asked Shepherd.

Standing shrugged. 'I'll head back to the States and see if I can track down Bobby-Ray.'

'Are you going to confront Markov?'

Standing tilted his head on one side. 'Do you want me to?'

Shepherd smiled but his eyes stayed hard. 'Why do you ask that?'

'I'm just wondering if you planned to have me go in as some sort of cat among the pigeons.' He held up the list. 'And you've even given me the names and addresses of said pigeons.'

'Hawks would be a better analogy than pigeons,' said Shepherd. 'But Markov isn't a target of ours. Whether or not he should be is a different matter, but there's no way my bosses would approve an operation targeting him and I certainly wouldn't be launching an operation off my own bat. I understand what you're doing, and I've always been a supporter of the underdog. If I can help you and Bobby-Ray with intel and guidance then I will, but that's the limit of my involvement. If you do find that Markov is behind Koshkin's death, then what happens then is your call.'

'Message received and understood,' said Standing.

'At the risk of repeating myself, be careful,' said Shepherd. 'And if it does turn to shit, make sure you keep my name out of it.' The tour bus came to a halt and the doors hissed open. Tourists came clattering down the stairs and out onto the street. 'I'll leave you here,' said Shepherd. He stood up and clapped Standing on the shoulder. He reached into his pocket and gave him a SIM card. 'If you need to talk to me again, use this.'

'Will do,' said Standing. He put the SIM card into his wallet as Shepherd got off the bus and walked away without a backward look.

Standing sat back in his seat and folded his arms as the doors closed and the bus resumed its journey. Spider Shepherd was one of the good guys, but he couldn't help but wonder why the MI5 officer was so eager to help. Was it because he had an affinity for the underdog as he'd said, or was there an ulterior motive at work? Not that it mattered. All that Standing cared about was getting back to LA and saving Bobby-Ray. But first there was someone he needed to talk to.

19

Standing stayed on the bus for another ten minutes, then got off and went back to his hotel, taking a circuitous route to check that he wasn't being followed. He waited until he was back in his room before calling Kaitlyn on FaceTime. It took her a while to answer. When she did, he could see that her room was in darkness and he realised that it was still the early hours in Los Angeles. He held the phone so that she could see his face and spoke clearly. 'Sorry,' he said. 'I can never get the hang of the time difference with LA.'

She smiled sleepily. 'That's okay, I had to wake up to answer the phone.' She laughed at her own joke and sat up blinking, her hair tousled. 'Are you okay?'

'All good,' said Standing. 'Hang on, if you're asleep, how do you know the phone is ringing?'

'It's in the bed with me, and I set it to vibrate,' she said. Then she laughed. 'That didn't quite come out the way I meant it to.'

Standing grinned. 'Have you heard from Bobby-Ray?'

She shook her head. 'No.'

'I'm flying back today or tomorrow,' he said. 'I'll text you with my flight once I've got my ticket.'

'I'll pick you up at the airport,' she said.

'I can get a cab,' he said.

She shook her head. 'I'll be there.'

He ended the call, pulled out the bits of the gun and silencer from under the mattress, then walked to the Thames. The Golden Jubilee Footbridges had been built either side of the Hungerford railway bridge that carried trains from the South Bank to Charing Cross Station. The bridges were popular with tourists but Standing was able to find a quiet spot near the middle where he dropped the gun parts into the water far below.

He crossed over to the north side of the river and there he caught a black cab to St John's Wood. He had it drop him around the corner from where Lipov lived. It was an apartment in a white-painted three-floored conversion. He pressed the bell for Nikolai's apartment and a few seconds later a Russian accent growled, 'Who is it? What do you want?'

'Mr Lipov? This is the police. I need a word with you.'

'About what?'

'I'm investigating the attack on your former employer.'

'He's dead.'

'Yes, I know. But we still have some loose ends to tie up. Look, I'd rather talk to you in person, Mr Lipov,' said Standing. 'It won't take too long. Or if you'd rather, we could go down to the station.' The door lock buzzed and Standing pushed open the door. Lipov's flat was on the second floor and the door was already open when Standing reached it. Standing took out his Military Identification Card and flashed it just long enough so that Lipov could see the photograph. He hoped that his English wouldn't be up to realising that it wasn't a police warrant card.

The Russian barely glanced at the ID. 'What do you want?' he said. He was big, an inch or two over six feet, and like most Russian bodyguards that Standing had come across, he had a weightlifter's build, with massive forearms and a thick neck. His head was pretty much square with slab-like teeth and a chin that looked like it would shrug off most punches. He was wearing a Lonsdale sweatshirt and jogging pants and had a large black G-Shock watch on his left wrist.

'I need to talk to you about what happened in Los Angeles,' said Standing.

The Russian frowned. 'I already spoke to the American cops.'

Standing smiled and nodded. 'Absolutely you did, but there was an attack on Mr Koshkin in London and that case is still open.'

'He's dead. Why do you care what happened in London?'

'Because the case is still open,' said Standing. 'Can we do this inside, Mr Lipov, I need to take notes and it's hard to do that while I'm standing up.'

For several seconds it looked as if the Russian wanted to slam the door in Standing's face but eventually he stepped aside to let him in. The door opened into a large high-ceilinged sitting room with a big TV on one wall and two windows overlooking the street. A door led off to a small kitchen and another opened into the bedroom. There didn't appear to be anything of a personal nature in the room other than a small MacBook laptop on a dining table by one of the windows.

There were two grey sofas set at a right angle around a glass-topped coffee table. Standing sat down on one.

Lipov dropped down onto the other sofa and leaned forward with his elbows on his knees. He stared at Standing aggressively with pale-blue unblinking eyes. It was the typical bodyguard's stare and with most people it would have worked, but Standing wasn't most people and he smiled amiably. 'So, when Mr Koshkin was poisoned, where were you?'

'In the car outside. He wanted to have the meeting in private.'

'Was that usual?'

Lipov frowned, clearly not understanding the question.

'Did he usually have meetings in private, or were you always there?'

'Fifty fifty,' he said.

'And who was with you in the car?'

'Max and Boris.'

'The men who died with Mr Koshkin in Los Angeles?'

Lipov nodded.

'They were your friends?'

Lipov shrugged. 'We worked together.'

'You joined the team after them, right?'

Lipov stared at Standing for several seconds. 'How do you know that?' he asked eventually.

'I've interviewed Mrs Koshkin,' said Standing.

Lipov nodded slowly as he continued to stare at Standing.

'So, you were a recent addition to Mr Koshkin's security team?' asked Standing.

'Yes.'

'And he took you with him to Los Angeles?'

'He took the three of us. And then he hired more security there.'

'Including the man who went on to kill Mr Koshkin?'

Lipov nodded. 'Yes.'

'That must have been quite something,' said Standing. 'Having a member of your team go rogue like that?'

Lipov shrugged. 'Shit happens.'

'You would have thought that Mr Koshkin would have taken more care over who he hired,' said Standing. 'I mean, how does that happen? How does a man as smart as Mr Koshkin manage to hire a man who then kills him? And kills the other bodyguards?'

Lipov shrugged again but didn't answer.

'What was his name? The bodyguard who went rogue? Bobby-Joe?'

'Bobby-Ray. Bobby-Ray Barnes.'

'That's right. He was some sort of special forces soldier, wasn't he?'

'Navy SEAL.'

Standing nodded. 'I hear they're tough, the SEALs.'

Lipov sneered and sat back. 'They're not so tough,' he said. 'The Spetsnaz, they are tougher.'

'Spetsnaz? What's that?' asked Standing, pretending to be ignorant of the Russian special forces term. In fact, Standing knew that Spetsnaz was a catch-all term for many special forces units in the former Soviet Union, including the Army, Navy and National Guard, plus various government departments.

'They are the Russian special forces,' said Lipov. 'Better than the Navy SEALs, better than the SAS, better than anybody.' He folded his massive arms. 'Best in the world.'

'Were you in the Spetsnaz?'

Lipov nodded. 'Five years.'

'Did you see any action?'

'Of course. Why not?'

Standing was pretty sure that Lipov was lying. Big muscles were okay for a bodyguard, but bulk was a hindrance when it came to combat. Virtually every SAS trooper Standing had ever served with had been below average height and whippet-thin. They tended to put on weight after they left the Regiment, but while serving they were usually as fit as the proverbial butcher's dog.

'Whereabouts?' asked Standing.

Standing was sure the Russian was lying by the way he shifted uncomfortably on the sofa. 'The Ukraine,' he said. 'And the Caucasus. Why are you so interested in what I did?'

Standing smiled and waved away the question. 'Just background,' he said.

Lipov's eyes narrowed. 'You said you would take notes.'

'I will, when I hear something I need to write down,' said Standing.

'Background is a waste of time,' said Lipov. 'Koshkin is dead.'

'Yes, he is,' said Standing. 'There's no doubt about that. Did you actually see Bobby-Ray shoot Mr Koshkin?'

'No, I was upstairs.'

'That's right. Max and Boris were with him. So what, you heard the shots?'

'I was checking the bedrooms. I heard shots downstairs. I went to see what was happening and he shot at me.'

'On the stairs?'

'Yes.'

'You were lucky.'

'Lucky?'

'Lucky that he didn't kill you. He killed Max and Boris.'

Lipov nodded. 'If I had been downstairs he would have killed me, too.'

'So where did he shoot Max and Boris? In the hall?'

'No, in the sitting room. They had just brought Koshkin in and were making sure he was settled. Once he was settled we would usually wait in the kitchen.'

'And they had already checked the downstairs area?'

'That was procedure. One of us would go inside first and when they were sure the area was clear we would take him inside.'

'But you brought him in before checking the upstairs.'

Lipov frowned. 'What do you mean?'

'Standard procedure would be to keep the client outside until the whole house had been checked. That's all I'm saying.'

'It was the way we did it. It was his house, anyway. We weren't expecting any trouble.'

'And who decided that you would check the upstairs?'

Lipov's frown deepened. 'What do you mean?' he asked again.

'Who was the leader of the security team?'

Lipov's jaw jutted up. 'There wasn't a leader. We all knew what to do.'

'So you were lucky?'

'Lucky?'

'Well, whoever stayed with Mr Koshkin died. That was Max and Boris. And the American. If you had been in the sitting room when Bobby-Ray started shooting . . .' He shrugged and left the sentence unfinished.

'You are asking a lot of questions about Los Angeles,' said Lipov.

'It's an interesting situation,' said Standing. 'And we think that whoever paid for the killing in Los Angeles probably also paid for the poison attack in London. Who do you think wanted Mr Koshkin dead?'

'How would I know?'

'Did you not have threat assessment briefings?' The Russian frowned again. Standing wasn't sure if it was the language or the concept that was confusing him. 'Didn't the security team ever discuss who might want to hurt your client?'

Lipov shook his head. 'We were just told to protect him.'

Standing nodded as he considered his next question. He wasn't used to interrogating suspects, he usually left that to the intelligence experts. His forte was action and combat, attacking the enemy with a carbine and grenades, and he didn't feel comfortable sitting on a sofa trying to outflank Lipov with words.

'When you came down the stairs, Bobby-Ray was in the hallway, right?'

Lipov's eyes narrowed. 'Yes.'

'And by then he'd already shot Mr Koshkin, Max and Boris. And the other American bodyguard.'

'Yes.'

'Did you have your gun out as you came down the stairs?'

'Of course.'

'And Bobby-Ray had his gun out, obviously.'

Lipov's eyes narrowed even more but he didn't say anything.

'I guess my point is that Bobby-Ray must have known you were upstairs. And he must have known that you would come down to investigate the shots. So he'd have been waiting for you. With a gun.'

Lipov nodded. 'That's what happened.'

'But he didn't shoot you, did he?'

'He did but he missed.'

'He's a Navy SEAL and you're not a small target. And he missed?'

'I fired at him.'

'Yes, you did. And you missed.'

'He was moving fast.'

'Really? So he was what, running for the door?'

'Yes. He was running for the door and I was shooting at him.'

'But he got away.'

'He was moving quickly.'

'But why didn't he shoot you?'

'What?'

'He shot Mr Koshkin. He shot Max and Boris and the American. What was his name?'

'Kurt,' said Lipov sullenly.

'That's right. Kurt Konieczny. He killed Mr Koshkin and three bodyguards, but then he doesn't kill you. He shoots and misses, right?'

'So?'

Standing shrugged. 'So Navy SEALs don't usually miss.'

'Like I said, I was shooting at him. Max and Boris and Kurt weren't shooting back.'

'Then there's the gun,' said Standing. 'The gun's a worry.'

'What gun?'

'Bobby-Ray's gun. He left it behind. Outside.'

'He'd done what he wanted to do. He didn't need it.'

'It had his fingerprints and DNA on it. A smart killer would have taken it with him.'

Lipov shrugged. 'People make mistakes.'

Standing looked at the Russian, his eyes hard. 'They do, don't they?'

The Russian stared back at him. 'Who are you?' he said quietly.

'I told you who I am.'

'You're not a detective.'

'What makes you say that?'

'Most British cops are overweight and out of condition. You look battle fit. And you haven't written a single note. Who the fuck are you?'

Standing could see the Russian tensing but he was big and had a lot of mass to move so he'd be slow, slower than Standing anyway.

'Mr Lipov, I'm just a police officer doing his duty . . .'

The Russian moved while Standing was talking, bending forward at the waist before pushing himself up off the sofa.

Standing moved at the same time and both men got to their feet simultaneously, the coffee table between them. Lipov said nothing, which confirmed that an attack was coming. Standing didn't say anything either. There was no point. What was going to happen was going to happen, no matter what he said.

Lipov was big and strong, which meant he was probably confident that he would be able to overpower Standing with just his hands. There was no weapon in sight and nothing on the coffee table that either man could use. Standing waited, his arms relaxed at his side, his eyes taking in everything. He began to count in his mind. One. Two.

Lipov's right hand bunched into a fist a fraction of a second before his arm moved back. Standing turned side on and lashed out with his right leg, putting all his weight behind a kick that caught the Russian in the stomach and sent him sprawling over the sofa. Three. Four.

Standing pulled back his leg, twisted around and stepped away from the coffee table into the space by the door. Close up, Lipov would be devastating, especially if he managed to get hold of Standing. He'd have the strength of a grizzly bear and Standing needed room to strike.

Lipov roared as he pushed himself up off the sofa again. Standing grabbed one of the wooden chairs from the dining table and smashed it into Lipov's left leg so hard that the wood broke apart. Lipov grunted but held his ground. Standing smashed what was left of the chair over the Russian's head and it disintegrated completely. Blood dripped down Lipov's forehead but he stayed on his feet, glaring at Standing. Standing had a chair leg in his hand, about two feet of splintered wood that was sharp enough to use as a weapon until he could grab something else. The kitchen was the best bet, but that was a good ten feet away to his left and running there would mean turning his back on the Russian. Standing was sure he could outrun the man but if he didn't get a knife straight away, Lipov would be on him.

Lipov bent down, grabbed the coffee table and upended it towards Standing. Standing jumped back and the glass top crashed on the floor just inches from his feet. Lipov rushed towards him and Standing lunged with the chair leg. He doubted it would make any impression on the man's barrel chest so he aimed at Lipov's throat, but the Russian was surprisingly fast and knocked it out of the way. His momentum carried him forward and he slammed Standing against the wall. His right hand grabbed for Standing's throat.

The chair leg was still in Standing's right hand and he stabbed Lipov in the ear. Lipov roared but didn't release his grip. Lipov grabbed the chair leg with his left hand and twisted it out of Standing's grasp. As he raised the chair leg to hit Standing, Standing brought his fist down on the man's nose and heard and felt the cartilage break. Blood poured down Lipov's face but the grip on Standing's throat was relentless.

Standing used both his hands to twist the fingers away from his throat. He raised Lipov's arm in the air then brought it back down and twisted hard, pushing himself away from the wall and forcing the Russian down. The Russian resisted but all he did was add to the pressure on his shoulder. He lashed out with the chair leg but Standing saw the blow coming and managed to avoid it. He brought his knee up hard into Lipov's chest and heard a rib crack.

Lipov jabbed with the chair leg again and this time caught Standing with a glancing blow to the thigh.

Standing stamped down on Lipov's instep, then kneed him again in the chest. This time Lipov lost his balance and staggered to the side. Standing kicked him on the

knee then fired off two quick punches to the man's chest.
It was akin to hitting a tree.

Lipov straightened up and raised the chair leg above
his head. Before he could stab with it, Standing slashed
him across the throat with the side of his hand. He felt
the trachea crack and for the first time the Russian regis-
tered pain. Blood was still pouring from his broken nose
and soaking into his sweatshirt.

Standing threw two more punches, aiming for the man's
solar plexus, but Lipov took them without flinching. They
were close to the dining table now and Standing grabbed
another chair. He jabbed the legs towards Lipov like a
lion tamer, first at his face and then lower down. Lipov
stood his ground. The Russian was breathing heavily but
didn't seem tired.

Standing knew the chair wouldn't do any serious
damage, but it would keep Lipov at bay for a few seconds.
He tried to move towards the door, but Lipov moved
with him, blocking any escape. Standing jabbed with the
chair again and Lipov swatted it away like a bear knocking
a salmon out of the water. The chair almost slipped from
Standing's grasp but he managed to keep hold of it. Lipov
seized the opportunity to rush Standing, but Standing
moved to the side as deftly as a matador avoiding a bull.
He brought the chair crashing down on Lipov's head and
again the chair smashed into several pieces.

Lipov bent down, then shook his head and straightened
up. Standing let loose a side kick that would have sent
most men hurtling across the room, but Lipov was so
heavy that it was Standing who lost his balance and
staggered back.

Lipov growled, dropped his chair leg and threw himself at Standing, wrapping his massive arms around him and squeezing. Standing struggled but Lipov had interlinked his fingers and locked them tight. He increased the pressure, forcing the air from Standing's lungs. Standing head-butted the Russian, his forehead slamming into Lipov's nose. Lipov grunted but tightened his grip. The blood pouring down his nose and running into his mouth made it hard for the Russian to breathe and he turned his head to the side, gasping for air. Standing took the opportunity to bite into the Russian's ear, grinding his teeth together and chewing through a lump of flesh and cartilage. Lipov screamed in pain and released his hold on Standing, staggering back as blood poured from his mangled ear.

Lipov lashed out with his fist, a lucky punch that Standing didn't see coming. It hit him on the left side of his chin and sent him crashing to the floor. He rolled to the side and hit one of the sofas. He braced himself for an attack from Lipov as he got to his feet but the Russian was staggering towards the kitchen.

Standing rushed towards him but Lipov had already ducked through the door and grabbed a knife from a knife block. He turned with the knife in his fist, grinning maliciously.

Standing stopped and raised his hands in front of his chest. The table leg had been a dangerous enough weapon but the knife was a game changer. It was a butcher's knife, long and pointed, perfect for trimming cuts of meat or slicing open a man's stomach.

There was a black bomber jacket hanging over the

back of an armchair and Standing grabbed it and quickly wound it around his left hand and arm.

Lipov was switching the knife from side to side as he advanced on Standing. His sweatshirt was drenched in blood and it was dripping onto the carpet.

Standing waited, rising up onto the balls of his feet. His mind was calm; there was no point in having any sort of plan. All he could do was to react, and he trusted his instincts.

Lipov's left leg moved forward as the knife arm went back. Standing moved, springing forward with his covered left arm out, his right hand pulling back and forming a fist. Lipov growled as he saw the attack but all his weight was on his back foot, so he could only move forward. He started to strike with the knife but the jacket was already blocking the blow. Standing's fist connected with the Russian's nose and he put all his body weight behind the punch, crushing the cartilage.

Lipov pulled back the knife and thrust it at Standing's chest but Standing managed to deflect it. The tip of the knife snagged in the jacket.

Lipov surged forward and Standing felt his legs collapse underneath him. He fell back, trying to keep the knife away from him. As he hit the ground, Lipov fell on top of him, knocking the breath from his lungs.

Lipov straddled Standing but wasn't able to pin Standing's arms to his sides, so Standing was able to toss the jacket to the side and grab the hand holding the knife. Lipov's left hand fastened around Standing's throat and squeezed.

Lipov was gritting his teeth together and staring at the knife as if he could move it by sheer force of will. Standing was pushing up with both hands and was just about managing to halt its progress. He grunted and twisted the blade so that it was pointing up, then he thrust upwards with all his might. The rapid movement took the Russian by surprise. The knife plunged into Lipov's chin and Standing pushed even harder. Lipov's body went into spasm and he released his grip on Standing's throat.

Standing gave the knife one final thrust and more than half the blade disappeared into the Russian's skull. Blood was pouring down the blade and along Standing's arms. Lipov's hand released the knife and Standing pushed it another inch or so until he couldn't push it any further. Lipov fell to the side and Standing wriggled out from under him. Lipov rolled onto his back. His chest was still moving. Standing bent down over him. The knife was still embedded in his chin. It had almost certainly gone through the roof of his mouth and into his brain, so death wasn't far away.

'Who hired you, Nikolai?' asked Standing.

The Russian glared at Standing.

'Just tell me, Nikolai? Who paid you to kill Koshkin?'

Lipov's chest shuddered and coughed and blood trickled from between his lips. His mouth opened slightly and Standing saw that the blade had speared the Russian's tongue. Lipov sneered at Standing. 'Fuck you,' he managed to grunt, then he shuddered one last time and went still, his pale-blue eyes staring sightlessly up at the ceiling.

Standing stood up. His hands were wet with the Russian's blood and it was all over his jacket and shirt.

He went over to the front door and peeped through the security viewer. The hallway was empty. There had been plenty of noise but hopefully anyone else in the building would just assume it was furniture being moved around. He stayed peering through the viewer for a full thirty seconds and no one appeared.

He took off his jacket and shirt, then went over to the Russian and pulled out the knife. He took it over to the sink and washed it carefully, then dried it with a cloth and used the cloth to put it back in the block that Lipov had taken it from. He washed his hands and arms under the tap, then used the cloth to wipe away any prints on the bits of chair lying on the floor, then dropped the cloth on top of the jacket and shirt.

He picked up the jacket that he had wrapped around his arm. Other than a couple of small nicks from the knife, it was in good condition, and there was no blood on it. He went into Lipov's bedroom and used the jacket to open a mirrored wardrobe. He pulled out a white T-shirt. It would have been tight on the Russian but it was loose on Standing and he pulled it on, then put the jacket on top. He checked his reflection in the wardrobe door and nodded.

He went back into the main room and looked around for anything that might identify him as Lipov's killer. When he was satisfied that he was good, he went back into the kitchen and picked up an empty supermarket plastic bag and put his own jacket and shirt into it. He took another look around, then used the cloth to open the door to let himself out, and to close the door behind him.

He went downstairs and used the cloth to open the main door, then put the cloth in the bag with his jacket and shirt. He slipped out and dumped the carrier bag in a skip outside a house that was being renovated before heading to the nearest Tube station. He'd done all he could do in London; it was time to go back to LA.

20

S tanding called Kaitlyn on FaceTime as he waited to board the flight to Los Angeles but there was no answer, so he sent her a text with his flight details. He slept most of the way. The queue at LAX immigration was, if anything, longer than on his first visit, and the man who scrutinised his passport seemed to have taken it as a personal affront that Standing was trying to get into his country. He was a big man but carrying more weight than was good for him, bald with a neck so thick that hands alone wouldn't have been enough to strangle him. He frowned at the passport, and his frown deepened. 'So you were here for, what, three days? Then you went back to the UK for two days. Now you're back.'

Standing grinned. 'I thought I'd left the stove on.'

The immigration officer stared at Standing with unblinking pale-blue eyes. 'You think this is funny?'

'I was just trying to lighten the moment,' said Standing. He stopped smiling and met the man's gaze. 'I was here to see a friend. Something cropped up back in the UK, business-related. I flew back to take care of it and now I'm back here to see my friend again.'

'Who is this friend?'

'Kaitlyn Barnes.'

'So a girlfriend?'

'Not really. She's the sister of a friend.'

'And you'll be staying with her?'

Standing nodded. 'Sure.'

'And what sort of business are you in . . .' he squinted at the passport again. 'Mr Standing?'

Standing knew that lying to an immigration officer was never a good idea. Retribution could be anything from the rubber-glove treatment to being put on the next plane back to the UK. 'I'm a soldier,' he said.

The man's eyes widened a little. 'You don't say. Who do you serve with?'

Standing met his gaze. Lying still wasn't a good idea but no serving member of the SAS ever admitted to being in the Regiment. 'I'm a para,' he said.

The immigration officer frowned. 'A para?'

'Paratrooper. Third Battalion, the Parachute Regiment.'

'So you jump out of planes and shit?'

'It's been known, yes.'

'Served out in the Middle East?'

'Some,' said Standing.

The man nodded. 'My father was in Operation Desert Storm.'

'Before my time,' said Standing.

'It's still a mess out there,' said the man.

'And probably will be for some time,' said Standing.

The immigration officer handed the passport back to Standing. 'Have a nice day,' he said. 'And thank you for your service.'

'Right back at you,' said Standing.

He walked out into the arrivals area. There was no sign of Kaitlyn. He took out his phone and called her on

FaceTime but there was no answer. He figured she was probably driving, so he headed for a coffee shop and ordered an Americano and a sandwich. He ate the sandwich and drank the coffee, then called her again. Still no answer. He frowned as he stared at his smartphone. It wouldn't take her much more than thirty minutes to drive to the airport from her apartment, though there was always the possibility that there had been an accident on the freeway and she'd been caught up in traffic. He ordered another coffee and sat down. He tried calling Kaitlyn every five minutes or so, but by the time he had finished his second coffee she still hadn't answered. He found her address on his phone and then went along to the taxi rank and took a cab to her apartment block.

He followed another resident into the building and went up the stairs to her third-floor apartment. He knocked on her door, even though he knew she wasn't going to answer, then let himself in with the key she had given him.

He dropped his bag in the hallway and walked towards the sitting room. There was an envelope Sellotaped to the mirror. It had his name on it in capital letters. MATT STANDING. If Kaitlyn had left the note, she would have just used his first name. He stared at the envelope for several seconds, wanting to delay the moment when his worst fears would be realised, then he reached out and pulled it off the mirror. There was a single sheet of paper inside the envelope and he unfolded it. TELL BOBBY-RAY TO GIVE HIMSELF UP OR HIS SISTER DIES.

Standing cursed. Whoever wanted Bobby-Ray dead now had Kaitlyn, and he was sure they were serious about their threat. But what was he supposed to do? He was no closer to knowing where Bobby-Ray was than when he had first arrived in Los Angeles.

He looked around the room. There were no signs of a struggle. He went through to the bedroom. The duvet was half off the bed and there was a pillow on the floor, but Kaitlyn could just have been a messy sleeper.

He rubbed the back of his neck as he walked into the kitchen and opened the fridge. He took out a beer and popped the cap off, then went back into the sitting room and dropped down onto the sofa. He had the envelope that Shepherd had given him in his jacket pocket and he took it out. He sat and drank his beer as he studied the list of Russian names. Two of them were in Los Angeles.

21

S tanding twisted the top off the bottle of water and took a long drink as he stared at the house across the road. It was a single-storey wooden-sided house with a new black BMW and a white Range Rover parked in the driveway, which suggested that Stanislav Yurin was at home. Standing was in Kaitlyn's Polo. The keys had been in the kitchen and the car had a full tank of fuel. It had taken him thirty minutes to drive to Yurin's house in Venice, just four blocks from the beach.

Standing took another drink of water. All Shepherd had given him was Yurin's name and address, and Googling hadn't come up with anything else. Standing didn't have a gun, but if Yurin was a high-ranking member of the Russian mafia he'd almost certainly have one, or have people around him who were armed.

His phone rang and he jumped. It was Kaitlyn calling, but he frowned when he realised that it was a regular call and not FaceTime. He answered the call but didn't say anything. For several seconds there was just static on the line, then a man spoke. 'Standing?'

'I'm sitting, actually.'

'Very funny,' said the man. He had a strong Russian accent, which both reassured and worried Standing. It confirmed that he was right to suspect that the Russian mafia were involved in the Koshkin killing and Kaitlyn's abduction, but it also meant that he was going up against some serious villains. 'Have you spoken to Barnes?' the man growled.

'I don't know where he is. Let me talk to Kaitlyn.'

'Tell Barnes that if he doesn't turn himself in, his sister is dead. And before she dies, she'll suffer a lot of pain.'

'I need to see Kaitlyn.'

'Fuck you.'

'Proof of life.'

'Fuck you twice. Tell Barnes he has twenty-four hours. He can call us on this phone.'

'I don't know where he is and he doesn't call me,' said Standing.

'And after we've killed her, we'll come looking for you,' said the Russian.

'Yeah, well good luck with that,' said Standing.

'Twenty-four hours,' said the man, and the line went dead.

Standing put the phone back in his pocket and took another drink of water. Twenty-four hours wasn't long. He put the cap back on his bottle and got out of the car. He had no game plan to speak of, he was just going to play it by ear. It wasn't the best way of going into action, but his instincts had never let him down so far.

He walked up the driveway. The blinds were down at the windows. He reached the house and went up to the front door. There was a doorbell on the right-hand side and he pressed it. He was breathing slowly and evenly and if there had been anyone on hand to take his vital signs, they would have found his pulse was a steady seventy-two beats a minute and his blood pressure was a healthy 120/80.

He pressed the bell again. The door opened, just a few inches. A man looked down at Standing. He was tall, well over six feet, and big. 'What?' barked the man. There was a large diamond stud in his left ear.

'Are you Stanislav?'

'Who the fuck are you?'

Definitely Russian. 'I'm the man asking to speak to Stan.'

Someone shouted from inside the house. Diamond Stud turned and barked again, this time in Russian. Standing shouldered the door, hard. He caught the man off guard and he staggered back. Standing pushed the door wide. It opened into a hallway. At the far end was a kitchen. There was a man sitting at a table with a cup of coffee in front of him. There were two doors to the right, both open. One to the left, closed. Diamond Stud snarled at Standing and reached down with his hand. He was wearing an LA Lakers sweatshirt and there was a gun-shaped bulge over his stomach. Standing punched him under the chin but even as the punch landed he knew it wouldn't do much more than annoy him. Diamond Stud weighed at least two hundred and fifty pounds and it was all muscle. Armchair warriors liked to say that the bigger they are, the harder they fall, which might well have been true but it required one hell of a lot of effort and some luck to get them to the ground.

Diamond Stud's right hand was still going for the gun. Standing kicked his left knee to get him off balance and almost immediately slammed his elbow in his temple.

Diamond Stud staggered back. The man in the kitchen was getting to his feet and grabbing something off the table. Like Diamond Stud he was a big man, wearing a tight T-shirt that showed bulging forearms covered in brightly coloured tattoos. The kitchen door blocked Standing's view so he couldn't see what the man was reaching for.

Diamond Stud roared, more in anger than pain, and tried to claw Standing's eyes. Standing grabbed the hand with both of his, twisted it at the wrist and then used his elbow to force him down. He resisted and Standing immediately moved in the other direction, pushing the arm back and exposing his chest. He let go with his right hand and grabbed Diamond Stud's gun from under the man's shirt. Diamond Stud's eyes widened in panic as he realised what was happening.

The gun was a Smith & Wesson M&P Shield, which, like the Glock, had the safety built into the trigger. Standing lowered the barrel and pressed the muzzle against Diamond Stud's right leg. He pulled the trigger and the gun kicked and Diamond Stud immediately sagged against the wall as blood erupted around the knee.

Standing stepped to the right and brought up the weapon. Tattooed Sleeves had reached the kitchen doorway and was holding a gun in his right hand. Standing immediately went into a crouch and pulled the trigger again. They fired at the same time but Tattooed Sleeves shot high. Standing fired twice and both shots hit the man in the right shoulder.

A third man appeared in the doorway to Standing's right and then ducked away.

Diamond Stud grabbed at Standing's left leg and Standing shot him in the shoulder. He fell back, cursing.

As he moved down the hallway, Tattooed Sleeves slumped to the kitchen floor, his shirt a mass of red. His mouth was working soundlessly and he was looking at Standing with a look of surprise on his face.

Standing walked quickly to the room where he'd seen the third man. He had the Shield up in both hands. If there had been anyone there to take Standing's vital signs, they would have found that his pulse rate and blood pressure were exactly the same as when he'd pressed the doorbell. He went through the door gun first, his head moving from side to side for maximum vision.

The man was standing by a desk, his right hand in a drawer. 'Hands in the air, now,' said Standing. 'If I see a gun, I pull the trigger.'

He slowly raised his hands and turned to face Standing. 'Are you Stanislav Yurin?' Standing asked.

'Fuck you,' spat the man.

Standing shot him in the leg. The man didn't go down; he stood his ground and continued to glare at Standing as blood dribbled through his jeans.

'The next one goes in your head and I'll go back into the hallway and talk to the other guys,' said Standing. He levelled the gun at the man's head and tightened his finger on the trigger.

The man jutted up his chin. 'I am Yurin,' he said. 'Who the fuck are you?'

Standing gestured with the gun. 'Get into the hallway so I can keep an eye on all of you,' he said. He moved into the hall and stood with his back to the wall. Diamond

Stud was sitting on the floor. He said something to Yurin. 'English!' said Standing. 'If I hear one more word of Russian I will put a bullet in whoever said it.'

Tattooed Sleeves was curled up on the floor and blood was pooling around him, glistening on the tiles. If he wasn't already dead, death wasn't far off. Standing felt no guilt about ending his life – it had been kill or be killed, and on the day Standing had been the better killer.

Yurin limped into the hallway.

'Sit down,' said Standing. He walked to the kitchen, stepped over Tattooed Sleeves, grabbed two dishcloths and went back to Yurin. He threw one at Yurin and tossed the other to Diamond Stud. 'Stem the bleeding. If we can tie this up in a few minutes, you can call 911 and get yourselves patched up.'

'Fuck you,' snarled Yurin, but he placed the cloth on his wound and applied pressure.

'Yeah, sticks and stones,' said Standing. 'Now where is Kaitlyn Barnes?'

'You think she's here? You fucking idiot.' Yurin spat at him but the spittle fell short.

'At least you're not denying you know what I'm talking about,' said Standing. He waved the gun. 'Where's your phone?'

'My pocket.'

'Take it out.'

Yurin did as he was told.

'Call your boss. Tell him a friend of Bobby-Ray Barnes is here and tell him that if he doesn't let Kaitlyn Barnes go I'll put a bullet in your head. And speak English.'

'He won't give up the girl,' said Yurin. 'You're wasting your time.'

'It's my time to waste,' said Standing. He gestured with his gun. 'Do it.'

Yurin sighed and called a number.

'Put it on speaker,' said Standing. 'And remember, no Russian.'

Whoever was at the other end of the line answered. 'It's me,' said Yurin. The person at the other end spoke in Russian. 'We have to speak in English,' said Yurin. 'There's a shithead here with a gun. He's shot Vlad and he's shot Roman. He's shot me in the leg and he says if you don't let the bitch go, he'll put a bullet in my head.'

'How did this motherfucker get into your house?'

'That's not the fucking point, is it?' said Yurin.

'I think it is. How the fuck does one man shoot three of you?'

'For fuck's sake, Denis, he's going to kill me.'

'No, he won't,' said Denis. 'If that was his plan he'd have done it already. Let me talk to him.'

Standing shook his head and pointed at Yurin.

'He doesn't want to talk to you.'

'Then tell him to go fuck himself.'

'I've got a bullet in my fucking leg, Denis.'

Denis began speaking in Russian. Standing stepped forward and grabbed the phone from Yurin. He killed the speakerphone and put the phone to his ear. 'Listen to me, Denis, and listen good,' he said. 'You need to give Kaitlyn back to me.'

'Who the fuck are you?'

'I'm a friend of Bobby-Ray's. You might have a problem

with Bobby-Ray, but that's nothing to do with his sister. You need to let her go now.'

'You don't tell me what to do, *suka, mudak*.'

Standing didn't know much Russian, but he knew the words for bitch and asshole.

'If you don't release her, I'll kill Yurin.'

'Kill him,' said Denis. 'He's a fucking liability anyway.'

'Suit yourself,' said Standing. He pointed the gun at Yurin, took aim, and fired twice. He ended the call and slipped the phone into his pocket.

Yurin stared up at him in horror. Both rounds had embedded themselves in the wall, a few inches above his head. '*Ty che, suka, o'khuel blya?*' he hissed. 'Are you fucking crazy, you bitch?'

'Would you rather I shot you in the head?' asked Standing. 'Because that's what Denis wanted, right?'

Yurin glared at him and didn't answer.

'Your boss couldn't give a damn if I killed you or not,' said Standing. 'You heard him. You mean nothing to him.'

Still Yurin said nothing.

'Here's what's going to happen, Stan. I'm going to find Denis and he's either going to release Kaitlyn or I'm going to kill him. Those are the only choices. And you're going to have to hope that I do kill him, because otherwise he's going to come after you.'

Yurin frowned, not understanding.

'When Denis finds out that I didn't kill you, he'll assume it's because you told me what I wanted to know. And he probably won't just kill you, right? He'll probably torture you first. That's what you Solntsevskaya guys do, right? You're big on torture?'

'What do you want from me, motherfucker? I don't know where the bitch is.'

'No, but you know where Denis is. And your best hope right now is to share that information with me.'

Yurin gritted his teeth and stared up at Standing, his eyes burning with hatred.

22

If there was any doubt about the services provided in The Dollhouse, the ten-times life-size cut-out of a sexy blonde dancer holding a glass of champagne on the roof was probably a clue. Plus the words GIRLS! GIRLS! GIRLS! above the door.

It was just after six thirty in the evening and Standing had parked the Polo across the road from the building to get a feel for the establishment. Other than the signage, it had the look of an industrial warehouse. There was a parking lot to the left with a dozen cars there, mainly pick-up trucks. There was a line of expensive SUVs lined up by the entrance under signs that said unauthorised vehicles would be towed away. Standing figured they belonged to the owners, which meant one of them probably belonged to Denis Volkov.

Once he had realised that Volkov had done him no favours, Yurin had given Standing Volkov's name, his address and told him that he used the Hollywood Boulevard strip club as his base of operations. Yurin's wound wasn't life-threatening but the man shot in the hallway needed medical attention and the one in the kitchen was dead. Yurin told Standing that he would take care of the body and that he had an off-the-books doctor who would tend to the injuries. Yurin's attitude had changed once he'd realised how little his boss cared about what happened to him, and Standing guessed that Yurin was already planning on taking over Volkov's operations once Standing's mission had run its course.

The gun he'd taken from the kitchen of the house was in the glove compartment. The Shield that he'd taken from the man who had opened the door had been a small, light gun, easy to carry as a concealed weapon but so small that it could only hold eight rounds in the magazine. He had fired seven, so he'd wiped his prints off it and left it in the house. The gun in the kitchen had only been fired once. It was a Beretta APX compact with twelve rounds left in the magazine. But Standing had pretty much decided that there was no point in taking the gun in with him. There was no obvious security outside and Standing was no expert on strip clubs but he was sure he wouldn't be allowed to walk in with a gun.

He turned off the engine and climbed out of the Polo. It was still hot, and sweat beaded on his forehead as he crossed the road. He pushed open the double doors and was immediately hit by a blast of cold air and a pounding rock beat. Two big men in black T-shirts were standing there and Standing was thankful he'd left his gun in the car. One of the heavies mimed for Standing to raise his arms and he did. The heavy patted him down roughly, then gestured for him to go through to the bar.

There were two long podiums, each with two dancers on it, and beyond the podiums was a bar with three bartenders – two men and a woman – wearing black T-shirts and jeans. Off to the left was a curtain and above it a sign that said VIP AREA and to the right was a door with a STAFF ONLY sign on it.

He walked over to the bar and slid onto a stool. The male bartender walked over. He was in his thirties, tanned and with his blond hair tied back in a ponytail. He gestured with his chin, his way of asking what Standing wanted to drink.

'Budweiser,' said Standing.

The barman pulled a bottle off a shelf, popped off the cap and put it on the bar in front of Standing without saying a word. As the barman walked away, Standing swivelled around on his stool.

All four dancers were topless, and from the look of it had invested in breast implants. Two were blondes, one was a brunette and one had hair that had been dyed a vibrant pink. All of the girls had at least one visible tattoo and the girl with pink hair had a full back tattoo of a leopard.

The curtain to the VIP area was pulled back and a bearded man in blue jeans and a red checked shirt walked out, followed by another topless blonde. As the customer headed out, the girl walked over to a booth where two men in suits were drinking whisky. One of the men got to his feet and the girl took him by the hand and led him through the curtain.

A girl appeared at Standing's side. She had black spikey hair that was a stark contrast to her pale white skin. 'Hey,' she said. She had thick black eyeliner and shocking pink lipstick.

He raised his bottle in salute. 'Hey back at you.'

'Do you want a dance?' Her accent was East European, Polish maybe.

'Perhaps later,' said Standing. 'But can I buy you a drink?'

'Sure,' she said. She nodded at one of the female bartenders and a pale-blue cocktail appeared within seconds. Standing didn't bother asking what it was or how much it cost. The key to any successful operation was intel, and so far Standing knew next to nothing about his target. All he had was a man's name, Denis Volkov, and a location, a back room at The Dollhouse. Volkov was always armed, Yurin had said, but that was to be expected. And he always had a minimum of three heavies with him. That was also to be expected.

'I'm Simon,' he said.

'Eva,' she said. He figured they were probably both lying about their names. She clinked her glass against his bottle. 'Are you on vacation or here on business?'

'A bit of both,' he said. 'So how long have you worked here?'

Eva shrugged. 'A few weeks,' she said, and Standing could tell from her body language alone that she was lying. Customers probably didn't like to hear that the girl they were chatting up had been sliding up and down a chrome pole for years.

She was young, he was sure of that, but there was a weariness in her eyes and dark patches under them that suggested sleepless nights or drug use or maybe both.

'It's a good place to work?'

She shrugged again. 'It is what it is,' she said.

There was a bruise on her right wrist. Several bruises. As if a hand had gripped her tightly.

Standing looked around the club. 'Answer me this,' he

said. 'We're in California, but there are no Hispanics dancing. Why is that? Does the boss not like Mexicans?'

Eva laughed. 'Plenty of Mexicans come for jobs but the boss never hires them. He says they can't dance.'

'Is that true?'

She snorted softly. 'Of course not. He brings the girls in himself, he doesn't hire walk-ins. Doesn't trust them.'

Standing nodded. The subtext was clear – Volkov and his men were traffickers and they brought their own girls. That almost certainly explained the bruises on Eva's wrist.

'So do you want a dance?' she asked. She had drained her glass and there was nothing in it now but ice cubes.

'Nah, I'm good, thanks,' said Standing. 'But I'll buy you another drink.'

She shook her head. 'I need dances,' she said. She flashed him a tight smile and walked away. She went over to a booth and began talking to some guys in jeans and denim workshirts. In less than a minute she had one of them by the hand and was leading him towards the VIP area.

A middle-aged man in a cowboy hat and a shirt with the name of a landscaping firm on the back waved a hundred-dollar bill in the air. A waitress went over and took the money to the bar, returning with a wad of single dollar bills. The two dancers on the podium moved towards him like sharks that had scented blood, but he ignored them and began to methodically count every note. When he'd finished he snarled and clicked his fingers to get the attention of the waitress. After she'd walked up to him, he began to harangue her for only giving him ninety-two singles. 'You've stolen eight bucks!' he shouted. 'What sort of fucking place is this! I want my eight bucks!'

The waitress said something to him but whatever she had said only made him angrier. He stood up and began shouting that he wanted his hundred-dollar bill back.

Standing watched as the two bouncers walked quickly across the club. Cowboy Hat didn't see them coming and he was still haranguing the waitress when he was grabbed by the scruff of the neck by the bigger of the two bouncers. The other punched him twice in the stomach, quickly and efficiently. Cowboy Hat doubled over and the bouncer who was holding his collar hauled him over to the exit. The bouncer who had done the hitting picked up the dropped banknotes, then hurried after his colleague.

The two bouncers took the customer outside and were with him for several minutes, presumably explaining the error of his ways. When they reappeared, the bigger of the two was licking his knuckles.

None of the customers had paid any attention to the fracas, though one of the dancers shouted over at the bouncers. Standing guessed that she was asking for the money, and from the way the bouncers gestured back at her, he guessed they were telling her to go fuck herself.

Standing sipped his beer. The door to the office remained closed. There didn't appear to be any CCTV cameras in the club, so whoever was behind the door probably wasn't aware of the disturbance. Hopefully, the converse would also be true and anything that happened inside wouldn't be heard by the bouncers.

Two men in suits appeared at the entrance and from the way the dancers all pointed their breasts in their direction it was clear that they were regulars. Both men were patted down by the bouncers, then headed to sit at one of the podiums. A waitress took their orders and both men handed over hundred-dollar bills.

Eva reappeared with her customer and took him back to his table, then took the hand of the guy he was with and walked with him back into the VIP area. The girl was clearly a trooper.

The waitress carried drinks over to the two new arrivals and gave them each a stack of dollar bills. The men took the money and they both tipped the waitress.

There were now three girls on the podium closest to the guys and they immediately went into overdrive, dancing around the silver poles as if their lives depended on it. The two suits were soon handing over money, usually tucking it into the thongs the girls were wearing.

Standing's eyes scanned the bar. He had no way of knowing how many men were in the office, or what weapons they were carrying. He slid off his stool and went over to the men's room, which was to the left of the office. There was a line of urinals and two stalls. He had hoped that there would be a window that he could use to get the gun into the building, but the only source of outside light was a line of glass blocks.

He went back to his seat, considering his options. He could either go into the office, or bring the men out. He was sure he could take out the two bouncers, but there were several dozen customers in various stages of inebriation and he wasn't sure how they would react if it kicked off in the club.

The two suits were being very generous with their money and were attracting quite a bit of attention from the customers and girls. The two bouncers were deep in conversation at the entrance. Standing put down his beer.

He headed towards the men's room. He took a quick look over his shoulder but no one was paying him any attention. He walked past the men's room and grabbed the handle of the office door and pushed it open. He took a deep breath and exhaled slowly. Game on.

23

There were five men in the room. Two were sitting on a sofa facing the door with their feet up on a long coffee table. One was sitting behind a desk, on which there was a big Apple computer. Another was sitting at a table looking at his smartphone. There was a man in an armchair reading a Russian newspaper. Next to him was a coffee-maker with two pots of coffee, presumably caffeinated and decaffeinated and even as he scanned the room Standing couldn't help wondering what sort of Russian mobster would bother with decaf.

There was a window opposite the door but it was covered by blinds and they were pulled shut. There were fluorescent lights overhead and a large floor lamp by the desk. To the right was a blue-topped pool table with the balls set up for a game.

All five men stared at him. Standing was fairly sure that Volkov was the man behind the desk, and his suspicion was confirmed when he stood up. 'Who the fuck are you?' he said, his hands on his hips. He was wearing a black turtle-neck sweater with the sleeves pulled up to reveal forearms covered with thick, black hair.

'I'm the guy who's just been cheated out of eight bucks,' said Standing. He closed the door behind him. 'I gave the waitress a hundred and she gave me back ninety-two singles.'

'Are you fucking serious?' said Volkov. 'You're bothering me about eight fucking dollars?'

'What sort of joint is this?' said Standing. 'You rip off everyone, do you?'

Volkov waved at the two men on the sofa and spoke to them in Russian. They got to their feet and walked towards Standing. No weapons that he could see. They were both wearing long-sleeved shirts and tight jeans, fashionable but not the greatest gear for a bit of rough and tumble.

The man holding the newspaper put it down. He was wearing a dark-brown leather jacket and Standing caught a glimpse of something metallic under his left armpit. He was thin and his wrists were protruding from the sleeves of his jacket. He had three large rings on his right hand, not a good idea if he planned to be pulling a trigger any time soon.

The heavy who had been studying his smartphone had put it down and he now had a large switchblade in his hand. The handle alone was close to nine inches long.

Standing stood with his hands at his side. 'I just want my money back,' he said, still playing the irate customer.

The bruiser approaching on Standing's left side was the bigger of the two, with a shaved head that glistened under the fluorescent lights. He had a spider-web tattoo across his neck and both hands were covered in ink. He had a wide chin with a dimple in the centre and a nose that looked as if it had been pushed flat against his face.

The other heavy reached into his pocket and pulled out a brass knuckleduster that he slipped over his right hand.

Standing went into overdrive. There were two fire extin-guishers fixed to the wall at the side of the door. One was a water extinguisher, the other filled with CO_2. Standing grabbed the CO_2 cylinder, ripped out the locking pin and pressed the trigger as he pointed the horn at the heavy with the knuckleduster. A jet of liquid CO_2 hit the man in the face. He coughed and spluttered and had no time to react as Standing slammed the base of the cylinder into his face. The bruiser slumped to the ground, the white foam on his face turning red.

The heavy with the tattoos pulled back his fist to hit Standing, but Standing was already aiming the horn and he pulled the trigger again, sending a stream of foam into the man's eyes and mouth. Standing stepped to the side and slammed the extinguisher into the man's stomach, then as he doubled over, Standing brought it crashing down on the back of his neck. He went down but he was still conscious and pushed himself back up, his hands slipping on the foam-soaked floor. Standing brought the cylinder down on the back of his head and he shuddered and went limp.

Two down, three to go.

The man with the switchblade was on his feet, coming around the other side of the pool table. The man with the newspaper had dropped it and was pulling out his gun. The fact that he was still in his armchair hindered his movement and he was having trouble getting the weapon out of its holster. Standing hurled the extinguisher at him, then grabbed a pool cue from the table.

The extinguisher hit the man in the chest and he roared in pain. The extinguisher fell to the floor and the man got to his feet, reaching for his gun again. Standing upended the pool cue, took two quick steps and slammed the heavy end against his right elbow. There was a loud crack as the joint broke and the man yelped. Standing hit him again, this time on the right knee, and again there was the satisfying sound of cartilage breaking. Standing slammed the cue into the man's stomach and the air exploded from his lungs as he bent over. Standing dropped the cue, grabbed the butt of the man's gun and yanked it from the holster, then slammed it down on the back of his skull. He fell heavily and lay still.

The gun was a Smith & Wesson Bodyguard .38 with a five-round cylinder. Not the most accurate of weapons but it packed a punch. Volkov was staring open-mouthed at Standing. If he had a weapon, he wasn't reaching for it.

The man with the flick-knife was coming around the pool table. He was holding the knife low, his thumb along the handle close to the blade, ready to stab upwards or slice. He looked like he knew what he was doing. Standing knew a dozen ways of taking a knife off an attacker but there was always an element of risk, so he swung the gun around and shot the man twice in the chest. The man staggered back, collapsed into the armchair, and the knife fell from his senseless fingers and clattered to the floor.

The familiar smell of cordite assailed Standing's nostrils as he turned to face Volkov. Volkov bent to open one of the drawers of his desk. 'Don't even think about going for a gun!' said Standing. He levelled his weapon at Volkov's chest. 'Keep your hands where I can see them.'

Volkov slowly raised his hands. There was a thick gold chain around his right wrist and a chunky gold watch on his left. He was big, a couple of inches over six feet, and the turtle-neck was a size too small, as if to emphasise his upper body muscles. Volkov glared at Standing, then nodded slowly. His eyes were a pale blue and he had the thousand-yard stare of a man who had taken the lives of others and done it without a shred of conscience. 'You're the motherfucker who killed Yurin,' he said.

It wasn't a question and Standing just shrugged. He had no intention of telling Volkov that Yurin was alive, albeit with a bullet in his leg.

'Who the fuck are you?' said Volkov. 'You a Navy SEAL like Barnes?'

'Where's the girl?' asked Standing.

'Fuck you. You think I'm scared of a gun?'

'Well, you've got your hands in the air, haven't you?'

The door behind Standing opened. He took a quick look over his shoulder and saw it was one of the bouncers. The bouncer didn't see the gun in Standing's hand and rushed towards him. Standing turned and slammed the gun against his temple. It stunned him but didn't knock him out and he managed to throw a punch that connected with Standing's shoulder before Standing hit him again with the gun. As the bouncer fell to his knees, Standing caught movement in the corner of his eye and he dropped into a crouch and whirled around. Volkov had a gun, a large revolver, and it kicked in his hand as he pulled the trigger. The round whizzed a couple of inches above Standing's head and buried itself in the wall behind him.

Standing brought his own gun up and instinctively pulled the trigger twice, a double tap that put two bullets in the centre of his chest. It was only as Volkov fell to the floor that Standing regretted his action. He'd wanted the Russian alive.

He hurried over and stood looking down at Volkov. His eyes were glassy and there was bloody froth bubbling between his lips. 'Where is the girl?' asked Standing, but it was too late. The Russian shuddered once and went still.

Standing bent down and pulled Volkov's wallet from his jacket and his keys from his trouser pocket. He had no way of knowing if the bouncer had come into the office because he'd heard the shots, or if it had just been bad timing.

He looked around the room. Volkov was dead. The bouncer was out for the count. The heavy with the knife was dead. The man who had pulled out his gun was face down on the floor, unconscious. The two guys he'd hit with the fire extinguisher were also out cold.

He put the wallet and keys in his own jacket pocket, then went over to the tattooed heavy and rolled him over. He slapped him on the face but it had no effect. Standing straightened up, went over to the door and looked out into the club. Girls were dancing, customers were drinking and there was no sign of the second bouncer. He slipped the gun inside his waistband, pulled his jacket over it and headed out, keeping his head down and pulling the door closed behind him.

The music was loud, and he began to think that it had covered the noise of the shots, but then he saw the bouncer standing by the exit with his phone up to his ear. The bouncer saw Standing and his eyes widened, and Standing knew immediately that he was either phoning the police or calling for reinforcements. Standing walked towards him and the bouncer backed away until he was against the wall. Standing hit him twice in the solar plexus, two punches in quick succession that pretty much paralysed him. Standing grabbed the phone and looked at the screen. It was a cellphone he'd been calling, so the cops wouldn't be turning up any time soon.

The bouncer bent over, gasping for breath, his hands clasped to his stomach. Standing put the phone in his jacket pocket and walked out. Two men in suits were getting out of a Jaguar and Standing turned his face away as he headed for his Polo.

24

S tanding checked in his rear-view mirror as he headed east along Hollywood Boulevard but there was no one following him. He pulled over to the side of the road and took out Volkov's wallet. It was a brown Louis Vuitton with slots for half a dozen credit cards. Volkov's driving licence was in one of the slots and Standing tapped the address into the Polo's SatNav. The house was a twenty-minute drive away in Glendale, according to the SatNav, but traffic was heavy and it took him almost twice as long.

Volkov's house was a single-storey modern home with a two-car garage to the side and a neatly cut lawn in front. Standing parked a hundred yards away and walked back slowly, looking for any signs that someone was watching the house. When he was sure that the house wasn't under surveillance he went up to the front door and let himself in with Volkov's keys.

He pulled out the Smith & Wesson as he closed the door behind him. There was a sitting room to the left and a dining area and kitchen to his right and a hallway that presumably led to the bedrooms. He stood in silence for a full minute, listening intently before moving quickly and efficiently from room to room. There was no one home and no animals. He put the gun away. Standing took out his cellphone and called the number that the bouncer had been talking to. Whoever it was didn't answer and the call went through to voicemail. Standing left a message. 'Call me back, *suka*,' he said.

He helped himself to a beer from Volkov's fridge and sat down at the kitchen table. He was halfway through it when his phone rang. 'Who the fuck is this?' barked a man with a guttural Russian accent.

'The man who's going to kill you if you don't let the girl go,' said Standing.

'You killed Volkov?'

'Where is the girl?'

'I don't have her.'

'Who does?'

'Who the fuck are you?'

'I'm the guy who's going to keep making your life a misery until you let her go.'

'Where is Bobby-Ray?'

'I don't know, and that's the truth. And the girl doesn't know either. No one knows where the fuck he is, so you're wasting your time with her. Just let her go.'

'After what you've done?'

'I didn't start this. But I will end it, you have my word on that. I will find you and I will kill you and then I'll ask whoever has the girl to give her to me, and if they don't I will kill them. Except I think you're the one who has her.'

There was silence for several seconds. 'Fine. You can have her.'

Standing frowned. The man had capitulated far too easily.

'You can come and collect her.'

'I'm not stupid,' said Standing.

'Then choose a neutral place and we will deliver her to you.'

It was an obvious trap, but it was his only chance to get close to the mobsters. 'The Hollywood Walk Of Fame,' he said.

'Are you fucking serious?'

'In one hour. By Steve McQueen's star.'

'Who the fuck is Steve McQueen?'

'You don't know Steve McQueen? One of the biggest Hollywood stars ever. *Bullitt, The Great Escape, The Getaway, The Magnificent Seven.* How can you not know who he is?'

'He is an actor?'

'Of course he's an actor. I'll see you at his Hollywood star in one hour. If the girl isn't there you'll be sorry.' Standing ended the call. It was definitely a trap. But it wasn't the first time he'd deliberately put himself in harm's way to achieve his objective. Hopefully it wouldn't be his last.

25

Humphrey Bogart walked up to Standing, took a drag on his cigarette and glared at him through narrowed eyes. 'Who the fuck are you?' he asked.

Standing smiled amiably at Bogart. 'I'd have thought the bowler hat, suit, bow tie, moustache and walking-stick gave it away,' he said. 'Charlie Chaplin.'

'Your real name, asshole,' said Bogart.

'What's the problem?' asked Standing.

'The problem is that Eddie McGee is Charlie Chaplin and has been for the last four years, ever since Ronnie Gilchrist died from the cancer.'

An Elvis impersonator in a white suit walked over, holding a rhinestone-encrusted guitar. 'What's going on?' he asked Bogart.

'This guy here's doing Chaplin and I told him we already have a Chaplin.'

Elvis glared at Standing. 'What the fuck are you playing at?'

Marilyn Monroe tottered over on high heels. 'It's okay,' she said in a child-like voice at odds with her very impressive cleavage. 'He spoke to Eddie earlier on. Eddie's cool.'

'Eddie's cool?' said Bogart. 'How the fuck can Eddie be cool?'

'I gave Eddie a couple of hundred bucks to borrow his outfit,' said Standing. Actually, he paid Eddie McGee five hundred dollars and he had gleefully accepted. McGee was one of the many impersonators who made a living on the Hollywood Walk Of Fame posing for pictures with tourists, there to visit the more than 2,600 terrazzo and brass stars embedded in the pavements along fifteen blocks of Hollywood Boulevard and three blocks of Vine Street.

Eddie was just about Standing's size and the suit fitted just fine, though Standing was wearing his own training shoes and he'd had to draw on the small moustache.

'Why would you do that?' growled Elvis.

'I'm playing a prank on a pal. He's coming here today with his wife and I'm going to surprise him.'

'Okay, that's all right then,' said Bogart. 'We can't be too careful. We get people all the time trying to break into this business and we have to protect our turf.'

'I understand,' said Standing. 'I won't be posing for tips, I'll just surprise my pal and then I'll go.'

Bogart took a drag on his cigarette then shrugged, turned up the collar of his raincoat and walked away. Elvis strummed a couple of chords and then he, too, went away. Two tourists had already grabbed Marilyn, and the husband was posing next to her as the wife snapped away with her phone.

Steve McQueen's star was on the south side of the 6800 block of Hollywood Boulevard, in front of the garish façade of the El Capitan movie theatre at the base of a six-storey office building. Standing stood in the shade of a juice bar as he kept an eye on the area around McQueen's star. He had parked in a side street and assumed that the Russians would do the same.

Most of the people walking up and down the pavements were tourists, many of them holding maps. The Russians were easy enough to spot because of the way they were dressed and the way they strode purposefully towards the McQueen star. The one in the middle was a big man wearing a black leather jacket. He had a goatee beard and wraparound sunglasses. The men either side wore hooded sweatshirts that Standing was pretty sure concealed handguns. They all had thick gold chains around their necks and wrists.

One of the hoodies pointed at McQueen's star and the three men gathered around it, scoping the area.

Standing called 911. A female operator answered almost immediately. 'You need to get to Hooters in Hollywood Boulevard, next to the El Capitan,' said Standing, using an American accent as best he could. 'There's four Arab-looking guys in there with backpacks and one of them has a gun. They're up to something. Jihadists, they look like. They keep talking in Arabic and looking around like they're going to do something.'

The operator asked Standing for his name but he ended the call and put the phone away.

The man with the goatee took out a mobile phone. As he turned, Standing spotted a large scar that zig-zagged across his right cheek. A few seconds later Standing's phone rang. He answered. 'Where the fuck are you?' asked the man, with a heavy Russian accent.

'Where's the girl?' asked Standing.

'Close by,' said Goatee. He was looking around but

Standing was on the other side of the road, shielded by a UPS delivery truck.

'That's not good enough,' said Standing. 'I want to see her.'

'You've got nothing to deal with,' said Goatee.

'I'm not dealing,' said Standing. 'I just want the girl. Give me the girl and I'll get out of your hair.'

Goatee looked around, then cursed. Standing heard him talk to one of his men in Russian and watched as the hoodie walked down the road and turned into a side street.

'We're going to get her,' said Goatee. 'Who are you?'

'I'm just a friend of Kaitlyn's.'

'And a friend of her fucking brother, no doubt.'

'We don't need a formal introduction, I just want the girl.' Standing knew that the Russians had no intention of letting Bobby-Ray's sister go. She was the bait. But it made sense for them to show the bait. So far as they were concerned, Standing was just one man and they were the Russian mafia. They believed their own publicity and in their minds it would be no contest.

'Where the fuck are you?' growled Goatee.

'I'm not far away,' said Standing.

Two elderly tourists, a man in a cream linen suit and his wife with blue-permed hair, waved at Standing and mimed taking a photograph. He shook his head and pointed at his phone. The man took out his wallet and showed Standing a twenty dollar note and again Standing shook his head.

'Here she is,' said Goatee. He was looking down the street, where two heavies were now walking back with Kaitlyn. One of the heavies was the guy in the hoodie, the new arrival was a short, squat man with curly hair, wearing an LA Dodgers baseball jacket. He was gripping Kaitlyn by the arm and she looked terrified.

Standing ended the call and put his phone away. The elderly couple started asking him to pose with them but he was already striding across the road towards Kaitlyn, swinging his walking-stick. She saw him when he was halfway across the road and did a double-take as she realised it was him. She tried to pull away from the man holding her, but he gripped her harder and pulled her back.

Standing kept walking. He started twirling his walking-stick.

Goatee frowned, then turned to the man next to him and pointed at Standing. He moved towards the road.

Standing pulled out his phone, tucked his stick under his arm and took several photographs of the man with the goatee as he walked. He put the phone away as he reached the pavement. He stopped about ten feet away from them. 'Let her go,' said Standing, the stick at his side.

Goatee grinned. 'That's not going to happen. Who the fuck are you supposed to be? Hitler?'

'Charlie Chaplin,' said Standing.

'Who the fuck is Charlie Chaplin?'

'A comedian from the days of silent movies.'

'A comedian? Well I'm not laughing, *mudak*.'

'You said you'd let her go,' said Standing.

'Just how stupid are you?' asked Goatee.

The two hoodies approached Standing, one either side. They grabbed an arm each. Standing didn't react. He could have easily disabled both men in seconds, but he stood passively, his eyes fixed on Goatee.

'Matt . . .' pleaded Kaitlyn, not sure what was going on.

Goatee spoke to the heavy in the baseball jacket and he took a firmer hold on Kaitlyn. A middle-aged couple looked up from one of the stars. Goatee glared at them until they walked away, muttering to each other.

'You're coming with us,' said Goatee. He opened his jacket with his left hand to show the butt of a gun nestling in a shoulder holster.

Two police cruisers came down the road and stopped in a squeal of brakes. Four uniformed cops began ushering pedestrians away from the Hooters window. Within seconds a large black van with SWAT signs on the side came roaring down the road. The Russian heavies looked around, wondering what was going on.

The rear doors of the SWAT van flew open and half a dozen armed cops piled out, dressed in black with Kevlar helmets and cradling carbines.

Standing stamped his heel down on the foot of the hoodie to his right. The man yelped and released his grip on Standing's arm. Standing hit the hoodie on his left with the stick, slashing it across his throat. He let go of Standing's left arm, gasping for breath. Standing poked him in the stomach with the end of the stick, then walloped him across the knees with it.

The uniformed police were shouting for everyone to move away. Two more cruisers arrived and they pulled across the road, blocking it to traffic.

Standing walked towards Kaitlyn. The heavy holding her was looking at the SWAT team, clearly confused.

'Matt!' said Kaitlyn again and the heavy turned to glare at Standing.

'You did this,' he growled.

'Let her go,' said Standing.

Goatee stood at Standing's shoulder. His right hand moved towards his gun but the SWAT team were now joining in the shouts for the pedestrians to clear the area and he realised that drawing his weapon wasn't an option. 'You bastard,' spat Goatee.

'Maybe I'm not that stupid after all,' said Standing. The heavy's left hand was still gripping Kaitlyn's shoulder and Standing smacked it with his stick. 'Let her go or I'll break it,' he said.

Pedestrians were running now and more cruisers were arriving to help block off the road around Hooters.

SWAT officers were taking up positions behind parked cars, bringing their weapons to bear on the Hooters window.

'*Suka!*' hissed Goatee. He said something in Russian to the heavy, who released his grip on Kaitlyn.

'Good call,' said Standing.

Goatee pointed his finger at Standing's face. 'This isn't over, *mudak*,' he said.

Standing shrugged and put his arm around Kaitlyn. 'It is for the moment,' he said.

Standing felt a hand grip his shoulder and he let go of Kaitlyn and whirled around, knocking the hand away and firing off two rapid punches to his attacker's chest. It was only when the second punch landed that Standing realised he was hitting a police officer, a large black sergeant. His bulletproof vest absorbed a lot of the impact but the punches still sent him sprawling across the pavement.

Standing grabbed Kaitlyn's hand and ran with her

across the road as the Russians hurried away. Uniformed officers were using blue and white police tape to seal off the area.

'What's happening?' asked Kaitlyn.

'Later,' said Standing. He hurried down the side road to where he'd parked the Polo. He helped her into the passenger seat before climbing in and driving off.

26

The waitress poured coffee into their mugs and Standing waited until she was out of earshot before speaking to Kaitlyn. They were in a diner a couple of miles from Hollywood Boulevard, sitting in a booth that gave them a view of the parked Polo. Standing had taken off the Charlie Chaplin outfit and was now wearing a denim shirt and black jeans. 'How did they get you?' he asked.

'I was stupid,' she said. 'They rang my bell and said it was a DHL delivery. I thought it might be from Bobby-Ray, so I opened the door and they Tasered me. They put a bag over my head and didn't take it off until I was in a room somewhere. It didn't have any windows so I don't know where I was.'

'Did they hurt you?'

She forced a smile. 'Not really. But the boss, Oleg, kept saying that if Bobby-Ray didn't turn himself in they'd kill me.'

'When they drove you to the house where they kept you, how long was it?'

'About an hour.'

'House or flat?'

'Flat? What's a flat?'

Standing grinned. 'Sorry, forgot. We call them flats, you call them condos.'

'It was a house. They had to let me out of the room to use the toilet and I could see a hallway and stairs.'

'See anything else that would tell us where you were?' She shook her head.

Standing took out his phone. He sent the two clearest photographs of Oleg to the number that Spider Shepherd had given him, along with a message. 'OLEG WHO?'

'What are you doing?' asked Kaitlyn.

'Using my phone-a-friend,' said Standing. He put the phone down. 'Is there anything else you saw or heard while you were their prisoner?'

'I read Oleg's lips on the way from the bathroom. He spoke on the phone to someone. I think he was speaking Russian because I couldn't understand what he was saying. When he finished the call he spoke in English, told his people that someone called Markov was coming around. Then they locked me up again so I never saw him.'

'Markov? You sure he said Markov?'

'Pretty sure. He was about twenty feet away but I had a clear view of his lips. Why?'

'Koshkin had a partner, Erik Markov. He arrived in LA shortly before Koshkin was killed.' He sipped his coffee. 'I'm pretty sure that Markov is involved in this. It might even have been him who ordered the hit on Koshkin.'

The waitress returned with their food. A steak for Standing and a cheeseburger for Kaitlyn. Kaitlyn picked up her burger and wolfed it down, slotting in French fries between bites. 'They didn't give me much food,' she said. 'And I need a shower.'

Standing grinned. 'No argument here.'

She looked worried. 'Do I smell?'

He laughed and shook his head. 'You look and smell fine,' he said.

'I don't want to go back to my condo,' she said. 'Not after what happened.'

'You need to stay well away,' he said. 'Oleg is going to be having your place watched, no question. He's not going to be happy about you getting away. We'll finish this and then check into a motel.' He chewed on a piece of steak. 'I just wish we knew where Bobby-Ray was. Have you checked your email?'

'Not since they took my phone,' said Kaitlyn. 'You think he'll try to contact me?'

'He has to eventually,' said Standing. 'He can't hide forever without help.'

Standing was finishing his steak when his phone beeped to let him know he had received a text. It was a reply from Shepherd in London. 'OLEG IVCHENKO.' And there was an address in the Hollywood Hills. He looked up and grinned at Kaitlyn. 'My phone-a-friend has come through,' he said.

27

'Whoever said that crime doesn't pay?' said Standing. He was looking out of the windscreen as he spoke, so Kaitlyn couldn't read his lips.

She tapped him on the shoulder. 'What?'

He turned to face her and smiled. 'Sorry, I keep forgetting,' he said. 'I said that crime doesn't pay, except for the likes of the Russian mafia.' He gestured at Oleg Ivchenko's house. 'I mean, how much do you think that place is worth?'

Kaitlyn shrugged. 'Eight million? Ten maybe. But it could be a rental.'

They were looking down on a large compound halfway up one of the hills that overlooked downtown LA. There were three buildings – a main two-storey house next to a large pool, a parking area with a garage with a tennis court behind it, and a small single-storey block next to the gated entrance. There were half a dozen vehicles parked near the garage including three black SUVs, a red Ferrari and a white Bentley convertible. As they watched from their vantage point, a fourth black SUV with tinted windows arrived and pulled up at the gate. Two big men came out of the block. They waved at the driver and the gate opened and the SUV drove in. The two men stayed where they were until the gate had closed again before heading back into the block. They didn't appear to be armed but they were definitely security.

It was eleven o'clock in the morning. They had spent the night in a motel in West Hollywood, which Standing had selected because its car park was hidden from the road. After a quick breakfast they had driven to the Gateway Mall on Santa Monica Boulevard. Kaitlyn was understandably reluctant to go back to her apartment to pick up clean clothes and toiletries, so Standing had taken her shopping instead. Now she was wearing a blue Gap shirt and jeans with a white pullover tied around her neck.

They watched as the SUV drove to the house. A man got out of the passenger side. A big man with a goatee and dark glasses, wearing a black suit. It was Ivchenko. Standing had bought a pair of high-powered binoculars from a military surplus store and he put them to his eyes and focussed on the man. 'That's him all right,' he said. Another man got out of the back of the SUV and followed Ivchenko inside the main house. The car drove over to the garage area. 'Do you think that's where they kept you?' asked Standing.

'Maybe,' she said. 'I never got to see outside, but there was definitely a gate and I felt the vibration of cars coming and going.'

'Maybe you were in the garage block,' he said. 'There don't seem to be any windows there, there could be storage rooms inside.'

Standing used the binoculars to methodically check out the compound. There were three men walking around the walled perimeter, dressed casually in loose baggy shirts or jackets that could easily have been concealing handguns. The wall was only about ten feet tall and easily climbable, but he counted eight CCTV cameras on the buildings that covered all the approaches to the compound, plus two on the wall by the main gate. The gate was the only way in.

The roof of the main building had two satellite dishes, a small one and another that was the size of a car. Dotted around the roof were several floodlights that illuminated the gardens at night. The compound appeared to be pretty much impregnable.

Kaitlyn tapped him on the shoulder and he lowered the binoculars and turned to look at her. 'Are you thinking of going in there?' she asked.

'I was,' he said. 'But I don't see how I can. It's a bloody fortress.' He shook his head. 'I can't understand why he's not behind bars. You know what they're into? Drugs, trafficking, racketeering. And I'm damn sure they killed Koshkin and framed your brother. The cops must know what's going on, but they're living like bloody kings as if they don't have a care in the world.'

Kaitlyn patted him on the knee. 'Big breaths,' she said.

'What?'

'Chill, Matt. Don't let it get to you.'

Standing looked at her for several seconds, then his face broke into a grin. 'You sound like my therapist.'

'You have a therapist?'

'I used to. I had anger management issues.'

'Seriously?'

Standing nodded. 'I still do. I have a tendency to react instinctively, without considering the consequences. Like when I hit that cop in Hollywood Boulevard.'

'He grabbed you. I saw that. You just reacted.'

'Yeah, but I hit a cop. And there's no excuse for that.'

'Matt, I saw what happened. He grabbed you from behind. You turned and hit him and when you saw he was a cop, you stopped. You didn't do anything wrong.'

He laughed. 'Yeah, well if I end up in court, I hope the jury sees it that way.'

'What did the therapist say you should do, about your anger management issues?'

'Like you said, big breaths. And chill.'

'She didn't give you medication?'

Standing shook his head. 'Basically she said I should count to ten. And she taught me square breathing.'

'Square breathing?'

'You breathe in for four seconds, hold it for four seconds, breathe out for four seconds, then hold it again for four seconds. And you keep doing that.'

'Does it work?'

Standing nodded. 'Actually it does. It's quite calming.'

'So you're better now?'

He chuckled. 'I guess so. The trick is to know when to use it.'

She frowned. 'What do you mean?'

'I'm a soldier, Kaitlyn. If I start doing square breathing in a combat situation, I'll be dead. In combat I have to react instinctively because it's kill or be killed.' He shrugged. 'The problems start when I'm not in a war zone. Like with that cop. I hit him and he'll be fine. But suppose the situation had been different and I'd had a gun in my hand. I could have shot him.'

'You'd have seen he was a cop and you'd have stopped yourself.'

'You say that, Kaitlyn. But when I'm fighting, it's as if my subconscious takes over and it does whatever it thinks is necessary to protect itself.'

'Because of the way you've been trained, right? Bobby-Ray's the same. You're trained to react quickly.'

'It was more than training. It's difficult to explain but when I'm in combat I function almost on remote control. Say we're in the desert and we're being fired upon. Okay, so we're trained not to panic or freeze, we're trained to look for cover and to return fire. And in the SAS we do a lot of training. But with me, it just sort of happens naturally. We can be taking fire from multiple attackers and I instinctively know where to go, and in what order to take out the targets. I don't panic, I don't even worry about it, I just do what I have to do. I don't know what it is that I do, but it's never let me down. Whereas I've seen guys make calculated decisions and come a cropper.' He shrugged. 'Like I said, it's only a problem when I'm back in the real world.'

She patted him on the knee again. 'Try a bit of square breathing while you decide what we're going to do next.'

He chuckled. He put the binoculars back to his eyes. A red minivan with tinted windows had pulled up at the gates and the two guards were back. The gates opened and the van drove in and then stopped. The guards moved to either side of the vehicle, looked in through the side windows and then waved it on. It drove slowly to the main house and pulled up. The side door opened and four pretty girls tottered out on impossibly high heels, two blondes, a black girl with waist-length dreadlocks and a Chinese girl in a bright red minidress with gold dragons on it. The front door had already opened and the girls went inside.

'Do you think they're hookers?' asked Kaitlyn, and Standing burst out laughing.

'I don't think they're dressed for housework,' he said.

She grimaced. 'You couldn't pay me enough money to sleep with a pig like that,' she said.

'Good to know.'

'Do you think they're on drugs?'

'Maybe.'

The front door had closed and the minivan was heading back to the gate.

'Why don't we go to the police?' said Kaitlyn. 'I can tell them I was kidnapped.'

'It would be our word against his,' said Standing. 'There's no proof.'

'We could tell the police that they wanted Bobby-Ray. That proves that they are connected with what happened to Koshkin.'

'It's all circumstantial, Kaitlyn,' said Standing. He gave her the binoculars and she put them in the glove compartment. 'The thing is, we're still no closer to finding out what happened that night in Bel Air.' He tapped his fingers on the steering wheel. 'We need more intel.'

'But everyone there that night was killed, right? Except for Bobby-Ray and the Russian guy.'

'There was another witness,' said Standing. 'Let's see if he can help.' He took out his mobile phone and called John Keenan. Keenan didn't seem pleased to hear from Standing, but agreed to meet him at a diner in Pasadena.

Standing put the address into the Polo's SatNav and thirty minutes later they were parking outside Tom's Famous Family Restaurant. Keenan was already sitting in a booth and he stood up when Standing and Kaitlyn walked over. Standing introduced Kaitlyn and Keenan shook hands with her. 'Bobby-Ray talked about you a lot,' he said.

'Nothing bad, I hope,' she said.

'He was very proud of you,' said Keenan. 'You're deaf, right?'

'As a post,' she laughed.

'But you can hear me?' Realisation dawned. 'You read lips.'

'I try,' she said.

The three of them sat down. Keenan already had a coffee and a waitress came over with menus.

'I ate at home,' said Keenan. 'But you guys feel free.' The waitress recommended Tom's Famous Pastrami sandwich so Standing ordered one with a coffee, while Kaitlyn went for a turkey and avocado sandwich and a Coke.

'So what's up?' asked Keenan as the waitress walked away.

'I spoke to Lipov in London,' said Standing.

'You called him?'

Standing shook his head. 'I went to see him.'

Keenan looked over the top of his coffee mug. 'And how did that go?'

'Not great,' said Standing. 'He attacked me which I took as an admission of guilt. But he wouldn't tell me anything.' Standing thought it best not to mention that Lipov wasn't in a position to say anything to anybody.

'Yeah, as I said, he wouldn't talk to our people either. He attacked you? He's a big guy.'

'He is,' agreed Standing.

'I'm surprised he didn't kill you.'

'He gave it his best shot,' said Standing. The waitress returned with Kaitlyn's Coke and a cup of coffee for Standing. They stayed quiet until she had gone. Standing leaned towards Keenan. 'Look, the night that Koshkin was killed, there were two drivers. Did they both see what happened?'

Keenan shook his head. 'One had already left. The other, Paul Dutch, was still outside in his vehicle. He saw Bobby-Ray run off.'

'This Dutch is a former SEAL?' asked Standing.

'Delta Force,' said Keenan.

'Can I talk to him?'

'He was interviewed by the cops on the night, and the following day. He saw Bobby-Ray running away from the scene but that's all.'

'I hear you, but I'd like the chance to talk to him. If that's okay with you.'

Keenan looked at Standing for several seconds, then he nodded and slipped out of the booth. He took his cellphone out and headed outside to make the call.

While he was outside, their food arrived and Standing and Kaitlyn tucked into their sandwiches.

After five minutes, Keenan returned. 'He's not far away, he'll be here soon,' he said as he slid back into the booth.

'Is he primarily a driver?' asked Standing.

Keenan nodded. 'He's good at it. Plus clients like him. He's good with wives and the like. He had a couple of problems with the cops when he first left Delta so he's not allowed to have a concealed carry permit but as a driver that's not an issue.' He was looking at Standing's sandwich and Standing pushed his plate towards him.

'Take half,' he said.

'You sure?'

'Go ahead,' said Standing.

Keenan picked up half of the sandwich and took a large bite out of it.

'So the night that Koshkin died, this Dutch wasn't armed?' asked Standing.

'No, we tend not to arm our drivers anyway. If there's any trouble they're told to get the client out of danger immediately rather than to start returning fire.'

'Where's he working now?'

'We've placed him with a Hollywood producer who's having a few problems at the moment, so Dutch's main job is to keep him away from the paparazzi. Easier said than done in this town.'

Standing was just finishing his sandwich when a black Towncar pulled up outside the diner. 'There he is now,' said Keenan. 'I'll bring him in.'

Keenan went outside as Standing sipped his coffee. A few minutes later Keenan returned with a tall man with a neatly trimmed beard. Standing stood up. Dutch had piercing brown eyes that scrutinised Standing as the two men shook hands. 'You're the SAS guy?' said Dutch.

Standing nodded.

'Bobby-Ray mentioned you a few times. Said he saved your life in Syria.'

'He took an IED blast in the back,' said Standing.

'Yeah. Blew his lung, so that was his SEAL career over.' He shrugged. 'Me, I was happy enough to move into the private sector, but Bobby-Ray wanted to be where the bullets were flying.' He grinned. 'That's ironic, considering how things turned out.' He looked down at Kaitlyn. 'You're the sister, right?'

'I am,' said Kaitlyn. She held out her hand and Dutch looked at it for a second or two before shaking it. He sat next to Keenan and ordered a coffee from the hovering waitress.

'I'm not sure what you want me to say,' said Dutch as the waitress walked away. 'I told the cops everything. It seems open and shut, right?'

'My brother wouldn't kill anybody,' said Kaitlyn.

'Darling, your brother was a Navy SEAL,' said Dutch. 'That's what he was trained to do.'

'I meant he wouldn't kill someone for money,' said Kaitlyn, folding her arms defensively.

'You think SEALs work for free?' said Dutch. 'Girl, you need to wake up and smell the coffee.'

Standing could see that Kaitlyn wasn't reacting well to Dutch's teasing, so he put up a hand to intervene. 'I think what Kaitlyn means is that her brother isn't the type to work as a killer for hire, and I agree with her on that. And that's what this killing looks like, right? Bobby-Ray had no connection with the victim, this wasn't a revenge killing or a moment of anger, this was an assassination and that's not the sort of thing that Bobby-Ray would get involved in, not in a million years.'

Dutch nodded. 'I was being flippant.' He turned to look at Kaitlyn. 'I'm sorry, I didn't mean to offend you. I like your brother, he's a good guy. But I saw what I saw. And I went into that room after he ran off and I saw the bodies.' He grimaced. 'It wasn't pleasant.'

'You heard the shots?' asked Standing.

'I heard a couple of shots, yes.'

'Just a couple?'

'I was in the car for part of the time. And then I was in the garage.'

'So how many shots did you hear?'

'Two or three.'

'But which is it? Two or three?'

Dutch looked sideways at Keenan. 'Am I being interrogated?'

'I'm just a stickler for details,' said Standing. 'I've no ulterior motive here.'

Dutch looked back at him. 'I hope that's true.'

'Paul, I don't think for one second that you were involved in what happened. But I'm equally sure that Bobby-Ray didn't kill Koshkin and the bodyguards.'

'Well, Nikolai Lipov says he did. And I saw Bobby-Ray running away.'

Standing nodded. 'You did, yes. So tell me, why did Bobby-Ray run and not shoot you?'

'Because he knew I wasn't armed. I wasn't a threat to him.'

'So he just ran?'

Dutch nodded.

'Did he have a gun?'

'Sure. The cops found it.'

'Did you see him drop it?'

Dutch frowned but didn't reply.

'It's a simple enough question,' said Standing.

'No, I get the question,' said Dutch. 'But now I think about it, I didn't see a gun in Bobby-Ray's hand. But the cops found it later.'

'Found it where?'

'Near the wall. Bobby-Ray went over the wall and they found the gun nearby.'

'And did Lipov go anywhere near the wall?'

Dutch nodded slowly.

'What are you suggesting?' said Keenan.

'I think Lipov killed the client and the bodyguards,' said Standing. 'I think he planned to kill Bobby-Ray, too, and make it look like he had done the killings.'

'Wow,' said Keenan.

'But Bobby-Ray ran and managed to get away. Lipov ran after him and dropped Bobby-Ray's gun by the wall.'

'You know this for sure?' asked Keenan.

'Lipov told me that he came down the stairs after he had heard the shots. But Bobby-Ray was a pro; if he really had gone rogue he would have shot Lipov. Lipov says he fired at Bobby-Ray and that scared him off but that's bollocks. Bobby-Ray was a highly trained Navy SEAL, he wouldn't panic under gunfire. Lipov was a big man, he'd have been an easy target.'

Keenan raised an eyebrow. 'Was? Past tense?'

'Is. Was. Whatever. I'm just saying, if Bobby-Ray had killed the client and three bodyguards, he wouldn't have baulked at killing Lipov. Or Paul, here. If he really had killed four people then why not kill five or six?'

Keenan sat back in his seat and linked his fingers together. 'Shit, this is a mess,' he said.

'So we need to clear it up,' said Standing. 'Because no one else will. The cops are sure that Bobby-Ray did it and the chances are that when they do eventually find him it'll go down badly.'

'And we're not going to be getting a confession from Lipov any time soon?'

'That horse has bolted,' said Standing.

'So that's it, then,' said Keenan. 'Paul here didn't see what happened and there were no other witnesses. None that survived, anyway.'

'Paul didn't see what happened, but he heard it. And he only heard two or three shots.'

'So?'

'So I'm thinking that Lipov must have used a silencer. That's how he was able to take down four men without them fighting back.'

'And he did it with Bobby-Ray's gun,' said Keenan.

'Which is another issue,' said Standing. 'At some point Lipov must have taken Bobby-Ray's gun away from him. Then he used that gun with a silencer to kill Koshkin and the three bodyguards. At some point Bobby-Ray fought back. Maybe Lipov had knocked him out and he came around. Lipov fired at Bobby-Ray but missed. Bobby-Ray ran. Lipov then used his own gun without a silencer to fire two shots in the hall. Those were the shots that Paul heard. Bobby-Ray ran and got over the wall, Lipov chased him and dropped the gun that the cops found.'

'But only Bobby-Ray's prints were on the gun,' said Keenan.

'So Lipov wore gloves.'

'He wasn't wearing gloves when the cops arrived,' said Dutch. 'It's LA, no one wears gloves.'

'And the cops searched everyone, right?'

Dutch nodded. 'And they got there within minutes.'

Standing nodded. 'So Lipov must have hidden the gloves and the silencer.'

'Not in the garden,' said Dutch. 'I was with him all the time. And I went back into the house with him.'

'Were you able to see him all the time you were in the house?' asked Standing.

Dutch frowned as he thought back to that night, and eventually he shook his head. 'I went in to check on the client. Nikolai was behind me. Then I checked on Kurt and the two Russians. At that point Nikolai was calling the cops. He definitely wasn't wearing gloves then.'

Standing looked at Keenan. 'There you are, then. I think that Lipov planned to kill everyone but Bobby-Ray, then he was going to put Bobby-Ray's gun back in Bobby-Ray's hand and shoot him with his own gun. Bobby-Ray managed to escape so Lipov had to run after him and plant the gun. But at that point he'd still have had the gloves and the silencer so he needed to hide them before the cops arrived.'

'Why didn't he leave the silencer on the gun?' asked Dutch.

'Because it wouldn't have had Bobby-Ray's prints on it,' said Standing. 'The CSIs would have spotted that there were prints on the gun but not on the silencer.'

Keenan nodded thoughtfully. 'So the silencer and the gloves are hidden somewhere in the house?'

'Probably in the hallway. Lipov wouldn't have had much time to dispose of them. So if we get the cops to do a proper search, the gloves will have Lipov's prints on the inside and Bobby-Ray will be in the clear.'

Keenan banged the flat of his hand on the table, hard enough to rattle the coffee mugs. 'Good job, Matt.'

'We shouldn't go counting chickens just yet,' said Standing. 'We need to convince the cops to do a proper search of the house.'

'I don't think that's a problem,' said Keenan. 'I can call

the lead detective on the investigation. We got on okay. Let me see if he's up for it.'

'When?'

'Hell, we can do it right now,' said Keenan. 'Strike while the iron's hot.'

28

John Keenan looked at his watch. 'Shouldn't be long now,' he said. He and Standing were sitting in the front of a black SUV parked outside the gates to a Bel Air mansion hidden behind a twelve-foot high wall, on which were posted signs informing would-be trespassers that armed security was close by. Kaitlyn had taken her Polo and driven back to the motel. Paul Dutch was sitting in the back, probing his teeth with a toothpick.

'They were okay to come by at night?' asked Standing.

'The lead detective practically insisted on it,' said Keenan. 'Craig Withers, his name is. Detective First Grade.' He nodded at a grey sedan prowling down the road towards them. 'That'll be him now.'

The sedan pulled up alongside their SUV and the passenger window wound down. 'You're sure about this, Mr Keenan?' growled a grey-haired man with a slightly bored tone that suggested he had heard a lot of lies in his career.

'As sure as we can be, Detective Withers. Otherwise I wouldn't have bothered you.'

The detective nodded. He must have had a remote control, because the large metal gates rattled open of their own accord. Keenan followed the sedan along a driveway that ran between two immaculately manicured lawns. In the middle of each was a stone fountain. There was a triple-width garage to the left of the house, which was whitewashed stone covered with ivy, with fake shutters either side of latticed windows.

'How much would this cost?' asked Standing. The metal gates rattled closed behind them.

'Ten million bucks, maybe,' said Keenan. 'Fifteen. They go for crazy money these days. But Koshkin didn't own it. He was renting it for a hundred thousand dollars a month. That's what I was told.'

The sedan pulled up in front of the garage and Keenan parked next to it. Standing and Dutch climbed out as Keenan turned off the engine.

Withers got out of the sedan. He was wearing a light-weight grey suit with a gun on his right hip. The driver was younger, a tall, thin black man with bookish spectacles. He was wearing a dark jacket and beige trousers and also had a gun on his belt.

'This is Matt Standing,' said Keenan by way of introduction. 'He served with Bobby-Ray out in Syria.'

'Yeah?' said the detective. 'I don't suppose you know where Barnes is, do you? It would make our lives a lot easier if he came forward and spoke to us.'

Standing shrugged. 'I'm sorry.'

Withers looked up at the house. There was Police CRIME SCENE tape across the front door. 'Tell me again what you think we'll find in there, Mr Keenan,' he said.

'We believe that the bodyguard who survived – Nikolai Lipov – carried out the killings and hid a silencer and a pair of gloves in the house.'

'I spoke to Mr Lipov at length,' said the detective. 'I didn't see or hear anything that suggests he was the killer. He fired his gun twice and both those slugs are accounted for.'

'We think Lipov used Bobby-Ray's gun to kill Koshkin and the bodyguards,' said Keenan.

Withers shook his head emphatically. 'Barnes had the gun on him and he dropped it in the garden.' He pointed away to his left where police tape had been pegged to the ground.

'Where were you when Bobby-Ray ran out of the house?' Standing asked Dutch.

Dutch moved to stand in front of the middle of three garage doors. 'Here,' he said.

'And where did Bobby-Ray run?'

Dutch pointed to the front door, then pointed at his route along the driveway and across the grass to the wall. 'That's where he went over.'

'Did you see a gun?'

Dutch shook his head. 'No. But I wasn't looking for one.'

'But you didn't see him drop a gun?'

'No,' said Dutch.

'And the wall is high, I'm not sure even a Navy SEAL could scramble over a wall that high with a gun in his hand.'

'That's the point,' said Withers. 'He dropped the gun to go over the wall.'

'But Dutch didn't see him do that,' said Standing.

Withers sighed in exasperation. 'I've seen the gun with my own eyes,' he said. 'It had Bobby-Ray's prints and DNA on it and there's no doubt that it was the gun that killed Mr Koshkin and his bodyguards.'

Standing nodded at Dutch. 'Where did Lipov go? After he came out of the house.'

'Same way that Bobby-Ray had gone. He saw him slipping over the wall and headed over there.'

Standing pointed at the crime scene tape. 'So Lipov was over there?'

Dutch nodded. 'That's where he was standing.'

'And that's where you found the gun?' Standing asked Withers.

Withers ignored the question but looked over at Dutch. 'Did you see Lipov drop the gun?'

'No. I was looking at the wall, so I wasn't watching him.'

Withers looked back at Standing. 'Lipov's prints weren't on Bobby-Ray's gun,' he said. 'His prints and DNA were on his own gun, but not on Bobby-Ray's.'

'Which is why we think he was wearing gloves,' said Standing. 'And if he went back inside still wearing those gloves and he didn't have them when the cops arrived . . .'

'Then the gloves are somewhere in the house,' Withers finished for him. He sighed.

'Along with the silencer he must have used,' said Standing.

'Why do you say that?'

'Paul only heard two or three shots. There were at least ten shots fired that night, so the sounds of some of them must have been suppressed.'

Withers stared at Standing with a frown on his face, then he slowly nodded. 'Right, then. Let's have a look around.' He gestured over at his companion, who produced a set of keys from his pocket and walked over to the front door. He pulled aside the police tape and unlocked the door. He went in first and switched on the lights. Withers went in next, followed by Keenan, Standing and Dutch. They gathered in the double-height stone-flagged hallway under a large wood and brass chandelier.

A wide stone staircase wound up to the bedrooms and four doors led off the ground-floor atrium.

'Where were the bullets from Lipov's gun found?' Standing asked Withers.

'Behind you,' said Withers.

Standing turned around. There were two yellow circles around small holes in the plasterwork at about eye level. They were numbered, one and two. Standing looked at the holes and then up at the staircase.

'What's wrong?' asked Withers.

'Where did they happen? The killings?'

Withers pointed at an open door to his right. 'In there. The sitting room.'

Standing pointed at the staircase. 'Lipov was up there. Coming down the stairs. Bobby-Ray supposedly comes out of the sitting room and into the hallway. They see each other. Bobby-Ray shoots at Lipov and Lipov shoots at Bobby-Ray. They both miss each other?' Standing went up the staircase, stopped at the halfway point. He pointed at the bullet holes as if he was aiming a gun. 'I don't see how Lipov's rounds went where they did. He was shooting high. But if he was here, he'd be shooting down.'

'He was being fired at,' said Withers.

Standing looked at the wall above the staircase. There was a single bullet hole, circled and numbered. Three.

'So Bobby-Ray fired once?' he asked.

'That's how we read it.'

'First, a Navy SEAL wouldn't just fire a single shot unless he was sure of a kill. He'd double tap. Two shots. Second, I don't see that Bobby-Ray would miss at this range. I saw him in combat and you can trust me when I say that he's not the type to panic under pressure.' He walked back down the stairs into the hallway. He mimed holding a gun and pointed his fingers at the two bullet holes. 'If you ask me, Lipov was here when he fired.'

'Why would he lie about that?' asked Withers.

'Because what he said happened, didn't happen,' said Standing. He walked back down the stairs and into the sitting room. There were two low black leather sofas either side of a carved wooden coffee table and around the walls were large pieces of furniture, mainly oak and teak, plus a couple of Chinese chests. There were French doors at the far end of the room, leading onto the garden. Standing stopped and pointed at the doors. 'And what was he doing going through the hall, anyway? Wouldn't it have made more sense for him to have gone out that way?'

'Maybe they were locked?' said Withers.

'One good kick would open them,' said Standing.

He looked down at the floor. There were three individual pools of blood. Keenan and Dutch were standing at the doorway as if reluctant to set foot in the room. Standing gestured at Dutch. 'Who was where?'

Dutch pointed at the sofa facing him. 'Koshkin was on the sofa. Shot in the face and chest.' He shuddered. 'It was a mess.' He pointed at the three patches of dried blood from left to right. 'Max, Boris, Kurt,' he said.

'How were they lying when you came in?' asked Standing.

'Face down,' said Dutch. 'They had all been shot in the back of the head.'

'None of them had turned?'

Dutch shook his head. 'No.'

Standing looked over at Withers. 'Which is why I'm sure that Lipov used a silencer,' he said. 'Paul didn't hear the shots outside and Lipov was able to shoot all three men in the back of the head.' Standing mimed shooting three times. 'Bang, bang, bang. He left Koshkin until the end because he knew that he wouldn't have a gun. Koshkin would have seen Lipov shoot the bodyguards but there was nothing he could do to save himself. Bang, Bang. Then, with the bodyguards down, Lipov went back into the hall. I'm guessing that he'd knocked Bobby-Ray out and taken his gun, then screwed in the silencer before carrying out the killings. As he goes back into the hall he takes off the silencer. Now maybe he didn't hit Bobby-Ray hard enough, maybe Bobby-Ray just has a thick skull, but when he gets back into the hallway, Bobby-Ray is on his feet. Lipov shoots at him twice with his own gun but Bobby-Ray is already running and the shots go wide. At this point Lipov realises that his plan to frame Bobby-Ray is turning to shit. He used his own gun to fire two shots at Bobby-Ray but to make it look like Bobby-Ray was the shooter he has to fire one round from Bobby-Ray's into the wall. Lipov does that, bang, then shoves Bobby-Ray's gun in his holster and gives chase. Bobby-Ray is over the wall before Lipov can get to him, and Lipov drops Bobby-Ray's gun on the lawn by the wall. Still wearing gloves so his prints aren't on Bobby-Ray's gun.'

Keenan nodded in agreement but Withers had a look on his face that was close to contempt.

'Then Lipov comes back into the house with Paul. Paul goes over to the bodies. While Paul is doing that, Lipov takes off his gloves and hides them and the silencer. Where were you exactly, Paul?'

Dutch moved into the room and went over to the sofa. 'I checked Koshkin first. A big chunk of his head was missing so I knew he was dead. Then I moved to check Max because I thought I saw his chest move but he was gone.'

'How long before Lipov joined you?'

Dutch shrugged. 'Thirty seconds, I guess.'

Standing went back into the hall. 'So Lipov had thirty seconds to hide the silencer and his gloves. I don't think he would have risked going upstairs, so that leaves him in the hallway or through one of the doors here.'

He opened one door and it led to a large well-equipped kitchen with a centre island and lots of gleaming stainless steel appliances. A second door led to a cloakroom, a third into a study lined with bookshelves.

'How do you want to play it?' Standing asked Withers. 'I'm sure the gloves and silencer are here somewhere, do we search together or split up?'

'You search with me,' said Withers. 'Detective Reid can work with Mr Keenan and Mr Dutch.'

'Sounds like a plan,' said Standing.

Withers took a handful of pale-blue latex gloves from his pocket. He gave a pair each to Standing and Keenan and Detective Reid gave a pair to Dutch. 'If any of you civilians find anything, don't touch it,' said Withers.

The men put on their gloves and began the search. Withers and Standing went into the kitchen while Reid, Dutch and Keenan headed to the study.

Withers stood by the island and pursed his lips. 'Two ways of doing this,' he said. 'Methodically, starting at one end and searching everywhere. Or try to think like he was thinking.'

'He only had seconds to do it,' said Standing. 'So he probably stayed close to the door.'

Withers nodded in agreement. He pulled open the doors to the fridge. 'Favourite hiding place for drug dealers for their cash,' he said. He began going through the freezer compartments.

Standing looked around. There were a lot of cupboards, and Lipov could have used any of them. But the body-guard would have known that once the police were called, the house would be a crime scene and he wouldn't be allowed back in. He had no way of knowing if the police would search the house, or how extensive the search would be. But if the police didn't search, even-tually the owner of the house would have access and he would probably have the house cleaned. Lipov needed a place that wouldn't be checked by the owner or the cleaner.

Withers had finished checking the freezer compart-ments and was now looking inside the main part of the fridge.

Standing rubbed his chin and looked up at the ceiling. It was solid plaster with beams running across it. He took one of the stools from the island and carefully climbed on top of it. His head was still a couple of feet from the ceiling as he looked around. He grinned when he saw the top of the fridge. 'Bingo,' he said.

'Bingo?' repeated Withers.

'On top of the refrigerator,' said Standing.

'You're shitting me,' said the detective, closing the fridge door.

'No one can see it and who cleans the top of a fridge?' said Standing, carefully getting down from the stool. He carried it over to the fridge and helped Withers to climb up.

The detective pulled a clear plastic evidence bag from his pocket and carefully put a bulbous black silencer and two latex gloves into it. Standing helped him down. The two men looked at the evidence bag in the detective's hand. 'Well, I'll be damned,' said Withers, shaking his head.

'So that puts Bobby-Ray in the clear?' said Standing.

'Sure looks that way,' said Withers. 'Assuming that it's Lipov's prints and DNA inside the gloves.'

'It will be,' said Standing.

He went into the hallway and called into the study. 'We found it, guys!' he called.

'Are you serious?' said Keenan. He came out into the hall.

'In the kitchen, on top of the fridge,' said Standing. 'The silencer and the gloves.'

'Awesome,' said Keenan. He high-fived Standing. 'Well done, Matt.'

Dutch came out of the study, followed by Detective Reid.

'So Bobby-Ray's off the hook?' asked Dutch.

'Damn right he is,' said Keenan. He grinned and as he did, Standing heard a pop behind him and Keenan's face imploded into a red mass. Standing moved without thinking, throwing himself towards the study door. As he moved, there was a second loud pop and a bullet thwacked into the wall behind him.

Keenan fell to the floor with a dull thud. Dutch's eyes were open in terror but he was frozen to the spot.

Reid's right hand was moving towards the gun on his hip.

There was a third pop but Standing was still moving and the round missed him by inches, passing so close that he felt the wind before it buried itself in the wall.

Standing didn't look over his shoulder. There was no point. He knew what was happening and seeing it happen wouldn't help him out of the situation. The shots were coming from the kitchen door and the only person in the kitchen had been Withers. The popping sound meant that Withers was using a silencer, either the one they'd found on the fridge or one that the detective had brought with him.

Reid had his hand on his gun and was about to draw it. A round smacked into the centre of Reid's chest and his jaw dropped. Blood immediately spurted down Reid's shirt and he staggered back, his arms flailing.

Dutch had thrown up his hands as if they would protect him, but his feet stayed rooted to the floor.

Standing went down, hit the floor with his shoulder and immediately went into a roll that took him past Reid.

As he straightened up, Standing was facing the kitchen and saw Withers with his gun in his hand. Withers was aiming at Dutch and he pulled the trigger. The gun kicked in his hand and the round hit Dutch in the throat. Blood splattered across the floor and Dutch collapsed.

Withers was already looking at Standing, his eyes widening. The gun began to move in Standing's direction. The detective had fired five times. The gun was a Beretta

Cougar which had eight .45 cartridges in the clip so Withers had three shots left.

Reid's hand was now hanging limply by his side. The strength was fading from his legs and he was starting to fall. Standing grabbed for Reid's gun, still in its holster. He pulled it out, registering immediately that it was a Glock so there was no safety to be flicked. He dropped low to make himself a smaller target and held the weapon with both hands. It was an unfamiliar weapon, so he'd need all the stability he could get.

Withers had the gun trained on Standing, but he was holding it with one hand and it was still moving, and when he pulled the trigger the shot missed Standing and hit Reid in the groin.

Standing fired twice, the two shots so close together that they almost sounded like one, a perfect double tap to the centre of the detective's chest. Withers was a big man and the Glock was a 9mm, so Standing fired a third shot to make sure, hitting him smack in the middle of the face. Withers fell back and his gun clattered to the floor.

Standing straightened up. Reid fell to his knees and then keeled over.

Dutch was dead, his eyes were wide and staring and blood was pooling around his neck.

Keenan had died the instant that the round had burst through his skull and sprayed brain and bone and blood across the wall behind him.

Reid was making a gurgling sound and Standing went over to him. The detective was lying on his side and blood was trickling from the chest wound onto the floor. Standing had seen enough chest wounds to know that there was nothing he could do. He sat down, taking care to avoid the blood on the floor. He held Reid's hand. 'Okay, just relax,' he said. He realised he didn't know the man's first name.

Reid tried to speak but all he could manage was a stifled grunt. Standing squeezed his hand gently. 'I'm here, Buddy. I'm here with you.'

There was a panicked look in Reid's eyes, a look that Standing had seen many times before. Reid was scared. It wasn't pain, the body's natural painkillers had flooded into his bloodstream the moment he had been shot. Pain came later, after the initial shock had worn off, but from the state of Reid's injuries, Standing knew that death was only seconds away. Standing squeezed his hand again. 'Think of the people you love, and the people who love you. Fill your mind with thoughts of them. Let them be the last thing you think of.'

Reid gave him the faintest of squeezes, then there was an almost imperceptible sigh followed by a shudder and stillness. Reid's eyes remained open but the life had gone from them. Standing let go of the man's hand and gently closed his eyelids. He stood up and looked around, getting his thoughts in order. From the moment Withers had started shooting, Standing had been operating on instinct, but now he had to think through what he was going to do.

Withers was an LAPD detective, there was no question of that. But he had killed his colleague without hesitation, on top of murdering Keenan and Dutch. And if Standing had been a fraction of a second slower, he'd also be dead on the floor. But why? Why had Withers come out of the kitchen shooting?

Standing went over to Withers and picked up the gun. The silencer looked tailor-made for the Beretta, which meant that the detective had probably brought it with him. That suspicion was confirmed when he found the evidence bag containing Lipov's silencer and gloves in the pocket of the detective's jacket. That meant that Withers had arrived at the house with at least the option of killing them. But why? The only reason that made sense was that he didn't want anyone to know that Lipov had killed Koshkin and his bodyguards. But why would an LAPD detective want to protect a foreign bodyguard with links to the Russian mafia?

He looked around the hallway. He was sure he hadn't touched anything there, but he had touched the stool and the cabinet under the sink in the kitchen. He took the Glock with him into the kitchen and used a cloth to wipe the gun clean, then he took it back into the hall and put it in Reid's hand. 'Sorry, Buddy,' he said. A cursory look at the crime scene would set investigators thinking that the two detectives had been shooting at each other.

He went back to the kitchen and carefully wiped the stool and the cabinet. Then he put the cloth in his jacket pocket. He walked around, checking that he hadn't left any footprints, then let himself out of the front door.

As he walked up to the main gate he remembered that Withers had used a remote control to open them. If he climbed over the gates he'd leave fingerprints and DNA, so he went back to the rear garden and went over the wall where Bobby-Ray had disappeared the night that Koshkin was killed.

He scaled the wall easily, dropping down into the neighbour's garden. The house was smaller than the one behind him and there was no wall, but there were several signs warning that the property was protected by armed security. Standing skirted the edge of the property and reached the road. He started walking north with his hands in his pockets, trying to look as casual as possible. The problem was that Bel Air wasn't the sort of place that people walked, certainly not at night. During the day there was the occasional jogger and people walking dogs, but any travelling was generally done in the air-conditioned comfort of an expensive vehicle. If a police car went by, there was every chance that he'd be stopped and questioned.

He reached Sunset Boulevard and relaxed slightly because there were more pedestrians around, heading to and from the area's many bars and restaurants. He walked east and by the time he was on the outskirts of West Hollywood he figured he was far enough away from the mansion to risk phoning Kaitlyn. He FaceTimed her and showed her where he was. She said that she'd pick him up and he told her to meet him at Mel's Drive-In on Sunset Boulevard, a Fifties-themed diner that was open twenty-four hours a day.

29

Standing was halfway through a mug of coffee when Kaitlyn arrived at Mel's Drive-In. She had changed into jeans that were ripped at the knees and a red leather jacket over a tight white top. She ordered a Coke and then watched his lips intently as he ran through everything that had happened. He found himself speaking faster and faster and eventually she reached over to hold his hands and told him to slow down. He laughed and nodded. She was so good at lip-reading that often he just plain forgot that she was deaf. When he'd finished, he sat back and sipped his coffee. 'And they were real cops?' she asked.

'The Withers guy was running the investigation into Koshkin's death,' said Standing. 'That's what Keenan said and I've no reason to doubt him. Whatever Withers was up to, his partner wasn't part of it, because Withers shot him without any hesitation.'

Kaitlyn shook her head in astonishment. 'It's no wonder that Bobby-Ray is hiding,' she said. 'He can't trust anyone.'

Standing nodded. 'True,' he said. 'Withers had a silencer with him, which means he had it all planned. He went into that house knowing he was going to kill everybody.'

'Why would he do that?'

'I wish I knew,' he said. He took out the evidence bag containing Lipov's gloves and the silencer, made sure that no one was paying them any attention, and showed it to her before putting it quickly back into his pocket. 'That proves that Lipov was the killer and not Bobby-Ray. But if Withers had managed to dispose of it, no one would ever know. The big question is, who can we trust now? How can we be sure that anyone else we approach won't be the same as Withers?'

Kaitlyn sat back and didn't say anything.

'Do you want to eat?' he asked.

She shook her head. 'My stomach is churning.'

Standing patted her hand. 'I'm sorry. I know how stressful this is for you.'

'It's got to be worse for Bobby-Ray,' she said. She sighed. 'I just wish I knew where he was.'

'He has to be running out of cash now,' said Standing. 'He won't be using credit cards or going anywhere near an ATM. Unless someone is helping him.'

'If he needed money, he'd come to me,' said Kaitlyn.

'Not if he thinks they're watching you. He'd be more likely to approach one of his SEAL pals. But then if he was doing that, surely he'd use them to get a message to me.' Standing grimaced. 'I think he's staying away from everyone. Wherever he is, he's not reaching out to anyone.'

'But he told me he wanted your help.'

'Sure. But then those two FBI agents turned up at his motel and tried to kill him. He has to be worried that if he contacts you or me, then our lives would be in danger.' He sipped his coffee. 'The problem is, we don't know who we can trust either. We're in exactly the same position as he is. We know we can't trust the FBI because of what happened at Bobby-Ray's motel. And tonight the lead investigator on the Koshkin killing shoots dead two men from Bobby-Ray's company and a cop. So we can't trust the LAPD. That doesn't leave us with much choice, does it?'

'But we've got the evidence that proves that Bobby-Ray is innocent. That's got to count for something, surely?'

'Not until we get it into the right hands,' said Standing. 'And that's the problem. We can call the FBI but how do we know that we can trust whoever turns up? Same with the cops.' He banged his hands down on the table. 'This is so bloody frustrating.'

Kaitlyn reached over and held his hands. 'Big breaths,' she said. 'Square breathing, remember?'

He laughed. 'Yeah, I remember. Sorry. It's just . . .'

'Frustrating. I know. We want to help but we don't know what to do. It'd be easier if we could just talk to Bobby-Ray.'

'Is there anyone he would go to for help? What about your parents? Where are they?'

'Redding,' said Kaitlyn. 'About eight hours' drive north of here. Do you think Bobby-Ray might have gone to stay with them?'

'If he wanted to protect you, he'd be just as keen to keep them out of it,' said Standing. 'So no, I think he'd stay away from them. What sort of place is Redding?'

'It's a small city, ninety thousand population or there-abouts. Mom and Dad were born there and never wanted to leave. Dad's a dentist and Mom was his hygienist, then she gave up work to bring up me and Bobby-Ray. She started to get Alzheimer's a few years ago and now Dad is her full-time caregiver, pretty much.'

'Sorry about that,' said Standing.

'It's early days,' said Kaitlyn. 'It's like she's forgetful. But she always recognises me when I go up to see them. She'll seem fine and then suddenly she'll leave the house naked or she'll put the laundry in the oven. She has to be watched all the time but she's still my mom.'

'Do you go back often?'

'Every few weeks. We used to go to our cabin in Trinity Alps for weekends but since Mom got sick we just stay at home now.'

'Trinity Alps?'

'It's a wilderness area in the far north of the state. About two thousand square kilometres of mountains and forests. They've got a cabin in what they call the Green Trinities, a forested area in the western half of the wilderness. Most of the land is government owned but there's still about two thousand acres in private hands. The cabin has been in Dad's family since the early nineteen hundreds. The Wilderness Land Trust keeps trying to buy it and if he doesn't sell they'll probably take it off him eventually.' Her eyes widened. 'Oh my God,' she said. 'The cabin. Why didn't I think of it before?'

'Do you think Bobby-Ray might be hiding out there?'

'It's the perfect place,' she said. 'The nearest neighbour is five miles away, there's no phone, no Internet, no nothing. It doesn't even have electricity.'

'Bobby-Ray would be able to live off the land,' said Standing. 'What about water?'

'There's a stream running through the land that goes to a lake. Oh my God, I bet that's where he is. The cabin.'

'There's an easy way to find out,' said Standing.

30

S tanding and Kaitlyn left for Redding not long after
dawn. They drove first to LAX, where Kaitlyn parked
the Polo in a long-term car park and they rented a Ford
Escape using Standing's credit card. It was then that
Standing realised he still had the evidence bag containing
Lipov's gloves and the silencer. 'I'm not sure it's a good
idea to be driving round with this,' he said, showing the
bag to Kaitlyn. 'If we get stopped we'll have a lot of
explaining to do.'

'There's a 24/7 left-luggage locker place about ten
minutes away,' she said.

'Will we have to show them what we're leaving?'

She shook her head. 'I've used it a couple of times, it's
all automated. You use a credit card or ID to gain access
and you choose your locker on a computer screen. You
don't even speak to a person unless there's a problem.'

The locker rental shop was in a small shopping centre,
underneath an accountant's and next to a hairdresser's.
As Kaitlyn had said, it was fully automated. Standing
used a credit card to open the main door. Inside, the
walls were lined with lockers of various sizes, most of
them able to take cabin baggage or full-size suitcases.
Standing used the same credit card to rent one of the

smallest lockers and he put the evidence bag inside. It looked a secure enough system, he thought, certainly a safer option than driving it around the state.

They headed for Redding, which the SatNav told them was an eight and a half hour drive. They stopped twice to refuel and eat, and it was mid-afternoon when they reached the outskirts of Redding. Standing was constantly checking for tails but it didn't appear that anyone was following them.

'Do you see your parents much when you're in England?' Kaitlyn asked as she put away her phone.

'My mother died when I was young,' said Standing.

'I'm sorry,' she said. 'That's awful.'

Standing shrugged. 'It happened a long time ago.'

'What about your father?'

'He's still alive, but I'm not in touch.'

'Wow, that's a pity. Bobby-Ray and I are still really close to our parents. I can't imagine not being close to them.'

'That's one of the reasons I joined the army,' said Standing. 'It became my family.'

'No brothers or sisters?'

Standing was never comfortable answering questions about his family situation – or lack of it – but he didn't want to be rude. 'I had a sister,' he said. 'She died.'

'Wow. I'm sorry. You've been really unlucky.'

'Yeah, I suppose I have,' said Standing. He concentrated on the road ahead. Kaitlyn must have realised he didn't want to open up about his family, because she didn't ask him any more questions.

The Barnes place was a two-storey wooden house with a pitched roof surrounded by a white picket fence. At the end of the drive was a mailbox in the shape of a red barn on a white post. There was a blue Chevrolet parked in the driveway. They drove past twice, checking for any surveillance, but there were no cars parked in the street.

'What do you think?' asked Kaitlyn after they had driven by the second time and parked up by the side of the road.

'It doesn't look as if they're being watched,' said Standing. 'And to be honest, there's no reason that anyone would expect him to go running to his parents.' He rubbed the back of his neck. 'Maybe we should just go to the cabin.'

'We can at least ask them if they've spoken to Bobby-Ray.'

Standing frowned. 'If they knew that your brother was in trouble, they'd have spoken to you about it, surely?'

She nodded. 'I suppose so. So that means the cops haven't talked to Mom and Dad.'

'It seems that way,' said Standing. He rubbed the back of his neck. 'There's definitely something going on with the cops. And it looks like it's at a senior level, too.'

'Matt, I really want to see Mom and Dad,' said Kaitlyn.

'Okay,' said Standing. 'We'll swing by one more time and if it looks good we'll go in. But if they don't know that Bobby-Ray is in trouble, then we don't tell them. The less they know, the better.'

She grinned. 'Deal,' she said.

They drove to the house again. There were still no signs of surveillance, so Standing pulled up behind the Chevrolet.

A flight of wooden steps led up to a shaded porch where a cushioned swing seat was hanging from chains.

Kaitlyn pressed the doorbell and smiled nervously at Standing. The man who opened the door was tall and balding with thin lips that broke into a broad smile when he saw Kaitlyn. 'Darling, why didn't you tell us you were coming?'

'It was a last-minute decision,' she said. 'Spur of the moment.' She hugged him and kissed him on the cheek.

Mr Barnes had pale-blue eyes and they blinked behind steel-framed spectacles as he looked over her shoulder. He frowned a little when he saw Standing. 'Is Bobby-Ray not with you?' He was wearing a cardigan that looked like it had been hand-knitted and had comfortable slippers on his feet. When she didn't reply, he held her by the shoulders and repeated the question.

Kaitlyn exchanged a look with Standing, then smiled at her father. 'He's working, Dad,' said Kaitlyn. 'This is my friend, Matt,' she said when she eventually broke away.

Mr Barnes shook hands with Standing. He had a soft grip but he looked Standing in the eyes as he shook. 'Are you a SEAL, too, Matt?'

'I'm British, Mr Barnes, but I served alongside your son in Syria.'

Mr Barnes eyes hardened a fraction as he released his grip on Standing's hand. 'Bobby-Ray said there was a Brit with him when the IED went off.'

'That would be me,' said Standing.

'It was the worst day of Bobby-Ray's life when they told him he had to leave the SEALs,' said Mr Barnes.

'Where's Mom?' asked Kaitlyn, and Standing knew she was trying to change the subject. Standing had to fight the urge to tell her father that Bobby-Ray's injuries had more to do with him being in the wrong place at the wrong time and less about him making a conscious decision to step in front of the blast. The position could just as easily have been reversed. There was no doubt that Bobby-Ray had taken the bulk of the blast and that had saved Standing from more serious injuries, but Standing didn't like the way that Mr Barnes seemed to be implying that he was responsible for what had happened to his son.

'In the kitchen,' said Mr Barnes. 'She's baking. You picked a good time to visit.'

Mr Barnes stepped to the side to let them in. There was a side table with a phone on it under an ornate mirror, and on the opposite wall were dozens of framed photographs, many of them school and college pictures of Bobby-Ray and Kaitlyn. There were several pictures of Bobby-Ray in the SEALs, a couple of them taken in the Middle East. Kaitlyn walked to the kitchen and Standing followed her as Mr Barnes closed the door behind them. The floors were bare oak, varnished to a glossy sheen, the doors were also gleaming wood and there were wooden beams overhead.

'Honey, guess who's dropped by unexpectedly!' called Mr Barnes.

'Who?' Mrs Barnes appeared at the kitchen door, wiping her hands on a cloth. She was tall and thin like her husband, her hair grey and loose around her shoulders, wearing a canary-yellow dress belted at the waist. She had no make-up on but her high cheekbones and piercing green eyes suggested that she had been a stunner when she was younger, and when she smiled she showed perfect white teeth. 'Darling!' she exclaimed when she saw Kaitlyn. 'What a wonderful surprise.' She rushed down the hallway to hug her. The hug was followed by two loud air kisses. 'Oh, you smell lovely,' said Mrs Barnes. 'What is that?'

'It's just my shampoo, Mom,' laughed Kaitlyn.

'It smells like apples.'

'I think that's coming from the oven, Mom.'

Mrs Barnes frowned, then laughed. 'You're right. Apple pie. And chocolate-chip muffins. Your favourites. Bobby-Ray loves my apple pie.' She frowned again. 'Where is Bobby-Ray?' asked Mrs Barnes. She frowned at Matt. 'And who are you?'

'This is Matt, he's a friend of Bobby-Ray's,' said Mr Barnes.

'Bobby-Ray is just busy, Mom,' said Kaitlyn. 'He couldn't come.' Standing could tell that Kaitlyn wasn't happy about lying to her parents, but he knew that there was no other option.

'It's been ages since I saw Bobby-Ray. Simply ages.' Mrs Barnes began to toy with her hair, winding it around her fingers.

'Mom, he was here last month. We both were.'

Mrs Barnes shook her head emphatically. 'That is such a lie,' she said. 'This is the first time you've been here in years. I was starting to think you'd forgotten about us.'

'Mom . . .' said Kaitlyn. She looked over at her father for support but Mr Barnes just shrugged.

'So where is he?' asked Mrs Barnes. 'Still fighting the A-Rabs?'

'Mom, Bobby-Ray left the SEALs six months ago.'

'Nonsense,' said Mrs Barnes. She looked over at the kitchen. 'Did I switch the oven on?'

'Yes, you did, honey,' said Mr Barnes.

Mrs Barnes nodded happily. She looked at Standing and frowned. 'Who are you?' she asked.

Mr Barnes flashed Standing an apologetic look. 'That's Matt, honey,' said Mr Barnes. 'He's a friend of Bobby-Ray's.'

Mrs Barnes looked around, confused. 'Where is Bobby-Ray?'

'He's working, Mom,' said Kaitlyn.

'Okay,' said Mrs Barnes. She turned and walked into the kitchen, bending down to look at the oven controls as if to reassure herself that she had switched it on.

'Do you want a beer, Matt?' asked Mr Barnes.

'A beer sounds good, thank you,' said Standing.

Mr Barnes went over to the fridge and took out two bottles of Budweiser. Kaitlyn raised her eyebrows expectantly and her father laughed and took out a third beer.

They sat around the table while Mrs Barnes went over to the sink and began washing dishes.

'Is the dishwasher broken?' asked Kaitlyn.

Her father leaned towards her and lowered his voice. 'It makes her happy, washing up,' he said. 'Just let her get on with it.'

They sipped their beers as Mrs Barnes carried on washing. 'Dad, I thought I'd take Matt up to see the cabin, is that okay?'

'Of course, but it'll be in a bit of a state. It's been a year since anyone was there.'

'We're not looking for creature comforts,' said Kaitlyn. 'Maybe just stay there for a night or two.'

Mr Barnes tilted his head on one side and narrowed

his eyes and Kaitlyn burst out laughing. 'We're just friends, Dad. Don't worry.'

'I'm not worried,' said Mr Barnes. 'To be honest, I had hoped that Matt here was your boyfriend. It's about time you had someone in your life.'

'Dad, I have lots of people in my life.'

'You know what I mean, Kaitlyn.'

Kaitlyn sighed. 'You're going to start on about grand-children again, aren't you?'

'My biological grandfather clock is ticking,' said Mr Barnes.

'Dad, you've only just turned sixty,' said Kaitlyn. She sighed in exasperation. 'I'm sorry about this, Matt. I didn't realise I was dragging you into an episode of *The Dating Game*.'

She raised her bottle in salute and he clinked his bottle against hers. 'We're good,' he said.

Mr Barnes looked at his watch. 'If you're planning on getting there tonight you'll need to leave soon. You don't want to be moving through the woods after dark.'

'We've got flashlights,' said Standing.

'It's always better to get there during daylight,' said Mr Barnes. 'And you'll need to take food, remember. And take water to be on the safe side. I don't know what state the stream is in. You might want to check the latrine, too.'

'We'll check everything, Dad, don't worry.' She grinned at Standing. 'We had some great vacations there when we were growing up. It really is in the middle of nowhere. Dad taught us hunting, shooting and fishing. That's prob-ably what gave Bobby-Ray his taste for adventure.'

'Where is Bobby-Ray?' asked Mrs Barnes, turning around from the sink.

'He's working, honey,' said Mr Barnes.

'Okay,' said Mrs Barnes and she turned back to her washing-up.

'What do the doctors say, Dad?' whispered Kaitlyn.

'They say she's still at the early to moderate stage,' said Mr Barnes. 'They're trying her on different cholinesterase inhibitors. She didn't react well to Aricept and she's on Exelon now, which she doesn't have any adverse reactions to. And they put her on Memantine a couple of weeks ago, which is supposed to help with memory and attention span, but I haven't noticed any improvement. Mind you, it hasn't got any worse over that period, so maybe it is working.' He shrugged sadly.

'Are you okay, Dad?' asked Kaitlyn.

He forced a smile. 'I'm fine now, I just worry what the future holds. At the moment it's amusing, at least until she wanders around without her clothes on, but it can only go one way, unless they come up with some sort of wonder cure. She knows who I am, and she recognises you, but the day will come when she won't and that scares me.'

Kaitlyn reached over and held his hand. Standing felt suddenly uncomfortable, knowing that he was intruding on a family matter and feeling worse because he had to take Kaitlyn away. But her father was right, they needed to be at the cabin before dark.

Kaitlyn looked over at him as if she had read his mind. 'We'd better be going,' she said.

Mrs Barnes went over to the oven, opened it and peered at the muffins and apple pie. 'Let me wrap these up for you to take with you,' she said. She slipped on oven gloves, pulled out the tray with the pie and placed it on top of the stove, followed by the muffins.

'They smell great, Mom,' said Kaitlyn.

'They do, don't they,' said Mrs Barnes. She looked around, frowning. 'Now where has Bobby-Ray got to?'

31

Dan Shepherd's phone rang. The caller was with-holding his number but he took the call anyway, though he answered with a laconic 'Yeah?' rather than identifying himself.

'And how are you this warm and pleasant day?' The accent was American and Shepherd knew immediately who it was. Richard Yokely. Despite the pleasantries, the only time the American called was when he wanted some-thing, so Shepherd was immediately on the alert. 'I'm fine, keeping the free world safe from harm. You?'

Yokely chuckled. 'The same, of course,' he said. 'And on that matter we need to talk. You're in the office?'

MI5 was based in Thames House, a Grade-2 listed building on the north bank of the River Thames, next to Lambeth Bridge. 'I'm afraid so,' said Shepherd. 'I'm between jobs at the moment so tied to a desk.'

'You'll appreciate some fresh air, then, and at least I can still smoke outdoors. How about that café near the Serpentine in Hyde Park?'

'I'll have to get a cab. Can't we make it closer?'

'It's sensitive, so I wouldn't want to meet you too close to home. And they do make a very good cup of coffee.'

Shepherd looked at his watch. 'Give me an hour.'

'It's yours,' said Yokely, and ended the call.

Shepherd sat back and sighed. He wasn't happy at being summoned across town, but whenever Yokely got in touch it was important. He wasn't one for social calls. Shepherd had crossed paths with the American several times over the years, but knew very little about him. At various points in his career, Yokely had worked for the Central Intelligence Agency and the Defense Intelligence Agency and quite a few other organisations that preferred to be known by their initials. He was also involved with the black ops group Grey Fox, a highly secret unit that reported directly to the White House. They weren't friends but Shepherd trusted the man as much as he trusted anyone within the intelligence community.

Shepherd was actually quite pleased to get Yokely's call; he'd spent the last week doing little more than overseeing three long-term undercover operations involving the penetration of right-wing groups that had been carrying out racist attacks in the north of England. The two men and one woman were experienced MI5 officers who needed very little hand-holding, so all he was doing was collating reports and offering the occasional piece of advice.

He arrived at Hyde Park ten minutes early and spent the time checking that he wasn't being watched. Yokely was already at an outside table with a black coffee in front of him, smoking a small cigar. He waved Shepherd over, then stood up to shake hands with him. Yokely was in his late fifties. His hair was greying but he was tough and well muscled, though his dark blazer, white shirt and dark-blue tie gave him the look of a BMW salesman. As always the black leather of his tasselled shoes gleamed as if they had been freshly polished, and he had a chunky gold ring on his right ring finger.

'Sorry about dragging you across town, Spider,' said Yokely. He waved him to a seat. 'You make yourself comfortable, the coffee's on me.' Yokely stubbed out what remained of his cigar and went inside the café as Shepherd sat down. There were plenty of people around, in the café and walking around the Serpentine, the forty-acre lake in the middle of Hyde Park, but no one was paying him, or Yokely, any attention. Shepherd was sure that the American had run his own counter-surveillance techniques before turning up at the meeting place.

Yokely returned with Shepherd's coffee and sat down. 'So, you look in good shape, Spider. Still running?'

'When I can,' said Shepherd. 'But watching my diet more than anything.'

'It's one of the annoying things about getting older,' said Yokely. 'By the time you can really afford to eat and drink the finer things in life, the doctors are telling you that they're all bad for you. When I was in my twenties I ate nothing but fast food and drank cheap beer and whisky. Now I can afford a decent steak and Châteauneuf-du-Pape and they tell me red meat is a killer and two glasses of wine is my limit.' He raised his coffee cup. 'And no more than two cups of coffee a day, they say.' He grinned. 'Fuck 'em,' he said. He sipped his coffee and smacked his lips. 'This is one of the few places in London where you can get a decent cup of coffee.' He looked around, then lowered his voice slightly. 'I want to talk to you about your friend Matt Standing,' he said.

'Friend is pushing it a bit,' said Shepherd. 'But I'm all ears.'

'Former Sergeant Standing is causing havoc and mayhem in the States at the moment, and I need to know if he's doing it with MI5's blessing or not.'

Shepherd's eyes narrowed. 'What sort of havoc and mayhem, Richard?'

'I'll come on to that in a moment,' said Yokely. 'The thing is, the SAS keeps its secrets a darn sight better than the police or the intelligence agencies. If he worked for the cops or the spooks I'd probably have a handle on him already, but you SAS guys keep your cards close to your chest. I know that he was a sergeant but is now a regular trooper, and I know that he was embedded with a Navy SEAL unit in Syria and handled himself well, but as for anything else, he's a man of mystery.'

Shepherd shrugged but didn't say anything.

'So what I need to know at this point is if Mr Standing is on an MI5 mission, or if what he's doing is at the behest of the Increment or some other secret-squirrel department that I'm not aware of.'

The Increment was an ad-hoc group that drew on the resources of the SAS and SBS for missions that were too dangerous or specialised for MI6 and MI5. According to the conspiracy theorists, the Increment had also been behind events such as the deaths of Princess Diana, Colonel Gaddafi of Libya and the former Serbian president Slobodan Milošević but the people who believed that also believed that the Americans had never walked on the moon and that George W. Bush was responsible for the attacks on the World Trade Center. Shepherd shook his head. 'He's not working for MI5, and I'm pretty sure he's not doing anything for the Increment.'

'That's what I thought, but I wanted to check,' said

Yokely. 'Now, you say you're not friends, but you are helping him, right?'

Shepherd looked pained. 'I think you're going to have to tell me what you have, Richard.'

'You mean I show you mine and you'll show me yours?'

'I don't mean to be difficult, but . . .' Shepherd shrugged.

Yokely took out his pack of cigars, selected one and lit it before continuing. 'Your Mr Standing is trying to help a Navy SEAL he befriended out in Syria, a guy by the name of Bobby-Ray Barnes. Barnes left the SEALs after he got hit by an IED. He had a collapsed lung, which they fixed, but it meant his diving days were over. So Bobby-Ray becomes a bodyguard and one night his principal and three of his colleagues are shot to death in a Bel Air mansion. Bobby-Ray goes on the run and Mr Standing flies out to offer assistance.' He took a long drag on his cigar and blew smoke up at the clear blue sky before continuing. 'Now, somewhere along the line either Mr Standing asks you for help or you offer it, but either way you start making enquiries about the Solntsevskaya syndicate, in particular about their West Coast activities.'

'Have you been spying on me, Richard?'

Yokely chuckled heartily. 'We're your allies, remember? The special relationship? We are constantly sharing intelligence and manpower. Our NSA works hand in hand with your GCHQ, so when you start asking about what the Solntsevskaya is up to on our turf, of course we're going to know.'

'And you're interested in the Russian mafia, are you?'

'Oh yes,' said Yokely. 'Very much so. So am I correct in saying that the intel you obtained on the Solntsevskaya was passed on to Mr Standing? In particular the details of Oleg Ivchenko and Stanislav Yurin?'

Shepherd grimaced. The American clearly knew everything. 'I gave him names and addresses, yes.'

'What about Denis Volkov?'

Shepherd shook his head. 'That's not a name I've come across,' he said.

'That's surprising because he's Yurin's boss. Well, was his boss. Volkov is dead now, along with a few of his minions. Yurin is apparently alive and well, albeit walking with a limp, and has already taken over from Volkov. Oleg Ivchenko is alive and well, but if Standing is on the rampage that could very well change soon.'

'And this is down to Matt, you think?'

'I'm sure of it,' said Yokely. 'But it's a lot more complicated than just a few dead Russian hoodlums, which is why I need to know the full extent of MI5's involvement.'

'Officially, there is zero involvement,' said Shepherd. 'Matt approached me on a personal level and asked for some help. I gave him a couple of names and addresses.'

'And Erik Markov?'

Shepherd nodded. 'As I'm sure you know, the principal who was killed out in LA was also the victim of an intended assassination here in London. His business partner – Markov – had connections with the Solntsevskaya.'

'You didn't think that he might take matters into his own hands?'

'He wanted to help his friend, that's all. Is Markov dead, too?'

Yokely smiled. 'Not yet. But the way things are going . . .' He shrugged and took another drag on his cigar.

'Is Matt in trouble?' asked Shepherd.

'I think the question that's better asked is whether or not he's in danger. And the answer to that is yes, because you do not fuck with the Russian mafia. But so far as trouble – legal trouble – goes, the cops aren't officially looking for him.'

'Officially?'

Yokely sighed. 'Spider, this is what we in the States call a regular clusterfuck. What's going down is so convoluted you'll need a road map to follow it.'

'Are you going to explain it to me?'

Yokely blew smoke up at the sky. 'What theories did you have for the attack on Koshkin in London?'

'Various,' said Shepherd. 'He was getting divorced, he'd fallen out with Markov, the Russian government wanted his scalp. Lots of options, but the fact that he died in LA put a stop to the investigation.'

'Well, what I can tell you is that Koshkin was sure that it was Markov that tried to have him killed. That's why he ran off to the US. He wanted to hurt Markov, and the way to do that was to tell the authorities how Markov helped influence the 2016 presidential elections. He had the smoking gun the FBI wanted and was prepared to hand it to them in exchange for protection and citizenship.'

'Erik Markov wanted to influence the election?'

'Markov just provided the money and the resources. He was doing it for the Solntsevskaya, who were almost certainly acting on behalf of the Kremlin. And Koshkin was the man who could tie it all together.'

'So it was the Russian mafia who had Koshkin killed, to keep him quiet?'

'That's what it looks like.'

'From what Standing told me, the plan was to frame an American for it. Bobby-Ray Barnes was supposed to have died in that house with the murder weapon in his hand. But something went wrong and Barnes did a runner.'

'And you believe that?'

'I believe that Standing believes it. I've no way of knowing if that's what happened. It does seem to me that if this Bobby-Ray is innocent then he should talk to the police.'

'That's where it gets complicated,' said Yokely. He took another drag on his cigar and blew a fairly decent smoke ring. 'Two FBI agents went to see Barnes at the motel where he was holed up. Not to arrest him but to kill him. They fucked up and ended up dead.'

'FBI agents? Real FBI agents?'

'Real, genuine, time-served Feds. But their loyalties were with the Solntsevskaya. That's the problem we've got with the Russian mafia now. They're everywhere. They've infiltrated the government, the police, the armed forces. They're like a cancer that's spread to all the vital organs.'

'So now they think Bobby-Ray is a Fed killer?'

'Spider, he IS a Fed killer. They were bad Feds, they were there on the Solntsevskaya's behalf, but they were still FBI agents.'

'But there's nothing in the media?'

'There's a media blackout. Someone high up in the FBI or the LAPD is making sure that the full details of what happened aren't released. It's been made to look like a drug-related killing. And the same thing has happened with Koshkin's assassination. That's been sold as a home invasion.'

'And the papers and TV are buying that?'

Yokely shrugged. 'Journalists these days just accept whatever line they're fed. Though that's just got harder after what happened in Bel Air yesterday. Two LAPD cops were killed in the very same house where Koshkin was killed, along with two members of the company that Barnes was working for.'

Shepherd's jaw dropped. Yokely held up a hand. 'I know, I know. Like I said, it's complicated. One of the cops was the lead detective on the Koshkin killing. The other cop was also on the case. Barnes's boss was killed along with the guy who was driving Koshkin the night he was killed. The only guns involved were those belonging to the cops. It looks as if Reid, the junior detective, shot the lead detective and the lead detective shot him and the two other men.'

'But Standing wasn't involved?'

'His name hasn't come up – yet.'

'So what do you think? That one or both of the detectives was working for the Solntsevskaya?'

'That's how I read it. Maybe the bodyguarding company guys said they had information for the detectives and the detectives didn't want it getting out. As I keep saying, this is complicated.' He took another drag on his cigar, exhaled, and followed it up with a sip of coffee. 'Your friend has gotten himself into a whole world of pain, Spider.'

'He's not my friend,' said Shepherd.

'Associate, colleague. Fellow warrior. Whatever. At the moment you're the only line I have to Standing. So my first question is, what's his family situation? Married? Siblings? Parents?'

'He's never been married. His father is serving a life sentence for murdering Standing's mother. He had a sister but she died.'

'So he's got no one. That's the first good news I've heard today.'

'Why's that?'

'Because if the Solntsevskaya get on his case they'll kill him and everyone he loves. That's what they do. How driven is he?'

'He's SAS, Richard. That should answer your question.'

'He won't stop?'

'Not until he's achieved his objective. And as I understand it, his objective is to help Bobby-Ray.'

'And he'd do that even if it meant putting his own life on the line.'

Shepherd nodded slowly. 'Sure.'

'That's what I figured.'

Shepherd sipped his coffee. 'My turn? To ask a question?'

Yokely nodded. 'Go ahead.'

'You know what's going on, obviously.'

'Most of it.'

'So why the hell don't you put a stop to it? You know Bobby-Ray didn't kill Koshkin, you know he was being framed . . .'

Yokely put up a hand. 'I've got to stop you right there,' he said. 'There are two issues here. There's the issue of whether Barnes killed Koshkin and the bodyguards. And there's the issue of what Matt Standing is up to and the waves he's creating. I have no clue as to whether or not Barnes killed Koshkin or if what Standing says is true and that he's been framed. But I do know for sure that the Solntsevskaya is mightily pissed off at Standing and that there will be repercussions.'

Shepherd nodded thoughtfully. 'And I'm guessing that those repercussions could help you in your investigation.'

Yokely laughed. 'You know me so well,' he said. He nodded. 'Your man Standing has banged into a right hornet's nest and so everyone is buzzing around like crazy. The fact that at least one very high-up cop is trying to keep a lid on what's happening is an eye-opener, and we've already seen things happening within the FBI that have given us another couple of leads that we weren't aware of. We already have two high-ranking Solntsevskaya officials and several soldiers in the morgue, and the way it's going there'll almost certainly be more. So yes, your man Standing is being very helpful indeed.'

'And what about Erik Markov?'

'Ah yes, the two billion dollar question.'

'Is that what he's worth?'

'And some,' said Yokely.

'Is he of interest?'

Yokely took another pull on his cigar.

'I'll take that as a yes,' said Shepherd. 'So you're looking for evidence that Erik Markov was meddling in the presidential elections? You had it within your grasp but lost it when Koshkin was murdered.'

'That's one way of looking at it,' said Yokely. 'But trust me, there were quite a few people who were relieved when Koshkin was killed.'

Realisation dawned and Shepherd raised his eyebrows. 'Of course, Grey Fox works for the White House. And the last thing the White House wants is for someone to come up with evidence that the Russians tampered with the US electoral process.'

'Not just the White House,' said Yokely. 'But yes, there are some dirty secrets that are better off not aired.'

Shepherd sighed through pursed lips. 'I see what you mean about it being complicated.'

'It's messy,' said Yokely. 'What we have is this triumvirate of the Kremlin, the Russian mafia, and a powerful oligarch. They all help each other, they all use each other and they all profit from each other. Koshkin and Markov fell out over business and Markov decided he wanted his partner killed. He probably used his Solntsevskaya contacts to arrange that, but they fucked up and Koshkin fled to the States. Koshkin decides that the best way to get back at Markov is to tell the authorities what he did, but as soon as he does that he incurs the wrath of the Kremlin. And Markov, of course. So either Markov or the Kremlin gets the Solntsevskaya to finish off what they started in London. Now that Koshkin is dead, everything should be fine and dandy, except for the fact that Barnes is on the run and Standing is on the offensive.'

'And what the White House wants is for all this to go away and presumably for Markov to get the hell out of Dodge.'

'Except Markov seems to be hanging around to see how the Barnes business plays out. Now the burning question I'd like answered is if Standing discovers that Markov is behind all this, what will he do?'

'Will he go for Markov?' Shepherd shrugged. 'I think he's more concerned about getting his pal out of trouble. Once Bobby-Ray is free and clear, Standing will back off. He's not the sort to go looking for trouble, but he will always fight his corner.'

'The problem is, the Solntsevskaya won't see it that way. No matter how this pans out, he'll be on their shit list for the rest of his life.' He took another pull on his cigar.

Shepherd stared at Yokely for several seconds. 'How do you want this to pan out, Richard?'

Yokely blew smoke up at the sky. 'It's not what I want that matters.'

'Your bosses, then. What do they want?'

'I think they'd be happier if Markov was no longer an issue.'

Shepherd's eyes narrowed. 'You want him dead? Is that what this meeting is about? You want to find out if Matt is capable of killing Markov?'

Yokely smiled. 'That's not what I said, and you know it.'

'But it would make the White House's life a lot easier, wouldn't it?'

'That I can't deny,' he said.

'That's why you were asking about his family situation, isn't it? Because if Standing does kill Markov, the Solntsevskaya will want revenge. Which means any family he has will be at risk.'

'I'm afraid that ship has sailed, Spider. As soon as Standing killed Volkov, his name went right to the top of their shit list.'

'I need you to promise me that Standing won't come to any harm,' said Shepherd.

'I can't promise that, but I'll do my best,' said Yokely.

'I'm serious, Richard.'

'So am I.'

32

Kaitlyn told Standing when to turn off the main highway. They drove down a narrow two-lane road that twisted and turned through thick woods. They saw the occasional SUV or pick-up truck passing in the other direction but for most of the time they were the only vehicle on the road.

They went down into a valley from where they could see rocky peaks towering over the forest, then the tree cover became so thick that Standing had to turn on the headlights.

They began to climb again and Kaitlyn told him to slow down. The turn-off she was looking for was so narrow that they could easily have missed it. It was a single track of rutted dried mud that wound its way through towering redwoods. Standing had to slow to ten miles an hour or so, as to have gone any faster would have risked damaging the vehicle. They bumped their way for about a mile along the track and then it opened onto a makeshift parking area of flattened grass with space enough for a dozen or so vehicles. 'This is it,' said Kaitlyn, though Standing had already brought the SUV to a halt. The undergrowth was head height around them and the canopies of the huge trees all but blotted out the sky.

Standing climbed out of the car and tucked the Beretta APX compact he'd taken from Yurin's house into the waistband of his trousers. 'If Bobby-Ray is in the cabin, wouldn't he have left his pick-up truck here?' he said, looking around.

Kaitlyn nodded. 'This is as far as you can drive,' she said.

'Is there anywhere else he could have left the truck?'

'This is the only track in,' she said.

Standing walked around, looking at the flattened grass, trying to see if another vehicle had been there. He saw some relatively fresh tyre marks and frowned as he saw they went to the edge of the clearing and ended at a large bush. He went over to the bush. Many of the branches and leaves were mangled and there were specks of oil splattered all over it. He pushed through and the next bush was in a similar condition and then he saw a flash of red in the undergrowth ahead of him. He kept pushing through the vegetation until he reached the rear of the truck. 'It's here!' he shouted.

Kaitlyn made her way through the bushes to him and nodded when she saw the vehicle. 'That's Bobby-Ray's,' she said.

'Then we know he's here,' said Standing. He slapped the tailgate. 'Clever move hiding the truck, but if we found it others could.'

'No one knows about the cabin, it's a family thing,' she said.

'I hope so,' said Standing. 'Come on, let's go surprise your brother.'

They went back to the clearing. Standing opened the rear door of the SUV and took out the carrier bags containing the provisions they had bought at a Safeway in Redding and a cooler in which Mrs Barnes had put the pie and muffins that she had baked. They also had two backpacks filled with clothes and toiletries. Standing took out his cellphone and checked it. There was no phone signal.

'It's always like that,' said Kaitlyn. 'There are some places high up where you can sometimes get a signal but it's patchy.' She shouldered one of the backpacks and picked up the cooler. Standing threw the other backpack on and picked up the carrier bags. Kaitlyn was already heading across the clearing to a small track that led between two bushes. It was barely a couple of feet wide and it zig-zagged through the undergrowth but Kaitlyn strode on confidently.

The sun was starting to go down but the tree canopy had already cut out most of the light. It reminded Standing of the jungle phase of his SAS training but without the energy-sapping rain and heat that he had faced in Brunei. And none of the bees, wasps, centipedes, snakes, spiders and scorpions that had made his life a misery for six weeks, or the mosquitoes that he had come to hate with a vengeance.

The track opened into a small clearing and Kaitlyn waited for him to catch up. 'It's not much further,' she said.

'It really is in the middle of nowhere,' said Standing.

'That's the attraction,' said Kaitlyn. 'The nearest neighbour is about five miles away. But it's not as heavily wooded as it is here, the cabin is up on a hill and there aren't as many trees.' She nodded at the carrier bags. 'Can I have a bottle of water?'

'Sure,' said Standing. He put the carrier bags down and pulled out two bottles of water. He gave one to her and unscrewed the top off the other before drinking greedily. Kaitlyn did the same. He wiped his mouth with the back of his hand and put the bottle back in the carrier bag. Kaitlyn put the cap back on her bottle and held it out to him. Standing took a step forward and his foot brushed against something. He looked down and saw a rope underfoot and then he heard a swishing sound and a rustle of leaves and the rope wrapped itself around his ankle and yanked him up into the air. Before he knew what was happening he was hanging upside down.

'Matt!' shrieked Kaitlyn.

'I'm okay, I'm okay,' said Standing. He tried to reach up to his ankle but the effort was too much and he dropped back, gasping for breath.

'What's going on?' she asked.

Standing was turning slowly. A rope had looped around his left ankle and he was hanging from it. The rope disappeared into the branches of the tree overhead. His right leg was swinging out to the side and his hip was burning. The blood was rushing to his head making it difficult to focus his eyes. 'Some sort of trap,' he gasped. 'See if you can cut me down.'

'I don't have a knife,' she said.

'Neither do I.' The gun was still in his belt but he couldn't see himself being able to shoot the rope.

He tried to grab his ankle again, but it was harder the second time and his hands couldn't even reach his knee. He fell back, his stomach muscles burning.

He was still spinning around slowly and Kaitlyn passed out of his vision, and then he saw a man in camouflage gear running towards him with a hunting knife in his hand. Standing put up his hands to protect himself and then Kaitlyn shouted. 'Bobby-Ray!'

The figure stopped and turned to look at her. 'Kaitlyn? What the hell?'

'Thank God,' said Kaitlyn. She ran to her brother and hugged him.

'What are you doing here?' asked Bobby-Ray.

Standing continued to swing around, his fingertips brushing the undergrowth. 'When you've got the time, you might think about getting me down,' he said.

Bobby-Ray chuckled. He went over to the other end of the rope, which was tied to a sapling. He hacked away with his knife as Kaitlyn hurried over and grabbed Standing's shoulders. She helped him upright as Bobby-Ray cut the rope, then Bobby-Ray walked over and hugged Standing. 'You crazy son of a bitch,' he said. 'How did you find me?' He had a hunting rifle over his back.

'Kaitlyn and I were talking and she remembered the cabin,' said Standing. 'We figured there aren't too many places where you can live off the grid without money, not at short notice.'

'I couldn't call you,' he said. He slotted the knife into a nylon scabbard attached to his right leg above the knee. There was a Glock in a holster on his right hip. 'I'm sorry. I'm pretty sure they can listen on any phones I use. I'm in deep shit, Matt. Deep, deep shit.'

Standing clapped him on the shoulder. 'I know, mate,' he said. 'But we're here to help now.'

'And we've got muffins,' said Kaitlyn, holding up the cooler.

'Muffins?'

'Mom made muffins,' said Kaitlyn. 'And an apple pie.'

'How is she?'

Kaitlyn grimaced. 'She's getting worse. One minute she was asking where you were, the next she was telling us you were off fighting Arabs. Or A-Rabs as she insists on calling them these days.'

'How's Dad coping?'

'Dad's Dad, right? He never complains.'

'Did you tell them you planned to come to the cabin?'

'Sure. We had to.'

Bobby-Ray looked pained. 'I just don't want anyone to know I'm here. For obvious reasons.'

'I said I wanted to show the cabin to Matt. I didn't say we thought you were here.'

Bobby-Ray forced a smile. 'It's all good,' he said. Then another thought struck him. 'What car did you use?'

'A rental,' said Standing. 'A Ford Escape.'

'You parked on the lot?'

Standing nodded.

'Maybe we'll move it tomorrow.'

'We found your truck,' said Standing.

'That's not good,' said Bobby-Ray. 'We'll fix that tomorrow as well.' He picked up one of the carrier bags and peered inside. 'Cheese? Bread? Eggs? Butter? Excellent. There's no fridge so most of my fresh stuff has already spoiled.' He looked into another carrier bag and grinned when he saw the six cans of beer. 'Even better,' he said. 'No ice, obviously, but we can chill them in the stream. Come on, let's get to the cabin before it gets any darker.'

33

Spider Shepherd thought long and hard before phoning Matt Standing. It was usually tricky trying to get a read on Richard Yokely, but the meeting in Hyde Park had given Shepherd a lot to think about. He had crossed paths with the American several times and it was always the interests of the United States that were Yokely's prime concern. On the surface, the main purpose of the meeting appeared to be so that Yokely could get information on Matt Standing. But Standing had been embedded with a Navy SEAL unit in Syria and for that to have happened the Department of Defense would have put him under the microscope, and Yokely would almost certainly have been able to see their file on him. Yokely asked about Standing's personality but he could have got that information from any of the men who had served with him in Syria. No, Yokely had an ulterior motive, Shepherd was sure of that.

Yokely already knew that Shepherd had given Standing information on the Russian mafia active in Los Angeles, he didn't need Shepherd's confirmation of the fact. So why was Yokely telling him that he knew? Was it a warning? Was he letting Shepherd know that he was on dangerous ground by helping Standing? Or did he want Shepherd to warn Standing of the danger that he was getting himself into. Yokely had been quite definite that he wanted Erik Markov out of the picture, or at least out of the United States. Was he hoping that Shepherd could somehow get Standing to kill Markov? Because that was out of the question.

Standing knew that he was going up against the Russian mafia, and he would know that killing one of the members would incur the wrath of the entire organisation. He didn't need Shepherd to warn him of the danger he was facing, but that did seem to have been one of Yokely's concerns. Maybe the American was just making sure that Shepherd was aware of the trouble Standing was in, but that would be a degree of altruism that Shepherd hadn't seen before.

Eventually Shepherd decided that if nothing else, he owed it to Standing to tell him that at least one member of the US intelligence agency knew what he was up to and that he needed to tread carefully. He made the call from a throwaway mobile, one of more than a dozen that he had in his desk, but it went straight through to voice-mail. He decided against leaving a message.

34

M r Barnes and his wife were sitting on the sofa watching television when the doorbell rang. Mr Barnes frowned. They weren't expecting visitors. Mrs Barnes started to get up. 'That'll be Bobby-Ray,' she said.

'Don't be silly, Sarah,' said Mr Barnes. 'Bobby-Ray's not coming. Sit yourself down. It had better not be those Mormons again.'

Mrs Barnes sat down and Mr Barnes pushed himself off the sofa, grunting as the arthritis in his knees kicked in. He walked unsteadily into the hallway and along to the front door. He opened it and frowned up at the three big men standing on the porch. They certainly weren't Mormons. They were all well over six feet, wearing leather jackets and dark trousers and with thick gold chains around their necks and wrists.

The one in the middle had a goatee and dark glasses and a scar that ran the full length of his right cheek. It was an ugly ragged scar that looked as if it was the result of a broken bottle rather than a knife.

'Can I help you?' asked Mr Barnes.

'You're Bobby-Ray's father?' asked the man.

'Has something happened?'

'When did you last see him?'

'A few weeks ago. Are you from his unit?'

'What about his sister? Did you see her today?'

Mr Barnes frowned. 'How do you know that?'

'I'll take that as a yes,' said the man. He had an accent. European or Russian maybe, thought Mr Barnes, but wherever the man was from he had a bad attitude, so he went to shut the door on him. The man thrust his foot in the gap and stopped him from closing the door.

'What do you think you're doing!' said Mr Barnes.

The man slammed his shoulder against the door with so much force that Mr Barnes staggered back into the hallway. Before he could speak, the man with the goatee had grabbed him by the throat and thrown him up against the wall. The man jabbed a nicotine-stained finger in his face. 'You do as you're fucking told or I'll snap your neck. Understand?' The grip tightened on his throat. 'I asked you if you fucking understand?' Mr Barnes tried to nod. His eyes were filling with tears. The man released his grip and Mr Barnes gasped for breath.

The two other men walked into the hall. One of them closed the door behind them.

'Who else is in the house?' hissed the man.

'Just my wife.'

'What about Standing and your daughter?'

'They left.'

'When?'

'A couple of hours ago.'

The man put his face up close, so close that Mr Barnes could smell garlic on his breath. 'Where did they go?'

'I don't know,' said Mr Barnes.

One of the men was peering at the framed photographs on the wall.

His wife appeared in the doorway of the sitting room. 'Who is it?' she asked. 'Is it Bobby-Ray?'

The man stepped away from Mr Barnes and turned to face her. 'We're friends of Bobby-Ray's,' he said. He flashed her a big smile. 'Old friends,' he said.

'Oh that's nice,' said Mrs Barnes. 'Would you like coffee? And I have muffins.'

The man grinned. 'Muffins sound good,' he said.

Mrs Barnes headed for the kitchen and the man followed her. Mr Barnes walked after them. He was trembling. The two other heavies brought up the rear.

Mrs Barnes switched on the kettle and gathered together five cups and saucers. Some of the muffins she had made earlier were on a plate on the table and she waved at them and told the men to help themselves. The three visitors grabbed a muffin each as Mr Barnes stood in the doorway, watching nervously. He had no idea what to do. The men were younger and bigger and stronger than he was, and the two guns in the house were hunting rifles locked in a steel case in the basement.

The man with the goatee nodded his approval at Mrs Barnes. 'These are tasty muffins,' he said.

'They're my mother's recipe,' said Mrs Barnes. 'She's dead now.'

'I'm sorry to hear that. I bet Bobby-Ray loves these muffins.'

'Oh, he does,' she said. She opened the fridge and took out a carton of milk. 'Bobby-Ray is out fighting the A-Rabs.'

'Is he now?'

She frowned. 'I think so.' She looked over at her husband, her frown deepening. 'Where is Bobby-Ray? Was he here today?'

'No honey, he wasn't here today.'

'But Kaitlyn was, wasn't she? I remember Kaitlyn was here. With her friend.'

'Just make the tea, honey,' said Mr Barnes.

The man with the goatee pointed a warning finger at Mr Barnes. He was smiling but his eyes were as hard as flint. 'Let your lovely wife talk, Mr Barnes.'

'She isn't well,' whispered Mr Barnes.

'She seems fine to me,' said the man.

'She doesn't know what she's saying.'

The man's companions walked over to stand next to Mr Barnes, intimidating him with their presence. He folded his arms and stared at the floor.

The man took another bite of his muffin. 'Kaitlyn is your daughter, isn't she?' he asked Mrs Barnes.

Mrs Barnes nodded. The kettle finished boiling and she poured water into a cafetière. 'She was here today. She took some muffins with her. And an apple pie that I made.'

'Did she now? Where was she going?'

'To the cabin.' She looked over at her husband. 'That's right, isn't it? Kaitlyn is going to the cabin with that nice man. What was his name again?'

The man looked over at Mr Barnes. 'The cabin, you say? Where is this cabin?'

Mr Barnes continued to stare at the floor.

'We used to go to the cabin a lot but these days not so much,' said Mrs Barnes, pouring coffee into the cups.

The man went over to Mr Barnes and poked him in the chest. 'The cabin,' he said. 'Where is it?'

Mr Barnes shook his head. 'Please,' he said, as tears streamed down his face. 'Please just leave us alone.'

35

Bobby-Ray led Standing and Kaitlyn through the woods, pointing out the occasional trap that he'd set. After about a mile the track opened into a clearing that bordered a large lake. There was a small log cabin with a wooden porch overlooking the water. There was a line of washing drying across the porch and two wooden rocking chairs. 'Home sweet home,' said Bobby-Ray.

Trees surrounded the lake and Standing couldn't see any other cabins or buildings. There was a small rowing boat on the shore with two oars inside.

'So no one else lives near here?' asked Standing.

'It's all a designated wilderness area, pretty much. Our land is this clearing, down to the lake, and about halfway up the hill. The nearest neighbour is over there.' He pointed to the west. 'But the guy who owns it is a lawyer in Sacramento and he's only here for weekends during the hunting season.'

There was a babbling stream running down the hill towards the lake. Bobby-Ray went over and placed the carrier bag containing the cans of beer into the stream.

The sky was darkening overhead and the brightest stars were already visible. Kaitlyn opened the door to the cabin and carried her bags inside. Standing followed her.

The floor was bare wood dotted with thick rugs. The furniture was old and battered, including a wooden coffee table and two overstuffed leather sofas with thick Native American blankets thrown over them. There was a rough wood cabinet and a wooden trunk, on which there was an oil lamp. Bobby-Ray came in behind them and propped his rifle by the side of the door. 'No electricity here, so we use lamps if we need light, and I brought a couple of flashlights with me,' he said.

'What about bathroom arrangements?' asked Standing.

Bobby-Ray laughed. 'Didn't Kaitlyn tell you?'

Standing shook his head.

'The toilet is on the edge of the clearing. A wooden hut over a hole. Every few months we fill in the hole, dig another hole and move the hut.' He laughed at the look of surprise on Standing's face. 'Come on,' he said. 'You've shat in enough plastic bags in your time. A hole in the ground is a step up from that.'

'I guess so,' said Standing.

'We shower using water from the lake,' said Bobby-Ray. 'We have a rubber bladder thing that we fill with lake water and we hang it up at the back of the cabin. There's a nozzle on the bottom and you get about two minutes of water from it. If you hang it up for three or four hours before you use it, the sun warms it.'

He went over to a kitchen area, where there was a wood-burning stove. 'Coffee?' he asked. There was a metal coffee pot and he put it on one of the hotplates, then opened the front of the stove and shoved in two chunks of wood. 'It'll take the beer an hour or two to chill.'

'Coffee sounds good,' said Standing, dropping down onto a sofa. There was an ornate dream catcher on the wall behind him, peppered with turquoise and blue beads. The cabin felt homely, albeit grubby. There was a layer of dust over most of the furniture and cobwebs in the ceiling corners.

Bobby-Ray made coffee while Kaitlyn took out the muffins and apple pie and put them on plates. Kaitlyn joined Standing on the sofa and Bobby-Ray sat in a matching leather armchair that was also covered with a Native American blanket.

'What are you doing here, Bobby-Ray?' asked Standing.

'Lying low,' said Bobby-Ray.

'You're hiding,' said Standing. 'I get that. But from who? The cops?'

'From everybody,' said Bobby-Ray. He picked up a piece of pie and bit into it. He nodded his appreciation at Kaitlyn. 'Mom makes a great pie.'

'Bobby-Ray, we went to the motel where you were staying,' said Kaitlyn. 'We found the FBI agents.'

Bobby-Ray nodded. 'They tried to kill me.'

'But you killed them?' asked Standing.

'They gave me no choice, Matt. It was kill or be killed.'

'What happened? How did you get into this mess?'

Bobby-Ray laughed. 'It's a long story.'

'We've got time,' said Standing. 'So tell me what happened. Right from the start.'

Bobby-Ray sipped his coffee and nodded. 'I was set up. One of the Russian bodyguards killed our client and was trying to frame me for it. He coldcocked me in the hall and when I came to he'd killed the client and the rest of the bodyguards. With my fucking gun. He started shooting at me and I barely managed to get out of the house. I went home and picked up my truck. With hindsight, not a smart move but I wanted to be mobile. No one was watching my place so I grabbed the truck and drove. Then I got a call from Faith Hogan, John Keenan's number two. She wanted to know what was happening and I told her. She told me that I should ditch my phone and buy a throwaway.'

'Why did she say that?'

'She said Keenan wanted to keep his distance until they were sure what had happened.'

Standing frowned. 'That's a strange thing to ask you to do,' he said.

'Not really. If the cops did think that Redrock was behind the killings, any calls afterwards might look like conspiracy. She said they needed to get all their ducks in a row before going to the cops with our side of the story.'

'That's what she said?'

'I think so, yeah. Pretty much. It wasn't my idea to chuck the phone, anyway. She said I should get a throw-away phone and find somewhere to lie low and then call her back.'

'Call her, not Keenan?'

'She said he was busy dealing with the fallout and that she had been assigned to babysit me until we'd got it resolved.'

Standing grimaced. 'Just so you know, John Keenan told me he'd never heard anything from you after the killing, that you just went dark and he had no idea where you were.'

'Fuck,' said Bobby-Ray. 'Faith must have been lying to me.'

'So what happened then?'

'So I got a throwaway phone and I called Faith Hogan back. She told me that I'm to stay under the radar and book into a motel, somewhere quiet where I won't be seen. At that point I start to get worried, it's like Redrock is distancing itself from me. So I'm thinking that maybe they're getting ready to hang me out to dry. And I can see their point, right? Lipov used my gun to kill the client and the other bodyguards. Who's going to believe that he set me up? Plus, he stayed in the house and I ran, which has to make me look as guilty as fuck, right?'

'It would have made everything much simpler if you'd stayed,' said Standing.

'He was shooting at me, Matt. And I wasn't armed.'

'I'm just saying,' said Standing. He shrugged. 'Anyway, that's water under the bridge. We have to play the hand we've been dealt.'

'Right,' said Bobby-Ray. 'So I was getting a bad feeling about the whole scenario then, which is why I called Kaitlyn and asked her to call you.'

'Bad feeling? What do you mean?'

'The way Keenan seemed to be distancing himself from me. I started to think that maybe I was being set up as the fall guy and wanted a friend in my corner.' He grinned. 'Thanks for coming, by the way.'

'No problem,' said Standing. 'You'd have done the same for me. So what happened then? What did you do?'

'I found a motel and I made another call to Faith. She wanted to know where I was and told me to stay there and not go out until she got back to me. So that's what I did. I sat and I waited. I kept the TV on but there was nothing about Koshkin being killed. Nothing at all. Then after a few hours there was a knock on the door and there's two Feds there, asking if I'm Bobby-Ray Barnes. How the hell they knew I was there I have no idea because I used an assumed name and paid in cash. But they knew. So I let them in. They ask me where I've been and why I'm in the motel, but they're being really weird, you know. They keep moving, in front of me and behind me and they keep looking at each other like something's about to happen. Then one of them says something to me and I answer him, and then I sense that the other one is up to something and I turn around and he's screwing a silencer into his gun.' He shrugged. 'I just went into overdrive, like you do.'

'We were there, mate, we know what happened.'

'It wasn't my fault, Matt, they were there to kill me. Why else would they have silencers?'

'You're preaching to the converted,' said Standing. 'We were attacked as well, by guys with automatic weapons. They killed the motel clerk and came this close to killing us.'

'What the fuck's going on, Matt? What have I gotten into?'

'It's all to do with the Russian mafia, and an oligarch who had it in for the client. A guy called Erik Markov. He wanted Koshkin dead and someone decided it would be a good idea to frame you for it.'

Bobby-Ray ran his hands through his hair. 'So I'm fucked?'

'There's good news and bad news,' said Standing. 'The good news is that we have definitive proof that Lipov and not you killed Koshkin and the bodyguards.'

'Seriously?'

Standing nodded. 'Seriously. We found the gloves that

he was wearing and the silencer he used and both will have his prints and DNA on them.'

Bobby-Ray's jaw dropped. 'No way.'

'He'd hidden them in the kitchen. I was in the house with John Keenan and Paul Dutch. But the bad news is that they're both dead.'

'What!'

'We went to the mansion with a couple of LAPD detectives, but when we found the stuff Lipov had hidden, one of the detectives pulled out a gun and started shooting. He killed his colleague and he killed Keenan and Dutch before I could stop him.'

'You killed him?'

Standing nodded. 'Eventually.'

Bobby-Ray cursed under his breath. 'What the fuck are we going to do? Who do we go to? We can't trust anybody. We can't trust Redrock, we can't trust the FBI and we can't trust the LAPD. That doesn't leave much, does it?'

'That's the problem, the Solntsevskaya are everywhere.'

'Solntsev-what?'

'The Russian mafia,' said Standing. 'Mean sons of bitches who have managed to infiltrate themselves into organisations around the world. They've got links to the Kremlin and make money from drugs, trafficking, arms, extortion. You name it, these guys do it, and they kill to protect their organisation.'

'So who do we go to, Matt?' asked Kaitlyn. 'We have the evidence, who do we show it to?'

'I'm going to need to sleep on that,' said Standing. He looked around the cabin. 'How many beds are there?'

'There are two bunk beds in there,' said Kaitlyn,

nodding at a door to their right. 'That's where Bobby-Ray and I usually sleep. Mom and Dad sleep in the main bedroom.'

'I've been using the bunk bed,' said Bobby-Ray. 'Why doesn't Matt sleep with me and you can have the other bedroom to yourself?'

'That's very brotherly of you,' said Kaitlyn.

'I just don't fancy sharing a bed with Matt,' said Bobby-Ray.

'Mate, we slept together in Syria often enough when we were on patrol.'

'For warmth,' said Bobby-Ray. He grinned at his sister. 'It can get really cold in the desert.'

'I'll take the big bed,' said Kaitlyn. 'You can have the bunk beds.'

36

It had been dark for several hours by the time the two black SUVs pulled up next to Standing's Ford Escape. There were three heavies in the first car, hard men that Oleg Ivchenko used as enforcers and assassins.

Ivchenko was in the front passenger seat of the second vehicle. Driving him was one of his most trusted operatives, a former Spetsnaz special forces soldier called Valeria Demidova. Demidova was female, in the sense that she had only X chromosomes, but there was nothing at all feminine about her, other than her name. Her first name meant strong and she was, as an ox. She had put on weight since leaving Spetsnaz and if anything that had made her even more formidable. Ivchenko had seen her take out three men single-handedly, and she had taken several punches to her square jaw with no signs of feeling them. She was wearing a black leather bomber jacket and blue Valentino jeans and with her close-cropped jet black hair most people who saw her assumed she was a man.

Sitting in the back was Ivchenko's nephew, a big bruiser of a man called Gregory Nesterov. Nesterov wasn't smart and sometimes had to have things explained to him twice, but he was fiercely loyal and Ivchenko trusted him with his life. Nesterov almost never left Ivchenko's side; he was with him night and day and even slept in the next room. Ivchenko was sure that Nesterov would take a bullet for him, because one night in Moscow he had done just that. That was in the days before Ivchenko had been sent to head up the Solntsevskaya's Los Angeles operations, back when Ivchenko was a foot soldier in Moscow, running a kidnapping ring that seized the children of wealthy Muscovites and held them until ransoms were paid. A rival gang had taken offence at one of the victims Ivchenko's team had chosen and had sent a group of armed thugs to teach him a lesson. They had ambushed him as he walked to his car and he had been shot in the hip before he managed to pull out his own gun and kill two of his attackers. He was too slow to get the third, who fired at point-blank range but Nesterov managed to throw himself in front of his uncle and took a bullet in the chest. Ivchenko fired at the attacker but he ran off. Ivchenko drove his nephew to hospital and he survived. Two weeks later Ivchenko found and tortured the shooter for a whole night before killing him and throwing his body parts into the Moskva river.

'What do you think, boss?' asked Demidova. She tapped her chunky fingers on the steering wheel. There was a single gold band on her wedding finger, the only jewellery she wore.

Ivchenko stroked his goatee thoughtfully. They had flashlights in the car, but the lights would mean that they would be seen and they would lose the element of surprise. In a perfect world they would have come with night vision equipment but the world wasn't always perfect, especially not the world that Ivchenko moved in.

Ivchenko looked at his wristwatch, a gold Rolex Cellini

Prince with two dials that told the time in California and
Moscow. 'It'll be light in four hours,' he said. 'We'll wait
and head to the cabin at dawn.'

'Right, boss.'

Ivchenko opened his window a few inches and lit a
cigarette. Four hours wasn't long to wait. He took out
his mobile and cursed when he saw that he wasn't getting
a signal, then smiled as he realised that no signal meant
that when the shooting started no one would be able to
phone for help.

37

S tanding heard a noise from the other side of the room and he sat up, reaching for his gun, immediately wide awake.

'It's me,' said Bobby-Ray. 'Don't shoot, I've got coffee.' He kicked the door closed behind him.

Standing blinked. Light was coming in through the thin curtains and he could hear birds singing in the distance. 'What time is it?' he asked.

'Time doesn't mean anything out here,' said Bobby-Ray. 'Dawn's breaking. I get up with the light and there's no point in going out when it's dark.'

Standing sat up. 'How long are you planning to stay here?'

'Until I know it's safe.'

Standing ran his hands through his hair. 'That could be forever,' he said.

Bobby-Ray sat down on the end of Standing's bunk and handed him a mug of coffee. 'The way I see it, at the moment everyone's out to get me. The Russian mafia, the FBI, the cops, even my own bosses. And it's clear that they don't want to take me in alive. Until that changes, I'm better off here.'

'We've got the evidence to clear you,' said Standing. 'We just have to get it into the right hands.' He sat up.

'They don't care whether I did it or not,' said Bobby-Ray. 'They just want me dead so that Lipov is in the clear. The Russians know exactly what happened, they don't care about the evidence. They just want to protect Lipov.'

Standing smiled ruefully. 'Yeah, well that boat has sailed.' He drank his coffee.

'What do you mean?'

'I didn't want to say anything while Kaitlyn was around, but Lipov's dead. It was pretty messy.'

'Messy in what way?'

'I was just talking to him and he attacked me. He was a hard bastard. He didn't go easily.'

'I'm sorry.'

'Sorry for what? It wasn't your fault. I only went to talk to him, he made the decision to take it to the next level. But it means that he's not in a position to ever tell what happened. Or more importantly, to reveal who paid him.'

'And who do you think paid him to kill Koshkin?'

Standing gulped down some coffee. 'His business partner, maybe. Erik Markov. He's connected to the Russian mafia. But with Lipov dead, I don't see that we'll ever be able to prove that.'

'But we can prove that Lipov killed Koshkin.'

'Sure. His prints will be on the inside of the gloves. And the silencer will fit into your gun.'

'You don't think they'll try to pin the silencer on me?'

'There's no way you could have hidden the silencer with the gloves in the kitchen,' said Standing. 'The problem is, who do we give the evidence to? We only get the one chance and if we get it wrong . . .' He shrugged and left the sentence unfinished.

'What about someone at Redrock?' said Bobby-Ray. 'It's in their interests to prove that it wasn't one of their employees who killed the client, right?'

'John Keenan would have been the best bet,' said Standing. 'He seemed a good guy.'

Bobby-Ray nodded. 'He was. What about Faith Hogan? His number two? We can't trust her, can we?'

Standing grimaced. 'She said she talked to Keenan but Keenan denied that you'd been in touch, so she can't have said anything to him.'

'So she's part of this? She's tied in with the Russians?'

'I think she has to be,' said Standing. 'From what you said, it wasn't long after you told her where you were that the FBI agents turned up.' He shrugged. 'Sure, it could be a coincidence, but if we do approach someone at Redrock we might be better doing it at a higher level. Keenan's boss, maybe. Though again, how do we know who we can trust?'

'You could put out some feelers. I reckon I'm safe enough here for a while.'

Standing looked around the cabin. 'I hope so,' he said.

38

I vchenko couldn't see much of the sky through the tree canopy overhead, but the little that he could see was starting to glow red. He climbed out of the SUV and lit a cigarette. He had napped over the past few hours but hadn't really slept. His nephew had been in a deep sleep for most of the night, snoring and occasionally mumbling to himself in Russian.

Demidova had stayed awake, sitting quietly and staring out through the windscreen, moving only to sip water from a plastic bottle. When Ivchenko got out of the SUV she joined him and stood with her hands in her pockets. Ivchenko looked at the two dials of his watch. It was ten minutes to six in California and ten to four in the afternoon in Moscow.

He walked around to the rear of the SUV and opened the door. There was a black nylon holdall there and he unzipped it.

The three men in the other SUV climbed out. Leo Sorokin, Niko Tarasov and Petr Okulov. They were all wearing hoodies and jeans, though Sorokin had topped his off with a leather jacket. They went to the back of their SUV and pulled the door open.

Ivchenko pulled an Uzi out of the holdall. It was one

of his favourite guns. The Israelis knew how to make weapons and the Uzi was hard to beat, certainly for close-up fighting against multiple targets. The version Ivchenko was holding was the Uzi Pro, with a grip and handguard made of polymer to keep the weight down, and designed to allow two-hand operation to reduce the tendency of the original Uzi to pull to the side when on automatic fire. The Uzi Pro weighed less than two and a half kilos and without a stock was just thirty centimetres long. There were three magazines in the holdall, each holding 25 cartridges. Ivchenko slotted one magazine into the gun and put the others into his pockets, one on the left, the other on the right.

He stepped away from the SUV and Demidova reached into the holdall. She took out a Kalashnikov AK-74, a weapon she had used extensively during her Spetsnaz days. Demidova always claimed the AK-74's lighter ammunition meant that it had less recoil and was marginally more accurate than the AK-47, though the only times she had used it in LA she had been up close and personal and accuracy hadn't been an issue. The only way to tell the two models apart at a glance was from the curvature of the magazine. The AK-74 magazine had less of a curve than the AK-47 and the designs were not interchangeable.

Ivchenko knocked on the side window and Nesterov opened his eyes. He rubbed them sleepily then nodded when he saw his uncle with the Uzi. He scrambled out of the SUV and went to join Demidova who was shoving a spare magazine into her pocket.

Sorokin, Tarasov and Okulov were slotting magazines into their weapons. Sorokin had a Kalashnikov AK-47 with a folding stock and Tarasov and Okulov both had

MAC-10 machine pistols, the .45 calibre version, with two-stage Sionics silencers that both cut down on the noise they made but more importantly, made them easier to control on full automatic when they would fire at a rate of more than a thousand rounds a minute.

Demidova walked over to Ivchenko, her AK-74 down at her side, muzzle pointing at the ground.

'I need you to take point on this, Valeria,' said Ivchenko. 'Okay?'

'*Da*,' said Demidova. '*Nyet* problem.'

'Barnes is a former Navy SEAL, so be careful,' he said. He saw her start to grin and he knew that she was about to tell him that Spetsnaz was the best special forces unit in the world and that Navy SEALs didn't scare her. He held up his hand to cut her short. 'Just be careful, that's all I'm saying. And watch out for the British guy, there's something about him that worries me.'

'*Nyet* problem,' she repeated.

Okulov, Tarasov and Sorokin walked over to join Demidova. Nesterov shoved a magazine into the butt of a Glock and shut the rear door of the SUV. Ivchenko waved him over.

'Valeria will lead us to the cabin,' said Ivchenko. He gestured with his Uzi at a small break in the undergrowth. 'We head that way. North-east. According to the old man, the cabin is about a mile along that track. When we get to the cabin, we kill anyone we find there. No one will hear us. We're in the middle of nowhere.'

'What about the girl?' asked Nesterov. He had been helping to run the syndicate's west coast trafficking operations and liked nothing better than breaking in new girls.

'By the time we've finished, they're all dead,' said

Ivchenko. 'But if you want to have some fun first, knock yourself out.'

Nesterov leered and nodded his approval.

Ivchenko nodded at Demidova and she headed for the track. Ivchenko patted his nephew on the back. 'Today you'll be blooded, hopefully,' he said, speaking in Russian. 'Your first kill.'

'I'm ready,' said Nesterov. He grinned. 'I'm looking forward to it.'

Demidova disappeared into the undergrowth and the rest of the Russians followed her.

39

Standing carried his mug of coffee out of the bedroom. He had pulled on the same clothes he'd been wearing the previous day. Bobby-Ray was adding wood to the stove in the kitchen area. He used a cloth to pick up the metal coffee pot and pour more coffee into Standing's mug. 'Fancy breakfast?'

'Sounds good,' said Standing.

'I've got eggs. And I can use the cheese and bread you brought. And the fruit.'

'What have you been eating since you got here?'

'I brought quite a bit of dry stuff with me. Pasta, canned stuff. And there are plenty of fish in the lake.' He nodded at his rifle, propped up against the cabin door. 'My plan was to go hunting for fresh meat at some point. The water from the stream that runs into the lake is drinkable but I brought plenty of water purification tablets with me.'

'So you could stay here for months?'

'If necessary, sure. But hopefully it won't come to that.' He put the coffee pot back on the stove. 'I've filled the shower bag for you if you want a shower. It's around the back of the cabin, and there's a towel there.'

'Cheers,' said Standing.

They heard a scream of pain outside, off in the distance. It went on for a second or two and then abruptly stopped.

Bobby-Ray rushed over to the door and opened it. The two men listened intently.

'What the fuck was that?' asked Standing eventually.

'A deer maybe. There are plenty of predators out here. Bear, mountain lion, coyote, bobcat.'

'It sounded human,' said Standing.

Bobby-Ray nodded. 'Yeah.' He picked up his hunting rifle.

Standing ducked back into the bedroom and reappeared a few seconds later holding his Beretta. 'Shall we wake up Kaitlyn?' he whispered.

He shook his head. 'She'll be safer inside.'

They listened again but heard nothing.

'The birds have gone quiet,' whispered Bobby-Ray.

'That's a bad sign,' said Standing.

Bobby-Ray nodded. 'Stick close,' he said. 'I'll keep you away from the traps.' He bent double as he ran out of the cabin to the edge of the clearing. Standing followed him, keeping the barrel of the Beretta pointing at the ground.

40

Ivchenko kept his hand clamped over his nephew's mouth and hissed at him to stop struggling. Nesterov's foot had gone through a thin layer of twigs and had been impaled by two sharpened sticks in the hole. The makeshift stakes had penetrated right through Nesterov's Nikes and the foot inside. The stakes were smeared with blood but there was something else, too.

'Shit,' said Demidova, a look of distaste on her face. 'He smeared the sticks with his own shit.'

'Why would he do that?'

'To cause infection. Punji sticks they call them. It's an old Viet Cong trick.'

'What do we do?' asked Ivchenko.

'We can leave the sticks in until we get him to an emergency room, but if we do that he won't be able to walk. If we pull the sticks out, he'll bleed.'

'He has to walk,' said Ivchenko. He tightened his hand over his nephew's mouth and whispered into his ear in Russian. 'This will hurt, but it will be over soon.' Nesterov began to struggle but Ivchenko held him firm. He nodded at Demidova. She grabbed Nesterov's ankle and pulled hard. Nesterov went into spasm as she yanked the foot off the stakes.

'Be a fucking man,' hissed Ivchenko, in English this time.

Nesterov was shaking and his eyes were closed. Ivchenko slowly released his grip on his nephew's mouth. Nesterov's face was wet with tears.

Demidova undid the laces of Nesterov's training shoe and pulled it off. Nesterov grunted and Ivchenko slapped his hand over his mouth again. Demidova took off Nesterov's bloodstained sock, unscrewed the cap off a bottle of water and poured it over the injured foot.

'We need to move,' said Ivchenko, standing up. He prodded Nesterov with his foot. 'Can you walk?'

Nesterov nodded.

'Then get your shoe back on and follow us,' said Ivchenko. He nodded at Demidova. 'Now we move, and we move quickly,' said Ivchenko. 'But we spread out. If they heard us they'll be heading this way.' He waved to the right and pointed at Sorokin and Tarasov. 'That way.' The two men grunted and started forcing their way through the vegetation on the right. 'Petr, to the left.' Okulov flashed him a thumbs-up and headed off.

Demidova started following the track again and Ivchenko tucked in behind her, trying to follow exactly in her footsteps, his Uzi clasped to his chest.

41

B obby-Ray stopped and held up his right hand, clenched into a fist. Standing froze. There was something moving through the undergrowth to their left. Bobby-Ray had his rifle at the ready, his head cocked to the side as he listened. There was more noise, off in the distance. The brushing of leaves and the snapping of a twig. Standing's finger was on the trigger of his Beretta and he scanned his surroundings.

Bobby-Ray unclenched his fist and moved forward. Standing followed him. A bush in front of them rustled and then a small deer dashed out, sprang to the side, leapt into the air and then ran between them. It disappeared off into the distance springing from side to side as if it feared they were chasing it.

Bobby-Ray flashed Standing a tight smile and they started moving again. Bobby-Ray pointed ahead then gave Standing an 'OK' sign and pointed to the left, letting him know the area was safe to move through.

They heard another rustle ahead of them and again they froze. Something was moving towards them and it was larger than the deer. They crouched down, senses on full alert.

They caught a glimpse of a big man wearing a dark

blue hoodie and jeans, cradling a MAC-10 with a large silencer. Bobby-Ray slowly hung his rifle across his shoulder using its sling and pulled his hunting knife from its scabbard. He looked over at Standing and Standing nodded. The quieter the better.

The man approaching them clearly wasn't used to walking through undergrowth and his progress was accompanied by the cracking of twigs and the rustling of leaves and the occasional Russian curse.

Standing couldn't hear anyone else nearby. They kept low until the man was almost on top of them and then Bobby-Ray sprang forward, pushing the MAC-10 to the side with his left hand and thrusting the knife into the man's temple. Standing pulled the gun from the man's grasp as Bobby-Ray lowered him to the floor. The man shuddered once and went still. They both froze, listening for any sign that they had been heard. Nothing.

Bobby-Ray wiped the knife on the ground and then slotted it back into its scabbard. The MAC-10 was much heavier than the Beretta but with the silencer on it would make a lot less noise, so Standing decided to use it instead of his handgun. He shoved the Beretta into his belt. Bobby-Ray was already moving ahead, his rifle back in his hands.

Standing checked the MAC-10. It was set to full automatic. With a fire rate of greater than a thousand rounds a minute it was the perfect way to waste ammunition. He flicked the selector switch to SEMI so that it would fire single shots.

Bobby-Ray stopped again, made a fist and then pointed off to the left. Standing listened. Two people. Trying to move quietly but failing. Bobby-Ray pointed for Standing to go left while he would go straight ahead.

Standing moved slowly, taking care where he placed his feet and trying to minimise contact with the bushes around him. He came across a massive cobweb, more than three feet across, with a black spider in the middle. He ducked under it, and when he straightened up he was looking at a big man holding a Kalashnikov AK-47 across his leather jacket. His eyes widened when he saw Standing but he was holding his gun awkwardly and he didn't have his finger over the trigger, so Standing had all the time in the world to aim his MAC-10 and put a bullet in the centre of his face. The back of the man's head exploded across the vegetation, glossy red against green, and he slumped to the ground. The silencer cut down on a lot of noise but it still made a loud popping sound.

Standing heard another rustle to his left and then three quick crunching steps and another man appeared. He was holding a MAC-10, the twin of the one Standing was using. Standing kept his left hand on the insulated silencer for greater accuracy and shot the man just below the throat. Blood gushed down over his hoodie and splattered over his gun, which dropped to the ground. The man had just enough time to raise his hands to his throat before the life faded from his eyes and he buckled and fell into a bush.

Bobby-Ray appeared at Standing's side. 'Nice work,' he said appreciatively. He slung his rifle over his shoulder and picked up the dead man's MAC-10. 'Don't mind if I do,' he whispered.

The two men stood stock still and listened. There

was complete silence around them. They stayed where they were, breathing tidally, in and out with the least amount of movement, as they concentrated on their surroundings.

G regory Nesterov winced as he finished tightening the lace on his Nike. He stood up slowly, then tried to put his weight on his injured foot. It hurt like hell and he could feel blood still oozing from the wound, but he was determined not to be left behind.

He heard a popping sound in the distance, followed by another shortly afterwards. He frowned as he tried to make sense of the sounds. Tarasov and Okulov had silencers on their MAC-10s but they usually fired rapid bursts.

Nesterov listened but didn't hear anything else. He checked his phone again but there was no signal. He put his phone back in his pocket, bent down and picked up his Glock. He gritted his teeth in pain as he straightened up. He took a step down the track, wincing again. He was going to make that bitch pay for this. His uncle had kept him away from the girl while he had her prisoner in his compound, but now it was clear she was up for grabs. He'd never had a deaf girl before and he wondered whether she'd be able to scream. He'd find out soon enough. But first he had to get to the cabin. He took another step, grunted, and then another. He'd make the bitch suffer before she died, he promised himself.

S tanding could hear Bobby-Ray moving off to his right. The track was further off to the left and Standing was heading in that direction. Moving through dense vegetation was a tense business at the best of times, but when you knew there were men with guns heading towards you, the tension became almost unbearable. In a combat situation where bullets were flying and shells were exploding, Standing's instincts would kick in and he would react without thinking. But moving through areas of limited visibility meant he had nothing to react to. All he could do was to wait for the enemy to appear.

He took another two steps and then stopped and listened. He heard a rustle at his two o'clock but figured that was almost certainly Bobby-Ray. He moved his head slowly from side to side. The thickness of the vegetation where he was meant that he couldn't see more than three feet ahead of him so he was depending on his ears. Something snapped over to his right. He turned towards the sound, his finger on the trigger of the MAC-10.

He pushed forward slowly. An insect buzzed by his ear but he ignored it. Sweat was dripping down his forehead and he wiped it away with his left hand. As he brought his arm away he saw Ivchenko, holding what looked like an Uzi. Ivchenko roared and pulled the trigger, sending a hail of bullets that smacked through the bush to his left. The Uzi was notoriously difficult to control one-handed, especially when it was set on automatic. Standing got off a shot with his MAC-10 but he was also holding his weapon one-handed and his shot whizzed over the Russian's head.

Ivchenko continued to spray bullets and Standing had to dive to the side, hitting the ground hard. He brought the MAC-10 up but all he could see was vegetation. He rolled over and came up in a crouch. The firestorm had stopped but almost immediately he heard the click of an empty magazine being ejected, followed by the click-clack of a fresh one being rammed home.

He heard two loud pops over to his right. That had to be Bobby-Ray's MAC-10 but there was no way of knowing if he'd hit his target.

Standing stayed low, sweeping his limited area of vision with his gun, his finger tensing on the trigger.

Something snapped over to his left and he whirled around but there was nothing to see, just bushes and trees. Then the leaves on the bush next to him exploded as bullets ripped through them and again he had to dive to avoid the carnage. He hit the ground and rolled and came up next to a redwood. He kept the tree at his back as he got up. The volley of bullets came to an end and once more he heard the metallic clicks as the magazine was replaced.

He heard a crack off to his left and a bullet thwacked into the tree so close to his head that fragments of bark peppered his temple.

A man was shooting at him with a Kalashnikov that

looked like an AK-47 but the sound was slightly off and he figured that it was probably a lower-calibre AK-74. He ducked just as a second round thwacked into the tree. He fired twice but the shooter had already disappeared. He bobbed his head from side to side, trying to see through the vegetation but it was too dense.

He moved away from the tree and as he did, the figure with the AK-74 popped up again, further over to his left. The carbine was up but Standing fired first. This time he had his left hand on the silencer to help absorb the recoil and he saw the round smack into the shoulder of his target. Then Bobby-Ray was on his feet rushing towards the figure, firing three times as he ran. All three hit their target and the figure fell back in a shower of blood.

Standing moved forward, knowing that Ivchenko was still in the vicinity with a fresh magazine in place. Bobby-Ray disappeared from view again.

Standing heard movement ahead but relaxed when he realised it was the figure with the Kalashnikov, twitching before death. As he got closer, Standing saw it was a woman, though her features were so masculine there had been no way of knowing that when he was shooting her. Not that it would have made a difference to the outcome. She had been trying to kill them and that was all that mattered. As Standing looked down at her she went still.

There was the rustle of vegetation off to his left and he swung his MAC-10 towards the sound. Ivchenko's tendency to fire off a whole clip at random made him far more dangerous than a professional soldier firing off single shots; there was no way of predicting when he'd fire or in what direction.

A twig cracked. Then another. Standing tensed and ducked down, his subconscious making himself a smaller target, even though the calculating part of his brain knew that it would make precious little difference if the Russian unloaded the weapon in his direction.

Despite the pressure he was under, his heart was beating normally and his breathing was slow and regular. He wasn't scared, or even worried. He had a task to do and he would carry out that task to the best of his ability until he was either successful or no longer capable of carrying it out.

There was a sudden thudding sound at his one o'clock, followed by another. It wasn't footfall, something had been thrown and he realised it was almost certainly Bobby-Ray, trying to cause a diversion. He was throwing something, rocks maybe, in the hope of attracting the Russian's attention. Standing took another step forward and then moved around a clump of saplings. He caught a glimpse of black between the fronds of a bush ahead of him and then he saw Ivchenko, his Uzi held out in front of him with both hands. Ivchenko tensed as he heard two more rocks fly through the undergrowth and thud into the forest floor.

Standing took a step forward to get a better view but his foot cracked a twig and Ivchenko started to turn. His head turned before his body and his eyes widened when he saw Standing. Standing's finger was already on the trigger and his left hand was holding the silencer steady. He squeezed off one shot and the round smacked into the Russian's shoulder. The Uzi started to fire but Ivchenko wasn't aiming, it was an automatic reaction to the shock of being hit. Standing fired again as Ivchenko continued to turn and the round clipped a chunk off the top of the Russian's head. Ivchenko was only about forty feet away but the MAC-10 was inaccurate at the best of times. The Uzi was still spraying bullets but most of them were thudding into the ground. Standing tightened his grip on the MAC-10, took aim again, and fired two shots in quick succession that both hit Ivchenko in the chest. The Uzi dropped from his fingers and the Russian fell backwards, arms outstretched, collapsing into a bush.

Standing's eyes were watering from the cordite in the air and he blinked away tears as he scanned left and right, wondering if it was over or if there was more to come.

44

Gregory Nesterov limped into the clearing. He could feel his training shoe filling with blood and he knew that moving was only making it worse, but he gritted his teeth and ignored his pain. He heard more rapid shooting off to his left as he walked slowly towards the cabin. It sounded like his uncle's Uzi. Sweat was pouring down his face and he was finding it hard to breathe; it was as if his chest was being held in an unforgiving vice.

The door to the cabin was closed and there didn't seem to be anyone around. He gently eased open the door and moved inside. His injured foot was throbbing but his heart was pounding and he barely felt the pain as he waved his Glock around, covering all the corners. There were two doors, one closed and one ajar. He moved to the open door. It was a bedroom, with bunk beds. Empty.

He turned and went back into the main room and over to the closed door. He held the gun in his right hand as he turned the handle with his left. The door was heavy and opened with a slight squeak. There were curtains over the single window but enough light was coming in to illuminate the figure lying on the bed. His heart pounded. It was the girl. She was wearing a white T-shirt and had her arms over the top of her blankets, her hair sprawled across the pillow. He licked his lips and when he swallowed he realised his mouth had gone dry. He felt himself growing hard as he thought about what he planned to do to her.

'Hey, dickhead.'

Nesterov turned to see Bobby-Ray Barnes in the doorway behind him.

'Not planning on hurting my sister, are you?'

Nesterov swung up his gun but Bobby-Ray already had the MAC-10 trained on Nesterov's chest and he pulled the trigger. The round ripped through Nesterov's heart. He crumpled and fell to the floor.

Standing joined Bobby-Ray at the doorway. 'I think that's the lot,' he said.

'For the moment,' said Bobby-Ray. 'They're not going to stop, Matt. This isn't over by a long way.'

'We'll see,' said Standing. He went over to the bedroom door and looked at the bed, where Kaitlyn was still fast asleep, her blonde hair in disarray over her pillow. He smiled and shook his head. 'She didn't hear a thing.'

'That's kinda the definition of deaf,' said Bobby-Ray, patting him on the shoulder. 'What do we do now? We've got six bodies. Do we call the cops?'

'I don't see how us calling the cops helps us. We don't know if we can trust the cops up here any more than the LAPD.'

'Do you want to bury them? We've got shovels.'

'What about the lake?' said Standing. 'It'll be easier and quicker.'

Bobby-Ray nodded. 'Probably best,' he said, closing the bedroom door. 'Let's see if we can get it done before sleeping beauty wakes up.'

45

It took Standing and Bobby-Ray the best part of two hours to dispose of the bodies of the dead gangsters. They carried them one by one to the lakeside and lined them up, side by side, close to the small boat. They filled the pockets of the corpses with rocks and then took them two at a time out into the middle of the lake. Before rolling them over the side and into the water, they used knives to puncture the lungs and slit open their stomachs. Bodies swelled up when they decomposed and allowing the gases to escape would keep the bodies on the bottom of the lake.

They dropped the guns the Russians had been using over the side, too. There was no way of knowing the history of the weapons and it wouldn't do them any good to be caught with guns that could be linked to previous murders.

When they'd finished their macabre task, they pulled the boat back onto the shore and went back to the cabin. Bobby-Ray made fresh coffee and boiled six eggs in a pan. He poured three mugs of coffee while Standing sliced bread and cheese and arranged it on three plates with some of the fruit they'd brought with them. He finished the plates off with the boiled eggs, then placed the coffee and food on the table.

Bobby-Ray went into the bedroom where Kaitlyn was still sleeping. He gently shook her shoulder to wake her up. 'Good morning,' she said sleepily. 'What time is it?'

'Time to get up,' said Bobby-Ray. 'Breakfast is ready.'

Kaitlyn followed him out of the bedroom and she sat down at the table, brushing her hair from her face. She picked up a mug of coffee, sipped it and nodded her approval. 'You always did make a great cup of coffee,' she said. She frowned as she saw the red flecks on his sleeve. 'Is that blood?'

Bobby-Ray looked down at the stains and forced a smile. 'I don't suppose you'd believe that I cut myself shaving?'

'What happened?' asked Kaitlyn.

'We had visitors, while you were asleep,' said Bobby-Ray. 'Don't worry, we took care of it.'

Kaitlyn frowned at her brother, then looked over at Standing. 'Visitors? What sort of visitors?'

'Oleg Ivchenko and his heavies,' said Standing, sitting down at the table.

'Why didn't you tell me?'

'You were asleep.'

'Matt! You could have been killed.' She looked across at Bobby-Ray. 'You, too. What were you thinking?'

'We were thinking that we'd take care of it and then make you breakfast, which we've done,' he said. He started to peel one of the boiled eggs.

'And what happened?'

Bobby-Ray shrugged but didn't answer. Instead he popped the peeled boiled egg into his mouth, whole.

Kaitlyn looked up at Standing. 'Matt?'

'Like Bobby-Ray said, we took care of it.'

'How many of them were there?'

'Six,' said Standing.

'Where are they now?'

Standing looked uncomfortable and didn't answer.

'Matt?'

'They're in the lake,' said Standing quietly.

'The lake?'

'Yeah. The lake.' He picked up a piece of cheese and ate it.

'I don't understand how you can be so relaxed about it? You killed six people.'

'Six people who came out here with the intention of killing all of us,' said Bobby-Ray. He picked up another of the boiled eggs. 'Anyway, it's over.'

'Except if Ivchenko found us, others could follow,' said Kaitlyn.

'That had occurred to us,' said Standing.

'So what's the plan?' asked Kaitlyn.

Bobby-Ray sat down at the table. 'We can't stay here, not after what's happened,' he said.

'So we go back to LA?'

Bobby-Ray looked at Standing. 'I think that's probably the best option, right?'

'I think we need to talk to Erik Markov,' said Standing. He picked up an apple.

'But he's the one who wanted Koshkin dead,' said Kaitlyn. 'He's going to want you dead as much as the Russian mafia.'

'But he's the one who can call them off,' said Standing. He bit into the apple.

'Why would he do that?'

'We explain to him that we'll be more trouble than we're worth.'

'You're going to threaten him?' said Bobby-Ray.

'He needs to know that we won't lie down and let him and his mafia mates walk all over us,' said Standing. 'What are they going to do? Keep sending gangsters to kill us and we keep killing them?'

'You think he'll just walk away?' asked Bobby-Ray.

'He's a businessman, right? An oligarch? He has to look at this like a profit and loss account. What does he gain by trying to kill us? And what does he lose?'

'So you get him to back off, what then?' asked Kaitlyn. 'The cops are still after Bobby-Ray.'

'We have the evidence that shows that Bobby-Ray didn't kill Koshkin. Once the cops have that, Bobby-Ray is in the clear and he can get on with his life and I can go back to the UK.'

'You make it sound so simple,' said Kaitlyn.

While Kaitlyn went to shower and change, Standing and Bobby-Ray packed everything and cleaned up the cabin. When Kaitlyn eventually came back into the kitchen she was wearing a blue UCLA shirt and blue jeans. They shouldered their backpacks and picked up the carrier bags and holdalls. Bobby-Ray had his hunting rifle over his shoulder and Standing had his Beretta tucked into his belt.

Bobby-Ray led them down the track and through the undergrowth to the parking area, where they loaded the bags into the back of the Escape. 'What are you going to do about their cars?' asked Kaitlyn, gesturing at the two SUVs.

'There's not much we can do,' said Bobby-Ray.

'If more mafia guys come, they'll see them,' she said.

'I don't see that matters,' said Standing.

'What about my truck?' asked Bobby-Ray.

'Leave it hidden for the time being,' said Standing. 'You don't want to be riding around LA in it, the cops will be looking for it.'

'I call shotgun,' said Kaitlyn, climbing into the front passenger seat of the Escape.

Bobby-Ray laughed and got into the back. He had his Glock and hunting rifle with him. The rest of the weapons had gone into the lake with the bodies.

It took just under two hours to drive back to Redding. Standing parked behind the Chevrolet. Kaitlyn got out of the car and went to the front door as Standing twisted around in his seat. 'Do you want to stay with your parents for a while?' he asked.

'Better not,' said Bobby-Ray. 'In fact, maybe I should just stay in the car and not see them. That way if the cops turn up, they don't have to lie.' He flashed Standing an uncomfortable smile. 'If I do talk to them, they're going to have so many questions.'

'I hear you,' said Standing. He got out of the car and went over to Kaitlyn, who was ringing the doorbell for the second time. Standing tapped her on the shoulder to get her attention. 'Maybe they went out,' he said, but Kaitlyn gestured at the car in the driveway. 'They never walk anywhere,' she said. She tried the bell a third time and when there was no response she took out her keys. She had a key to the door on her ring and she slotted it into the lock and turned it.

Standing put a hand on her arm and nodded for her to stand to the side. He pulled out his Beretta. She frowned and opened her mouth to speak but he put his finger to his lips and shook his head. He looked over his shoulder at Bobby-Ray in the car.

Bobby-Ray understood immediately and got out of the Escape with his Glock.

Standing pushed open the door. Almost immediately he heard a buzzing sound. That and the smell of decomposition told him all he needed to know. He kept his finger on the trigger as he moved down the hallway but the buzzing sound intensified as he got close to the kitchen, so he was pretty sure there was no one else alive in the house.

Bobby-Ray was at his shoulder and Standing looked across at him. Their eyes met and Standing could see the pain in them.

Bobby-Ray turned to look at his sister, who was just behind him. 'Wait here,' he mouthed.

'What's happening?' she asked, trying to peer around them.

'Just stay outside!' he hissed. 'Wait here until we tell you it's safe to come in.'

Kaitlyn went out onto the porch, hugging herself as Bobby-Ray and Standing moved down the hallway to the kitchen. Standing went in first. Mrs Barnes was lying on the floor by the stove. Her face had been beaten to a pulp and her dress was a mass of blood. Flies had settled on her face while others buzzed around.

'Oh my God, no . . .' moaned Bobby-Ray. He rushed over to his mother and knelt down next to her. 'Mom . . . Mom . . .'

Mr Barnes was sitting at the kitchen table, upright but as dead as his wife. His wrists had been separately tied to the legs of the table opposite him, forcing his arms out, and all of his fingers and thumbs had been hacked off. The table was awash with blood that had dripped down to the floor. The man's head had slumped onto his chest. One of his ears had been sliced off and his nose had a deep cut from the top to the bottom, revealing the cartilage within.

Standing shuddered. The Russians had tortured and killed Mr and Mrs Barnes, presumably to find out where the cabin was.

Standing put his hand on Bobby-Ray's shoulder and squeezed. He knew there was nothing he could say. It wasn't just that his parents were dead, it was the way they had died. Standing could only imagine the horror of their last moments. 'I'm sorry, mate,' said Standing. He'd seen countless dead bodies over the years, and been responsible for many of them. But this was different. This wasn't combat, this was the murder and torture of innocents. Standing understood warfare, he had no qualms about taking lives when it was necessary, but he doubted that he had it in him to chop off the fingers of someone just to get information from them. Cold-blooded torture wasn't in his nature, though if anyone was trying to kill him he would do whatever was necessary with zero feelings of guilt.

Standing looked over at the sink. Dozens of flies were buzzing over the discarded bloody fingers. There was a pair of pliers in the sink, and two bloody knives.

'My God, Dad!' shouted Kaitlyn.

Bobby-Ray stood up, whirled around, grabbed his sister and hustled her down the hallway, away from the kitchen. Standing could hear Kaitlyn sobbing as Bobby-Ray took her into the sitting room. Standing looked around the kitchen, wondering what to do. Calling the police wasn't an option, at least not while they were in the vicinity. But he wasn't comfortable with the idea of leaving the bodies where they were, covered in flies.

The smell was still turning his stomach. He got a bottle of water from the fridge and took it through to the sitting room. Bobby-Ray was sitting on the sofa with his arm around his sister.

Standing offered her the bottle of water and she took it but didn't open it. 'I'm so sorry, Kaitlyn,' he said.

'Why?' she asked, looking up at him with tear-stained cheeks. 'Why would they do that to my parents? They never hurt anybody, not in their whole lives.'

'Ivchenko wanted to know where the cabin was,' said Standing.

'Why didn't Dad just tell them?'

'Because he wanted to protect us,' said Bobby-Ray.

Standing nodded in agreement but he knew that Mr Barnes wouldn't have been able to stand that degree of torture for more than a few seconds. He would have told them what they wanted to know almost immediately, but the mutilations had continued. Mrs Barnes had been hit in the face and shot in the chest, so death had probably come reasonably quickly, but her husband had been hacked away at until he had bled to death from his injuries. Standing was sure that Ivchenko had done that because he'd wanted to see the man suffer. He'd taken pleasure from the killing, something that Standing had never been able to understand.

'This is all my fault,' said Kaitlyn. 'You said we should have gone straight to the cabin but I'm the one who said we should visit them and now they're dead. I should have listened to you. Shit, shit, shit.' She started to sob again. Bobby-Ray hugged her but there was nothing that Standing could do or say to make her feel better. He didn't want to walk away but at the same time he felt almost embarrassed by her grief.

The fact that the men who had killed Mr and Mrs Barnes were all dead themselves didn't make Standing feel any better. And there was an unfairness to the fact that the Russians had died quickly and with guns in their hands, while Mr Barnes had died while he was tied to a kitchen table as his fingers were hacked off one by one. He wondered whether Mrs Barnes had died first or if she had been forced to watch her husband being tortured. He shuddered. His phone buzzed in his pocket and he took it out. It was Spider Shepherd.

He walked through into the hallway and took the call. 'Where are you?' asked Shepherd.

'Still in California.'

'How's it going?'

'Not good.'

'What happened?'

'Best you don't know the specifics, that way you at least have plausible deniability.'

'That doesn't sound good.'

'Yeah. That's an understatement.'

'Have you spoken to Bobby-Ray?'

'I'm with him now. And we've got evidence that proves he didn't kill Koshkin.'

'So that's good news.'

Standing grimaced. 'The Russians killed Bobby-Ray's parents,' he whispered. 'I'm at the house now. It's a mess.'

'I warned you, the Solntsevskaya are dangerous bastards.'

'You were right. They came for us and we took out half a dozen of them. The family has a cabin upstate. We got there last night and they attacked us first thing.'

'They won't stop, Matt. They'll keep on coming.'

'Maybe,' said Standing.

'There's no "maybe" about it. They're relentless. Look, come back to the UK, let the Regiment protect you. No one's going to get to you in Stirling Lines.' Stirling Lines was where the 22 Special Air Service Regiment was based, on the site in Herefordshire that used to be RAF Credenhill. It was one of the most secure places in the UK.

'What about Bobby-Ray and Kaitlyn? I can't abandon them, Spider. That's not going to happen.'

'They can go into witness protection.'

'Mate, the FBI has tried to kill Bobby-Ray already and an LAPD detective tried to slot me. The Russian mafia are into everything. I don't know who we can trust.'

'So what's your plan?'

'That's a work in progress at the moment.'

'What's the evidence you've got?' asked Shepherd.

'The gloves that Lipov was wearing, and the silencer he used when he shot Koshkin and the bodyguards. He hid them in the kitchen. Bobby-Ray's gun was found – without the silencer – in the garden near where Lipov was standing. It's all good stuff, we just have to get it into the right hands.'

'Just so you know, Lipov is now dead, here in London. Someone shoved a knife into his skull after what seems to have been an epic fight.'

'No great loss to the world,' said Standing.

'The cops think that Lipov knew his killer because he seems to have let him in.'

'I'm sure he had a lot of enemies.'

'You're probably right,' said Shepherd. 'But whoever killed him was obviously skilled at unarmed combat because a lot of punches were thrown before the knife went in. And Nikolai Lipov was a big, powerful guy.'

'You know what they say, Spider. The bigger they are, the harder they fall.'

'Sure, if you know what you're doing. Just be careful, Matt. The cops aren't looking for you but if they do . . .'

'I hear you. And thanks for your concern. By the way, Koshkin's former partner, Erik Markov. He is still in the Four Seasons in LA?'

'So far as I know. I've got a watch on his movements so as soon as he leaves, I'll be informed. Why do you ask, Matt?'

'Best you don't know.'

'Plausible deniability?'

'Markov is the problem here. He's the one who paid for Koshkin to be killed, he's the one tied up with the Russian mafia and ultimately he's the one who framed Bobby-Ray.'

'Be careful, Matt.'

'I always am.'

'No, you're not. You have a tendency to shoot from the hip. And Markov has the resources to shoot back.'

'I have to put an end to this, Spider. I can't spend the rest of my life looking over my shoulder. And neither can Bobby-Ray.'

'Just be careful. And think it through.'

Standing chuckled. 'I promise to count to ten before I do anything stupid.' He ended the call.

Standing took Kaitlyn out of the house and put her in the back of the Escape while Bobby-Ray locked up. Standing got into the driving seat and Bobby-Ray got into the back with his sister. She sobbed quietly most of the way back to Los Angeles.

They checked into a motel in West Hollywood, booking two rooms with a connecting door. They hadn't eaten all day, so they went into a nearby diner. Kaitlyn ordered a coffee but said she didn't want to eat. Standing and Bobby-Ray ate burgers and drank coffee. Kaitlyn stared out of the window. Standing could see that she was in shock, but there was nothing he could do or say to make her feel better.

'The way I see it, there's only one way out of this, and that's to get to Erik Markov,' said Standing. 'He's the one who wanted Koshkin dead. And he's the one who is in bed with the Russian mafia. If we can get him to call off the dogs . . .'

'You think he'll do that?' asked Bobby-Ray.

'If we put the right sort of pressure on him.'

'And how do we do that?'

Standing grinned. 'I have a plan.'

47

Bobby-Ray tapped out the number. 'It's ringing,' he said. Standing was on the bed holding a bottle of beer. He raised it in salute. Kaitlyn was in the next room, dozing.

Faith Hogan answered the call with a curt 'yes?'

'Faith?'

'Who is this? It's almost midnight.'

'It's Bobby-Ray, Faith.'

Hogan gasped. 'Bobby-Ray? Where are you?'

'I'm in LA. But I have to stay under the radar, Faith. I'm in big trouble.'

'You know that John's dead, Bobby-Ray. He was shot in the house where Koshkin was killed. Paul Dutch is dead, too.'

'I know. I know.'

'Bobby-Ray, they're saying you did it.'

'What?'

'They're saying you killed them. And two cops.'

'I wasn't there, Faith. It was nothing to do with me.'

'Then you need to tell the LAPD that, Bobby-Ray. I'll pick you up and we'll get our lawyers involved and we'll get this sorted.'

Standing was frowning over at Bobby-Ray. 'What?' he mouthed.

'It's okay,' mouthed Bobby-Ray and he flashed Standing a thumbs-up. 'Faith, listen to me. I've got evidence that proves I didn't kill Koshkin and Kurt and the Russians.'

'What sort of evidence?'

'Nikolai Lipov killed them. I've got the gloves he was wearing and the silencer he used in my gun the night he shot Koshkin.'

There was silence for several seconds before she spoke again. 'How did you get them?' she said eventually. 'You said you weren't in the house.'

'I wasn't. But I have the evidence and it proves he's the killer, not me.'

'Then you need to give that evidence to our lawyers. Then we can go to the LAPD and make this right.'

'It's too dangerous, Faith,' said Bobby-Ray. 'They're trying to kill me.'

'Who are? Who's trying to kill you?'

'I don't know. The cops, maybe. Or some crazy Russians. There's all sorts of shit going on.'

'And I can help you, Bobby-Ray. Bring the evidence to me and we'll go and see the lawyers.'

'If I get picked up with the evidence by crooked cops then I'm dead,' said Bobby-Ray.

Standing grinned and gave Bobby-Ray the thumbs-up.

'Where is it? This evidence?' asked Hogan.

'A left-luggage place, near the airport.'

'Then I'll see you there,' she said. 'You can give it to me, and I'll take it to the lawyers.'

'I'm not talking to the cops,' said Bobby-Ray. 'Not yet.'

'You don't have to,' said Hogan. 'I'll take the evidence to our lawyers and they'll make sure it's protected. Then I'll get them to advise us on what to do next.

You can stay under the radar until all our ducks are in a row.'

'That's what you said last time, Faith.'

'It's got more complicated since then, what with John being killed. But we can bring you in, Bobby-Ray. I swear.'

Bobby-Ray kept quiet, as if he was considering her offer.

'Bobby-Ray, are you still there?' she asked eventually.

'I'm here, Faith.'

'Where's here?'

'Just a motel.'

'I'll come there.'

'No,' he said quickly. 'All right, I'll see you at the left-luggage place. Three hours from now. I'll text you the address. But come alone. I'll give you the evidence and we'll take it from there.'

'You're doing the right thing, Bobby-Ray,' said Hogan.

'Just make sure you come alone,' said Bobby-Ray, and he ended the call.

'Do you think she bought it?' asked Standing.

'I think so. But she's a smart one.'

'You told her about the evidence. She needs to get that, and this is her only chance.'

'She'll bring back-up.'

'Let's hope so. Because we need her on CCTV working with the Russian mafia. If we have that, we can tie her into the killings.'

'She's going to try to kill us, Matt. You know that.'

Standing raised his beer bottle and grinned. 'She can try.'

48

S tanding parked the Escape a short walk away from the left-luggage outlet. He had his Beretta in his belt under his jacket and Bobby-Ray had his gun tucked into the back of his jeans. They walked towards the shop, eyes watchful. It was three o'clock in the morning and there was no traffic on the roads. They had left Kaitlyn in the motel. She had wanted to go with them but they had insisted that it was too dangerous.

The woman standing in front of the shop was short, not much over five feet, though her high heels added a couple of inches. She had shoulder-length dyed blonde hair pushed back from her eyes with a pair of Dior sunglasses, which seemed incongruous to Standing, considering that it was the middle of the night.

She was wearing a dark-blue suit and carrying a Louis Vuitton shoulder bag. She smiled and waved when she saw Bobby-Ray and walked towards him, her high heels clicking on the pavement. 'I'm so glad to see you,' she said. 'We've all been so worried.'

'This is my friend, Matt,' said Bobby-Ray. 'Matt, this is Faith Hogan. My boss.'

Hogan held out her hand. Her nails were bright red and pointed. She had a firm grip when she shook and the nails bit into his flesh. 'Pleased to meet you, Matt.' She released her grip on his hand. 'But I have to say I was expecting Bobby-Ray to be alone. You didn't say anything about bringing a friend when we spoke on the phone.'

'I'm the one who put the evidence in the locker,' said Standing. He took out his wallet and used his credit card to open the door. 'After you,' he said.

She smiled and stepped inside. As Standing moved to follow her, three big men in bomber jackets ran up holding guns. One grabbed Standing by the collar and jabbed a gun into his neck. Another pulled Standing's Beretta out, while the third kept his gun aimed at Bobby-Ray's face. 'Faith, what's going on?' asked Bobby-Ray. The heavy reached around Bobby-Ray's back and relieved him of his weapon.

'Let's take this inside, shall we?' said Hogan. She held open the door and the three heavies pushed Standing and Bobby-Ray through.

When they were all inside, Hogan closed the door. The three heavies stepped back, keeping their guns trained on Standing and Bobby-Ray.

'Who are these guys?' asked Bobby-Ray. 'Are they with Redrock?'

'From the bad clothes and the body odour, I'd say they're Russians,' said Standing.

'Fuck you, *suka*,' growled one of the heavies.

'There you go,' said Standing.

'I wouldn't go upsetting them, if I were you,' said Hogan. 'They're already very unhappy at what you did to their friends.'

'So you're in with the Solntsevskaya?' said Standing.

'Just get the evidence out and we can be on our way,' said Hogan.

'You've no intention of taking it to the cops, have you?' said Standing.

'Just do as you're told,' said Hogan.

'And if I don't? What will you do? Shoot us?'

'We'll do whatever's necessary,' said Hogan.

Standing smiled. 'You know it's over for you, don't you?'

She frowned. 'What are you talking about?'

Standing pointed up at the small black dome in the corner of the unit. 'CCTV,' he said. 'Everything you've done has been recorded and is on the company's mainframe. You and your mafia friends with guns.'

She smiled coldly. 'No one's going to be checking the footage,' she said. 'They only do that if they think something's wrong and there's been no damage, no violence, nothing. No harm, no foul. Now open the locker.'

'Go fuck yourself.'

A white SUV pulled up at the side of the road. Hogan smiled. 'Here we are,' she said. 'This might change your perception of the situation.' The rear door of the SUV opened and another heavy got out. He was bearded and wearing a heavy black leather jacket. He looked around, then reached into the back of the vehicle and pulled out a girl wearing a sweatshirt and cut-off jeans. The heavy marched her towards the shop, a gun jammed up against her neck. It was Kaitlyn.

'You bitch!' shouted Bobby-Ray.

'Is that any way to talk to a lady?' said Hogan. 'Now, if you continue to give me any problems, just think what will happen to your lovely sister. What these guys will do to her . . .' She faked a shudder. 'Well, better we don't go there. Just give me the evidence.'

Standing glared at her as he walked over to the locker. He tapped his date of birth on the keypad and the locker opened.

'Stop!' shouted one of the Russians as Standing reached inside. Standing slowly stepped back, raising his hands to show that he wasn't a threat. The heavy groped inside the locker and pulled out the evidence bag. He handed it to Hogan. She looked at it and smiled. 'And these will have Lipov's fingerprints on them?'

Bobby-Ray nodded. 'If you give them to the cops, they'll know that Redrock wasn't involved in the killing.'

'That's not going to happen,' she said. 'Right. Outside.'

The heavy holding Kaitlyn had reached the window of the shop. He still had his gun pressed against her neck. It was a Ruger SP101 hammerless revolver with rubber grips. It was a .357 magnum but the calibre was irrelevant because at that range anything would kill. The heavy saw Standing looking at the gun and he grinned, showing two gold front teeth. He jabbed the barrel savagely against Kaitlyn's neck and she yelped.

'I don't think so,' said Standing, turning to look at Hogan. Three figures appeared from behind the shop. Stephen Fenn, John McNally and Simon Farrant. All were dressed casually in sweatshirts and tracksuit bottoms and all were holding Sig Sauer P226 MK25s, the favoured handguns of Navy SEALs. The heavy holding Kaitlyn kept his gun pressed into the side of Kaitlyn's neck and backed away from the SEALs as they covered him with their weapons.

Standing grabbed the evidence bag off Hogan.

'Everyone needs to stay calm,' said Standing. 'If bullets start to fly then the cops will come and the CCTV will be checked and that'll be that.'

'So what are you suggesting?' said Hogan quietly.

'You just walk away. I'll give the evidence to the cops and the heat will be off Bobby-Ray. Redrock is clean and you get on with whatever it is you do for the Russians. We don't care. We just want to get out from under all this shit. You can tell Markov that he's in the clear, the cops aren't going to be looking at him or the Solntsevskaya organisation. They'll have the evidence that Nikolai Lipov was the killer and he's dead.'

'Lipov's dead?' asked Hogan.

'As a doornail.'

'How did that happen?'

'He cut himself shaving. In London.'

Hogan's eyes narrowed. 'You killed him?'

Standing flashed her a tight smile but didn't say anything.

Hogan continued to stare at Standing, but then she shook her head. 'That's not going to fly,' she said. 'If we walk away, you'll go to the cops. You'll show them the evidence and the CCTV footage and then they'll come for me. I'm not stupid. There's no way you'll keep quiet about this, not after everything that's happened.'

'So you can run,' said Standing. 'It'll take them time to go after you. You've got money. All your Solntsevskaya connections. I'm sure they'll fix you up with something in Moscow.' Standing looked at his watch. 'I'd go now if I were you,' he said. 'The clock's ticking.'

She continued to stare at him with undisguised hatred.

'Tick tock. Tick tock.'

Hogan slowly raised her right arm. Within seconds half a dozen men came running down the stairs from the upper level of the mall and fanned out behind the Navy SEALs, big men carrying an assortment of weapons including Uzis and MAC-10s.

Hogan smiled at Standing. 'I'll see your three Sig Sauers and I'll raise you a hell of a lot of firepower,' she said. 'Now hand me that evidence bag and step outside.'

Standing shook his head. 'I'm not going anywhere with you,' he said. 'If you want to kill me you're going to have to do it here. And we'll fight back, and that'll cause so much damage the cops will come.'

'I know, and they'll check the CCTV. But if you do that, you and Bobby-Ray and the lovely Kaitlyn will be dead.'

Outside the shop, the heavily armed new arrivals were taking the Sig Sauers off the Navy SEALs.

'We'll be dead anyway if we go with you,' said Standing. 'You can't afford to leave us alive.'

'Let's take this one step at a time, shall we?' said Hogan.

'You leave my sister alone!' shouted Bobby-Ray. He roared and lunged at Hogan but one of the heavies clubbed his gun against the back of his head and he fell to his knees.

'We're not going anywhere, Faith,' said Standing quietly. 'Because if we walk out of here, we're dead.'

'Oh, you're going,' said Hogan. 'You're walking out with us or you'll be carried out, but you're going.'

The man behind Standing prodded him in the back with his gun. Standing started to count under his breath. One. Two.

'We don't have all night,' said Hogan.

Bobby-Ray got to his feet, shaking his head.

Three. Four. Five. Standing knew he had to fight. If he left with the Russians, he was a dead man. Better to die fighting than to be shot in the back of the head.

'Are you counting?' asked Hogan. 'Are you fucking kidding me?'

Six. Seven. Standing's mind was racing but he couldn't see that he had any options. Not survivable ones, anyway. Eight, Nine.

Outside the shop, the Russian thug holding Kaitlyn fell to the ground. His gun clattered on the tarmac next to him. His face was a bloody mess. He'd been hit by a large calibre round. Kaitlyn staggered back, her hands over her mouth, her eyes wide with terror.

A second Russian fell. His Uzi clattered on the ground. He juddered once and then went still. There was blood on his chest. Hogan frowned. 'What the hell?' she said.

The man at Standing's shoulder was staring out of the window. Standing elbowed him in the stomach, then backfisted him in the face. Standing grabbed the gun and slammed the butt into his temple. He went down, out cold.

Standing pointed the gun at the remaining heavies. 'Drop them,' he said, his finger tightening on the trigger. They did as they were told and raised their hands.

Outside the shop, a third thug went down, his MAC-10 falling from his lifeless fingers. The rest of the Russians dropped their weapons and raised their hands, looking around them fearfully as they tried to work out where the shots were coming from.

Bobby-Ray got unsteadily to his feet. 'Snipers,' he said. 'Fenn brought snipers.'

'I don't think they came with the SEALs,' said Standing. Hogan was staring out of the window, clearly confused by what was happening.

A convoy of black vehicles sped along the road and came to a halt at the entrance of the mall. There were five SUVs with tinted windows and two windowless vans. The side doors of the vans slid open and men in overalls rushed out. Men in suits carrying Glocks piled out of the SUVs. Within seconds, the men in overalls had carried the Russians who had been shot into the van.

Three of the suits came into the shop, grabbed the Russians there and bundled them out. Two men in overalls came in and picked up the man that Standing had knocked out. They dragged him outside, zip-tied him, then carried him over to the vans.

Standing went outside. 'Who are you?' he asked one of the men, but he was ignored.

The guys in suits quickly and efficiently zip-tied the wrists of the surviving Russians. Their weapons were loaded into one of the SUVs, which quickly drove off, and the zip-tied heavies were put into the vans with their dead colleagues. The side doors slid closed and the vans sped off down the road accompanied by two of the SUVs.

Hogan walked out of the shop, frowning in confusion.

Fenn, McNally and Farrant picked up their Sig Sauers and stared after the departing vehicles. 'What the fuck just happened?' asked Fenn.

There were two SUVs still parked at the side of the road. The front passenger door of the lead vehicle opened and a man climbed out. He was in his late fifties but still fit, with a strong jaw that he jutted up as he walked over to the left-luggage outlet. He was wearing a dark-blue blazer, a pale-blue shirt and a dark-blue tie with black stripes. His shoes were tasselled, the black leather gleaming as if they had just been polished.

The three Navy SEALs moved to block his way.

'Who are you?' asked Fenn, his gun down at his side.

'That's not really your business, son,' said the man.

Fenn gestured with his gun. 'You should just turn around and get back in your car, old man. You've no idea who you're messing with.'

The man's eyes tightened a fraction, but he continued to smile. He had a chunky gold ring on his right ring finger and a Rolex Submariner watch on his left wrist. 'You'd be wrong there, son,' he said. 'I know exactly who I'm messing with. You're Petty Officer Second Class Stephen Fenn, a valued member of SEAL Team Six. Your colleagues are John McNally and Simon Farrant, and gentlemen, I would like to thank you all for your service and I admire the way you stepped up to help a friend and former SEAL. But your work here is done and it's time for you to drive back to Coronado.'

Fenn frowned. His gun was still pointing at the ground, but he began to raise it.

'Just in case you're thinking of getting physical in any way, I suggest you take a look at those green dots dancing on your chest,' said the man amiably.

Fenn looked down and his eyes narrowed when he saw the two green dots over his heart. They were joined by a third.

Fenn looked up at the adjoining building but couldn't see the snipers.

'It would obviously be very awkward indeed if this

should escalate, Petty Officer Fenn. You can trust me, Bobby-Ray is in good hands.'

Two men in dark suits were walking purposefully over from the SUVs. They were in their mid-thirties and had the look of men who had served in special forces.

Fenn looked over at Standing, but Standing was equally confused.

'Who are you with?' asked Standing.

'That's really no concern of yours, Mr Standing,' said the man. 'But I'd like to think that I was a friend of Daniel Shepherd and if he was here I'm sure he'd happily vouch for me.' He held out his hand for the evidence bag. 'I'll take that if you don't mind.' Standing gave it to him and the man slid it into his pocket.

'What the fuck is going on?' asked Hogan. 'Are you with Redrock? Who sent you?'

'You are to go with my men, Ms Hogan,' said the man.

'I'm not going anywhere,' she said.

A green dot appeared on Hogan's chest. Then another. 'Are you going to shoot me?' she asked.

'I hope not,' said the man.

The two men in suits walked up and stood either side of Hogan.

'You need to go with them now,' said the man.

'Go where?'

'Wherever they take you to,' said the man. 'You really don't have a choice in the matter.'

One of the men reached to grab her arm but she shrugged him away and swore at him.

'Please, don't make this any harder than it has to be,' said the man with the tasselled shoes.

Hogan gritted her teeth. She looked as if she was about

to hurl a tirade of abuse at him, but then the fight went out of her and she walked over to the SUVs, escorted by the two men in suits.

The man looked at his watch. 'I'm afraid we're going to have to move things along,' he said. 'Mr Standing and Mr Barnes need to come with me, you Navy SEALs need to get back to your base. We have another appointment and time's a wasting.'

Fenn stared at the man for several seconds and then slowly nodded. He tucked the gun into his belt but the three green dots continued to dance on his chest. 'If anything happens to them . . .' Fenn left the sentence unfinished.

The man smiled. 'Your threat is duly noted,' he said.

Fenn stared at the man, then nodded slowly and walked away. McNally and Farrant followed him.

Hogan had climbed into the rear SUV with the men in suits and a few seconds later it drove off.

The man waved at the remaining black SUV. 'Let's go, gentlemen,' he said. He smiled at Kaitlyn. 'And lady, of course.'

'Who are you?' asked Standing.

The man smiled brightly. 'The name's Yokely,' he said. 'Richard Yokely.'

49

The SUV pulled up in front of the Four Seasons and Yokely climbed out. Standing, Kaitlyn and Bobby-Ray joined him and together they walked into the lobby. They rode up to the top floor in the lift. Yokely said nothing and although Standing and Bobby-Ray exchanged looks, neither of them broke the silence.

When the lift doors opened they were met by a broad-shouldered man with close-cropped hair, a square jaw and a white scar on his upper lip. He was wearing a dark suit and there was a slight bulge under his left armpit.

'Everything in hand, Gerry?' asked Yokely.

'All good,' said the man. Yokely walked towards a set of double doors. They were opened by another man in a suit, this one bearded and wearing tinted glasses. He stepped aside to let the visitors in and then closed the doors and stood with his back to them, his hands clasped over his groin. The suite was enormous, with floor-to-ceiling windows looking out over the city, two long, low sofas and a dining area. Erik Markov was sitting on one of the sofas. There was a man standing behind him, tall with a broken nose and a military haircut, holding a Glock.

'Everything all right, Peter?' asked Yokely.

'He's been as good as gold,' said the man.

'His bodyguards?'

The man nodded at one of two doors at the far end of the suite. 'In the master bedroom. David's watching them.'

'Excellent,' said Yokely. He smiled down at Markov.

Markov glared back at him. 'Who the fuck are you?' he growled.

'My name's Richard,' said Yokely.

'Who do you work for? CIA? DIA? NSA?'

'Let's just say I work for the big guy.'

'And you're here to kill me?'

Yokely shrugged. 'That was my first thought. But what would that achieve?' He raised his eyebrows. 'Well, I suppose killing you would stop you telling anyone how you interfered with the elections. And it would take the pressure off Bobby-Ray and Kaitlyn.'

The Russian frowned. 'Who the fuck is Kaitlyn?'

Yokely reached inside his jacket, took out a Glock, and gestured with it. 'Moderate your language when you're talking about a lady, Erik, or I might teach you a lesson by putting a bullet in your manhood. Kaitlyn Barnes is the sister of Bobby-Ray here, and Bobby-Ray is the man you intended to frame for the death of your former business partner, Mikhail Koshkin. She's also the girl that Oleg Ivchenko and his team of thugs tried to kill up in the Trinity Alps, though obviously that didn't go as planned.'

Kaitlyn glared at Markov. 'You had my parents killed, you bastard,' she hissed.

Yokely raised a hand. 'To be fair, it was Ivchenko who did that. I don't think Erik here even knew that Ivchenko went to see your parents. But I'm sure he knew that Ivchenko wanted Bobby-Ray dead.'

'Shoot him,' said Bobby-Ray. 'Or give me the fucking gun and let me do it.'

'What is it you want?' Markov asked Yokely.

'What do I want? World peace and a wife as pretty as Taylor Swift whose father owns a distillery would be a start.' Yokely chuckled. 'But seriously, Erik, what I want is for you to leave Bobby-Ray and Kaitlyn and Matt alone. Now, I could achieve that by killing you here and now, but the problem with that is that your mafia friends might decide that revenge is a dish they want to cook up at any temperature, and then my friends will be spending the rest of their lives looking over their shoulders.' Yokely frowned. 'You know, even as I say that, I can't help but think that killing you is the best way forward.' He pointed his gun at the Russian's chest and the man flinched. Yokely grinned at his reaction. 'Tell me this, Erik. Do you know why so few Russians get kidnapped by Muslim terrorists?'

Markov didn't say anything.

'It's not a rhetorical question,' said Yokely. 'ISIS and the rest take hostages all around the world and more often than not they end up killing them. But very rarely do they take Russians, despite there being an extensive Russian presence throughout the Middle East. Why is that?'

Markov shrugged. 'I don't know,' he said, his voice a hoarse whisper.

'Then let me enlighten you,' said Yokely. 'It goes back to the Eighties when we had what they call the Lebanon hostage crisis. More than a hundred foreigners were taken hostage, mainly Americans and Western Europeans. Then in 1985, Hezbollah kidnapped four Russian diplomats in Beirut. They wanted Moscow to stop pro-Syrian militiamen from firing on Muslim troops in Tripoli. Not the capital of Libya, obviously, there's another Tripoli in the north of Lebanon. Anyway, the shelling of Tripoli continued and the Muslims killed one of the diplomats, Arkady Katkov. The Russians weren't happy, obviously, but instead of just bleating about it, they took action. Decisive action. The KGB kidnapped and killed a relative of a Lebanese Shia Muslim leader. Before they killed him they castrated him and they sent the balls to the Hezbollah leader, along with the threat that if the remaining diplomats weren't released they would do the same to the rest of the man's relatives. The diplomats were released within days and ever since, the likes of ISIS and Al-Qaeda have tended not to take Russians hostage.'

Yokely looked over at Bobby-Ray and Standing. 'Did you guys know that?' The two men shook their heads. He smiled. 'There you go then, you live and learn.'

Yokely looked back at Markov. 'You're probably wondering what the point is of that little history lesson.' He used his left hand to fish a mobile phone out of his pocket and kept his weapon trained on the man's chest as he switched it on and flicked through to a photograph. 'You've got a nephew in Dubai. Young Alexei.' He looked over at Bobby-Ray and Standing. 'Nasty piece of work, Alexei is. Traffics in young girls and specialises in waterboarding them if they don't earn enough. Clever, because of course waterboarding doesn't damage the merchandise.'

Yokely looked back at Markov. 'Anyway, a few hours

ago some of my colleagues castrated and killed Alexei. Or the other way around. I didn't care which, to be honest. And we decided against couriering the body parts to you, I figured a selfie would do the trick. Well, not a selfie, obviously, because Alexei is dead.' He held out the phone and showed Markov a photograph of a mutilated body on a blood-soaked bathroom floor. Markov winced and looked away.

'I've got a close-up of the face, if you want to be sure,' said Yokely, but the Russian shook his head and Yokely put the phone away. 'The people I work with have a list of two dozen relatives of yours, starting with your wife and two sons and ending with seven or eight cousins back in Moscow. So here's the threat, Erik. Listen and listen well. I need you to convince me that no harm will come to Bobby-Ray, Kaitlyn and Matt. I need to believe that you and your Solntsevskaya friends will forget all about them. If I'm not convinced that you are prepared to forgive and forget, then I'll kill you now and bad things will happen to all your relatives over the next few days. But if you can assure me you will now let bygones be bygones, then I'll walk away. With the proviso, of course, that if you renege on the deal, you and your relatives will . . .' He shrugged. 'Well, I don't need to finish that, do I? You don't get to be a billionaire oligarch by being stupid, do you?' He shrugged again. 'So what is it, Erik? Deal or no deal?'

The Russian stared at Yokely and then slowly nodded. 'Yes,' he said. 'We have a deal. They will not be harmed, not by me or by anyone in the Solntsevskaya.'

'And just in case you're thinking that this is all down to me, never forget that the list is with my organisation and has nothing to do with me personally. If ever you try to attack me, the same rules apply.'

'Of course,' said Markov.

'Then I shall bid you a good evening,' said Yokely, putting his gun away. He tilted his chin at Bobby-Ray and Standing. 'Are you gentleman coming or staying?' He grinned at Kaitlyn. 'And lady, of course.'

50

Colonel Davies kept Standing waiting for fifteen minutes before seeing him. He looked up from his desk and smiled as the trooper walked into his office and stood to attention. 'Good to have you back, Matt. Everything go okay?'

Standing nodded. 'Yes, boss. All good.' He had arrived back in the UK early that afternoon and taken the train to Hereford. Bobby-Ray and Kaitlyn had seen him off at LAX. Bobby-Ray had quit Redrock and had already signed on with another security company. The mysterious Richard Yokely had assured him that the LAPD had closed their investigation into the killings in Bel Air, as they now knew that Nikolai Lipov was the killer and had himself been killed in London. The British police would be investigating Lipov's murder, but Yokely had made it clear that wasn't his problem.

'You were able to help your friend?' asked the Colonel.

Standing nodded again. 'Yes, boss.'

'That's good. Friends are important. Sometimes I think they're more important than family. As they say, you don't choose your family, but you choose your friends. Are you ready to start the training sessions with the Met's CTSFOs? They arrive tomorrow.'

'Ready, willing, and able, boss.'

'Good to hear it. And the anger management? You're keeping that temper of yours under control?'

'Doing my best, boss.'

'Good man. Let's keep it that way. If you can keep on the straight and narrow, we'll get those sergeant's stripes back on your arms before too long.'

'Yes, boss.'

TWO WEEKS LATER

Richard Yokely was sitting at the same table as the last time Shepherd had met him in Hyde Park, but this time Shepherd went inside the café to buy his own coffee. The American was smoking one of his small cigars. The weather was cooler than it had been on the previous occasion and Yokely was wearing a black cashmere overcoat that he had unbuttoned to reveal a pale-blue pinstripe suit. 'Your call was unexpected,' said Yokely as Shepherd sat down. 'I thought everything was shipshape and Bristol fashion, as you guys say.'

'I don't think anyone has actually said that in a hundred years or so,' said Shepherd.

'Maybe not, but I personally do love all the naval terms in your language. Loose cannon, a shot across the bows, cut and run, know the ropes. Wonderful that the terms are still used even though you're no longer a naval power.' He smiled and sipped his coffee, studying Shepherd over the top of his cup.

'I just wanted to talk through a few things with you, and it's always better to do it face to face.'

'Absolutely,' said Yokely. 'So fire away.' He smiled. 'I'm not sure if that one is nautical or not.'

'All shipshape, you said. No loose ends?'

Yokely shrugged. 'All's well that ends well,' he said.

'How so?'

'Your friend Matt Standing is back in Hereford, Bobby-Ray Barnes is off the hook and has signed up with a new security company, and Erik Markov has moved back to London for the foreseeable future. The cops now know that Nikolai Lipov killed Mikhail Koshkin and that case is closed, and we have identified half a dozen Russian mafia plants we didn't know existed before.'

'Faith Hogan is talking?'

'We can't shut her up,' said Yokely. 'She'll be in witness protection for the rest of her life, but given the choice she had, I think she can count herself lucky. She's given us the name of a judge, which is going to be very interesting if it pans out. I tell you, Spider, this is really going to hurt the Solntsevskaya organisation, big time.'

'That's good news.'

'Damn right it is,' said the American. He took a long pull on his cigar and blew smoke up at the sky.

'How long have you been working on this, Richard?' asked Shepherd quietly.

Yokely held the cigar away from his lips. 'Why do you ask?'

'Just interested,' said Shepherd. 'That phone call where you asked me about Matt Standing and his family situation, you made it sound then as if that was the first you'd heard about him.'

'It was,' said Yokely.

'But the fact that Mikhail Koshkin was in LA and

preparing to talk to the authorities, that wasn't new to you, was it?'

Yokely's eyes narrowed but he didn't say anything.

'And the whole Erik Markov thing, his alleged involvement with the presidential election, that wasn't new, was it? You knew about that?'

'I heard about Koshkin, obviously,' said Yokely. 'Quite a few people were interested in talking to him.'

'Talking to him about Erik Markov?'

'What else?'

'Because Erik Markov used his company's expertise and finance to influence the election?'

Yokely grinned. 'Allegedly.'

'So when you phoned me about Standing, it was because he had become involved in an operation of yours. An existing operation.'

'I think operation is putting it a bit strong,' said Yokely. 'You popped up on my radar because you were asking questions about Mikhail Koshkin's murder and that led you to the Solntsevskaya organisation.'

'And you had an ongoing operation to expose what the Solntsevskaya were doing?'

'See now, that's a bit vague,' said Yokely. 'We've known for some time that the Russian mafia has been infiltrating various branches of government, law enforcement and the justice system.'

'And you thought that Standing could help you, right? That's why you were asking me about what he had in the way of family, because there would be repercussions to what he was doing.'

'He was getting himself into a lot of trouble, that was for sure.'

'He was helping a friend,' said Shepherd.

'A friend in need, as they say. Yes, he was.'

'A friend who had been framed for the murder of Mikhail Koshkin. Tell me, Richard, had you been looking at Koshkin's murder before I started asking questions in London?'

'It was a high-profile killing.'

He had avoided answering the question, Shepherd noted. Yokely was very good at that. 'Well, not according to what was in the papers. It was described as a home invasion. Why would you be interested in a home invasion?'

'Koshkin's name came up and he was obviously a person of interest.'

'But you presumably knew that Markov was involved in the election?'

'Allegedly,' said Yokely.

'Allegedly or not, your people knew that he was involved.'

Yokely shrugged but didn't say anything. Shepherd could tell that the American was a lot less confident than when he'd started the conversation.

'So what was your interest, Richard? The fact that Koshkin was a wealthy oligarch or the fact that he was about to spill the beans on his former business partner.'

'It was a package deal, I suppose.'

'Really? You see, I get the impression that you were looking at Koshkin before he went to America. I think you knew that he was getting ready to hurt Markov by revealing what he knew about the election fixing.'

Yokely smoked his cigar and watched Shepherd carefully.

'There are a couple of things that are worrying me, Richard. The first involves the attempt to kill Koshkin in London, if that's what it was. I mean, we've got a professional assassin or assassins using a very clever poison, and yet all said assassin or assassins can do is make him ill.'

'People make mistakes.'

'They do. Indeed they do. But if you go to all the trouble of poisoning a person, you might at least make sure they get enough of it in their system to kill them.'

Yokely flicked ash onto the ground but didn't say anything.

'So that got me thinking that perhaps the plan wasn't to kill Koshkin, but to make him think that Markov was trying to kill him. Why? Because someone wanted Koshkin to spill the beans about what Markov had done. That someone must have been very happy when Koshkin flew to the US and offered to talk. But a lot less pleased when he was murdered for real shortly afterwards.'

Yokely took another pull on his cigar.

'Was it you, Richard? Were you working some scheme to get Koshkin to roll over on Markov?'

Yokely smiled thinly. 'You know perfectly that if that was the case, I couldn't tell you.'

'I realise that, Richard. But let me continue my train of thought. Let's assume it was you behind the plan to get Koshkin to the US. You must have been pretty pissed off when he was killed, but then I think you saw a way to turn that to your advantage when those two FBI agents turned up dead and Matt Standing arrived in LA. At that point you realised just how well connected Erik Markov was, and how far the Solntsevskaya had penetrated the

US justice system. All you had to do was keep tabs on Standing and Barnes and see who moved against them. And that's what happened, right? This operation is crippling the Solntsevskaya, so it's been a success. And I'm guessing it has given you leverage over Markov that you can use in the future.'

Yokely took another pull on his cigar.

'But I don't understand why you didn't pursue Markov. I would have thought the whole point of the operation would have been to see him jailed for his manipulation of the US election.'

Yokely blew smoke. 'Perhaps it would be better if we spoke hypothetically,' he said.

'Go for it,' said Shepherd.

'Okay,' said the American. 'Hypothetically, yes, the plan might well have been to get Koshkin to roll over on Markov, to get him to produce the smoking gun that would show that Markov manipulated the presidential election and that he was doing that at the behest of the Russian president. If it could be shown that the Russian government interfered with our elections, well, that's a stick that could be used to beat them again and again.'

'Of course,' said Shepherd.

'So, hypothetically speaking, you can imagine how upset investigators were when it started to look as if Markov wasn't working for the Kremlin. He was doing it for the Solntsevskaya. It was all about money. And power. And nothing to do with the Russian government. Then it became a whole different story. If the public were to find out that Russian gangsters influenced an election and that those same Russian gangsters have infiltrated our cops, our legal system and our government, then how can we expect people to trust those organisations? And a government depends on trust. If the public starts to believe the entire system is corrupt, then they'll stop cooperating with it, and that way lies anarchy.'

'So best to suppress the whole thing? Make it just go away?'

'No, it'll be dealt with. But quietly, with as little public scrutiny as possible. We're making a start with Faith Hogan's testimony but there's a long way to go.' He flicked ash and took a sip of his coffee. 'What's the other thing that's troubling you, Spider? You said there were a couple of things that were troubling you.'

Shepherd flashed the American a cold smile. 'You won't like it.'

'You're among friends.'

'I hope that's true, Richard.' Shepherd sighed. 'Okay, here it is. Bobby-Ray was holed up in the cabin his parents owned, all the way up in Trinity Alps.'

'Lovely part of the world,' said Yokely. 'Very rustic.'

'So I've heard,' said Shepherd. 'Matt and Bobby-Ray's sister go to see him there, and are followed by Oleg Ivchenko and his Solntsevskaya heavies. Despite being outmanned and outgunned, Bobby-Ray and Matt emerge victorious.'

'To be fair, highly-trained super-fit special forces soldiers are likely to wipe the floor with untrained thugs, no matter what the odds.'

'Agreed,' said Shepherd. 'And I'm sure you took that into consideration when you pointed Ivchenko in the direction of Bobby-Ray's parents.'

Yokely's jaw tightened.

'I spoke to Matt, and he tells me that the Russians

attacked the cabin in the early hours of the morning, just after dawn, about six or seven hours after he and Kaitlyn got there.'

'So?'

'So that implies that the Russians didn't have the Barnes house under surveillance. If they had they would have seen them arrive and then followed them up to Trinity Alps. There would have been no need to wait for dawn.' He took a sip of coffee and was impressed that his hand was rock steady. 'So it looks as if they turned up at the home of Bobby-Ray's parents after Matt and Bobby-Ray's sister had left.'

'That makes sense.'

'At which point they tortured and killed Mr and Mrs Barnes to get the location of the cabin.'

Yokely's eyes had hardened now and he was no longer smiling. 'What are you suggesting, Spider?'

Shepherd shrugged. 'I suppose we're still talking hypothetically, aren't we? In which case, hypothetically speaking, I guess that someone wanted that confrontation between Matt, Bobby-Ray and the Russians, because that someone would have known that Bobby-Ray and Matt would win the day and that they would then go after the man behind it all, Erik Markov. A fair enough plan, except that whoever tipped off Ivchenko must have realised that he was putting Mr and Mrs Barnes in danger.'

'Maybe whoever it was assumed that the Russians wouldn't hurt the couple.'

'Do you think so, Richard? The Russian mafia? You think they'd think twice about hurting anyone if it suited their purpose? You yourself warned me about what dangerous bastards they are.'

'We're talking hypothetically, remember?'

'Are we, Richard? Are we really?'

'I assumed we were.'

Shepherd stood up. 'As you said, all's well that ends well. Except for Mr and Mrs Barnes, of course.'

Yokely grimaced. 'That was never part of the plan. Trust me.'

'Trust you? Can I? Really?'

'We go back a long way.'

'No question of that. But you do tend to put your government's interests above all else. And in this case, Mr and Mrs Barnes paid a terrible price.'

'I never thought that the Russians would kill them. You have my word on that. To use the vernacular, shit happens. It was a mistake, and a mistake that will be on my conscience for the rest of my life.'

'I'm sure that will be a great comfort to Bobby-Ray and Kaitlyn.'

'I think Bobby-Ray and Kaitlyn realise that Oleg Ivchenko killed their parents, and that Ivchenko and his men got what they deserved, out there in the woods. They got their revenge.'

'Maybe,' said Shepherd. 'I just hope they never find out who told Ivchenko that they were heading up to Redding.'

Yokely shrugged again. 'We'll cross that bridge if and when we come to it,' he said.

Shepherd shook his head sadly. 'How do you live with yourself, Richard? The things that you do?'

Yokely smiled but there was no warmth in it. 'Is that a hypothetical question?' he asked.

Shepherd sighed in frustration, turned and walked away.

Don't miss Stephen Leather's next
explosive standalone thriller

THE RUNNER

Sally Page is an MI5 'footie', a junior Secret Service Agent who
maintains 'legends': fake identities or footprints used by real
spies. Her day consists of maintaining flats and houses were the
legends allegedly live, doing online shopping, using payment,
loyalty and travel cards and going on social media in their
names – anything to give the impression to hostile surveillance
that the legends are living, breathing individuals.

One day she goes out for a coffee run from the safe house from
which she and her fellow footies operate. When she comes back
they have all been murdered and she barely escapes with her
own life. She is on the run: but from whom she has no idea.
Worse, her bosses at MI5 seem powerless to help her. To live,
she will have to use all the lies and false identities she has so
carefully created while discovering the truth . . .

Available to order now

HODDER